FALLING FOR THE PROTAGONIST

FALLING FOR THE PROTAGONIST

BEX GOOS

An Aria Book

First published in the UK in 2026 by Head of Zeus,
part of Bloomsbury Publishing Plc

Copyright © Bex Goos, 2026

The moral right of Bex Goos to be identified
as the author of this work has been asserted in accordance with
the Copyright, Designs and Patents Act of 1988.

All rights reserved. No part of this publication may be: i) reproduced or
transmitted in any form, electronic or mechanical, including photocopying,
recording or by means of any information storage or retrieval system without prior
permission in writing from the publishers; or ii) used or reproduced in any way for
the training, development or operation of artificial intelligence (AI) technologies,
including generative AI technologies. The rights holders expressly reserve this
publication from the text and data mining exception as per Article 4(3) of the
Digital Single Market Directive (EU) 2019/790.

This is a work of fiction. All characters, organizations, and events
portrayed in this novel are either products of the author's
imagination or are used fictitiously.

9 7 5 3 1 2 4 6 8

A catalogue record for this book is available from the British Library.

ISBN (PB): 9781035919024
ISBN (eBook): 9781035919062

Cover design: Jessie Price

Printed and bound in Great Britain by Clays Ltd, Elcograf S.p.A.

Bloomsbury Publishing Plc
50 Bedford Square, London, WC1B 3DP, UK
Bloomsbury Publishing Ireland Limited,
29 Earlsfort Terrace, Dublin 2, D02 AY28, Ireland

HEAD OF ZEUS LTD
5–8 Hardwick Street
London, EC1R 4RG

To find out more about our authors and books
visit www.headofzeus.com
For product safety related questions contact productsafety@bloomsbury.com

For Susan, my mother, who taught me to march proudly to the beat of my own glockenspiel

One

The back corner of the bar known as Bonne Nuit echoed with the jovial, slightly manic titters and squeals that could only belong to a group of women who were two hours into a bachelorette party. Emmy Miura kept smiling as the feminine chaos surrounded her and she tried to tamp down the deep, heartfelt longing she felt for her comfy pants. They were at home all alone, probably missing her. She couldn't remember the last time she'd left them for so long on a Saturday night. Trying not to sulk, she shifted until the strapless cocktail dress she'd bought for the occasion—at her sister's subtle insistence—settled a little more comfortably around her.

"Deep breaths," her best friend of a million years, Sarah, murmured to her.

"I am a bad person for wanting to leave."

"You are a good sister for staying."

That was one way to look at it, and Emmy did enjoy seeing May's happiness, which was flowing more freely than the happy hour specials. Her sister, adorned with a sparkling headband coated in curlicues of metallic ribbon, was leaning over to listen to one of her friends. Whatever the friend said lit up May's face.

"Yes!" she cried. "Yes, absolutely. I have to tell the story. I don't even care if some of you already heard it a million times. Emmy, cover your ears."

Emmy immediately went on alert. "Why?"

"Because I'm going to tell—shh, seriously, guys, this is good—I'm going to tell the story of how me and Victor met. Emmy hates this because she is a cynic and a nonbeliever, but I'm telling it anyway because it is my party!"

"Oh, Jesus."

"How did they meet?" Sarah asked.

"She went to a sex psychic," Emmy muttered under her breath.

"Sorry. Run that by me one more time?"

Emmy gestured to her sister, indicating Sarah should listen to May, and repeated, "She went to a sex psychic."

As May launched into the story, Emmy clearly recalled her own version of events as if they had unfolded only yesterday. In reality, it had been months ago. Not enough months, Emmy thought, to justify the rock on her sister's finger. But Emmy's opinion didn't matter. May was head-over-heels, or so she said, and had expressed zero doubts about her future with Victor.

"It all started with the worst date of my life," May recited, hamming it up for her intoxicated audience. "Seriously, I matched with this guy, and he was cute, but I should've turned him down when his profile said one of his hobbies was 'Observing.' What even is that? Anyway, he was so proud of himself for choosing a casual setting for our first date so there would be no pressure. I know this because he told me that was why he had chosen Bunkers for our date on what happened to be half-price wing night. He claimed he wasn't aware of this, but he ordered two baskets of wings, so the jury's out."

Emmy knew the details of this date as if she'd been there. She'd received an infuriated and defeated text that very night detailing the colossal failure. It had hurt Emmy's heart because her sister had been convinced true love was right around the corner, but it kept evading her. Still, May's relentless optimism kept her going out on first date after first date.

Then, a few days later, a different text pinged its way onto Emmy's phone. It was one of her sister's signature superlatives, and it promised to be an interesting one.

> Just had the most amazing experience of my life!!! Meet me at Coffee Fix on ur lunch break! I've got pictures!!!!!

A little uncertain of what pictures May could have to show her—and curious why said pictures couldn't be texted or emailed—Emmy had joined May at their favorite coffee shop as requested. May waved her over to a table for two by the window. She was sipping from a steaming mug and tapping away on her phone. A second mug waited for Emmy, and she gratefully took a sip of the triple shot latte after she sat down.

"One second... There! My dating profiles are gone," May announced proudly, putting her phone down on the table.

"Profiles plural? How many did you have?"

"Three. But they're gone now because I just had a session with a sex psychic."

Emmy had always disparaged moments in books and movies when, after receiving a shocking bit of news, a character did a spit take. It felt unrealistic to her. But she nearly had to eat her words as coffee poured back out of her mouth and into the mug mid-sip.

"Excuse me?"

"Don't go all Emmy on me. Just hear me out. I found this little boutique in the Cities that sells romance novels and sex toys and stuff. I was feeling down after that last date, so I went inside to see if I could find something to cheer myself up. Turns out, the place was brand new which is why I'd never seen it before. Just opened a couple weeks ago. The owner—Lucy—is a sex psychic. She had her own deck of sex Tarot cards that she illustrated herself."

May picked up her phone again, this time to open her photos, and showed Emmy a picture of a Tarot spread. Emmy felt her eyebrows climb all the way up into her hairline.

"That is... a lot of penises."

"Vaginas, too," May added cheerily. "And boobs."

"Okay..."

"So anyway, she said she'd do a reading based on what I was looking for. You know, one-night stand, casual relationship, that sort of thing. I told her I wanted the real thing. I was looking for Love with a capital L."

"Oh God, May. How much did she charge you?" Emmy demanded.

"Not a penny, Ms. Cynic. She said the reading was free since it was for true love, except I got the idea it would have been free anyway, but I was welcome to purchase something from the retail side of the shop. I did. Got myself two adorable vibrators."

"What do you need two for?"

"They're different colors."

"Ah, of course."

"So anyway," May continued, "she does this reading for me, and get this... she tells me how I'm gonna meet the guy, what he's gonna be like. Hold on, I took notes."

"You took notes about your sex Tarot reading from the sex psychic."

"I told you not to go Emmy on me!" May shot back without taking her eyes off her phone.

Emmy rolled her eyes and waited. From the sound of things, her sister had been taken in by a smooth-talking saleswoman, but at least the cost hadn't been too high. As long as May was being truthful about not having to pay for the reading—and as long as she hadn't given the sex psychic her social security number in order to solidify the psychic vibrations or whatever—the consequences weren't too dire. The financial consequences, anyway. More worrying to Emmy at that moment were the emotional consequences when said mystery man failed to make his portended appearance. But they'd burn that bridge when they got to it.

"Okay, here it is. So first she did a three-card reading for me. Past, present, and future. Basically she said I was pushing too hard instead of sitting back a little and letting fate take its course." She swiped through the pictures on her phone. The more excited she got, the more she mixed Japanese in with her English. May had always been more inclined to slip into Japanese than Emmy. "*Look!* Look right here. I drew—she had me draw the cards, not her—I drew the Five of Testicles. She said that meant in the past I was too easily taken in by flattery and false promises, which is like *every* date I've ever had, *ne*? So then I got Edging, reversed, which I think means upside down? Anyway, she said that means it's time to change my approach, and then, and *then*, I drew The Lovers! *Mite! Kawaī desune?*" Another picture, this one of two people as entwined as it was possible for two people to be. They covered each other in such a way that it was impossible to determine gender, which Emmy admitted to herself was a nice touch. She wasn't sure she'd go so far as to call it cute, as May had. "It's the one card she didn't reinvent, Emmy. She said nothing needed to be changed or updated about lovers meeting, you know? And she said it meant that I was going to find true love!"

"May... this is all very... interesting." At her sister's snort, Emmy decided to shoot straight. "I think this is bullshit."

"I know you do, sweets. But I swear, it was unreal. We did way more than this. She told me things that she should *not* have known, not even if she'd somehow anticipated I was coming and stalked me on social media. Even better, she got it. She told me I wasn't wrong to look for love, and the stigma against online dating and dating apps was outdated... no pun intended. But she also said I should stop trying to force my happily ever after. And look at this picture." She tilted her phone screen, swiped again. "The guy I'm going to meet. She told me to draw three cards, and this is what I got. I forget what they were all called, except this one I think was the Ten of Dildos, but I took notes on what she said. He's going to be confident, a problem-solver, but not arrogant. Good at making deals, sharp, and intelligent. She said that meant he'd likely have a job where he had to wear a suit to work and use his intellect, something to do with the law or media. That was her guess, anyway. And then he's going to be intensely devoted, sometimes um… *chotto mate*…" She paused to scroll down and read through her notes. "Sometimes to the point of stubbornness, but he will also have a playful side."

"Sounds like your ideal man."

"Yes! I'm so excited to meet him."

"I don't suppose the sex psychic told you where to find him," Emmy said, dryly.

"She told me I'd meet him when our jobs brought us together."

That could mean anything. May was a makeup and hair stylist who worked for Elegancia, a somewhat pricey event planning company. They took on everything from bar mitzvahs to weddings to corporate fundraisers. If the mystery man she was supposedly destined to meet wore a suit for a living, he might be part of a fundraiser. Or he could be at a cousin's wedding, a niece's bat mitzvah. It was so open-ended, and it left a lot of wiggle room for the supposed psychic. Emmy wanted to say all this out loud, but her sister was flying high on caffeine and dirty Tarot cards. It seemed wrong to drag her back down to Earth. They finished their coffee, made small talk about work, laughed about something their father had texted them. It was all perfectly normal. Emmy hoped her sister would be able to hold onto her optimistic and sunny attitude when Mr. Perfect failed to show his face. A part of her hated this stupid psychic for setting May up for such a huge disappointment, but Emmy reminded herself May was an adult and would be able to live with the consequences of her own actions.

One month, two weeks, and six days later (May had absolutely counted), May's boss, Ando, decided the company was ready to take on an online marketing campaign to advertise within the Twin Cities as well as farther out into North Dakota and Wisconsin. They took May and a few other coworkers to an ad agency where they had scheduled a meeting with three people who wore suits to work every day. One of those three people was Victor Coronado, a witty, intelligent, determined man who didn't let May leave the building without his phone number.

Emmy still refused to believe in psychics.

By the time May finished telling the story of how she'd come to meet and fall in love with Victor, her audience was rapt. A chorus of "awws" followed the conclusion, and Emmy forced her eyes to hold still, though they ached to roll.

"Emmy, you look like you swallowed a lemon wedge," May noted with a giggle. "Your superpower is being able to remain skeptical in the face of incontrovertible proof."

"Seriously," said Sheila, May's best friend and coworker. "What was this place called? I'm tempted to go check it out."

"It's called Meet Cute," May supplied. "But I thought you were still going strong with Danielle?"

"Going strong and banging like hammers, but that doesn't mean I couldn't use a psychic reading on our sexual health. Or a new dildo."

This was met with a combination of high-pitched laughter and clinking glasses as the women toasted to all things sex. Emmy smiled and shook her head, squeezing Sarah's hand when she sensed her friend was about to make a comment.

"I'll tell you my side of it later," she said under her breath.

"Good. Because I have a lot of questions."

The night was still young for many of the partygoers, but Emmy noted the time and sighed. She hated to leave—or rather, she knew May would hate for her to leave—but it was getting late.

"You're going?" May asked when she saw Emmy nudge Sarah and get to her feet.

"If I stayed, I'd just rain on your sex psychic parade," Emmy pointed out with a self-deprecating smile. "Besides, I have work tomorrow."

"You're working on Sunday?" one of May's friends asked, aghast.

"I'm a concierge. They don't always ask me to work weekends, but I fill in when I can. Anyway, this was super fun. I can't wait for next week!" This last part was said with genuine feeling, and Emmy followed it with a long hug for her sister. "I'm so glad you're happy," she whispered. "Going to be the best wedding ever. I'll talk to you later."

"Thanks for coming, sweets."

Emmy and Sarah said goodbye—they'd carpooled since they lived so close to each other—and made their way out to Sarah's car. Her friend had volunteered to be the designated driver so Emmy could cut loose a little at her sister's party. As soon as they were buckled in, the questions started.

"Your sister really thinks she met her fiancé because of a novelty deck of Tarot cards?"

"Yes."

Sarah shook her head. "She is literally the happiest person I've ever met, and she believes in fairy tales. Sometimes I wonder how she can be that sweet without ever being obnoxious. But she just... isn't. It's a mystery."

"If I ever figure out the answer, I'll let you know."

"Have you been to this sex psychic place?"

Emmy snorted in response.

"You're not tempted at all?" Sarah asked.

"I'm good. Me and romance aren't talking right now."

Sarah winced. "Oops. Can't even blame the wine for shoving my foot in my mouth. I only had one glass all night."

Emmy waved away her concern. "It's fine. I'm mostly over it. Just not looking to ask fate to send me another guy yet."

"I can understand that. It's good that May's happy with her guy, and that's enough for me."

"Yeah." Emmy smiled a little wistfully. "Me, too."

Emmy put on her beloved comfy pants as soon as she was back in her apartment. She paired them with a loose t-shirt, then went about the soothing routine of checking on her plants. The window boxes had been one of her first purchases when she'd moved in. One day, she told herself, she'd have a house with a real garden that she could play around in. For now, she tested the dampness of the soil and satisfied herself that the light rain they'd had a couple days back had been sufficient to keep the brightly colored pansies feeling happy and healthy. She'd done the arrangement herself and thought they looked bright and inviting. Pansies had always been a personal favorite. Back inside, she checked on her snake plant, which she affectionately called Sir Hiss. It probably wouldn't need water for weeks yet, but she liked to run her fingers over the waxy leaves. Her peace lily got a sip of water, as did the little thicket of bamboo in the handmade ceramic pot that May had gotten her for her last birthday.

Satisfied that all her plants were thriving, she flopped back in bed. Her ears soaked in the sweet silence of her apartment, and her boobs breathed twin sighs of relief at having been released from the confines of the torture device known as the strapless bra. Of course, with the silence came the worries that had stayed buried under a pile of drunken chatter for the past several hours. If this marriage didn't work out… but no, that thought was too cynical even for her. Emmy resolutely pushed it away, blinked back unexpected tears, breathed deep. She knew Victor well enough by now, and he was great. She could admit to herself that he matched the description Sex Psychic Lucy had provided all those months ago, but that was hardly proof of ESP. Plenty of people fit those characteristics. She was beginning to drift off into a post-party coma when her phone lit up. May was calling. Was something wrong? They'd only left the party a half hour ago. She hit answer.

"What's up?"

"Hey, I have a favor to ask you."

Emmy could hear the murmur of the bar in the background, so May was clearly still at her party. In the bathroom maybe. "What favor?"

"Go see Lucy."

"You're kidding."

"I'm really not. Monday is your day off, right? Go into the Cities and talk to her. Tell her I sent you. I bet she'll remember me. You could at least do me a solid and tell her about Victor, thank her for me."

"May, listen…"

"No. I don't have time to listen to all your reasons why you won't do this one harmless thing. I have to get back before my friends get worried that I'm throwing up or having a meltdown or something. Just go. You can be there and back in a couple hours. If she tries to charge you a ton of money, you can walk right back out. But you need to do this. You need to remember what it's like to have fun and be a little reckless. Maybe…"

"Maybe what?"

May's sigh came through loud and clear. "Maybe you need to do something like this for, you know… closure. A symbolic gesture to prove you're really done with The Asshole. It could be… cleansing."

Emmy highly doubted that, but she decided this wasn't worth an argument. She didn't have to go. Though she didn't make a habit of lying to her sister, she could easily say she went, make up a story about how her dream dude was right around the corner with an engagement ring and an enormous box of chocolates. That would make May happy and save her the gas money it would take to drive all the way into Minneapolis.

"Fine. I'll go on Monday."

"Yes! Thank you! I love you!"

"Yeah yeah."

After they hung up, Emmy brushed her teeth, then grabbed a book off her nightstand. It was a romantic thriller she'd read before, but sometimes she just needed to escape into a world where good was guaranteed to prevail over evil. Reading novels where characters existed in a wholly just world, where evil got its comeuppance and heroes ended up married… Well, it made her understand why Shakespeare's comedies had been so successful. The formula still worked.

She fell asleep reading, as she often did, and dreamed of ridiculous nonsense that successfully wiped all thoughts of romance and happily ever afters—or lack thereof—from her mind.

Two

The impulse to stalk her ex on social media was usually fleeting. But it was a slow day at the hotel, and as her lunch break crept closer, Emmy kept looking at her phone. It was past eleven, so checkout time was good and done. She gave in to temptation and tapped on the app, typed her ex's name into the search bar. Her face immediately went hot from shame she wished she didn't feel; he didn't deserve that emotion from her. Maybe "humiliation" was a better descriptor. There he was, toasting the camera with one hand while holding his phone out with the other. Leaning into the selfie with him was the woman he'd started seeing a suspiciously short time after Emmy had broken up with him. The woman he felt comfortable taking home to meet his family. So white she looked like she could get a sunburn from a sunny-side-up egg.

The photo was captioned only with #loveofmylife.

Before she could think about it, she was looking up directions from her apartment to Meet Cute. It wasn't such a long drive. And she shouldn't lie to May about something that would be easy enough to accomplish without subterfuge. May had said she needed closure, and it was starting to feel like her sister was right. She tapped the button to save the route and decided she'd go in the morning, if only to make sure Lucy the "psychic" was as harmless as May had made her out to be.

The trip into the Cities went by easily as Emmy spent the time listening to a true crime podcast that Sarah had gotten her addicted to—not everything could be a sugary story with a happy, righteous ending. She found the little shop after a bit of searching. She'd expected a garish facade with pictures of crystal balls and/or genitalia. Instead, she walked right by the place before checking her phone and noting her mistake.

The storefront was simple. Understated, even. Through the window she could see a bookshelf lined with romance novels—if the passionately entwined cover models were any indication—and a few precisely arranged displays of sex toys. Before too many people could see her peering into the window of a sex shop, she pushed her way inside and let the door close behind her. She smelled jasmine and, beneath that, a hint of an earthy smell that reminded her of reading an old, well-loved book. There didn't appear to be anyone else in the store, which would have felt unsettling in any other kind of retail establishment, but in this case, she didn't mind being alone and unobserved. It was easy to tell where the psychic readings took place. There was a wooden table in the corner with ladderback chairs on either side. The table runner had an astrological motif, and there were candles on a little wall-mounted shelf behind the whole setup. Since the candles were lit, Emmy assumed they were most likely responsible for the jasmine smell.

"Oof, what did he do?"

Emmy jumped and turned to see a woman approaching her from around one of the bookshelves. Though May had never described the psychic, Emmy knew she was looking at Lucy. She was gorgeous. Olive skin, full lips, long lashes. Her hair was dyed bright red and cut close to her scalp. Other than a colorful dress and a few bangles on her wrist, she didn't look like the clichéd image Emmy had formed in her mind. The woman looked at her expectantly, and it was at that point that Emmy remembered she'd asked a question.

"What did who do?"

"The ex. I'm sensing a guy. He must have done something pretty shitty to make you come here when you never would have set foot in here otherwise."

Emmy felt goosebumps break out on her arms and cursed her nerves for daring to be spooked by the comment. She steeled her resolve—psychics did *not* exist—and narrowed her eyes.

"Did May call you?"

"May? Oh! You must be Emmy! She told me so much about you."

"Yeah, I'll bet she did."

Lucy laughed. "Not *that* much, chickadee. But it's okay to be skeptical. How is May?"

Emmy didn't want to answer. Worse, she wanted to lie. She wanted to tell this woman that May was fed up with waiting for the mystery man she'd been promised and was currently sitting at home eating her way through the frozen dairy section of Trader Joe's. But the thought of saying anything like that weighed too heavily on her conscience, so she had no choice but to tell the truth.

"She's getting married this coming Saturday."

"Yes!" Lucy actually did a fist pump, making her bracelets jingle cheerfully. "I was hoping it would happen for her. She was such a sweetheart. I hope she comes back to tell me about him."

"I'm sure she will."

"So, what brings you here?"

Another chance to lie was mentally waved away. Emmy figured she might as well test the woman's so-called powers.

"My ex posted a selfie with the white girl he's ready to take home to Mommy and Daddy."

"Ugh. That dick."

"Well, you don't have to be psychic to figure that out."

Lucy's laugh poured out again, a deep, rich sound that struck Emmy as confident and somehow sexual. She wondered if Lucy practiced it in the mirror every day.

"Are you going to test me, then?"

"What do you mean?" Emmy asked, trying not to let it show that she'd literally just been thinking about doing that.

"You don't think I'm psychic. I think I am. Don't you want to see which one of us is right?"

Damn it, she was really good at this. But Emmy wouldn't be taken in by some cold reading and fancy guesswork.

"Yeah, alright. You going to give me a sexy Tarot reading?"

"If that's what you want. Have a seat."

"How much?"

Lucy cast an amused glance her way. "Free of charge, just like it is for all my first-time customers. You're welcome to browse the retail section when we're done, but that's your choice." She swept over to the table and pulled out a chair. Raised an eyebrow in silent challenge.

In for a penny, in for a pound. Emmy sat down across from her. Lucy had the deck of cards on the table already. She laid a hand over them—displaying a manicure with deep blue nails dotted with specks of yellow and pink—and met Emmy's gaze. Her expression was surprisingly sober, showing none of the jocular attitude from a moment ago.

"I'm going to have you take this stack of cards and mix them up. Use your non-dominant hand, and try to keep your mind relaxed. Sometimes we start with a question, but in this case, I think I want to do a basic three-card draw. Past, present, and future. Let's see where you were, where you're at, and where you're going. Sound good?"

Emmy swallowed and nodded. It was hard to react with derision when the woman who sat opposite from her was acting so serious. There was also something in her eyes, something like sympathy, and it made Emmy uncomfortable. What did Lucy the Sex Psychic know of her? What right did she have to pity her? Still, Emmy wouldn't back away from this. When Lucy told her to, she knocked the stack of cards over, began mixing them with her right hand. There was something hypnotic about watching them twist and turn, spinning, diving under one another, slipping across the table.

"Stop when it feels right," Lucy murmured. "Then draw the first card that catches your eye and turn it over."

Emmy stopped a moment later, went with the obvious and turned over the card that was on top of the mass. The woman on the card was upside down, but unmistakably a bride. Her hand-drawn dress had just the right amount of froth on the skirt, a tight bodice, a sweetheart neckline. She held an eclectic bouquet of flowers. Roses and daisies and daffodils, a few sprigs dotted with what might have been bluebells. There was no veil, and her hair cascaded down her back in a sweep of waves that flowed like a waterfall.

"The Bride," Lucy said quietly. "Reversed." Without warning, she reached out and took Emmy's hand, held firm but not tight. Her eyes were on the table, not the card, her gaze a little unfocused like she was trying to remember something she'd forgotten. "It was a bad breakup. Harder on you than him. It was a game for him, a diversion. Every time you tried to get him to commit, he dodged and evaded, but in a way that turned it around on you. It was never a relationship, not in any way that counted. When it ended, you came to see that, and it broke your heart that you had allowed it to be real for you."

Emmy wanted to slap away the hand that held hers. She wanted to leave right then and there. Had May really told this woman so much? Why? Had Lucy pushed for information on the off-chance Emmy would come in to see her? Was she preparing all along for this exact moment? The reminder of everything that had gone wrong with Andrew—or, The Asshole—was an arrow that hit its mark with painful precision. She'd had no time to build up a defense. But she didn't want to let Lucy win. She forced herself to sit and breathe through it.

"What did he do?" Lucy asked, meeting Emmy's eyes again. "There's something there. Something big, but I can't get at anything specific."

"Didn't May already tell you?" Emmy snapped.

Lucy shook her head slowly, sadly. "Ask her. When we're done here, before you tell her anything else, ask her how much we talked about you when she was here."

"Believe me, I will."

"Do you want to stop?"

"No. This is just a game. I don't run from games."

"Okay then," Lucy said, setting The Bride aside. "The next card is your present. Pick one."

Emmy didn't look. Didn't think. She pulled a card and flipped it. An arrangement of four condom packets with an upside-down number 4 in the middle. She wanted to laugh, but there was no room for humor in the moment.

"The Four of Condoms. I'm not surprised." Lucy ignored Emmy's eyeroll and continued. "You're shutting everyone else out. Friends and family are kept at a distance. Deliberately or unconsciously, I'm not sure. Certainly you're making sure to avoid romantic entanglements. Avoid the topic, avoid men. There's too much fear in you right now that you'll repeat past mistakes, and you're not ready to be vulnerable like that again. No shame in it. But I'll tell you this: your loved ones might begin to worry when they notice they're at arm's length. It could hurt them if you don't let them in, especially if they're used to being let in. It seems to me like part of you is resisting the good for fear of the bad. Yes, you could get hurt again, but there could be something beautiful just out of reach, too. It's right there, but you won't take it." When Emmy said nothing to this, Lucy gestured at the cards. "Pick your future."

It was all or nothing now. What would be the point in stopping? Emmy reached out for a card. When she flipped it, she saw two others beneath that were also face up. With the card in her hand out of the way, the other two were visible. Lucy's eyebrows rose.

"Let's see them all, if that's what they want."

Emmy set her card down, and Lucy pulled out the other two so they sat in a row of three. First, a card that was right-side up, with an image of two people leaning toward each other over a tall, round table. From the looks of it, it was a high-top table at a bar. They had drinks in front of them, and they were smiling in a way that said very plainly they were into each other. The middle card showed five condoms. The ones in the corners were unrolled and pointing toward the fifth, a packet in the center. The number 5 was upside down. The last card was an intricately braided belt with a padlock instead of a buckle.

"Getting Lucky," Lucy said, tapping the first card. "Big change is coming, Emmy. That much is clear. Then we have the Five of Condoms, reversed. You're going to end up in a situation that seems awful and overwhelming. You'll hate it, but eventually you'll come to understand that it's the best thing that could have ever happened to you. It will be healthy for you to come to this realization." Lucy smiled as she tapped a fingernail on the locked belt. "The Chastity Belt, reversed. Makes sense. You're going to be free of a heavy weight, metaphorically of course. Some burden or demon that has been latched onto you will be banished for good. From the looks of things, these two cards are qualifying the first. You'll have to go through something seemingly terrible, but when you learn to accept it, you will simultaneously be able to free yourself of something that's been holding you back." Lucy smiled, all warmth and encouragement. "The end result? Big life change. That's not so bad, huh?"

Emmy stared at the cards, still finding it difficult to reach for the humor she wanted. It should be so easy to laugh this off. One of the cards was covered in condoms, for God's sake. Plus, it had all been super vague. Any person could be told they had a big life change coming. That was the point of psychic readings. Say something that could apply to almost anybody, then let the person decide how their life fits that prediction. But the first two cards, the ones about her past and present, still hit too close for comfort.

"I don't think you're interested in doing a sexual strength reading or finding out what kind of man your soulmate is going to be," Lucy said gently.

Silently, Emmy shook her head. She stood up, backed away from the table. "You could have said anything. No matter what card came up, you could have found a way to say something that sounded like it applied to me. That's what cold reading is."

"I suppose that's true." Lucy stood and put her hands in the pockets of her flowy dress. "The cards have set meanings, so all I have to do is recite one or two of those meanings, make it sound like I'm applying it to you. It's a pretty easy con."

"But you don't ask for money for it."

"Not the first time."

"How much does it cost the second time?" Emmy asked, wondering if May had already been back, if she'd already spent an arm and a leg to figure out what her and Victor's children would look like.

"Twenty-five bucks per question."

"If you're the genuine article, why did you set up shop? Why try to capitalize on your special gifts?"

"Because I can't buy a carton of eggs with energy readings alone."

Emmy shook her head, refusing to believe it. Any of it. "You have psychic powers specifically linked to sex, but you don't go public with it? Get on TV? Do talk shows? Write a book?"

"I never said my powers were linked to sex."

Emmy gestured frustratedly all around them. She was getting increasingly agitated with each passing moment, and she had no idea why. Maybe it was because Lucy was looking at her with that vaguely pitying expression again. Whatever the reason, there was a restlessness living under her skin now that hadn't been there before she'd entered the shop.

"My powers are linked to strong feelings," Lucy clarified, accurately interpreting Emmy's gesture. "I don't like the idea of making my living by reading people who feel extreme hatred or depression, though, and I don't think you can blame me for that. Those kinds of emotions can weigh on you. If you're not careful, you start to lose track of which ones belong to other people, and you start to take on all that negativity as if it's your own. So… sex. Love and lust. Romance. Arousal. They're happy things, wouldn't you say? I like being a part of other people's happiness."

It all made so much sense. Too much sense. Emmy kept looking for the cracks in the arguments, the truth behind the facade. But there was nothing there. If this woman was a con artist, she was working a very long game, nickel-and-diming her marks twenty-five dollars at a time.

"For what it's worth, I feel what he did to you. I don't know the specifics, but I can feel it, and I'm sorry."

Emmy did not want to burst into tears in front of this woman. She turned abruptly away, walked to the bookshelves, and took a few deep breaths. When she was steady again, she looked at all the brightly colored spines in front of her, ran her fingers over a few of them. The smell of books was stronger here, for obvious reasons, and it contributed a lot to the return of her equilibrium.

"Do you believe in all this?" she asked without turning around.

"All what?" Lucy asked from behind her.

"Romance. Happily ever after. Soulmates. Do you believe in all that, or are you a cynic looking to make an easy buck off of saps and hopeless romantics?"

"That's a good question, one I'm surprised more people don't ask." Emmy begrudgingly respected that Lucy took a moment to think before answering. She spoke carefully as if weighing her own words for truth. "I believe in the human spirit. People who want to be happy deserve to be happy. I believe in the potential of happiness because not everyone has it. Even people who claim to be on top of the world are sometimes empty inside. So yeah, I guess I'm a hopeless romantic because I want to believe in the best possible version of everyone."

Emmy pulled a book off the shelf at random. "Sometimes I buy these just to laugh at them."

Lucy shrugged. "Books like that are meant to be entertaining, right? If they make you laugh, if they amuse you, then job done."

Emmy had to admit she'd been deliberately dismissive of the genre to see how Lucy would react. She had expected a staunch defense of romance novels, and was more relieved than she wanted to admit that she hadn't gotten one. A part of her found Lucy likable, *wanted* to like her. That didn't mean she was ready to admit out loud that sometimes she bought romance novels so she could escape, just for a little while, into a world where happiness was guaranteed.

"You've been rereading the same three books for long enough," Lucy said cheerily. "Treat yourself to something new to keep on your nightstand."

Do not reply to that, Emmy counseled herself. *A lot of people reread books. A lot of people keep books on their nightstand. It was a lucky guess.*

"Maybe I'll buy something utterly ridiculous so I can laugh at it."

"As long as you choose one that speaks to you. I'm not the book police. Browse as long as you like. I'll be around if you need anything."

Three

Emmy read the back cover of the book in her hand, saw it was a historical romance. Not her thing. Too hard to think past the chamber pots. She picked up another, read the synopsis, put it back. Some of the authors' names were familiar, but most were not. In fact, some of the biggest names in romance were conspicuously absent. That was kind of cool. It was like Lucy was giving other writers a chance to shine. She picked up a book, saw the title was *Light the Way*, and nearly put it back again thinking it was a religious romance. The cover simply depicted a man with bulging muscles embracing a gorgeous woman with a curly cascade of coppery hair. That image could be used for any subgenre of romance. Just to be sure, she flipped it over and read the synopsis. No, not religious. A slice of life romance where the male lead—Will—was a nurse. That was an unusual role for the sexy mantagonist, and it kept her reading. He lived in Cobalt, Massachusetts, apparently. A more romance novel town name she'd never heard. Feeling curious, she took out her phone and googled it.

Yeah, no Cobalt, Massachusetts. There were, however, many Chevy Cobalts for sale in Massachusetts.

Shaking her head at the author for naming the fictional town something so cutesy—and at herself for feeling the need to look it up—she finished skimming the back of the book. When she got to the part of the synopsis that introduced the female lead, she nearly laughed out loud. Bright Ammerman? This author named her female lead *Bright*?

"Okay, I'm getting this one," Emmy announced to the room at large.

"Bring it on over!" Lucy called without missing a beat.

Emmy found her at a cash register tucked away in the back corner, behind a display of strap-ons. She handed Lucy the book, spared a moment to appreciate the nondescript brown paper bag that Lucy grabbed from beneath the counter.

"I haven't read this one," Lucy commented. "You'll have to let me know if you like it."

Emmy didn't respond, only watched as Lucy scanned the barcode on the back cover. Rather than the expected beep of success, the machine made a disgruntled noise. Frowning, Lucy pointed the scanner at the book from farther away. It didn't work.

"Weird. Hold on."

She put the book on the counter and began typing the ISBN into her computer. A moment after she hit enter, she frowned at the screen.

"I must have forgotten to enter this one into my system before shelving it," she said, more to herself than to Emmy. She picked up the book again and looked at the front cover.

When she next spoke, it was if she were addressing the book itself. "I swear I triple-checked my stock. How did you get out there on the shelf? Did you sneak in?"

"I guess even psychics make mistakes, huh?" Emmy said, unable to keep the smug expression off her face.

"Psychic, but still human," Lucy said with a smile. She quickly flipped through some of the pages, ran her fingers over them. Frowned, cocked her head.

A prickle of unease skittered up Emmy's spine, followed immediately by disgust with herself. What was she doing letting herself be taken in by Lucy's performance? To compensate, she made sure to sneer as she asked, "Are you sensing bad vibrations?"

Lucy shook her head slightly, clearly not at all bothered by Emmy's derisive tone. "I'm getting... something." She shrugged and closed the book. "I'm sure it's just an echo from the previous owner. It's clearly used. But it's still in good shape! How about I ring it up at my standard pre-owned price?"

"That's fine." Emmy handed over her card and waited while Lucy slipped the book and the receipt into the bag.

"Thanks for coming," Lucy said, and she sounded sincere. "Tell May to come see me and tell me all about her guy."

"I will."

"I'm sorry you couldn't hate me."

"What makes you think I don't?"

Lucy reached out and tapped the bag in Emmy's hand. "You didn't have to buy a book. Come on back if you ever have a burning romantic question you're willing to pay twenty-five dollars to answer."

"Thanks."

Emmy left the shop feeling confused. Far from hating Lucy, she felt a reluctant kind of admiration for her. The supposed psychic had been right; Emmy didn't hate her, and she was a little disappointed about that. Still, there was a bright side. She could now definitively say that May had not been taken in by a con artist. At least not in any way that would be harmful. Lucy wasn't psychic, but she meant well. Good enough.

With her new book in hand, Emmy got into her car and started the uneventful drive back to her apartment. It was her day off, but she couldn't start reading until she'd checked a few things off her to-do list. She had to check in with May, get groceries, call the dress place to make sure the final alterations on her maid of honor gown were complete. The steamy romance between Will and Bright would have to take second place to the mundane tasks of real life.

May texted her before she arrived home that evening.

> Did you do it? Did you go see Lucy???

> Yes, she is very happy for you

> Yay! What did she say to you? Did you get a reading????

> Apparently I'm in for a big life change and other vague nonsense

> Boo! No being a stick in the mud I'm calling you in 2 minutes

There was no avoiding it. Emmy set her stuff down and kept her phone out knowing that May would make good on the threat. Sure enough, her phone lit up a couple minutes later. She answered and was immediately assaulted by a heartfelt, if not entirely pitch perfect, rendition of "My Heart Will Go On."

"*Gomen, gomen,*" May apologized immediately. "*Chotto mate.*" Emmy waited as requested. She heard a dull sound that must have been a door closing because everything instantly went quiet. "You still there?"

"Yes. Where the hell are you?"

"Rehearsal dinner for the Nash wedding on Friday night. This was the only time they could do it, and they asked the whole team to stick around for a while to make sure there were no hiccups."

"Uh huh. Celine sounds a little off. Did she forget to warm up?"

"Huh? Oh! Ha. Yeah, that's the sister of the bride who is convinced she is the next American Idol or X-Factor or whatever. The bride's a genius. She convinced the sister to sing at the rehearsal instead of the actual wedding. Told her it would be more intimate and personal that way."

"And she bought it?" Emmy asked.

"Ah... maybe."

"She's totally going to grab the mic at the reception," Emmy predicted.

"Oh, yeah." May giggled. "It's the thought that counts?"

"You say that now. Wait 'til I get up on stage on Saturday and start belting out—" She paused, took a deep breath, and let loose with, "I-I-I want to tha-ank you... for giving me the best day of my life."

"I double dog dare you," May said after a beat of silence. "I will do your chores for a month if you do that."

"Don't think I won't. That's a good deal for me. I hate doing dishes."

"Okay, you've distracted me long enough. What did Lucy tell you? I want the full story. Not just the Emmy version."

Damn. She'd just started thinking she'd gotten May off topic enough where she'd forget to swing back around to the psychic. There was no point in trying to put her off. Emmy decided to get it over with instead. She recounted the details as close as she remembered them.

"Huh," May said once she'd finished. "That... sounds a lot more dire than mine did."

"If she really is psychic, then she definitely sensed I wouldn't be taken in by puppies and rainbows and unicorns."

"Oh, and I would?"

Emmy winced. "That's not what I meant. Exactly."

May laughed. "I absolutely would, and you know it. Not just would. *Did*. And now I'm getting married on Saturday!"

"Okay, point to you."

"Yes! I love points! Seriously though, thanks for going. I know you only did it for me. Did you at least have fun?"

"Yeah, I guess. She wasn't what I expected, I'll give her that."

"Wow, high praise coming from you." May paused. "Oh, shoot. Ando just texted. I have to go. Talk to you later?"

"Yeah. Go do your thing."

"Later, sweets. Love you."

"Love you, too. *Mata ne*."

That hadn't been too painful. May was happy. Lucy and her weird Tarot deck were in the past. Emmy was glad to wash her hands of the whole thing. She was tired from a day of running around and finalizing wedding plans. It was barely ten when she gave in to fatigue, changed into her cozy pajamas with rubber ducks on them, and scooted under the covers. She'd nearly forgotten about her new novel until she caught sight of it on the nightstand. She had just enough energy left to give it a try, so she cracked it open.

While flipping through the first few pages, she paused on the dedication.

For you

That was unusual. Emmy frowned for a moment, then moved past it. The author had dedicated her book to her readers. It was a nice sentiment. Didn't mean the author had no family or friends to dedicate the book to. That was too sad a thought. Emmy wouldn't allow sad thoughts to pollute the happy romance world she was about to enter. She found the first chapter and began to read.

The book quickly proved to be a worthwhile purchase. The writing was a little flowery for her taste, but the emotions were genuine, and Will felt like a real person. It was interesting to note that he appeared to be the protagonist of the novel, though she had no doubt she'd be treated to Bright's perspective soon enough. Usually the romances she read focused on the female lead. She welcomed the change of pace. After succumbing to a jaw-cracking yawn, she continued into chapter two, interested to see what Will would do now that his car had broken down.

Will indulged himself with some creative curses as he turned the key in the ignition and listened to his car sputter and gasp like a man dying of thirst in the desert. The check engine light had flashed for only a second before the car had died. Very helpful. With a sigh, he yanked out his keys and palmed the little flashlight keychain that had been a gift from his grandfather. His grandfather, who had left him his house. His grandfather, who had believed in luck favoring the prepared. His grandfather, who had died surrounded by his family, surrounded by legacy and love.

Will knew nothing about cars, but...

"Come on, Gordon," he muttered. "Let's see what we can see."

With Gordon leading the way, he popped the hood and pushed out of the car.

It took Emmy a moment to realize that he wasn't talking to an imaginary friend; he'd named his flashlight Gordon. Was that a *Flash Gordon* reference? She wasn't sure whether she should be impressed or disgusted by the pun. At least the book was eliciting genuine reactions from her. Shaking her head, she found her place and continued to read.

Though he'd never told anybody that he'd named his flashlight all those years ago when his grandfather had gifted it to him, he still felt a twinge of embarrassment whenever he thought about it or talked to the little inanimate object.

"Well, you should," Emmy said, stifling another yawn. "It's fucking embarrassing."

Gordon illuminated the engine, the tubes, the battery, the dust-caked container for windshield wiper fluid—which he had once again forgotten to replace despite the continued insistence of the light on the dash. He tried to see anything that was wrong, begged the fates to let him find something he could fix then and there. It was too late to get to work on time, but if he could fix the car, he could eventually make it there to finish his shift. But he still didn't know anything about cars, and the fates were still cruel. Tired, resigned, defeated, he pulled his phone out of his pocket to call a tow.

Emmy read through Will's journey to the mechanic, his somewhat contrived meet-cute with Bright, with requisite flirtation, and a rapid-fire description of his workday after he finally made it to the hospital. She could tell she was approaching the end of the chapter—Will had just crawled into bed—and thought she could push through before calling it a night. Her bookmark was ready.

Twenty seconds later, the book flopped unceremoniously onto the floor as Emmy dropped off to sleep.

Four

She woke several hours later and blinked the sleep out of her eyes. So much for making it to the end of the chapter. She patted the bed around her, then looked over the edge and spotted the book sprawled on the floor. Scooping it up, she quickly skimmed through until she found the last page she remembered reading and slipped her bookmark into place. She left the closed book on her nightstand next to the other three that had been living there for the past several months. Lucy's uncannily accurate words came back to her, and Emmy frowned. It had to have been a lucky guess, damn it. But she still felt petty enough to gather up the books and put them back on her book/plant shelf, which stood sentry next to her work/plant desk and across from the cooking/plant counter in her kitchenette.

She'd stumbled upon her obsession with plants at a young age. Her parents had unwittingly opened that door for her by being utterly hopeless with all things floral.

Emmy grabbed everything she would need for her workday and prepared to leave the apartment. She was a few steps from her car when her phone lit up with an incoming call.

"Hey, Mom," she answered, sliding into the driver's seat.

"Hey yourself. Do you have a minute?"

"I'm heading into work, but I can talk while I'm driving."

"Ah, *sōdesuka*. I was going to ask if you could swing by the house."

"Why? Is everything okay?" Emmy asked.

"Yes, everything's fine. May's wedding present arrived!"

"That's great! See, I told you it would be here in time."

"You never miss a chance to say, 'I told you so.'"

Emmy could hear the smile in her mother's voice, and her own mood responded to it. "That's me. Queen of Correct. So why do you need me?"

"I want you to see it. I could text you a picture, but I think it has a better effect in person."

"Okay." Emmy thought about wedding prep, work, any other obligations that might have snuck onto her schedule. She didn't think she had anything else going on that day. "I'll come by after work, okay? You can make me dinner."

"I can? How lucky for me."

"When did you get so sarcastic?" Emmy asked with a laugh.

"I learned from the best. I'll see you tonight. Text when you're on your way. Love you."

"Love you, too."

Emmy hung up, still smiling to herself. Her mother always did that for her. She had a way about her. And, since her mom could no longer hear her, she allowed herself one quick sigh of relief. All the shipping delays on May's present had also gotten Emmy pretty worried about timing.

Of course, May would have happily accepted a gift after her honeymoon, but Emmy knew it was important to her parents that the gift be presented at the rehearsal dinner as planned. They had contributed financially to the wedding, but that was a gift to the couple. This... this was just for May.

Emmy didn't find work at the hotel boring by any means. She'd tried other career paths that hadn't panned out, but so far this one suited her well enough. She was content with it. Usually. Except this particular shift dragged by. She went through most of it by rote. Check notes from managers and night audit, one early check-in at ten, four checkouts at eleven. She did what was expected of her, and when time lagged, she resisted the urge to go anywhere near social media.

Traffic that evening was the usual, but she eventually swung into the driveway of her childhood home. The door opened before she could reach it, and her mom pulled her inside.

"You have to see it! It's all set up now."

Emmy allowed herself to be guided to the spare room—which had been her room once upon a time. She inhaled once, quickly, at the sight of the gift, then let her breath out slowly on a sigh.

"It's beautiful, Ma. *Hontō ni.*"

The antique vanity gleamed with fresh polish, but it still felt old. The way the grain of the wood stood out, the elegant curves of the legs, the detailed pattern of roses carved into the mirror's frame. The brass drawer pulls showed just a touch of tarnish, which Emmy thought added charm to the overall effect. A lace runner was draped artistically over the length of the table. It perfectly accented the delicate silver and enamel makeup brushes, compacts, and combs that were laid out on top of it.

Her mother stepped forward and pulled the stool out from under the desk.

"This is the only thing we had redone," she said, tapping the newly upholstered cushion. "The seller recommended it."

"It's perfect," Emmy said. "Absolutely perfect. I always knew you loved May more than me."

"Your dad and I thought we hid it so well!"

Emmy laughed. "Cat's out of the bag. It's okay. Second best is still a silver medal, if you think about it."

Her mother put her hands on her hips. "What makes you think you get silver? We gave that to Sarah ages ago."

Emmy pretended to pout.

Her mom gave her arm a playful smack. "We love you both equally and you know it. When you get married, you can have all the Japanese maple trees you want. I'll even throw in a trowel."

Emmy's joy dimmed a little. "I'm gonna hold you to that."

Her mother's face fell. She apologized quietly and gently in a mixture of English and Japanese.

"*Daijōbu*, Ma. I'm happy to wait to get married rather than hook myself up to an asshole."

"Smart girl." The hand that had slapped her playfully a moment before now pulled Emmy in for a quick squeeze.

They stood for a moment in silence, admiring the splendor of May's gift, until Emmy heard her father's quiet footfalls. They turned to see him standing in the doorway.

Like his wife, he was wearing casual clothes that he'd changed into after work. He wore a Twins cap over his salt-and-pepper hair and house slippers over white socks. He raised his eyebrows, and said in his typical quiet, deadpan way, "I was promised dinner." Then he smiled that little smile that popped out anytime he told a joke, even when he tried his hardest to maintain a poker face, and held his arms out. Emmy went to him and let him hug her close.

"Let's eat," she said, her head still resting against her father's shoulder.

They shared a homecooked meal of steak, rice, and salad. The conversation centered around the wedding, naturally. There wasn't going to be much else to talk about until it was well over.

Emmy helped her parents clean up after dinner, then said her goodbyes. She didn't bother telling them that she planned to check on their garden before she left; they knew.

She called it her parents' garden, but Emmy knew it was hers. She'd done everything from planting seeds, to pruning and deadheading, to setting up a decorative fence around the perimeter. She'd also slipped a single gnome in among the perennials. It had been a joke at first, but then May had bought a cheerful, porcelain lucky cat to be the gnome's friend. Then, not wanting to feel left out, her father had added a scarecrow he'd picked up from a craft fair. The decorations should have clashed, but they looked deliberate, fun, and… homey, Emmy decided, brushing some stray dirt off the cat's head.

Yes, it had once been a bare patch of dirt. She didn't blame her parents for letting it go. They both worked full-time, and neither one had any particular interest in plants.

Why had she decided to take it over? She couldn't quite remember now. Fourteen years old, still getting used to high school, still trying to figure herself out. Maybe hearing her parents' perfunctory discussions about repurposing the space over the years had gotten to her. All she remembered was that, one day, she'd simply looked at the bare ground and decided it was going to be hers.

It started with her typing "How to garden" in the search bar of the secondhand laptop she kept on her desk.

She took notes on everything from planting schedules to pruning, common gardening mistakes to recommended soil brands. One YouTube tutorial taught her how to tell the difference between plants that had been over-watered versus under-watered. Another, run by a native Minnesotan, taught her all about what soils and pesticides to avoid in order to protect the local, lake-based ecosystem. The more she researched, the more determined she became. She started a list of plants she wanted to try growing, what supplies she needed, and how much everything would cost. Her parents gave her a weekly allowance, and she had plenty saved up. It relieved her to learn that dirt was, well, cheap. As were most seeds. It cost a little bit of money to mail a soil sample to NDSU for analysis, but she considered it an investment.

After several weeks of extracting every morsel of knowledge to be found in various blogs, videos, and articles, Emmy deemed her preparation complete. She remembered the moment when she set her pen down and closed her computer, feeling ready for the next step.

"I'm gonna have May take me to the hardware store after we drop you off." She had turned around in her seat and frowned down at her best friend. "What are you doing?"

Sarah, her dirty blonde curls tied back in a frothy ponytail, was sitting on the floor, surrounded by scraps of paper and several magazines that had already seen the business end of her scissors. She finished cutting out yet another picture from the magazine sitting in her lap before she answered.

"It's for art class," was the only explanation she offered. She held up the picture of the slender, grinning model, then severed her head with one decisive snap of the scissors. Then she frowned. "The hardware store? Why?" Her eyes tracked to the closed laptop. "Oh, my God! Are you finally done with all the nerd stuff?"

"I keep telling you, it's not nerd stuff. It's research."

"Which is nerd stuff," Sarah countered easily.

"You're cutting the heads off supermodels," Emmy pointed out.

"Yeah, but that's art nerd stuff."

"Oh, right. So different."

Sarah started to pack up her magazine clippings and gather the trash. "I'm just saying, you buy some seeds, you throw them on the ground. It's not that complicated."

Emmy shook her head, smiling at what she knew was feigned disdain on her friend's part. "You should host like… a *bad* gardening YouTube channel. 'Hey, guys, today I'm going to teach you how to plant flowers.'" She mimed holding a fistful of seeds and spiking them at the ground like a triumphant football player. "'And there you go! All done! Like and subscribe! Catch you next time.'"

Sarah laughed. "Honestly, that could work. But I'll stick to art nerd shit."

Emmy went to her nightstand to get her wallet, only to discover that it wasn't there. She was sure she'd left it next to the lamp, but maybe... nope, not in the drawer either. To be certain, she pushed around the various knickknacks, odds and ends. She did find a flash drive she'd been looking for a couple weeks back, so that was a plus.

"What are you doing?" Sarah asked.

"Looking for my wallet."

Sarah watched Emmy move to her desk, open one drawer, then another. "You spent a hundred years taking notes on how to grow plants, but you can't find your wallet? You are the most organized disorganized person I know. Or is it disorganized organized person?"

Emmy dug into her dresser. "I'm not disorganized."

"You are looking for your wallet in your underwear drawer."

"Which is organized, in case you didn't see. Aha!" She pulled the wallet out of the middle dresser drawer. "I put it in with my jeans."

"Why?"

"I dunno. I guess I thought I'd be wearing jeans the next time I needed it."

Since she was currently wearing a comfy pair of sweats, Sarah could only sigh at her and shake her head.

"No more throwing shade," Emmy ordered her friend. "Let's go get May."

They made their way out of Emmy's room, and Sarah waited in the hall, her backpack slung over one shoulder, while Emmy went to tell May they were ready to leave. May's door was open, but when Emmy stepped up to the threshold, she saw her sister was on the phone. She appeared to be listening intently to whoever was on the other end of the call. With the phone squeezed between her shoulder and her ear, she tested out a new eyeshadow palette, rubbing a stripe of color on the back of her hand, blending it a little, holding it up to the light. Emmy saw at least four different colors on her already.

"Okay, hold on," May said suddenly. She looked up, noticed Emmy in the doorway, and shot her a quick apologetic look. "No, wait. Just take a second. Did you talk to him about what Izzy said?" She paused to listen to the response. "I get that, but listen to me, you need to do this face-to-face. Not because he deserves it, but because *you* do. Wait until you're calm. Then talk to him. You're jumping to so many conclusions." More listening. Emmy could hear the vague buzz of May's friend as she responded. May brushed another careful line of color on her hand. Then nodded. "That sounds good. See? You can do this. You have a plan. Text me as soon as you're done talking to him. I want to know what he says. Okay? Okay. Yeah… I'll be here. You can do this!"

"You should start charging people for dumping all over you like that," Emmy said after May had hung up.

"Nah." May closed the eyeshadow, then put it on her overburdened, but meticulously organized, makeup shelf. "She'd do the same for me."

"When has anyone ever had to let you dump all over them?" Emmy asked. "When have you ever caused drama?"

"It could happen." At Emmy's dubious look, she laughed. "What can I say? I enjoy life."

"No one enjoys life," Emmy countered. They left May's room and Sarah automatically fell into step with them. "I think you've got something else going on to make you so happy. I know you're not on drugs…" She cocked her head. "Are you a robot?"

"Maybe she's a serial killer," Sarah suggested. "I heard about this one guy who had like a wife and kids and stuff, and everyone at work said he was nice, and he always smiled and helped his neighbor get her groceries out of the car, but he killed like a thousand people."

They piled into May's car. May only shrugged at the serial killer comment. "Guess you'll never know," she said, smirking at Sarah in the rearview mirror. "But you better stay on my good side!"

"Wow, that made me shudder. Like actually." Sarah wiggled a little as if shaking off the chill. "Please don't kill me. I have an algebra test on Monday."

"Okay. Since you asked nicely."

They continued to casually discuss serial killers during the drive to Sarah's house. When they arrived, Emmy turned around from the front seat to say goodbye.

"See you tomorrow, darling."

They tapped the tips of their index fingers together in their usual gesture of farewell. Sarah's older sister, Beth, had once told them it made them look like lesbians. The comment was so baffling and funny that they'd begun crafting an increasingly fanciful hypothetical love story for themselves that involved houses all over the world, fabulous wealth, and plenty of scandal. There was also a single paparazzo named Gregolas who followed them everywhere they went, desperate to capture a single shot of their infamous finger touch. In the way of younger siblings, they also started doing it more often when Beth was around.

"I need to go to the hardware store," Emmy said as May pulled away from the curb.

"Okay."

May drove her to the store without any question or complaint. She followed Emmy through the garden section. From the way she kept checking her phone and shooting off texts, Emmy guessed that her friend had confronted whoever they were supposed to talk to. She was glad May would have something to keep her occupied. Taking the folded list out of her pocket, Emmy got to work filling the cart with pots, seeds, soil, and tools.

She still remembered the smell, earthy and comforting, which had been new to her at the time. She'd gone home that evening and begun planting. Made a mess. Her patient parents had believed her when she said she'd clean it up, and she'd made sure to do so before going to bed.

The very next morning, even though she knew nothing was going to be growing yet, she checked her little seedling pots. It became a routine, something she did after she woke up and before she brushed her teeth. The feeling that had blown through her the day she'd seen the first sprouts poking out of the soil... it was indescribable. She'd created something. She'd made seeds *grow*. Green and delicate and new. A dozen at first. Then a dozen more. And more yet. Building everything up over the years until the once-bare patch of dirt was overflowing with life.

One of her fondest memories was a bright Saturday morning when her father had appeared with a brand-new lawn chair. Without a word, he'd set himself up in the shade with a newspaper and a can of pop. That was the first day of many when her father found time to just hang with her while she gardened. Occasionally her mother would join him, or straight up steal his chair. May even stopped by to ask questions sometimes, though she kept herself firmly on the lawn and cast wary glances at the dirt.

Standing in the garden she'd made herself, one that had been hers for half her life now, Emmy ran her fingers over a rose petal. If she went to the closet in the mudroom right now, she was pretty sure she would find that same fold-up yellow lawn chair. It was hard not to find reasons to linger, let the good memories wash over her, but eventually she had to leave. What would the neighbors think if they saw the Miuras' daughter standing idly in their garden like she was joining the gnome, the lucky cat, and the scarecrow? Maybe that was her calling, she mused as she walked to her car.

Emmy Miura: Lawn Ornament.

It would make for fun business cards at least.

Sighing a little, she turned the key in the ignition and headed for home.

That night, after getting into her favored duck pajamas, Emmy cracked open her romance novel to see how handsome nurse Will Barrett was doing. The narrator treated her to a tour of the hospital. She met Will's best friend, Jared, an attractive Black anesthesiologist who had been burned by love once before in a messy divorce. The narrator didn't explicitly describe him as attractive, but Emmy figured it was implied since he was a character in a romance novel. She wondered if Jared was going to end up the subject of a follow-up novel. At the moment, she felt fairly certain she'd be interested enough to read it.

Her eyes began to droop as Will sat drinking alone at the neighborhood gastropub after a bad day at work. Then

Bright showed up unexpectedly, and it turned into a date of sorts.

"Flirt harder," Emmy muttered sleepily after Bright pulled the classic giggle-and-touch-hot-guy's-arm maneuver. "I don't think you're being obvious enough yet."

"I haven't seen you around town much," Will said, sipping his beer. His bad mood had flown away on swift wings the moment he'd heard Bright's laugh.

"Mm, and you won't for a while yet. I'm still looking to hire more part-time help for my shop. Until then it's work, work, work," Bright replied, smiling sweetly.

"Work, work, work," Will repeated with a nod.

Emmy yawned as she pushed herself to at least finish the scene, but she only managed to read the rest of Will's dialogue.

"Welcome to my world."

Emmy didn't feel the book slip from her fingers as she dropped instantly to sleep.

Five

She woke up, groggy and disoriented, with sunlight blasting directly into her eyes. Squinting against the glare, she considered whether she'd be able to convince her body to fall back asleep if she put a pillow over her head. She had no idea what time it was, but it felt too early to be awake.

"What the fuck!"

The panicked male shout had Emmy shooting out of bed, adrenaline pushing her from drowsy to wide-awake in the span of a second. She whirled around to see an enormous dude, wearing nothing but a pair of plaid boxers, gaping at her.

"What the *fuck*?" he repeated, with a slightly more interrogative inflection.

"Who the hell are you?" Emmy asked in response, trying to tamp down her panic. Her head swiveled as she took in her surroundings and absorbed the fact that the unfamiliar man came paired with an unfamiliar room. "Where am I? Did you..." She paused, swallowed, and took a small step back. This was bad. Really bad. "Did you drug me?"

"Are you kidding me?" the guy demanded. He ran his hands through his hair in pure agitation. "Jesus, no I didn't drug you. You're the one who showed up in my house. You don't get to make any accusations here."

"Okay, hold on. Hold on. Just for a second." Emmy put up both hands, palms out, as if she could press pause on life. Her brain whirled. She wished this were a dream, but knew without a doubt that she was awake. Awake but... possibly losing her memory. Or her mind.

Then her eyes tracked back down to the guy's boxers.

Plaid boxers.

"Um..." he said, clearing his throat. He didn't say "What the fuck" a third time, but his expression did. She watched him grab a pair of sweats out of his dresser and slip them on. He'd had them neatly folded, she noted. Who folded sweatpants?

Focus, Emmy, she ordered herself. Then she remembered the book. What about plaid boxers made her think of the book?

Wearing nothing but a pair of plaid boxers, Will flopped into bed and... something, something, something.

She'd read those words recently, more or less. She hadn't memorized the damn book. But this one detail sure was sticking out at the moment.

"Plaid boxers," Emmy whispered, and she could feel the blood draining out of her face.

"What?"

Emmy swallowed, looked back up at the guy. Movie star handsome. Clearly worked out—a rigidly defined six pack was on full display and she'd seen the way his biceps bulged when he ran his hands through his hair. Over six feet tall.

Tousled brown hair, tan skin, and... he was too far away to tell for sure, but she was starting to think his eyes might be hazel.

"What's your name?"

She barely recognized the sound of her own voice. Was that buzzing in her ears an auditory symptom of panic?

He looked like he wasn't going to answer, but something on her face must have demonstrated the importance of the question. "Will."

"I think I'm going to be sick."

Emmy rushed out of the room, found a bathroom, locked herself inside. She pulled her hair back and leaned over the sink, maintaining that position until she was sure that her stomach wasn't going to turn inside out. Then she looked into the mirror. Yep. She was still her. Still wearing ducky pajamas. Apparently, she had completely departed from reality. Was she still in her apartment and hallucinating the book character guy? Or was her apartment just another layer of the delusion? Maybe she'd never been sane. Except... hallucinations weren't supposed to be this real, were they? How could she know? Feeling her hands tremble, Emmy reached out to grip the edge of the sink. She needed to focus. Follow the logic. She could do this. Sure, it seemed like logic had abandoned her, but she could bring it back. She could find it. There had to be a reasonable explanation. There *had* to be. She was *not* in a book.

"You're not in a book," she said to her reflection. Her stomach threatened to heave again, and she ruthlessly swallowed the nerves back down. "You're not in a book," she repeated, forcing strength into her thready voice. "And you're not leaving this bathroom until you figure out what's really going on." Her shell-shocked expression stared back at her, and she cursed under her breath. "I'm going to be in this bathroom for a long time."

While she was in the bathroom, Will pulled on a shirt and tried not to panic. He'd gone to bed alone the night before. It wasn't like he'd gone on a drug and alcohol binge after a fourteen-hour shift and brought someone home. He'd been lucid... or as lucid as a sleep-deprived person can be. So where the hell had the woman come from? The fact that she was just as uncertain about that as he was made him uneasy. *More* uneasy. When the door creaked open and she emerged from the bathroom, he took in her appearance. Pale. Too pale. But beautiful. God he wished he could ignore that, but he had eyes, didn't he? Her hair, dark brown with hints of caramel highlights, fell in soft waves down her back. Eyes that were wide and dark. Lips that were perfectly full, slightly parted now as she breathed slowly in through her nose and out through her mouth. No, he couldn't deny he found her appealing on a physical level. But that didn't change the fact that she wasn't supposed to be in his house.

"Okay," she said, and her voice was strained. "There are only two possibilities here."

"I think there are more than two."

She shook her head, dismissing his interjection. Then she met his gaze. Her eyes were... haunted, if he had to pick a word. "I need to tell you what I know. It's going to sound insane, but this whole situation is insane. I just need you to listen to me."

Will was trying to recall everything he could about mental disorders from his courses in college. It was clear this woman needed help, but he wasn't the man for the job. He was a nurse in the pediatric wing for fuck's sake. He knew all the names of the *Paw Patrol* dogs, could recite trivia about *Thomas the Tank Engine* as if he had created the series. He'd seen so many of Blippi's videos that he might as well consider the suspender-clad show host a close personal friend. None of that helped him in this situation. How was he supposed to talk this woman down from what was clearly a psychotic break?

Humor her, he decided. Humor her until a better solution came along.

"What do you need to tell me?" he asked, keeping his voice as calm and gentle as he could manage.

It sounded like he was talking to a wounded animal. Emmy tried not to feel offended as she organized her thoughts. She would probably have reacted the same way if the roles were reversed.

"Last night... I fell asleep reading a book," she began. "The main character in that book was named Will Barrett." She saw Will's eyebrows wing up, and the look in his eyes gave her the impression he was deciding between fight or flight. Seeing no other recourse, she plowed on. "Sometime in the first few chapters, Will Barrett fell asleep wearing only a pair of plaid boxers. I fell asleep last night in my apartment—in *my* bed—in suburban Minnesota, and I woke up this morning in your bed." She paused to take a breath, then let it out slowly. "Either I have gone deeply and irrevocably insane and you are a hallucination, or I am somehow... in that book."

Insane was right. Will wanted to take a step back, but the woman posed no real threat. She didn't have a weapon, and she was… dainty. He was pretty sure he could take her if it came to a hand-to-hand fight.

"I'm not a hallucination," he said, trying for calm and rational.

She arched an eyebrow. "So you're a book character, huh?"

"No, I'm going to go with option three."

When he didn't expound, Emmy gestured for him to continue. He shrugged. "I don't know what it is, but it's definitely more logical than me being a book character."

She nodded. "Right. I can hope for that. And, for what it's worth… I'm sorry. However I ended up here, I didn't mean to, and I'm sorry I scared you. As soon as I figure out how, I'll get out of your hair."

"I could drive you home."

"To Minnesota?"

"No, not to Minnesota." This was a truly surreal conversation. What was he supposed to say to her? If she was having a mental break, there was no point in trying to be rational. Weirdly enough, other than telling him a truly wild story about him being in a book, she wasn't acting like she'd dissociated. Her gaze was clear and direct. Her speech wasn't slurred. She responded to him and to the situation in an appropriate way, or as appropriate as was possible given the circumstances. There were no physical tics, no nervous gestures. He didn't see any indication of self-harm in the form of scars, cuts, missing hair, chewed lips. "Are you *sure* you live in Minnesota?" he tried.

"Yes, of course. I…" Emmy paused, realizing that she was not going to be able to reach into her pocket, grab her wallet, and show him her driver's license. She didn't make a habit of putting her wallet in her pajama pants. "I'm… in my pajamas."

"Yes, you are."

She looked down at herself. "I'm not wearing a bra."

"No comment."

"Fantastic."

"No comment again."

"I wasn't talking about my tits."

To her surprise, he smiled. The sheer sex appeal in the expression—Lord, he had a dimple in his left cheek—actually made her mouth go dry.

"How can you look at me like that and *not* believe you're a character in a romance novel?"

"It was a *romance* novel?" His disgust was evident, the sexy smile wiped clean as if it had never been.

"Look, you don't even believe me, so why are you acting offended?"

"You didn't mention it was a romance novel when you first brought it up."

"I... thought you might be offended."

"Ha!"

"Okay, shut up for a second!" Emmy closed her eyes, thought hard. She was in a strange place with no money, no ID, and no way to prove what was real. Unless... maybe she could pull a Lucy and tell him something about himself? Except that would do nothing to help her discern what was real. If he was her hallucination, *he* wasn't the one who needed convincing. She needed to think of a way to convince *herself*. Even if she could confirm it was a hallucination, at least that would give her a heading, a place to start. Closing her eyes, she visualized what little of the world she knew so far. What was something she would definitely recognize as a figment of her own imagination? Will didn't work for this experiment. He looked only vaguely like the cover model on the book, and her imagination had conjured up some kind of faceless apparition with fantastic muscle tone. Mentally, she cycled through what she'd read.

It struck her in the very next second.

She opened her eyes, looked up at him. "Go get your keys."

His expression instantly became wary. "Why?"

"Because I need to see Gordon."

Will felt like all the air had been sucked out of the room. Heat flooded his face as embarrassment washed through him, but that quickly cooled to an icy dread. There was something wrong here. Was she playing a prank? Even that explanation wouldn't make sense. He'd never spoken the name of his damn flashlight out loud in front of another person before. He'd barely spoken it out loud at all, even when he was alone.

"How do you—" He had to stop to clear his throat as his voice had gone hoarse. "How do you know that name?"

His tone recaptured Emmy's attention, and her expression softened into something apologetic. "I'm sorry. I know this is... weird." She wrinkled her nose at that. Will could guess what she was thinking. Weird? What a stupid, inadequate word. The word that could describe this situation hadn't been invented yet. "Can I just see him? It?" she asked.

It felt strange to move now, like his joints were full of glue. His keys hung on the hook by the door to the garage. Gordon dangled among them. Wordlessly, he lifted the keys off the hook and handed them to her. Emmy took them, separated Gordon from the rest, and stared. She didn't say anything for a very long time, but her breathing hitched like she was holding back a sob. Finally, she whispered something, her voice strained.

"What?"

"It's red," she repeated, then pressed her lips together to stop them from trembling. After taking a deep breath through her nose and letting it out slowly, she ran her finger over the flashlight and spoke again. "It's red... and it's a cylinder."

"Yeah? What does that mean?"

She looked up at him, and her eyes were full of unshed tears. "When I read about it... I pictured it blue and with that traditional flared shape on one end." She paused, twisted the end of the cylinder to turn it on. Stared without seeming to see for another beat of silence. Finally, she twisted it again to turn it off. "I pictured a little button on the back to turn it on and off."

When she reached out to hand the keys back, they jingled because her hand was shaking. He took them and replaced them on the hook more due to habit than a conscious decision. He was still watching her, waiting for the pieces to click. He was also still reeling at the fact that she'd known he'd named his flashlight.

"Did you name it Gordon because of *Flash Gordon*?" she asked, smiling weakly.

"Yeah. I was seventeen and thought I was clever."

"That was my guess."

"Can I ask... why you're so sad now?" Will said carefully.

"I'm sad because... if I was hallucinating this interaction, this house, this... flashlight... based on a book I'd been reading... then the flashlight should have looked how

I imagined it. If this is a world conjured up by my mind, everything should look how I imagined it, shouldn't it?" She pressed a hand to her mouth for a moment before speaking again. "I prepared myself for proof that this was all in my head. I didn't consider, even for a second, the possibility that instead I'd prove to myself that I'm really in a book. But I just don't see any other explanation right now, and I'm freaking out."

Will didn't want to respond because her reasoning made a little too much sense. He was right there with her, reeling from the implications of what she'd said and done. She absolutely should not have known Gordon's name. However, he was not ready to take the same leap as her. There simply had to be some other explanation for what was going on.

"Are you trying to convince me that I'm a book character and you were... what? Magically transported into the book?"

Emmy threw her arms out in a helpless gesture. "I don't know. I don't know what to think. This shouldn't be real. This *can't* be real." She paused, frowned a little. "That damn sex psychic."

"The damn what?"

She shook her head. "Look, I have to go find something to wear besides my duck pajamas, and you're probably going to be late for work again."

"Again?"

"Yeah, after your car broke down, you were—"

"Woah, hold on." Will held up a hand to stop her. "My car didn't break down."

"It didn't? But I read... Wait, what day do you think it is?"

"It's Thursday."

Emmy tried to adjust to yet another mental blow in what had been a long series of them. She'd fallen asleep on a Tuesday. How was this happening? Was she really in a book? Jesus, was she missing from the real world? What would May think when she missed her wedding due to being trapped in a fucking romance novel?

No. Stop. One step at a time, Emmy.

"Okay... okay. That means what I read hasn't even happened yet. Your car broke down in the beginning of the book. You had to go to a mechanic and that's where you met your love interest."

"Stop saying me! It's not me!"

"Right. Sorry. Will, the book character, has a meet-cute at the mechanic." She paused, bit her lip. How much should she reveal? More detail meant he might believe her quicker, but too much, and she might change something. "Her name is Bright."

"Come again?"

"Bright. Her name is Bright. Like the opposite of dim. That's literally how she says it. If meeting a beautiful woman named Bright doesn't convince you you're in a romance novel, I don't know what will." When Will just stared at her, she steeled herself for the next step. "So, you have to get to work. I have to get away from here. And I don't have any money..."

"You want me to give you money."

"Enough for a change of clothes, yes. I'd also like a shirt or something so I can cover my bra-less tits."

"You're insane," Will said incredulously.

"We've established that."

"Fine! Whatever. Just... just go. I hope you find some answers because I don't think you're going to get what you need here."

He reached into his wallet, pulled out a few bills. Then he went to his bedroom, returned a moment later with a sweatshirt. It was ten sizes too big, but that was perfect as it fell to her hips, looked a bit intentional, and was baggy enough to obscure her lack of bra. After digging in the hall closet, he came out with a pair of black men's sandals. They were huge on her, but they had Velcro straps that allowed her to make them somewhat tighter.

"Thanks."

"No problem, uh..." He paused, pointed at her.

"Emmy." She sighed. She already knew his last name. It seemed fair to balance the scales a little. "Emmy Miura."

"Right. No problem, Emmy Miura. Good luck out there."

"Same to you. Sorry in advance about your car trouble." She hesitated, then shrugged. There was no reason to start holding back now. "You should buy more windshield wiper fluid when you get the chance."

She walked out the door while Will gaped at her.

Six

Emmy didn't know where she was going, but the weather was great, and fresh air hit the spot just at that moment. She hadn't seen much of the town of Cobalt, Massachusetts, through the lens of the novel, but this place sure felt like it. She had a long walk down a rural road ahead of her—miles if the context clues in the book were any indication—before she reached any kind of civilization. No problem. She didn't want to interact with anyone else. She needed to be alone with her thoughts and the sunshine. The flashlight had been red. Okay. So maybe the sex psychic had magically transported her into a romance novel as some sort of misguided payback for Emmy's skepticism. All she had to do was figure out how to escape the book and get back to reality. Preferably before Saturday. She really didn't want to miss the wedding.

A car pulled up beside her. No, a pickup truck. Emmy longed for a can of pepper spray. Where had the truck even come from? She hadn't heard it coming. Had she been that lost in her thoughts?

The dude who leaned out the window was ruggedly handsome. Flannel work shirt, a few days' worth of scruff on his face, and—it turned out—a husky voice made for pillow talk.

"You lost, honey?"

"Nope." Emmy kept walking.

"I can give you a ride into town."

His truck kept pace with her. She wondered if there was a corn field somewhere she could disappear into if she needed to run.

"I need to walk, and I don't like taking rides with strange men. But thanks anyway."

"You sure? I don't feel right leaving you like this."

Emmy worked up a cheery smile. "I'm sure! You move right along. I'm fine."

"Okay..." He looked her up and down. "You're not in some kind of trouble, are you, honey? I can help you."

"I'm not in any trouble. I like wearing oversized clothes. It's a quirk of mine."

He laughed. "You're a little spitfire."

"Mm," she replied noncommittally. "This little spitfire is doing just fine on her own, so..."

"Alright then." He flashed her a quick, sexy smile. "It's sure been interesting talking to you. You stay safe now."

He didn't sound certain about leaving her, but she just kept smiling—*nothing to see here, move it along*—until he shrugged and picked up speed. When the truck was no longer in view, she let out a breath. That interaction had certainly been the perfect weird cherry to top her crazy sundae. Good thing it was over.

An hour later, sweaty, slipping out of her overlarge sandals, and with the sleeves of her borrowed sweatshirt rolled up, she found a promising street. Grateful for the freshly repaved sidewalk as it made maneuvering in Will's sandals easier, she kept walking until she reached a quaint little commercial area. The first thing she did was spend some of Will's money on an iced latte. While she stood off to the side, waiting for her order to come up, she desperately wished she had her phone. She didn't realize how attached she'd been to it until she caught herself reaching into her pocket for it at least ten times in two minutes. It was disconcerting to realize she had no idea what to do with her hands or where to look. She settled for putting her hands in the pockets of the sweatshirt and watching the baristas make drinks. That felt normal enough.

"Rough night?"

She turned to see a guy standing next to her. He had a phone in one hand. She almost asked to borrow it. He wore black glasses, a gray cardigan, and tight black jeans. He was tall, lanky, and handsome.

"Slept like a rock. Just need coffee." She shrugged and turned back to watching the baristas work.

"I hear you. Have you been here before? They have a great dark roast."

He had either missed her attempt to brush him off or purposefully ignored it. Emmy decided she'd trade her left eye for her phone. Nothing said "Leave me alone" like staring at your phone. Where the hell was her drink?

"I've heard it's good coffee," she said without looking at him.

"Stellar coffee. I've been coming here for years. Do you want to grab a table?"

"No, I have to run. Busy day."

He opened his mouth to say something else, but she was saved by the chipper barista who handed over her latte. Emmy thanked the girl, spared a quick farewell smile for Lanky Glasses, and escaped out the door.

She didn't think she'd find a lingerie boutique right there on the corner of Quaint Avenue and Wholesome Lane—even if she *was* in a romance novel where such things were often essential—but she did score big with a yoga studio that had a little storefront attached to it. Fifteen minutes later, Emmy emerged wearing a sports bra under her rubber duck camisole top, a new pair of yoga pants, and a pair of cheap flip flops. She'd had just enough funds. Any more, and she would have bought a shirt that didn't look like it was made for a toddler. Still, this was more than good enough to get by. Now all she had to do was sit somewhere and contemplate her situation. It stood to reason that, if she'd gotten into a romance novel, there had to be a way back out. She refused to believe otherwise. Also, given that she was in a romance novel, she had a pretty good feeling she'd find a cute little park somewhere nearby.

She found one three blocks away.

Sitting on a bench that was remarkably free of bird poop and dead leaves, she leaned back and let her mind wander.

Two minutes later, she was interrupted by yet another hot guy. This one was wearing a t-shirt and loose jeans, with a worn messenger bag strapped across his body, and he looked a little harried. His phone was in his hand, but he wasn't looking at it. Emmy wondered what the repercussions would be if she simply snatched the thing from him and ran. The phone was currently unlocked, its owner distracted, and she had a real chance of getting away before he thought to run after her. Then she could use it to... What? Call the real world? Text her sister? She didn't even know frickin' Will's phone number.

"Anyone in there?"

"Hm?"

Hot Guy Number Three was looking at her expectantly. "I asked if you could give me directions to 8th Street?"

"Oh! No, sorry. I'm not from here. Just... visiting."

"Oh yeah? Where are you from originally?"

"Minnesota."

"No kidding? I just visited a cousin there last month." He actually sat down on the bench next to her, all set to lengthen their conversation. "He has a lake house. What brings you out this way?"

"A sex psychic."

"Uh... really."

Not so glad you sat down next to me now, are ya, buddy?

"Yeah, really. How about you? You went from being lost to being ready to sit down and shoot the shit with me pretty quickly. Must not be urgent for you to get wherever you were going."

"Uh..."

He actually looked like he was short-circuiting. She was about to let him off easy, tell him she had to get going, when yet another hot guy walked up.

"Hey, is this guy bothering you?"

This one was muscular from the tip of his nose to his pinky toe. Running shorts, a white tank that was trying its very best to contain his pecs, and tennis shoes, along with the earbuds he yanked out of his ears, made it clear he'd been out jogging. He was looking at Lost Guy with suspicion, and Emmy found herself in the awkward position of trying to defuse the situation without appearing interested in either of them.

"I was just leaving." That seemed safe.

"Hey, I didn't mean to scare you off," said Lost Guy.

"Listen, buddy, you need to back off," said Muscular Jogger.

Lost Guy stood up. "You're the one who needs to take a step back, bro."

While they were amping up for a fight that Lost Guy was most likely going to lose, Emmy slipped away and darted out of the park, her flip flops thwacking the pavement in a way that would have been humorous if she weren't terrified that the sound would draw the two men's attention back to her. Glancing over her shoulder, she didn't see anyone following her. She turned back around just in time to see a yellow Lab barreling toward her. Before she could gather breath to scream or curse—she wasn't sure which would have been her first instinct—the dog had her on her ass. On the plus side—such as it was—the dog was not rabid. He'd knocked her down out of sheer enthusiasm at meeting a new person and was clearly intent on bathing every inch of her face with foul-smelling kisses, but that was the worst of it.

"Hi. Stop. Ew. Please. Good dog."

"Dizzy! Jesus Christ, get off her!"

A sense of foreboding overcame Emmy as an attractive thirty-something guy pulled the dog off her and wrestled him until he was standing still. The guy's wavy brown hair fell just so over his forehead. His big green eyes were full of concern and apology. When she took his offered hand so he could help her to her feet, she felt the brush of calluses.

"I am so sorry. Sit! *Sit*, Disaster."

The dog, with a bit more physical and verbal cajoling, plopped his butt on the sidewalk. His tongue lolled out of his mouth in a grin and his tail continued to wag steadily.

"You named your dog Disaster?" Emmy couldn't help asking.

"No, I named him Dizzy because he was always chasing his tail. Then a couple weeks after I got him, I unofficially changed it to Disaster because he is one." Emmy got a glimpse of a charmingly apologetic grin when the guy turned his attention back to her. "He escaped the yard when my niece opened the gate. She's kind of a disaster, too, if I'm being honest. Don't tell my sister I said that. Are you alright?"

"I'm fine," Emmy said, reaching back to swipe dust and gravel from the sidewalk off her butt. She winced at the brief contact. Just what she needed—a bruised butt to cap everything off.

"Are you hurt?" His voice was full of concern.

"I'll live," she replied, using the excuse of gathering up the clothes she'd dropped to avoid eye contact with him. "I was just heading home, so…"

"Do you want to stop by my place for some water or something? I live a couple blocks away. The least I can do is give you a chance to catch your breath since my dog assaulted you." He smiled again in a way that would definitely have caught her interest if she weren't already more than fed up with attractive men accosting her every five feet. "I'm Simon, by the way."

"Hi, Simon. Which direction is your house?"

He pointed.

"Okay, I'm headed in the opposite direction actually," she lied. "Thanks for rescuing me from your dog. You better get him home."

"Alright, if you're sure. I don't want you to—"

"Ma'am, is everything alright?"

Emmy wanted to groan, but stifled it. It was a cop who had spoken. God knew where he'd come from. Just the sight of the crisp blue uniform had her back going up, and she clutched the roll of Will's borrowed clothes closer to her body as if it were a shield. But the cop's eyes showed only polite concern.

"Are you hurt, miss?"

This would make six hot guys who'd approached her if she included Truck Guy. All white, her mind supplied unhelpfully. Typical romance novel. Was it too much to ask for one person of color? She wanted to continue fleeing, but decided to take advantage of the situation.

"I'm not hurt. Simon was just heading home."

The cop glanced at Simon, who looked put out by the interruption. "I'll take it from here, thanks."

"Alright. Sure. Come on, Dizzy Disaster."

Simon got a firm grip on the dog's collar and headed off down the street.

"Did his dog attack you? Do you want to file a report?"

"No, it didn't attack me. I'm really fine, except..." She tried her best to look lost and helpless. "I forgot my phone at home and I'm getting kind of frantic. Do you think you could give me a ride?"

"Sure. Come on."

He cast a look over his shoulder as if checking for attackers. Feeling grateful for the reprieve, she got into the car with him, waited while he radioed his partner or dispatch or whatever to give an update. Then froze up when he asked for her address.

"Um… I don't remember, if I'm being honest. I live with Will Barrett. Do you know him?"

"Will? Yeah, I went to high school with him. I didn't even know he was seeing someone, let alone living with someone."

He pulled away from the curb and started back toward the little country road that led toward Will's house.

"I'm not seeing him. Just staying with him. He's a friend. We uh… met online. This is my first time seeing his place in person, which is why I haven't memorized the address."

"Oh, sure. That makes sense." *Did it?* The lie had sounded obvious to her own ears. But the cop seemed entirely convinced. "Well, tell him I say hi, okay? Norton Graff. *Officer* Norton Graff."

"Sure." Was she supposed to be impressed by the "officer" part?

Emmy turned and stared out the window, willing the ride to be over. She knew Will wouldn't be happy to see her back at his place, but she didn't know where else to go. If one more guy flirted with her, she was going to start screaming at the top of her lungs and never stop. She felt her entire body unclench when the house came into view. The cop pulled to a stop in the driveway, then turned to smile at her.

"So, if you're not seeing Will, does that mean I have a chance?"

The scream bubbled up. Part terror. Part frustration. A touch of rage. She swallowed it down, took a breath.

"No. I'm not seeing Will, but I do have a boyfriend."

Something changed in him. He looked confused. Like a dog who hears a noise but can't determine where the sound is coming from. Then he just shrugged.

"Okay. See you later."

She got out of the car, and he drove off. Emmy made it to the door, then dropped onto the front step, pressed her head into her knees, and screamed.

Seven

Will sat in what the mechanic passed off as a waiting area—two beaten-up vinyl chairs, a wall-mounted TV, and a water cooler. He smelled gasoline, could easily see right into the shop where the two brothers who owned Kerry Brothers Auto Repair argued about something. How had Emmy known his car would break down? Had she sabotaged it before sneaking into his home and climbing into bed with him? Was there a subtle way to ask if a car showed signs of sabotage? He didn't think he could pull it off. She'd said he'd be late for work, and he was. Normally he'd be freaking out, but the work freakout was going to have to wait until he'd finished losing his shit over everything else that had happened that day. He had a lot of thinking to do. His mind was a maelstrom of suppositions, suspicions, possibilities, entanglements, and questions. He had pitifully few answers.

And then, like someone had flicked a switch in his brain, everything went blank, and he couldn't think at all.

The woman who walked past him into the shop was devastating to the senses. Tall and curvy with sun-kissed skin and a smile that simply enthralled him. He watched her trot over to the Kerry brothers, handily interrupt their argument, and strike up conversation. He couldn't hear what they were talking about, but the sound of her laugh carried to him. When she tossed back her head of honey-colored curls, he followed the movement like she was a hypnotist keeping him focused on a watch. She wore torn jeans and a paint-stained t-shirt, but she made it look like a fashion statement. Without realizing, he stood and took a few steps closer. It was enough for him to catch bits of the conversation. Even her voice was alluring. She sounded happy. Carefree.

"Anything you feel like you can part with," she said. "I'm thinking old tools, nuts, bolts, springs, gears. I can pay you! Should have led with that." She laughed at herself, that joyous sound that had him by the throat.

"We can look around," said Marlon Kerry, the older brother. "Can you hang out a minute?"

"I'm sorry, I should be getting back to my shop. Super easy to find. It's right down the street. I just opened two weeks ago."

"Yeah, I think I seen that place," commented Ed Kerry. "You sell weird furniture and pottery and such, right?"

"That's exactly right. Feel free to come in and browse or drop off odds and ends. Anytime."

"We sure will," Marlon said while Ed nodded.

"Thank you! You guys are super sweet. I'll let you get back to work."

She turned back to the waiting area. Both brothers, Will noted, took a moment to appreciate her ass. Then they went back to arguing.

"Hi," the woman said, and Will realized he was in her way.

"Sorry." He stepped aside to let her pass, then blurted, "Do you think you could use a bunch of Canadian coins?"

"What?"

"I overheard some of your conversation, and I have this pile of Canadian coins sitting in my car that I don't know what to do with. It's not enough to exchange at the bank, but it's enough that I feel bad throwing them away."

"Oh! Cool! Yes, absolutely. If you're willing to part with them, I'd be happy to take them." She stuck out her hand. "I'm Bright."

The world stopped turning. Will stopped breathing. The lights in the waiting area seemed to lose their brilliance. There was a weird pressure inside his skull, like someone was leaning on his brain.

He didn't take her hand. The possibility that this was all some sort of practical joke or scam orchestrated by the mysterious Emmy Miura was getting more and more unlikely.

"Sorry, you said your name was..."

"Bright, yeah. Like the opposite of dim. A far cry from the Brittanys and Jessicas of the world, I know." She giggled, and the sound that had been so appealing only moments ago now grated on him.

He forced himself to take her hand and shake. He almost made a comment about her name. It felt like he should. She'd practically invited him to. But he didn't have it in him. "Will."

"Nice to meet you, Will. Do you have your car here?"

She was asking about the coins. He'd already forgotten about them. Strangely, there appeared to be a response waiting in his head. He felt it making its way from his brain to his mouth. *Yeah, they're working on it now. Mysterious car disease. How about I bring them by your shop later?* But he didn't want to say that. At the last second, right when he opened his mouth to say those words that did not feel right, he forced himself to say the first random thing that he could come up with.

"I ate a jellyfish for breakfast."

"That would be great! Thank you!"

She was still smiling like they were having a pleasant, somewhat flirtatious conversation.

"I want you to eat a jellyfish."

"Yep! I'll be there. The shop's open Monday through Friday, eight to five. But sometimes I stay past closing, so don't rush."

"I'm going to fill your house with jellyfish."

"Perfect. Looking forward to it. See you, Will!"

She practically skipped away. Will's chest was tight. Too tight. He couldn't remember how to breathe. He'd just told the woman he'd fill her house with jellyfish, and she had reacted like he'd told her... if he was being honest, the words he'd wanted to say. Every time she'd spoken, there were words waiting in his head. She'd responded to those, the unspoken ones.

Fuck.

Fuck fuck fuck.

He was in a fucking romance novel.

Eight

He didn't go to work. Nassir, his supervisor, probably didn't believe him when he said he was feeling sick, though he hadn't been lying entirely. He *did* feel sick, just not from any kind of virus. But it didn't matter what his supervisor thought. Maybe Nassir was currently staring at a wall, wondering what to do now that Will wasn't in his life when he was supposed to be. No, that would be crazy. This whole situation was insane. Will couldn't believe he was even entertaining the idea that he was in a book. He kept trying to reason his way to a different conclusion, but he couldn't think past the endless litany of "What the fucks" that filled his brain. He drove home in his freshly tuned up car with his body on autopilot. When he pulled into his driveway, he couldn't truthfully say he remembered how he got there. He saw Emmy sitting on his front step, staring into space. Feeling numb all over, he got out of the car and approached her. She looked up at him and smiled sadly.

"Shouldn't you be at work?"

"I called in sick."

She nodded, gestured behind her. "You locked the door. I'm sorry. I know you wanted me to leave your life forever, but I didn't know where else to go. These guys kept…"

Despite himself, he felt a surge of dread. What had happened to her? Was he going to have to go cave some guy's face in? "These guys kept what? Are you okay?"

"Yeah, I'm fine. It's nothing like that." She stood up, brushed off her yoga pants. Then she handed him a bundle of cloth. His brain was so scrambled, it took him a full ten seconds before he remembered he'd loaned her clothes that morning. "I kept having meet-cutes."

"What?"

"Meet-cutes," she repeated while he tucked the rolled-up sweatshirt under his arm and unlocked the front door. "Hot guys kept coming up to me and trying to flirt. No matter where I went. There were two at once in the park. Then a dog knocked me down and the owner tried to get me to come back to his place. I escaped because a cop showed up out of nowhere. He drove me back here, and then he asked me out."

"What'd you say?"

She gave him a look. "I said 'No need for a date, big boy. Go ahead and show me your *nightstick*.' What do you think I said? I told him no and got the hell out of his car." She ran her hands agitatedly through her hair. "He says hi, by the way. Norton Graff. Apparently you know him."

"Yeah. He's a dick."

When they were both inside, he closed and locked the door. Then he just stood there and stared. He stared at his home and wondered if it was really his home. He'd inherited it from his grandfather, and now he was standing there wondering if he had fond memories of a man who'd never existed. Nothing he'd taken for granted yesterday could be trusted today.

"You alright?" Emmy asked quietly.

"I feel like I'm standing on a mountain of sand and it's just... sliding away beneath my feet."

He noted Emmy's wince. She had been the one to open the door to the possibility that his world was fiction. He didn't see any reason to blame her for this, but it was possible she blamed herself. She reached out and gently touched his arm.

"Do you have alcohol?" she asked.

"Yeah."

"Okay. Let's drink and you can tell me about your day."

He looked down at her, took a moment to focus, then nodded. "I've got tequila but no mixers."

Emmy smiled. "My favorite recipe."

They sat on the couch passing the bottle back and forth. Glasses didn't seem necessary right at that moment. Will told Emmy about his encounter with Bright, how all of Emmy's predictions had come true, right down to the "opposite of dim" comment. When he got to the jellyfish conversation, she put her hand over her mouth. At first, Will thought it was a gesture of shock and compassion. But when he finished by telling her about Bright's final comment and exit, a muffled snort escaped, revealing that she was trying to hold in her laughter. He gave her a look.

"Oh, come *on*! I'm sorry. Sincerely sorry. But I have to know where the jellyfish came from. Of all the random things to test her with..."

"It just popped into my head, okay?"

She let out a peal of tequila-soaked laughter. Will felt his lips twitch, then gave in and chuckled with her and at her. She did not hold her liquor well at all. He decided to defend himself.

"I *wanted* it to be weird. I needed to be absolutely sure that..." He paused, shook his head. "I just needed to be sure."

Emmy calmed down enough to reach out and squeeze his knee. "For what it's worth, I really am sorry. I didn't do this on purpose."

"I believe you. But... it's done. Now I have to figure out how to keep living my life. Unless..."

"Unless?"

"I don't know what will happen if you find a way out of... the book. Don't know if I, y'know, existed before you came here. Might not exist again if you leave."

"Fuck. I didn't think about that."

"Pretty much all I can think about," Will muttered, taking another slug of tequila.

Emmy took the bottle back, sipped, shuddered. "If it helps, I have no idea how to get out of here. You might be stuck with me in... indef... indefibly? What is that word?"

"Indefinitely?"

"Yes!" She gestured at him with the bottle. "You might be stuck with me indefinly, and then you won't have to worry about unexisting."

"Sure. I'm willing to bet my existence on that."

She nearly punched him when she tried to thrust the bottle back into his hands. He took it from her, helped himself to one last gulp, then capped the bottle. "I'm cutting you off."

He got up to store the considerably lighter bottle of tequila on top of his fridge. Then, thinking ahead to the morning, he grabbed two cups and filled them to the brim with water.

"*Nomisugita*," Emmy muttered as he wandered back in, a little more unsteady on his feet than he would have liked.

"No me what huh?" he asked. He set the glasses on the coffee table, then plopped down unceremoniously beside her. He could have sworn the couch made an "oof" sound. Or maybe that was him.

"*No. Mi. Su. Gi. Ta,*" she enunciated, a look of pure concentration on her face. He wished the look wasn't absolutely adorable. All he wanted to do now was pull her into his arms and cuddle. He was not usually a cuddler. "It's Japanese for 'I drank too much.'"

"You can't pronounce 'indefinitely' but you remember how to say an entire sentence in Japanese?"

"Fewer syllables in Japanese."

He hated that she had him counting on his fingers. "It's the same. I think." He looked at her, holding his fingers out still. "Isn't it? Say your thing again." She repeated it, and he counted as she spoke. "It's the same."

"Fine! Whatever. Japanese is just easier right now."

"How much do you know?"

"I know enough to get by. Used to speak it more when I was a kid. But I still know the important stuff. Like... basic conversational stuff. I can say 'Watch out!' and I can tell someone I'm from America and I can ask where the bathroom is. Everything else is incremental."

Will considered the three sentences and decided they were pretty useful in any language. "I think you mean incidental."

"Blame the tequila."

He toasted her with his water and drank half the glass. When she only stared at hers, he put it in her hands.

"You'll thank me later."

She shrugged and drank more slowly than he had. They sat in silence for a couple minutes. Will stared at his TV. If he turned it on now, would it even work? Or would his newfound self-awareness make the TV play only static? He was afraid to check. Maybe tomorrow he'd try to browse Netflix.

"This one guy in the coffee shop used the adjective 'stellar,'" Emmy said into the silence. "Who the hell says 'stellar' anymore?"

"I have no idea. He sounds like a tool."

"He probably was. He sure didn't pick up on my fuck off signals," Emmy grumbled.

"Maybe you need to work on clearer fuck off signals."

"I don't know. I'm pretty good at those already. I think he was just…" She wiggled her fingers. "Bespelled or something. The romance novel forced him to try to be in a romance."

"Or he saw a hot chick in a coffee shop and decided to try his luck," Will suggested.

"I was wearing a man's sweatshirt, oversized sandals, and duck pants."

"And still."

She waved this away. "Anyway. I don't think I'm escaping this book tonight, so um… can I bunk here? I'll sleep on the couch."

Will sighed. "I've got a spare bedroom. Come on, I'll get you a toothbrush. You can borrow a shirt to sleep in if you want."

★

As Emmy snuggled down under the covers in Will's guest room, she welcomed the weighty pull of sleep. Maybe this really had been a dream and she would wake up at home where she belonged. Then Will would be rid of her. He could...

Her eyes shot open. He could... *what*? She'd ended up in Will's house after falling asleep. Would she return to her own bed by falling asleep again? Would that make Will cease to exist as he had feared? What would that make her? Not a murderer. Not that. But... just the thought of being responsible for his existence—or lack thereof—made her feel sick to her stomach. More sick than she already felt after downing half a bottle of tequila. Will needed to know her suspicions. It was unfair of her to keep them to herself, knowing she might wake up in the morning having ended him in her sleep. She was halfway out of bed when she paused, reconsidered. Should he know? Or would keeping it to herself be more... *God*... merciful?

Feeling lower than she'd ever felt in her life, she crept out of bed and tiptoed over to his door, which he'd left ajar. He was already asleep. The dim hall light cast a dreamy glow into his room and showed her that his sleeping face was relaxed and peaceful. Her gut clenched, and she felt the sting of tears gathering in her eyes. How could she wake him up just to tell him he might not be real in the morning? Clutching one arm around her stomach, she retreated to her room. Back in her borrowed bed, she allowed a few tears to slip free as she gave in and closed her eyes. Sleep came quickly on the heels of the tequila binge, and her pillow dried her tears as she drifted off.

She woke in the same bed the next morning and felt a strange mixture of relief and disappointment. On the one hand—Yay! She hadn't murdered Will. On the other hand... Well, she was still stuck, wasn't she? She needed to leave at some point. It was impossible to say how time was passing back in her world, but she doubted time there had simply paused when she disappeared. Then again, she'd gone to sleep on a Tuesday night and woken up on a Thursday morning. In a book. So what the hell did she know?

Feeling groggy and desperately grateful for the spare toothbrush Will had found her the night before, she got up to use the bathroom and brush away the taste of old tequila. A few minutes later, the smell of bacon guided her to the kitchen. Will was at the stove. Coffee in the pot. She felt like kissing him. Then remembered that would be a supremely bad idea. Best to maintain a platonic relationship with the hunky romance novel character.

"Morning," she said, helping herself to some coffee. He'd kindly left a mug out for her.

Will turned to her, and his eyes flicked up and down. She knew what he saw—her hair was mussed, she was wearing nothing but his t-shirt, and her eyes were still half closed from sleep. In other words, she was a mess. But the way his gaze lingered for a moment before he turned away said maybe he didn't think so.

"Sleep okay?" he asked.

Emmy thought of her crisis of conscience the night before. "Fell asleep almost immediately. Thanks for letting me crash here."

"I'm not about to turn you out on the street. You can bunk here until... until you don't have to anymore."

"Thank you," she said quietly, knowing he was hurting still.

"I hope you're okay with bacon and toast for breakfast."

"Sounds great." She thought of the way he'd looked at her a moment ago. "I'm just going to go change."

"You're fine with what you're wearing."

She let out her breath in a quick laugh. "I'll bet *you're* fine with what I'm wearing. But yeah… just give me a sec."

When she returned wearing the outfit she'd purchased the day before, he'd already set the table. The toaster popped right as she walked in, so she detoured there to grab the toast and drop it onto the waiting plate.

"I want to buy more clothes," she commented as she sat down, "but I don't want to take more of your money. And I don't think I can stand any more meet-cutes."

"Don't worry about my money. My grandfather left me a chunk, and, given the circumstances, I'm not really worried about spending it."

"That's generous of you, but there's still the problem of the hopeless romantics out there waiting to pounce on me."

"I'll go into town with you today. If anyone tries to sweep you off your feet, I'll intervene."

Emmy thought this over as she munched on a slice of bacon. "That could work."

"For you, yeah. I'm still wondering if I'm going to accidentally wander into a scene from a book. Is anyone going to interact with me normally? Or is everyone besides you going to be on some kind of script?"

"I don't know. I only read the back cover and like… five chapters." Another thought struck her. "Maybe… maybe that's how I get out. You know, if the book reaches its conclusion…"

Will looked at her with sheer disbelief written all over his face. "I'm not going to force myself to fall in love with some woman I don't even like so you can get out of this."

"I'm not saying you have to. I'm brainstorming, okay? This is a ridiculous situation. Is some part of me still back in the—" She caught herself before she said real world. "In my world? Or am I gone? Physically in the book? My sister's wedding is on Saturday." She had to pause to swallow back the pain and panic that statement induced, but some of it leaked out anyway. "How long before she notices I'm gone? Will she report me missing? Delay the wedding? What if I never get out?" Feeling agitated, she got up to pace the room. "Do you know what my unexplained disappearance would do to my family? And even if I do get back, I might find out I lost my job from being gone with no warning. That, and I'd have to live with the possibility that I might have taken your life."

She felt his hands on her shoulders and nearly leaped out of her skin. She'd thought he was still sitting at the table. Gently, Will turned her around. His eyes found hers, his expression steely.

"We'll find you a way out," he said quietly. "And when we do… I want you to take me with you."

"What?"

"You think I can let you leave me behind now that I know the truth? No way. I want out. Take me back with you to the *real world*." The way he emphasized the words made it clear he'd known earlier what she'd been about to say.

"That's not possible."

"You're going to talk to me about 'possible' when we're standing here in a book. We're in a *book*!" he repeated in a near shout. "So yeah, you're going to find a way out. That's one promise. Here's another one. When you get out, I'm going to go with you."

He was right. She had no concept of what was possible or impossible anymore. That line had been redrawn when she'd woken up in his bed, and she didn't know who had erased it or where they'd put the new one. Hell, why not? She'd try to take the protagonist of the novel out of the book.

"Okay," she said. "Now take me into town so I can buy shirts without getting hit on. Then we can come up with some kind of plan to get us out of here."

When they got into his car a few minutes later, Emmy caught Will staring at the cupholder.

"Planning a trip to Canada?" she asked. "Wait… no. You were going to give those to Bright, weren't you?"

"I was, but not anymore. I'm staying far away from her."

Emmy didn't say anything else as he started the car and pulled out of the garage. But her curiosity got the best of her.

"Maybe I could bring them to her for you."

He cut her a quick look before returning his eyes to the road, his brow furrowed in confusion. "Why?"

"Will you hate me if I admit I'm curious?"

"Let me think about that…"

She punched his arm.

"Ow! Okay, I won't hate you. But what if you go in there and end up with twelve guys all looking to woo their way into your pants?"

"Oh… right. Damn." She fell silent and looked out the window.

Though she was trying not to pout, she must have looked disappointed, because Will rolled his eyes and said, "Fine. I'll go with you to take the coins to her. But if she starts hitting on me, I'm out of there."

"Deal."

She'd named her store Bright Ideas.

Emmy and Will stood outside staring in silence for a conspicuously long time, but Emmy was too preoccupied to care if she earned some funny looks.

"This is…" she said, not knowing how to finish the thought.

"Yeah."

"What does she even sell here?"

Emmy studied the window display, saw a vase bursting with flowers on a tiny end table that appeared to be made, at least in part, of old license plates. Beside the table was an easy chair that sported a cushion with Rosie the Riveter on it. The words "Girl Boss" occupied the speech bubble in lieu of "We Can Do It!"

"Jury's still out," Will said in response to her question. "Let's get this over with."

They pushed their way inside. Aside from two old women who were browsing and chattering, Emmy didn't see any other people in the store. Most importantly, she didn't see any sexy men (besides Will). She hadn't been accosted at all since going out with Will. She had a shopping bag loaded with clothes dangling from her hand, and she'd purchased them without so much as a single unwanted "Hey there."

They found Bright at the register, rearranging a display of... yep, those were bracelets made out of denim. Jean bracelets. Jacelets? When Bright saw Will, she smiled broadly.

"Hey, you! Welcome to Bright Ideas. Thanks for coming!"

"Yeah, no problem," Will mumbled, taking the coins out of his pocket and placing them unceremoniously on the counter. "Feel free to toss these if you can't find a use for them."

"Oh, I'm sure I'll think of something." She swept them off the counter and into her hand. "Thank you so much!"

"Did you make everything in here yourself?" Emmy asked.

Bright blinked at her as if she hadn't realized Emmy was there. Then the smile was back. "Not all of it. Some of the pieces are acquired from local artists, but I found all the antiques you see on display, and I restored some of the wood furniture. I mostly make jewelry and decorative items. We hope everyone can find something unique here. Variety is the name of the game." She shook her head, looking a little self-conscious. "I'm sorry. I'm giving you the whole sales pitch and I haven't even introduced myself. I'm Bright."

"Emmy."

"Nice to meet you, Emmy. Feel free to browse. Let me know if anything catches your eye. I'm just going to put these in the back so I don't lose them."

With that, she walked away. Not even a wink or a flirtatious giggle for Will. They stood there for a few seconds, then Emmy shrugged. "She doesn't look how I pictured her, but she's sweet. Pretty. You sure you don't want to…"

"Yes. I'm sure."

"Okay, well she didn't appear overly interested in you. Did you have any sense that you were acting out a scene there?"

"Maybe for the first part, but as soon as you spoke to her, that feeling went away. Did you see her face? It was like talking to you broke her out of the scene."

The idea hit them at the same time, and they turned to stare at each other wide-eyed. When they were together, men didn't hit on Emmy, and Bright didn't hit on Will.

Emmy couldn't believe it. Not only had the events of her life led her to be trapped in a romance novel, but to add insult to injury, they were going to have to rely on one of the most clichéd and contrived romantic comedy plots known to man.

They were going to have to pretend to be in a relationship.

Nine

"No way."

"Listen, it's a solid idea," Emmy insisted. "It'll keep all the NPCs off our backs while we figure out a game plan."

They were having lunch at a local diner at Emmy's insistence. She'd wanted to test her theory that being together with Will would stop the onslaught of eager single men. So far, it was playing out exactly as she'd hoped. While there were men in the restaurant, several of them potentially single, not one had looked her way. Will shook his head as he poked at his lemon meringue pie.

"This is ridiculous."

"Yes. Obviously. It's also going to save us a headache or two." Emmy reached over and stole a bite of his pie. He gave her a disgruntled look and she shrugged. "You weren't eating it. Anyway, we can pull this off so long as we come to an agreement about one thing."

"Just one?" Will asked sarcastically.

"Yes. This is important. Look at me." He rolled his eyes but obliged her, meeting her gaze. "If somebody—*anybody*—insists that we kiss each other to prove we're in a relationship, we are going to say no. We are going to tell them that's a fucking weird request and that we're not going to kiss for their amusement."

Will looked dubious. "Why would anyone ask us to do that?"

"Happens all the time in romcoms. That's always the worst part of the stupid pretend-to-be-involved plot. The two protagonists will inevitably encounter someone who's like, 'Oh, you're engaged? That's so sweet! Give each other a kiss now. Come on.' And for some reason they are super insistent, but the characters never tell them to stop being creepy. They just shrug like, 'Welp, I guess we have to lock lips now, or our whole charade is blown.'"

"That's moronic."

"Sure is. And we're not doing it."

"Okay. I can agree to that," he said after a moment's consideration. "We tell people we're in a relationship, but we never demonstrate it in any way."

"That's right. You can hold my hand if you feel so inclined—"

"Gracious of you."

"—but that's it."

"Fair enough. We can give that a try. I'm going to quit my job."

Emmy's eyes bulged. "Huh? What? Why?"

Will shrugged. "What's the point? I don't even know if my medical knowledge is real or if it's all yadda yadda'd by some author who bookmarked WebMD on their browser."

"Yeah, but... it's your job. What are you going to do all day?"

"I don't know." He spent a few seconds brooding over that. "Something different. I'll figure it out. I'm not going to quit with no notice. It feels wrong, even if my shift supervisor is an NPC. I'll put in my two weeks. We'll go from there."

"Two weeks. Crap. Am I going to be here that long?" At his look, she amended her statement. "Are *we* going to be here that long? My sister's going to start freaking out soon if she hasn't already. My whole family is going to go berserk. And Sarah... man, I wish I had Sarah here. She always keeps a cool head."

"Who's Sarah?"

"My best friend. She wouldn't let me freak out if she were here. She can just look at you and make you feel like she knows everything, and she never worries unnecessarily about anything." Emmy toyed absently with her coffee mug. "There are so many people whose lives will be disrupted by this. I hate it. I hate that they might be scared for me, that I can't tell them I'm okay."

Will reached out and laid his hand gently over hers. She looked at him and felt somewhat comforted by the sincere compassion in his eyes.

"We can only solve the problem that's right in front of us," he said quietly. "You can explain everything to your family and friends when you get back."

Emmy studied him in silence for a moment. "You're awfully confident."

"Have to be. No other way to make this whole situation work out."

"You're sure you want to come with me? You don't even know what my world is like. Plus... you'd be leaving your family behind. What about your siblings? Your parents? Are they..."

Will took his hand off hers and ate a bite of pie before answering. "No siblings. My parents own a farm up north."

"And you're okay leaving them? Do you hate them? That would be convenient."

He gave her a look. "No, I don't hate my parents." His expression turned somber. "I love them. They were good parents. Still are. I just..."

Will wasn't able to finish the sentence, wasn't even sure what he'd been planning on saying. He was too busy wondering if his parents were real. Had he ever been born? Or had he just popped into existence at age twenty-eight? Every time he tried to wrap his head around it, he felt a mild buzzing headache begin at the back of his skull. Emmy clearly sensed his turmoil as she chipperly changed the subject.

"Okay! Game plan. I need a phone, I need transportation, and I need access to every library and bookstore in a ten-mile radius."

"I get the first two, but why libraries and bookstores?"

"It's a shot in the dark, but I was thinking maybe if a book got me into this mess, then a book will also be the key to getting me... *us* out."

Will considered this, shrugged. It was as good a place to start as any. They finished their pie and coffee as they discussed strategies and theories, planned out next steps, and bartered over how much he was willing to spend on a phone for her. Emmy pointed out she needed 5G so she could search for bookstores and get directions, maybe take notes if she found something interesting. She'd want to save those notes to the cloud, obviously. Will capitulated on that, but remained firm when it came to getting her a car. Emmy relented when he pointed out that she couldn't rent or drive a car without a driver's license. She briefly toyed with the idea of making a fake, but without the proper tools and knowhow, it seemed like a futile effort.

"You do realize this means you're going to have to be my chauffeur whenever I need to go somewhere," Emmy pointed out on the drive back to Will's place.

He shrugged. "You don't exist in my world. Where would you even need to go besides a bookstore every once in a while?"

"You expect me to just hide out in your house like some kind of poltergeist you haven't gotten around to banishing?"

"Yeah, I guess. It'd be nice if you didn't make all my electronics short out. But I'll understand if you can't help yourself."

Emmy crossed her arms over her chest and glared. It took a few seconds, but when he realized she wasn't going to respond, he looked over at her again.

"What's that look for?"

"I'm going to want to go places," she stated.

"Fine. Jeez. I'll take you places."

"Good. That's all I needed to hear."

By the time they got back to the house, it was already late evening. The last of the sunlight trickled over the horizon, and Emmy was exhausted from running all over town. It was a good kind of exhausted, though, because she knew she was making progress. Armed with a phone and new clothes, she would be able to start her search for a way out of this book.

The first thing she did was put her new wardrobe away in her room. It was funny that she already thought of it as her room. That might be a worrying development considering she didn't want to form any attachments to this fantasy world. Even if, she thought as she wandered into the kitchen and saw Will frowning over a box of pasta, there were some things she wouldn't mind getting attached to. She leaned against the kitchen doorway and watched him as he pulled the makings of dinner out of his cabinets. Not only was this guy stupid hot, but he was surprisingly good company. She just wished she hadn't had to upend his entire life.

"I've got work tomorrow," Will said later while they shared a meal of pasta in spicy red sauce, crusty bread, and Caesar salad from a bag.

"From when to when?"

"Six to two."

"If you're not too tired after your shift, maybe you could take me to the library? I want to get started on my search."

"We'll see. What're you going to do while I'm at the hospital?"

"I don't know. I'll try to sleep in, watch some TV or something. I'll probably end up going stir crazy after like thirty minutes. Then who knows what mischief I'll get up to?" She narrowed her eyes at him. "You better back up all your files in case I decide to short out your electronics."

He grinned at that and pointed at her with his fork. "That was good. Good callback." He speared more pasta, chewed thoughtfully. "What're you going to search for at the library?"

She took a sip of her drink, trying not to notice the solid line of his jaw as he chewed. "I don't know exactly. Romance novels. There might be something there. I want to see if the book we're in exists in this world, for one. Maybe it will act as a doorway or something. Other than that, I'm going to try to find the solution to the problem by eliminating everything that isn't."

"Very Sherlock Holmes of you."

"Hey, if it ain't broke, don't fix it. His methods are sound. Except for the cocaine and opium and stuff." She gestured at him with a jerk of her chin. "If I'm Holmes, does that make you Watson?"

"Yeah, I guess so. Nurse Watson."

She cocked her head. "Why not doctor? Since we're on the subject."

Something in his expression closed off, and she realized there was a story there.

"I didn't have the money for medical school, and I wanted to work with patients as soon as possible. Being a nurse puts you in the thick of things. You learn a lot, connect with people. More than doctors do sometimes. It felt like a good fit for me."

"You being a nurse is the reason I bought the book."

That clearly surprised him. "Why?"

"It was new and different. So many romance novels feature these Manly Men—with capital M's—who are best friends with their gym and only have traditional-gender-role-approved Manly Man careers like contractor or FBI agent. Nurse was new and refreshing. It felt... real."

Will didn't respond to that. It was ironic, he thought bitterly, since real was the one thing he didn't feel about himself at the moment. But also sweet, he had to admit. He liked that she admired his work. He had never been ashamed of being a nurse; it made him proud to have a career where he could help people every day. Still, hearing the admiration in her tone was a soothing balm over his beleaguered psyche. Dinner with her was normal enough. Conversation with her was deep enough. Enough to keep the questions at bay for a few minutes.

"Thanks for dinner," Emmy said, rising to clear her plate and his. "You're a pretty good cook."

"When I have the time. Usually I'm too tired to make anything. I end up eating handfuls of granola and chasing it with a protein shake."

Emmy shuddered, amusing him. "Tell you what, for as long as I'm here with you, I'll take cooking duty when you're too tired for it."

"That would be... great. Thank you."

"Don't mention it. Least I can do, considering."

He helped her clean up the dishes, then they went their separate ways. The questions started to leak back into his mind as he showered, brushed his teeth, and prepared for bed. By the time he was under the covers, his brain was spiraling out of control.

How was it he could sleep and dream when he wasn't real? Did the author write his dreams? Were his subconscious fears fueled by whatever character development had been deemed necessary to propel the story along?

Praying for peace, Will swallowed the sleeping pills he'd picked up that morning, closed his eyes, and waited for unconsciousness.

Ten

Will was gone by the time Emmy blearily blinked her eyes open in the morning. She could hear the emptiness of the house, knew she was alone even before she wandered into the kitchen to prepare breakfast. It was insane that she found herself missing Will's company, but she accepted that this was a natural result of becoming dependent on him. Not just that, she had to admit, but comfortable with him as well. She shoveled cereal in her mouth as she thought about her next steps.

She was worried about May. What was her sister doing right now? How long had Emmy been gone in her reality? Had she already been fired for missing work? Those questions were closely followed by an endless series of what-ifs, many of them involving scenarios in which she never found her way back to the real world. Emmy gulped coffee in the hopes that caffeine would ward off the headache she felt coming on. Then she pushed back from the table and made her way to the little office at the end of the hall.

Will's computer was black and sleek. The tower hummed when she booted it up, and the keyboard immediately lit with a full spectrum of colors. He had carefully arranged speakers, and a chair that looked like one could live in it for days. Her temporary roommate was a gamer in his off hours. That much was clear. She typed in the password Will had given her. He, understandably enough, hadn't wanted to buy her a computer when his functioned just fine. When the desktop appeared, she raised her eyebrow at the *Full Metal Alchemist* desktop background. He had interesting taste. Emmy pulled up Google and typed her name into the search bar. She found plenty of information about The Emmys, something she was used to, but her social media profiles didn't pop up. She tried again with her full name—Emmy Haruka Miura. There were some women named Emmy, some people with her middle and/or last name, but none that lived in Minnesota. Just to be sure, she googled May Naoko Miura. Sarah Chaya Tillman.

Nothing.

The Everett Hotel existed, but that didn't help much. She didn't have to call the front desk to confirm she did not work there in this world. Feeling desperate, she picked up her cell and dialed May's number. She'd had the same number all through childhood, and at some point Emmy had memorized it, more through osmosis than any conscious effort. The phone rang once. Twice. Her free hand was squeezed into a tight fist, the nails digging into her palm.

"Hello?"

It was a woman's voice, but not her sister's. Still, she had to try.

"Hi... is May there?"

"I'm sorry?"

"I'm looking for May Miura. My sister."

"Oh, I think you have the wrong number."

Actually it's the right number, Emmy thought as she apologized and hung up. *Just the wrong reality.*

She knew Sarah's number as well, but accepted the futility of dialing it. Turning back to the computer, she searched for her new best friend, Lucy, the mechanical keyboard clacking loudly in the otherwise silent room. She looked for any hint that the sex psychic operated in this version of Minneapolis. Google provided her with some very interesting results—even with Safe Search on—but none of them indicated that Lucy was in business. It didn't help that she only had a first name to go off, maybe not even an accurate first name if Lucy was short for something.

"Damn it," she muttered at the screen.

The headache threatened to sink its teeth into her despite the jolt of caffeine. This was fruitless. Maybe a trip to Minneapolis would help. She could look and see if the sex psychic was there. Until she saw with her own eyes that Lucy was—or wasn't—running her business in this reality, she'd never be at ease. It was entirely possible that the way out was the same as the way in—not through a book, but through the psychic who sold it to her.

But it wasn't like she had money for a plane ticket. Maybe she'd be able to convince Will to fund her trip, though he'd probably want to make it a one-way ticket just to get her out of his hair. No... fuck. It would have to be a bus ticket. Airports were finicky about things like seeing valid ID before letting people on planes. Taking the bus to Minnesota would be a days-long trip, but it might be worth it. Still, there was no use thinking about it when any possible conversation about it was hours away. She needed to do something to keep her mind off the situation, to keep from wondering if her family was okay, if her job still existed. Her headache still lingered on the periphery, so she decided to go outside to get some fresh air.

A moment later, she stood on the front step, breathing deeply, staring out at miles of green grass and a picture-perfect blue sky perfectly punctuated with cottony clouds. It sure was idyllic, she'd give the writer that. The scene was perfect for romance. In comparison, the shrubs and flowers that bordered the front of the house looked a little... lackluster. Emmy chewed on her lip for a moment. Would Will be upset if she... zhuzhed things up a bit? Given the look of the landscape bed, he didn't care much about it. Therefore, he couldn't be mad if she messed with it, right? Especially if she made it look better.

Decision made, Emmy wandered around to the back of the house. A place like this was bound to have a shed.

"Bingo," she said when she found it.

The door squeaked when she opened it. The first thing she saw was a shiny riding mower, which explained how Will kept his immense lawn trimmed. Unfortunately, it quickly became clear that the mower was the only thing there that he made regular use of. There was a pitiful collection of gardening tools that had gathered rust and dust in equal measure. Spare landscape rock was piled in the corner. A bag of potting soil slumped against the wall like a drunk man sleeping off a couple shots too many. On one shelf was what had to be an antique watering can, likely one that Will's grandfather had bought in his youth.

"No wheelbarrow," she muttered to herself. "Fine. I could use the workout."

Rolling up her proverbial sleeves, Emmy began transporting what she needed to the front of the house, starting with the rocks. Once she had enough to work with, she grabbed the potting soil. Finally, she grabbed a trowel, a hand rake, a weeder, and a pair of pruning shears that whined in protest when she tested their ability to open and close. With the sounds of leaves rustling in the breeze and the occasional bird call for background music, she got to work. This was what she needed to keep her mind off everything else. Dirt and flowers. The satisfaction of using the weeder to hook and pull stubborn weeds. When she saw how much work she had to do, she belatedly realized she'd need a trash bag. Or two. The first was quickly filled with undergrowth, dead leaves, and a few of the most prominent weeds. With the bulk of the dead and the annoying out of the way, she set to work pruning the shrubs with the reluctant shears that could barely close due to all the rust. The sun was warm, but not unbearably so. Plus, the breeze kept her cool. She paused in her work only to grab a glass of water. After gulping down half of it, she pressed the cool glass to her forehead for a moment.

By noon, she'd finished pruning. Then she had to face the fact that several of Will's perennials would be better off put out of their misery. Others were salvageable, but there were going to be some empty spaces. Maybe she could arrange landscaping rock over the dirt. She had plenty. Wiping the back of her hand over her forehead, she looked back at the shed. It seemed a shame to waste the tools she had at her disposal. The antique watering can called to her. She ran and got it, looked it over as she walked back to the front of the house. Rusty and rustic. It could work. She tested the handle on top, found that it was loose. Using the weeder, she pried first one side, then the other free. The handle went into her second garbage bag. She opened the potting soil and dumped some into the watering can. Then she carefully dug around a peony that didn't look too worse for wear. She placed the plant inside the watering can, used more potting soil to keep it in place. Then she arranged the new planter in the empty space, built a little wall of rock around it so it looked purposeful. Sitting back on her heels, she took a good look.

"Yeah. He can't get mad at me for this. No way."

A couple hours later, she decided she'd done all she could do with the tools at hand. She cleaned up the garbage and debris and returned the tools to the shed. Next stop: the shower. The cool water felt like heaven. She stood for a good thirty seconds just letting it run over her, soaking her hair, washing away the first layer of sweat and dirt. Then she soaped, shampooed, conditioned, combed. It was a long process. When she stepped out of the bathroom, wearing fresh, clean clothes, she saw that Will was home. He was in the process of hanging his keys on the hook, so she assumed he'd just walked in.

"Hey."

"Hey." His brow was furrowed slightly. "Did you hire somebody to do stuff with the plants out front?"

Emmy raised an eyebrow. "I'm a little low on funds right now, so no, I didn't hire anybody. I did it myself."

She didn't know if she should be flattered or insulted when his eyebrows lifted in a show of stunned surprise. "*You* did that? By yourself?"

Suddenly self-conscious, Emmy shrugged. "I told you I'd go stir-crazy before long. It kept me out of trouble." She glanced up at him through her lashes. "Do you not like it?"

"To tell the truth, I've never thought about the bushes much. But they look great. About as good as they did when my grandpa was still alive. I saw what you did with his watering can. Very cool. He would have loved that."

"Really?"

"Yeah, for sure. Maybe I should take you to get some more supplies. You can tackle the side of the house next. Do you do this for a living? Back in… you know… your realm."

She snorted at the word choice, then shook her head a little. "No, not for a living. It's just a hobby."

"Some hobby. You could go pro if you wanted to. Guaranteed success."

She waved that off. "Are you too tired to take me to the library?"

"I've gotta shower, but then I'm good to go. Just hang tight."

Much as Emmy had done earlier, Will stripped off his clothes and stood under the spray of the shower. He'd had a tough time at work, tougher than usual because he kept wondering what the point of saving lives was when none of the lives were real. Fortunately, a lot of his job was so familiar to him now that he could do it in his sleep. His body had carried out several tasks through muscle memory alone. Still... he wished he could just forget about Emmy's unexpected appearance for a while. Not Emmy herself: she was fun and interesting, and a good gardener, apparently. But if he could just forget the circumstances of her being there... Will sighed, closed his eyes, and stuck his head into the spray. A drink sounded good. Maybe he'd hit the bar while Emmy was doing her thing at the library. Then again, would it be any better if he sat alone at a bar? Even with alcohol, he'd still be alone with his own thoughts. On top of having a never-ending stream of questions running through his head, he'd be the sad sack who was drinking alone.

He texted Jared as soon as he got out of the shower.

A couple seconds later, Jared sent back the two beers emoji.

Having secured a drinking buddy, he went back out to find Emmy. She was standing behind the couch in a pose he recognized as yoga. For a moment he just stood there watching her stretch and bend, the way her body moved fluidly from one stance to the next. She looked so serene that he felt bad interrupting her. And, yeah, watching her move like that was giving him some pleasant thoughts. When it looked like she was pausing, he cleared his throat. She opened her eyes, rolled her body back into a relaxed position.

"Hey, didn't hear you walk up."

"No worries. You ready to go?"

"Yeah, let me grab my phone."

She dashed over to the table, snagged her phone, and slipped it into her pocket.

"Have you considered what might happen if you go to the library alone?" he asked. "What if you get surrounded by single guys?"

"In the library?" she asked incredulously.

"Given your previous experiences, I would say that there's no logic behind this particular phenomenon."

"Fair point. I'll just be incredibly rude." She wrinkled her nose. "Some would say I'm a natural at it."

"And if that doesn't work?" He couldn't keep the anxious edge out of his voice.

Her expression softened. "I'll be okay. I promise. But if anything starts to feel off, I'll call you, okay?"

"If you're sure."

"Totally. I've been working on my fuck off signals. I practiced them in the mirror this morning."

Will laughed and shook his head. "Okay. I'm convinced. Let's go."

They drove to the library, arguing the whole time about which radio station to listen to. Will's car was old, practically a relic. He didn't have the luxury of hooking up his phone and shuffling his music library. He pulled into the parking lot as he told her this, effectively ending the heated discussion. Will didn't bother parking. He stopped at the curb, looked up at the brightly lit brick building. He didn't understand what she thought she was going to accomplish there, but appreciated her need to do *something*.

"Keep me posted," he told her before she got out of the car. "I'll be a couple minutes away whenever you're done for the night."

"Sounds good. Thanks, Will." She paused with one leg out of the car, smiled sadly at him. "I appreciate you indulging me. It's probably futile to look for answers here, but I have to start somewhere."

Since he'd just thought essentially the same thing, he smiled back. "You never know. See you later, Sherlock."

"Bye, Nurse Watson."

Eleven

"Hey, man, what's up?"

Will looked up from his drink as Jared slid onto the barstool next to him. They had often met for drinks at The Bell & Whistle, a local gastropub run by a wise-cracking, easygoing middle-aged couple from Ireland. This could be any normal evening for him, except this time Will was wondering if Ireland even existed in his world. If he bought a plane ticket and flew there, would the landscape around him turn into a 404 Error? Something to ponder later. Emmy would laugh if he asked her. He liked hearing her laugh.

"Earth to Will."

"Nothing's up," Will said quickly. He signaled for Callie, the sweet, young bartender with mile-long legs and strawberry blonde hair, to get his friend a drink. "I got the first round."

"Appreciate it. You sure you're okay? Nassir said you quit."

"I did." He studied Callie. Wondered if she was written to be gorgeous for some plot-related purpose or just because it was expected of a bartender in a romance novel.

"Fuck me. Really? I thought he was full of shit. What happened?"

Jared was an anesthesiologist. They had started around the same time, clicked over bad break-room coffee when they discovered a mutual love of *Final Fantasy* and bad medical dramas from the '80s and '90s.

Before he responded, Will made sure to check for a script in his head. If this scene with Jared turned into some kind of surreal book experience, he wasn't sure he could handle it. Thankfully, the only words that came to mind were ones he wanted to say. He still felt a deep stab of pain over the distance he now felt between himself and his best friend. Jared was looking at him with earnest interest, one hand wrapped around his beer. His ring finger was conspicuously bare. Will had been his best man four years ago. Six months ago, Jared and Macey had divorced. It had been amicable enough, and there were no children, but Jared had needed a friend to lean on. Will had been there for that, too.

And maybe none of it had happened. Maybe none of it mattered.

"I don't know where to start. I just... woke up one morning questioning everything about my life."

"Little young for a midlife crisis, buddy."

"Yet here we are."

"So you quit your job. Did you at least buy a Ducati while you were at it?"

No, but the idea appealed. Will spared a moment to consider how that would work out. He could ride across the country with Emmy behind him, her arms wrapped around his waist. Nothing but the open road, the roar of the engine, and the countryside flying by. Should they wear helmets? Could they die? Would the book allow it? Jesus, he was starting to think of the book as a god. He rubbed his hand over his face.

"Not yet," he replied. "It's a possibility, though."

"At least do me the favor of taking me with you when you go to buy it. What's next besides potential motorcycle ownership?"

Will sipped his beer, but he barely tasted it. This was where it got tricky. He couldn't tell his friend the truth—that he was hoping to find a way to transport himself permanently out of this world and into what he now considered to be the real world.

"There's this girl," he found himself saying. The words weren't part of a script, but he'd been surprised by them nonetheless. Hadn't had a chance to fight them off. Possibly because they *weren't* scripted. He just hadn't realized he'd want to say them.

"Okay, now we're talking. This calls for a pitcher." Will waited obligingly while Jared signaled Callie. He gulped down beer, hoping it would go straight to his head. Then his friend turned back to him. "Where'd you meet her?"

"Uh… funny story, actually."

"The best meet-cutes start with those words."

The use of the phrase gave Will a jolt. He hadn't even considered the rules here. If he wasn't real, and he did in fact live in a romance novel—both things he truly believed by this point—were his feelings for Emmy his own? Was he predisposed to start falling for any attractive woman in his path? Was he afflicted with Meet-Cute Syndrome just as Emmy was? Quickly, he glanced over at Callie. Nothing there. He'd felt some sort of way for Bright, but that had dissipated as soon as he'd realized the truth of their circumstances. Feeling a little more confident about the state of things, he turned back to Jared, prepared to make up a story of some sort. He could say he and Emmy had woken up in his bed, explain away the suddenness of it with a night of hard drinking on both their parts, although he didn't think Emmy would appreciate it. But as it turned out, he didn't need to explain a thing. They were interrupted before he could begin his careful prevarication.

"Hey, Will!"

Both men looked up at Bright, who was standing there smiling, with eyes only for Will. Jared raised his eyebrows, clearly noting how easily he'd been ignored. Behind her back, he flicked his glance at Bright to silently ask if this was the woman Will had been talking about. Will gave a quick, subtle shake of his head.

"Hey, Bright. Didn't know you were here."

"I just came in. I do dinner here at least once a week. Geoffrey and Molly make the best shepherd's pie."

Panic clawed its way up Will's chest as he felt words pressing at the inside of his mouth again, trying to wriggle their way out. Damn it, was this a scene from the book? Why hadn't he felt this way when it had just been him and Jared? He resisted the urge to invite her to sit down, agree with her about the food, and ask her to share a shepherd's pie and a drink with him. Right when he was about to open his mouth—maybe to scream something about one or more sea creatures—Jared pointedly cleared his throat. Bright jolted slightly and looked at him, her brow furrowed in confusion.

"I'm sorry… I'm interrupting."

An awkward silence ensued. Will let out a relieved breath. Bright looked utterly perplexed as she stared silently at Jared, and Jared looked like he was trying to decide whether to be offended or amused by the whole situation. As soon as Jared had cleared his throat, the script in Will's head evaporated. The only explanation he could come up with was that, in the book, he'd been drinking alone. This must have been a scene where he and Bright developed their relationship or something. But he'd invited Jared to the bar with him instead of going alone, rendering the romantic scene impossible. Thank God he'd decided against the pity party and texted his friend. Recovering quickly, he smiled good-naturedly at Bright.

"Jared, this is Bright. Bright, this is my friend Jared."

"Bright?" Jared asked.

"Yeah, like the opposite of dim," she murmured, almost as if it were a knee-jerk response. "It's um… it's nice to meet you." She finally recovered, smiled, stuck out her hand. "I'm sorry. I don't know where my head is at. It's nice to meet you," she repeated with more confidence.

Jared shook it. "Same goes. You own that new store, don't you? Bright Ideas?"

She smiled a little self-deprecatingly. "Yeah, that's my place." She shrugged. "The name was right there."

"I like it. Gotta work with what you got, right?"

"Yeah, exactly."

Jared moved over one seat, leaving a stool open between him and Will. "Grab a seat. Order one of those shepherd's pies."

Will raised one eyebrow. Their dialogue—he hated to think of it that way, but couldn't help it—was almost exactly what his and Bright's should have been.

Bright cast Will an uncertain glance. "You don't mind?"

"Not at all. We're just hanging."

"Okay." She sat, then regarded him curiously. "Is uh… is Emmy not here with you?"

Again, Jared gave him that questioning glance behind her back. This time, Will gave him a slight nod. "She's at the library. Doing some research."

"Late night research. Is she a grad student?"

It occurred to him he had no idea what her career was. She'd mentioned missing work and being worried that would lead to her being fired, but that left a lot of possibilities. And she'd made it clear the landscaping and gardening thing was just a hobby. Where did that leave him?

"She's a writer, actually," he improvised.

"Oh yeah? Like a journalist or…?"

"Romance novels," Will said and took another gulp of beer.

"No kidding."

"Must be good in the sack," Jared commented.

Will gave him a look. "Really, man?"

Bright giggled, accepted the cocktail Callie set in front of her with a grin and a thank you. "I can't speculate on whether writing about romance makes you automatically good in bed, but I can say that's a fascinating career. Good for her. Have you been together long?"

It was a probing question, and Will was grateful for it. Maybe this would help set the world to rights so he wouldn't feel like he had to dodge Bright at every opportunity. "Not too long. A few weeks. It's still new."

Something passed over Bright's face for a moment. It looked like regret and a kind of... grief. Again, she paused, as if unsure how to process this. Then she nodded, smiled again. "She seemed nice. I'll have to read one of her books sometime."

"I'll bring you a copy." If she asked about it later, he'd grab a book at random and claim the author's name was Emmy's pen name.

"Thanks!"

Conversation moved on to how Jared and Will had met. Jared told most of the story about Will's short-lived stint in the obstetrics wing where Jared still worked. As soon as Bright heard he worked in the hospital, she pressed Jared for details. He was happy to oblige. Before Will knew it, Bright had changed her empty cocktail glass for a pint glass and was sharing the pitcher of beer with Jared. All the better since Will had to drive soon. At least he thought it would be soon. He hadn't heard from Emmy yet. He checked his phone, sipped at his beer. It was getting late. He wondered how Emmy was doing at the library by herself. She'd seemed certain that she could handle any wayward men who tried to ask her out, but...

"Looking for a text from your lady?" Jared asked.

"Yeah. She must be really deep into the research."

"Look at those puppy eyes. You are *gone*, man."

"Shut up, Jared."

Bright touched Will's arm. "I think it's sweet."

"See?" he said to Jared. "She thinks it's sweet."

"So sweet I'm getting a cavity. You gotta work on razzing people, Bright. Single folks are supposed to stick together."

"We are, huh?" Bright studied Jared as she sipped her beer. "What makes you so sure I'm single?"

"Not sure, pretty lady. Just hoping. So... am I right?"

She watched his face for a moment, then smiled slowly in a way that spoke of hidden depths that any man would be happy to explore. Jared's throat worked as he swallowed.

"I am," she said simply. "My last relationship went up in flames shortly before I moved here."

"Sounds like a story."

"Maybe. How about you? No way someone who looks like you stays single for long, and it's clear you've got game."

They were completely involved with each other now. Will was oddly fascinated by the turn of events. And, if he was honest with himself, a little hurt at how easily he'd been cast aside. He'd get over that, though. Checking his phone again and seeing no texts from Emmy, he finished his beer and—though he craved another drink—switched to water. When he still hadn't heard from her after he'd polished off the whole glass—as well as the plate of cheese fries Jared had abandoned in favor of flirting with Bright—he decided it was time to check in on her. He left a generous tip beneath the empty water glass and slipped out of the bar. Neither Jared nor Bright looked his way.

Emmy was going to like this story. He couldn't wait to tell her. It was a little weird how much he was looking forward to seeing her, considering how recently they'd met and how little time they'd been apart that evening, but he couldn't deny that he felt more at ease with her than he was on his own. Or with any of the... characters was the right word, he supposed. Even if it made him cringe to think of his family, friends, and coworkers as characters. The lack of texts probably meant Emmy was deep in the stacks and not thinking about checking in with him. Still, if no news turned out to be bad news, he wanted to be there for her.

The library was only a few blocks away—*everything* was only a few blocks away in Cobalt—and he navigated the streets just fine. A part of him wondered what would happen if he got pulled over. He didn't think he was over the legal limit, but a breathalyzer might say different. That probably wasn't supposed to happen in the book. He kept an eye on his rearview, but the street was quiet. He made it to the library with no incidents, parked in a spot by the front entrance, and went inside.

Twelve

Emmy was surrounded by romance novels. She'd wanted to skip over the fantasies, the historical romances, the magical realism, but what if the author who'd written the book she was in had branched out? The Google searches for the author and the book had turned up nothing, unsurprisingly. But that didn't mean there wasn't a clue in a book somewhere. At the moment, she was exploring the possibility that the author existed in this world, but had a different name. Or a different pen name. As such, she couldn't take any chances; she would look at every single romance novel in the library. But, since she needed to start somewhere, she had only pulled those that had been published between 2016 and 2018.

There were three stacks on the table in front of her. The biggest one was books she had skimmed and rejected. The names didn't match and the writing styles were vastly different. Opposite the rejects was the pile she'd yet to go through. In front of her was a smaller pile of maybes. The names didn't match—not that she expected them to, as Big Brother Google had declared the author nonexistent—but the writing style was similar. It was still anyone's guess if she was supposed to look for the book she'd been reading—the one she was currently in—or a book that was about her. Maybe, just maybe, she would find a book about Emmy Miura that she could read in order to get back to her world. Then again, maybe she wasn't supposed to look for a book at all. There was always the possibility that she was only going to get out if Will agreed to somehow force himself to fall in love with Bright, and she couldn't ask him to do that. There was also the galling possibility that there was no way out, and she was stuck long-term in a world of make-believe. Last night, lying in her borrowed bed, she found her mind constantly wandering back to this possibility, that she was trapped forever. That she'd never see her friends or family again. Never find her way back to a world that she belonged to. Then she remembered that Will was feeling the exact same way, and he only felt that way because of her. Any time she felt like giving up, she thought of him rather than herself. For him, she would keep going. Until she was old and gray if she had to.

Good God, she hoped it didn't come to that.

When she heard footsteps behind her, she assumed Will had come to find her. How long had it been anyway? She checked her phone and was shocked to see she'd been at this for hours. Good thing Will was here. Her brain needed a break.

"You must be a fast reader."

She looked up with surprise and some trepidation to see one of the guys who'd tried to ask her out on her first unfortunate sojourn into town. She recognized the messenger bag. Was it Lost Guy? She couldn't put a name to his face, but she was pretty sure that was because he hadn't introduced himself at the time. When she only stared blankly, he coughed uncomfortably and shrugged.

"Lots of books," he mumbled. "We met the other day in the park. You were going to give me directions, but then that jogger came up and started hassling us. I lost track of you after that."

"Oh. Yeah. Sorry about that, but I was um… late and I had to run."

"Hey, no worries. As soon as you left, he backed off. Good thing, too. I think he was getting ready to punch me."

"I'm glad that worked out." Emmy didn't like sitting there while he was standing. He kind of towered over her. Not much would change if she stood up—he was still tall enough to tower over her—but it would at least put her in a position to beat a hasty retreat. She got to her feet, purposefully putting her chair between them. "I was just heading out actually. It's later than I thought, so…"

"Hey, no worries. I just wanted to say hi. We didn't get to finish our conversation last time."

To her recollection, there hadn't been much of a conversation. "It's fine. I didn't have much to say."

"Maybe we could find something to talk about over dinner. You like Italian?"

"Um… no. I mean, no to the dinner. I'm seeing someone."

His brow furrowed in confusion. "Since when?"

"What do you mean 'since when'? What does that matter?"

"I mean… it doesn't. It's just… I guess I got the wrong impression. I thought we were getting pretty deep into a flirt session back in the park. You know, before The Hulk thought he needed to smash."

"I was not flirting."

"Felt like it to me."

She shook her head. "If I gave you the wrong impression, I'm sorry. The point is, I'm seeing someone, so I'm going to pass on dinner. Thanks for the invite, though. It's really... flattering."

"I... okay. Sure. Well, maybe I could give you my number. Text me if you change your mind."

"Look—"

"Hey, Em. Everything okay?"

Fake relationship or not, Emmy could have kissed Will at that moment. As soon as he walked up, slipped his arm around her shoulders, her world felt steady again. It wasn't until that moment that she realized she'd been more than just uncomfortable when she was alone with Lost Guy; she'd been afraid.

Lost Guy frowned up at Will, who had a good four inches on him. "This keeps happening. If I didn't know any better, I'd say you were some kind of magnet for big, beefy dudes."

"It does seem that way," Emmy said, allowing herself to smile and lean into Will. "Anyway, as I was saying, I'm seeing somebody." She laid her hand over Will's chest to emphasize her point, and *damn*, that man had one fine chest.

"Oh, this is the guy." He sized Will up, looked disappointed by his own conclusions. "You're together."

"Yep."

He nodded and shoved his hands in his pockets. "Okay. Well."

Emmy allowed herself a sigh of relief when he shuffled off. Will's arm stayed around her as the door swung shut behind him. Then he touched the side of her face until she looked up at him.

"Are you okay?" he asked quietly.

"Yeah. For sure."

She was trembling, though. He clearly felt it because he slowly turned her until she was pressed more fully against him. Both his arms were around her now, holding tight. Emmy couldn't stop herself from pressing against his strong, solid form as she fought to stop the tremors rippling through her.

"Shh," he murmured. "It's okay. Your body went into fight, flight, or freeze mode and you've got some extra stress hormones running around inside you. It'll pass."

She let the comforting warmth of his voice wrap around her and soothe her ragged nerves. "I don't know why I reacted like that," she told his chest. "I don't even know where he came from. He was just... *there*, and he wouldn't take no for an answer. It was so stupid, but I was starting to get really itchy about the whole thing, like if he didn't leave me alone..." Her voice trailed off as another shudder ran through her. Apparently she'd been more affected by the situation than she'd realized. Will's only response was to run his fingers over her hair. It felt so good to be held like that.

Too good.

Emmy made herself step away. "Anyway, it doesn't matter. You showed up to pretend to be my boyfriend just in time." She smiled up at him. "Thanks."

Will had to fight the quick punch of lust that her simple, unguarded smile incited. All he'd done was walk up and stand by her, but she made him feel like a hero. She looked so sweet with her hair mussed—presumably from running her fingers through it as she pored over novels—and he had the impression that sweet was rare to see from her. He had to remind himself that they were only in a pretend relationship, and they were in no position to turn the fake into the real.

But he wasn't going to forget the way she'd felt in his arms anytime soon.

"You're welcome," he said, forcing himself to act casual. "Find anything?"

"Bupkis. But there are more books. Way more. Give me a minute to make notes and then we can get out of here."

Will helped her put books away since she felt bad leaving so many of them on the return shelf at once. Then they went out to his car. Once she was buckled in, she reached out and touched his arm.

"Thanks," she said quietly. "For real. I don't know how you appeared right on time, but I'm glad you had my back."

"No problem. I got a little worried when you didn't check in." He turned to look behind him as he backed out of the space. Then he shifted into drive and paused to raise his eyebrows at her. "And get this—I left Bright with my friend Jared at the bar. I think it was supposed to be a scene from the book, something between me and Bright. But I messed it up when I invited Jared along. They didn't even notice me leaving. Too busy flirting with each other."

"You're kidding. Bright was flirting with another guy while you were sitting right there?"

"Yeah. And the funny thing is, they kind of clicked. They had this whole banter thing going, and she smiled at him in this slow, sexy way. He nearly swallowed his tongue."

Emmy blinked at him. "That is so weird."

"Yeah. I don't know what it means or if it's going to mess with... I don't know... the fabric of the universe." He ran a hand through his hair and tried not to think about taking a drink of something stronger than beer when they got home. "You want to go back to the library tomorrow?"

"Yep. I've gotta try something." She studied him for a moment. "You okay?"

He looked over at her, saw the earnest and concerned expression on her face. It warmed something inside him. Every minute with this woman made it harder and harder to remember why he shouldn't—*couldn't*—fall for her.

"As okay as I can be," he told her. "Don't worry about me."

"Can't help it. We're in a worrying situation. Oh! Speaking of... I googled myself today. And my sister. And the sex psychic. Nothing."

"Man. That sucks."

"Yeah, I don't exist. It's weird." Emmy wrinkled her nose in consternation. "But I was thinking maybe I should find my way to Minneapolis. I know the internet didn't turn up anything, but maybe the sex psychic is there anyway. Maybe I have to physically go to her, like a quest or something."

"Minneapolis, huh? I guess I can check flights when we get back."

"Well... no. I don't have ID, so no airplane for me. We'd have to take the bus."

"We?"

A hint of a blush crept into Emmy's cheeks. "Or I. Me. If you don't want to go. I'm not saying I want to leave tomorrow, but maybe we could discuss it once your notice is up?"

Will shrugged. "Sure. Why not?"

He doubted the answer to their problems lay in Minnesota, but he did have some interest in exploring the country. His thoughts about flying to Ireland earlier held true for other parts of the U.S. as well. Did Minneapolis exist? It might be worth figuring it out, though he didn't know what that knowledge would change; whether it existed or not, he was still in a fantasy world. His hands tightened briefly on the steering wheel. He felt the strain, saw his knuckles go white, and then the relief from relaxing his muscles. It was important to remember he was alive. Or at least he was some version of alive.

"So," Emmy said into the silence. "Bright and Jared."

"Yeah, looks like. Oh, and you might have to write a romance novel real quick. You know, when you get some free time."

"What? Why?"

Will smiled as he explained the conversation he'd had with Jared and Bright. She let out a surprised laugh when she heard the lie he'd invented.

"A romance novelist, huh? That's the best you could come up with?"

"It was on my mind. I panicked."

Emmy shook her head, but she was smiling. "I'm not gonna write a book so you can save face. We'll burn that bridge if and when we get to it."

"Yeah, I figured as much. I didn't have a choice about the lie. I never got around to asking you what you do for a living." He paused a moment. When it became apparent she wasn't going to fill him in, he nudged her with his elbow. "So? What do you do?"

Emmy fidgeted with a loose thread on her shirt. "I'm a concierge at a midrange hotel halfway between my apartment and the Cities."

"Which cities?"

"The Twin Cities. Minneapolis and Saint Paul."

He glanced over at her and noted she was still looking down. Her voice had gone quiet and hesitant for what might have been the first time in their short acquaintance. "What's wrong with being a concierge?"

She shrugged. "Nothing really. It's a job. It pays the bills. It's just not exciting."

"Not every career has to be exciting."

"Right."

"How did you come to be a concierge at a midrange hotel halfway between your apartment and the Twin Cities?" he prompted.

"Well, first I went to community college and tried really hard to discover my calling, whatever that ended up being. I was pretty open-minded about it. You know, like maybe an eagle would roost outside my window, and I would think 'Aha! I'm meant to be a wildlife conservationist!' Or I'd join a music appreciation club and discover my passion for composition. But that didn't happen, so I majored in Business Management with a minor in Hospitality. Not because those areas captivated me, but because they seemed to cover a lot of ground career-wise. Straight out of college, I tried my hand at managing a restaurant, but I couldn't stand the stress. After that, I tried being a bank teller. Respectable; less stressful. The problem was, when I wasn't worrying about bank robbers, I was bored out of my mind." She paused, looked down at her hands, which twisted together in her lap. "I'm rambling."

He crossed his arms on the steering wheel and leaned forward. "That's okay. It's a good ramble."

Noting his position, Emmy looked around and appeared surprised that they'd gotten back to the house and he'd already stopped the car.

"Wow, when I wrap myself up in self-pity, I don't hold back."

"You weren't wrapped up in self-pity," Will told her, and got out of the car. He waited for her to do the same. "You were telling me about yourself. I, for one, think it's admirable that you refuse to settle for anything less than a perfect fit when it comes to your work. A lot of people would get into a rut and think there's no way out, or no reason to try to get out. You were self-aware enough to recognize a poor fit, and brave enough to start over from scratch. Multiple times."

Emmy simply didn't know what to say to him. He was just like her parents and her sister—self-assured and confident in his career path. Like her family, he had clearly felt a pull toward the career he wanted and needed in his life, and he'd pursued that path without straying or hesitating. Emmy, meanwhile, had wandered around in some kind of proverbial maze, questioning her own judgment at every turn.

She couldn't think of a way to reply to him without saying something clichéd like, "You wouldn't understand," so she said nothing as she followed him into the house. Will either didn't notice her silence or didn't mind it, because he rolled right through it.

"So why not landscape design? You're clearly good at it and passionate about it."

"Yeah, but I don't have any real experience with it." She didn't mention that she also took courses in ecology, biology, and soil composition at college, but was too scared to major in anything so specific. It was too embarrassing to admit that she'd chickened out every time she let herself think seriously about turning her gardening hobby into a career. It had always felt like her true calling… right up until she faced the prospect of trying and failing. She'd kept waiting for a sign, some definitive proof that she could, and *should*, do it. "My parents both have brown thumbs, so they left all the gardening and stuff to me when I still lived at home. I stop by every now and then to check on things. That's pretty much all I've done aside from touching up your yard. I'm good with plants." She shrugged. "It's just a knack, though."

Will stopped in the kitchen to grab a bottle of whiskey. He slung her a look of confusion. "Why does that mean you can't make a career out of it?"

Emmy was getting flustered. She noted the bottle in his hand, but didn't say anything. It wasn't her business if he wanted to follow up a trip to the bar with a nightcap. "Because it's a hobby. I'm not professionally trained. I just watched some YouTube videos and read Wikipedia articles."

Will shook his head slowly as if he couldn't comprehend the words coming out of her mouth. "You think you can't be a landscaper because you don't have some kind of certificate or license for it? Lots of people do things they didn't train for."

"Look, I know it's not that late, but I had a long day and I'm tired. Can we pick this up another time? I'm probably going to crash in a minute."

She was very obviously trying to escape, and she had no doubt he was aware of that. It was a relief when he said good night without calling her out for her cowardice. He went to the cabinet to grab a glass for his whiskey. Emmy made her retreat while he poured.

Thirteen

The days bled into one another. Emmy split her time between researching in the library and working on the exterior design of Will's house. His two weeks' notice was almost up, and she was no closer to an answer about how to get out of the damn book. With each fruitless visit to the library, she became more certain that she was pursuing the wrong course. Meanwhile, if time was passing normally in the real world, she'd missed her sister's wedding and then some. It hurt to think about her family, to wonder how they were handling her disappearance. The only way she could stop fretting about it was to convince herself that time had stopped when she'd been pulled into the book. Or maybe she was only a projection of herself. Maybe her real body was lying comatose in her bed. Her family would still be worrying about her—likely while watching over her in a hospital bed—but at least they wouldn't think she'd been kidnapped. Or worse. The problem with the coma theory was that it meant there was no way to pull Will out of the book with her.

Her brain started to throb whenever she had too much downtime. Fortunately, she never felt lost or overwhelmed when she was working on the landscaping outside Will's house. She had a pile of new supplies thanks to a trip to the hardware store Will had insisted on a few days prior. As she finished filling a window box with potting soil, she thought again about the conversation they'd had at the hardware store in town. She couldn't help but smile a little at the memory.

"Fresh herbs in the window box would be good," she'd said, more to herself than to him, as she perused a shelf of small green plants in their flimsy, disposable pots. "You cook enough where they'd actually get used, and they'd smell really good, too."

"I don't know if I can identify enough herbs to make it worthwhile. I mostly use the dried stuff in the conveniently labeled shakers."

Emmy cast him a withering look. "You want flowers, you can have flowers. I'm just saying, a lot of people are using homegrown fruits, vegetables, and herbs these days. It's efficient and organic and cottage-core and it saves you from having to go to the grocery store every time you want a tomato for a sandwich."

"Or I could make a sandwich without tomatoes on it."

Emmy whirled on him, brandishing a tiny pot of basil. "Look, buster, you're the one who insisted on bringing me here, so stop sassing me."

"Sassing?"

"Yes. You're being sassy. Stop it. You're going to have a window box herb garden and you're going to like it."

"Yes, ma'am," Will said, valiantly trying to hide his grin.

"That's better." Emmy added the basil to the cart and tossed in an assortment of seed packets for good measure, vowing to sort through them later. She didn't know if she'd be at Will's place long enough to watch seedlings grow into flowers—in fact, she hoped she wouldn't be—but she enjoyed the process of planting enough to make the purchase worth it.

Then they'd moved on to a display of perennials, already blooming and giving off an assortment of fragrances.

"You can arrange taller flowers along the edge of the house," Emmy told Will. "A lot of these plants thrive in partial shade, which is perfect for your house because it faces south. Then you get some mossy rocks to break up the pattern a little, throw in something unexpected. Oh! Maybe a fountain. No… a birdbath. An old one to match the style of your grandfather's watering can. Is there an antique shop around here?" She turned to look at him and caught him smiling at her. "What?"

"Just a hobby?"

Emmy felt her cheeks get warm. "A hobby that isn't worth doing unless you do it right."

"Emmy, you're talking about antique birdbaths. Maybe it's time to consider turning your hobby into a career."

"Not this again," she grumbled, wheeling the cart away.

"What's stopping you? You have the skills and the passion. You're obsessed with herbs, and you can spend twenty minutes staring at one packet of seeds. It sounds like a no-brainer."

"Yeah, until I find out that I'm competing with people who have been landscaping all their lives. People who studied it, got certifications, won prizes. People who have crews of dozens of people working for them. And I'll be sitting there hoping some grandma who lives in my neighborhood takes pity on me and asks me to prune her rose bushes."

"Or... you could do up grandma's garden real nice and she could tell all her grandma friends. Then, after you've done up all their yards, their worthless kids can come for a visit, see what you've done, and then you've got more customers."

Emmy raised an eyebrow. "What makes them worthless?"

"Because they never call, and they only visit on major holidays."

"Oh, sure. Obviously."

Will fell silent. She thought he was finally ready to drop the subject. She thought wrong.

"You could try it out for however long you're here. I bet there are tons of people in town who would love to redo their yards, and there wouldn't be any pressure because none of it is real anyway."

"It would feel real to me."

"That would just help motivate you to give it your all."

"If I agree to try it, will you stop pushing this?" she snapped.

"Yes, because then I'll have won."

Emmy opened her mouth to argue, found she couldn't come up with a good comeback, and snapped her jaw shut. Will just smiled at her in that smug-yet-charming way that only a romance novel protagonist could pull off.

★

With all the elements put together, it did look professional. Emmy worried her lip with her teeth as she studied her work. Yeah. Professional. Right? Maybe the plants looked a little haphazard, but she hadn't wanted neat little rows for Will. And the antique birdbath did look absolutely perfect tucked in among the foliage. There were three antique shops in Cobalt to choose from, thank the romance gods.

"Wind chimes," she whispered to herself. "All it needs now is a good set of wind chimes."

She checked the time on her phone. Will would be home soon. She hoped he had enough energy to drive her to Bright Ideas. She could skip the library for one afternoon. Before she went in to take a shower, she grabbed the rusty old gardening tools from the shed. She'd already replaced them with new ones, and she had a great idea how to put these to good use.

"Do you think Bright would let me nap on one of her antique couches while you talk to her about trash art?" Will asked later as he drove her toward town.

"First of all, it's not trash. It's your grandfather's old tools, and they deserve your respect. Second… no. I don't think she'd mind if you took a nap. She probably has a back room or something, though. No need to make yourself part of the display floor." He felt Emmy's gaze on him, studying him. He knew he looked and sounded fatigued, and she must have noticed, because she added, "I told you we could wait a day if you needed to."

"I'm fine," he told her. "I wouldn't have agreed to go if I didn't want to. I'm just a little worried about seeing Bright again."

"Why?"

He sighed. "I had another book scene at the hospital today. It hit me out of nowhere. I don't think I can handle it if I end up in one today."

Emmy turned more fully toward him. "What happened?"

Will didn't want to recount it. More than anything, he wanted to forget it. He wanted to go back to a time when he thought he was a person with a purpose and a life to lead. But that wasn't in the cards.

"There was this kid who was recovering after surgery. Appendicitis. It went fine, but they're keeping him overnight just to be sure. The parents caught it late, and the appendix was severely inflamed. I was doing my rounds, and I saw he was crying and clutching this stuffed owl his mom had brought him."

He remembered it too well. The words had been there, and he'd wanted to fight them. But how could he when they perfectly aligned with what he wanted to say and do? This wasn't a casual conversation with Bright in the waiting room of a mechanic. A child was suffering. He'd had no choice but to go through with the script.

"Hey, buddy, what's wrong?"

The kid had looked up at him with big brown eyes. His name was Lamar Booke. He was six years old, and he was spending the night in the hospital.

"It's my fault," Lamar said, his voice small and pitiful.

Will heard the words in his head before he spoke them, and he resented them even as he understood the kid needed them.

"What's your fault?"

"We were supposed to pick up our dog today from the shelter place. My tummy hurt a lot, but I didn't want to say anything because I wanted to get our dog. She's really pretty. My mom has a picture on her phone. I had to wait because the people had to come and look at our house and stuff. I really wanted a dog for forever."

"Nothing wrong with that. Dogs are great."

"Yeah, but my tummy hurt real bad and I didn't say anything. I heard the doctor talking to my mom. He said it was lucky we got here in time because it was real bad. My mom was crying. I made her cry."

Will sat on the edge of the bed and took the boy's hand. "You didn't do anything wrong, Lamar. Your mom was probably crying from relief because the doctor was telling her you're okay."

At that moment, Lamar's mother walked back into the room. Her face fell when she saw Will.

"Is everything okay? Did something happen? I just stepped out for a minute to take a call from his dad." Panic rose in her voice. "The reception in here is so spotty. Is he okay?"

"Everything's fine, Mrs. Booke," Will said quickly, allowing the words that weren't his to flow out of him. "I was just checking in with Lamar and telling him how brave he is."

Her smile was watery and so full of love for her son. "So brave, sweet pea. And guess what!"

"What?"

"Daddy just called. Look who's waiting for you at home." She turned her phone so her son could see, and Will could tell the boy was looking at a picture of his new dog because his face lit up.

"My dog!" Lamar pointed to the screen and smiled at Will. "Look, mister! That's my dog now!"

The sugar sweetness of the scene would delight romance readers everywhere, Will thought bitterly. But he gamely looked at the screen, saw a picture of a gangly dog who looked like a cross between a greyhound and a husky. The result was pretty cute.

He opened his mouth and let the words come. "Look at that. She's happy to be home." He patted the kid's arm. "Rest up, buddy. You're going to have a lot of playing to do when you get home."

Will had slipped into a parking spot a block down from Bright Ideas while he'd spoken. They were parked, but Emmy made no move to get out of the car.

"You did a good thing, Will."

"I did what I was supposed to do," he countered. "It was all written. I can't describe how... *used* I feel. Fucking Pinocchio has more autonomy than I do. You have no idea how frustrating this is."

"You're right," she said quietly. "I can't even imagine it."

He shook his head before dropping it back against the headrest and closing his eyes. "I shouldn't be taking it out on you."

"Who else?" she asked. "I'm here for you if you need me. No script. No all-powerful author calling the shots. If you need to vent, go for it."

When he opened his eyes again and looked at her, he saw that she meant it. "Thank you. That might just keep me sane for a while longer."

"That's a change of pace for me. Usually people find themselves telling me that I'm driving them crazy."

"You're just misunderstood."

She laughed as she unbuckled her seatbelt. "That's what I'm always saying."

Will followed her into Bright Ideas. Bright had a salesclerk working for her now, a young twenty-something girl with purple hair and a nose ring. The girl smiled when she saw them walking in and waved.

"Welcome in! Feel free to browse."

"Thanks," Emmy said. "I'm actually looking for Bright, though. Is she here?"

"Yeah, let me go get her for you."

They wandered a bit while the twenty-something went to find Bright, eventually stopping at a wall of paintings depicting naked men with beer bottles in place of their penises.

Will studied the artwork with a quizzical expression. "What is this supposed to mean? Is it a commentary on men or alcohol? Or sex?"

"All of the above, probably," Emmy said. "Maybe you should get one. Support local artists."

Will managed a smile. "I'm more of a whiskey guy."

Emmy silently pointed to a painting on the end that depicted a prominent Jack Daniel's erection.

Will sighed. "I walked right into that one."

"Hey, guys!"

"Saved by the manic pixie dream girl," Emmy whispered, making Will snort.

They turned to greet Bright. Her curly hair was tied up with a bandana and she wore a denim bracelet on her left wrist.

"Good to see you! Bianca said you needed something from me?"

"I have a request," Emmy told her. She held out the bag that contained the old gardening tools. "Do you think you'd be able to freshen these up and turn them into a wind chime?"

Bright took the bag and looked inside. The expression on her face turned to pure delight.

"Absolutely! What a good idea. I can work with this tonight. Could you pick it up tomorrow?"

Emmy glanced at Will, who nodded. "Yes. We can come back tomorrow."

"Excellent. This is going to be a lot of fun. I can't believe I never thought of doing anything like this." She started walking toward the back. Will and Emmy followed. "I'm going to give you the Bright Idea discount. In that you gave me a new bright idea. It's a discount that I made up just now."

"I appreciate it," Emmy said.

"Since you brought me the tools, I only need to charge you for the supplies to assemble the chime and the labor."

Bright named a price that made Will's eyebrows shoot up, but Emmy didn't bat an eye. Bright ran Will's credit card for the fifty percent deposit she'd requested, then took the tools back to her office.

"It'll be worth it," Emmy assured him. "I keep wanting to offer to pay you back, and then I remember my wallet doesn't exist in this realm."

He shrugged. "I'm trying to remember that money doesn't mean much to me anymore."

"I appreciate you spending it anyway." On an impulse, Emmy pushed herself up on tiptoe to kiss his cheek. "Thank you. I'm excited to see what Bright comes up with."

He didn't respond, only stared at her mouth long enough for Emmy to feel her blood start to hum. There was no mistaking his intent. The man was thinking about kissing her. Interestingly enough, she didn't back away. And when he started to lean in, her lips parted, seemingly of their own accord.

Then Bright bounced back into view. Will's back snapped straight. Emmy closed her mouth, pressing her lips together for good measure.

"All set!" Bright declared. "Oh, almost forgot, here's your receipt! I'll see you tomorrow afternoon!"

"Yeah, thanks." Will stuffed the receipt in his pocket.

Neither of them spoke as they got back in the car and started home.

Emmy was sure he'd been about to kiss her. She was slightly less sure that she'd been about to kiss him back, but it had felt that way in the moment. What happened to keeping her distance from the romance novel protagonist? She silently chastised herself as Will drove home with his eyes fixed on the road ahead. No entanglements with the fictional man. None. No matter how sexy he was. And sweet. And funny.

Damn it.

She was about to suggest that they make out just to break the tension when Will spoke.

"I've got an early shift tomorrow, so I'm going to hit the hay. I'll take you to pick up your wind chime when I get back." His eyes held a glint of humor when he flicked his gaze over to her. "But if it's ugly, I'm taking it back and exchanging it for one of those beer-penis paintings. And I'm gonna hang that painting in your room as punishment."

Emmy laughed. "That's fair enough."

Just like that, they were on even footing again.

Fourteen

Will wanted to call in sick. He didn't want to risk another encounter with a book scene in the hospital. If he was honest with himself, he occasionally found ways to convince himself that he was insane to think he was in a romance novel. Sometimes he managed to find his way around to believing it was all some kind of joke or... cosmic coincidence. Then he'd be slapped in the face with a Scene—he thought of them as having capital S's—like the one with Lamar. It was like being doused with ice water. A fierce wakeup call that yanked him out of denial and shoved the truth in his face.

He didn't call in sick, and he went through his shift the next day constantly on edge, waiting for the next Scene to sneak up on him. By the end of his shift, he was so exhausted, he didn't have it in him to feel relieved that there hadn't been any. Then he remembered he was going home to Emmy and her silly wind chime. Something lifted inside of him at the thought of it. He found himself hoping more than ever that she would somehow find a way to get them both out of the book. And soon. Emmy was a solid silver lining in the dark gray cloud of his life, but he hated that she was stuck in the book with him. He wanted to start a life—a *real* life—with her in it.

"Will."

He turned to see Nassir approaching him and cursed silently to himself. One more minute and he'd have been out of there.

"What's up?" he asked, resigning himself to the delay.

"I wanted to check in with you, see if you're still set on leaving us. I know we already discussed this, but I want to reiterate that a mental health sabbatical is an option."

"I know, Nassir, but I'm sorry to say that my mind's made up."

His supervisor nodded. "Alright, let me try one more tactic. I know working around sick kids can take its toll. Trust me, I've seen it happen time and time again. Maybe you'd like to request a transfer?"

Will was already shaking his head. "I'm quitting, Nassir. I appreciate your concern, but I need to take a different direction with my life."

Nassir sighed. "Okay. Okay." He slapped Will companionably on the arm. "Go home. Get some rest. And…"

"And?"

Nassir looked like he wasn't sure he should continue the thought. Then he said, "If you need to talk to someone, I can recommend several counselors who are experienced with working with healthcare professionals. All you have to do is say the word, and I'll grab you a couple business cards."

Will worked up a smile. "Thanks. I'll keep that in mind."

He didn't realize so much of what he was feeling was on display for all to see. As he made his way to his car, he told himself he was going to have to suck it up. He didn't need every person he knew offering him therapy recommendations or shoulders to cry on.

When he pulled up to the house and saw Emmy standing outside fiddling with a window box, he realized he already had the only shoulder he needed.

"Isn't it beautiful?" Emmy crooned. "She might be weird, but she sure can pull through when it counts."

Will glanced over at the wind chime that clanked a bit discordantly where it dangled from Emmy's hand. "Did you have to take it out in the car?"

"Yes!"

"Okay."

"I'm going to hang it up right away. I saw the perfect place today. There's already an eye hook stuck in the overhang."

Will smiled to himself at her enthusiasm over hanging a wind chime. How could she not see that this could be the calling she'd been searching for? He hoped that working on his yard was slowly opening that door for her.

"I just need a step stool," Emmy said, studying the eye hook.

"I've got one in the laundry room," Will said. "Or I could hang it for you."

"Oh. Yeah. You should hang it. It's your grandfather's tools and your house." She looked seriously put out as she held the chime out to him, inciting another series of clanks from the suspended tools.

Will didn't take the chime from her. "Emmy."

"What?"

"Do you want to be the one to hang the wind chime?"

"No." She was looking somewhere off to the side of his head, refusing to make eye contact.

"Emmy."

"You're going to think I'm stupid and obsessive."

"Try me."

She let out a breath and looked down at the chime where it dangled from her left hand. Absently, she gave it a little swing to make the tools collide and sing in their own unique way.

"It's like... the finishing touch," she said quietly, her tone bordering on apologetic. "I guess I want to be the one to put the cherry on top, so to speak. But you're right that it doesn't make sense to go get a step stool when you're standing right here," she rushed on. "I can watch you hang it. That'll be fine."

Will was pretty sure she had no idea how endearing it was that she offered to make this sacrifice for him. Far from finding it stupid, he thought it was incredibly sweet that she was so dedicated to the project.

"I have an idea," he told her. "A compromise. Go stand under the hook."

"Okay..." She side-eyed him for a second, then turned to do as he asked.

Will stepped up behind her. "Get ready."

"Ready for wha—Eep!"

The squeal jumped out of her before Emmy could call it back. Will's hands were on her waist, and before she could even begin to process that, she was airborne. He lifted her straight up, and she didn't hear a single grunt of effort. Emmy easily hooked the chime in place, then waited while he slowly—perhaps more slowly than necessary, she thought—lowered her back down. Her body slid against his in the process, and it sent heat shooting from her toes to the roots of her hair. The guy had some serious *moves*. His hands remained on her waist, and he used them to turn her until she faced him. Her heart pounded as she looked up into those warm hazel eyes. Slowly, his gaze never leaving hers, his hand traveled up the side of her body before it came to rest on the side of her face. His skin was warm and rough against her cheek, and she felt her breath catch when he allowed his thumb to slip down and graze her lips in an intimate caress.

When he leaned down, she told herself to step away. She couldn't let this happen. She couldn't become entangled with the main character of a romance novel she was trapped in.

Then his lips brushed hers ever so lightly, and she melted. Her resolve simply slipped away as his mouth caressed and tempted. He didn't deepen the kiss, didn't up the tempo or the intensity. He simply… lingered on her lips, taking little tastes, changing the angle only slightly to touch one corner of her mouth and then the other. Emmy was on the brink of begging him for more when he pulled back.

"We got interrupted back in Bright's shop. I like to finish what I start."

"Uh huh."

"You alright there?" he asked.

His self-satisfied grin was enough to snap her out of her lust-induced stupor. "I'm great. I'm uh…" She cleared her throat. "I need to see the wind chime. Um… thanks for the lift."

"Anytime." He made that one word sound like a sexual promise, and she felt her throat close for a moment.

Turning away from him, she looked up and saw the garden tools dangling above her head. They swayed with the breeze, as they were meant to do, and reminded Emmy that she had successfully reinvigorated the landscaping of this house all by herself. The extent of her accomplishment made her feel warm and fuzzy. Bright had done a great job cleaning up the tools so they were no longer stained with rust, but they still showed signs of age that gave the piece character.

"Done and done," Emmy said, the kiss momentarily forgotten amid the warm glow of success.

"I guess all that's left is to check with the client to see if he likes it." Will smiled and said apologetically, "I've been so far up my own ass lately, I don't think I've even looked at what you've done with the place."

Emmy forced herself not to wring her hands while he stepped back and took in the scene before him. He put his hands on his hips as he scanned the plants, the fresh rock accents, the decorative moss. After a moment that stretched to eternity in Emmy's mind, he let out a long, low whistle.

"Wow."

That sounded promising. "Wow" was good, wasn't it? Unless he meant "Wow, I've never seen anyone fuck up this badly."

"You like it?" she asked.

"I love it, Em. You were right about the birdbath. But even more important to me is, I think my grandfather would have loved it, too. He treasured this house, and you enhanced it without taking away from its charm. He'd have gotten a kick out of the wind chime, too."

Emmy threw up a hand to ward off further praise and covered her eyes. The grandfather comment had done it. She was choking on unshed tears. After a deep breath, she lowered her hand and looked back at Will.

"You really like it? You're not just saying that?"

Will walked over to her and pulled her into an unexpected hug. He didn't say a thing for a moment, just let her press her face into his chest and breathe in his scent as she tried to regain her composure. He was so warm. So solid. With his arms around her, she felt safe and cherished. It was a heady experience. Then he bent down so his lips were near her ear, and goosebumps broke out all over her body.

"I really like it, Emmy," he murmured to her. "You made it look professional but not stuffy. It's still open and welcoming. Not everyone would have understood that this house needs that."

"Thank you," she told his shirt.

"No, thank *you*. I know I bullied you into doing this, but I'm grateful to you for letting me."

"Me, too."

He pressed his lips against her temple, held them there for a few seconds, allowing both of them to relish the contact. Then Emmy reminded herself she was not supposed to be embracing him or pursuing anything other than friendship. With what she considered admirable self-control, she pulled herself together and stepped back from him.

"So… my turn to cook?" she asked.

"Yep." He was still smiling at her in that way that said he would be more than happy to pick up their earlier kiss where they left off. She pointed a warning finger at him. "Hands off."

"Yes, ma'am."

"I mean it. The last thing I need is a steamy tryst with a romance novel character."

Because she was walking past him into the house as she spoke, she didn't see how her words wiped the grin right off of Will's face.

Fifteen

Emmy gave up on trying to find a magical book in the library. It was hard to set that idea aside because then she'd have to admit she didn't have any others. It also meant she didn't have anything to occupy her time while Will was at work. She'd toyed with the idea of expanding what she'd done with Will's yard, but she knew it looked great the way it was. She wouldn't have capped it off with the I-have-finished-redecorating-this-yard wind chime if she'd thought it still needed work. Because of that, she was sitting inside nearly vibrating out of her skin with restlessness. She'd browsed various streaming services, tried a few shows, flipped through channels, and eventually landed on a public broadcast woodworking show.

The host, a man with a fantastic mustache and a surprisingly soothing voice, was describing the process for safely and securely clamping wood to the workbench without leaving marks on the material. Within minutes, despite having no interest in woodworking, Emmy found herself contemplating the practicality of having Will buy her a table saw. She was saved from going down that mental rabbit hole by a knock on the front door. More than grateful for the distraction, she immediately jumped up to answer it. By the time it occurred to her that this wasn't her house, and she probably shouldn't be opening the door for people, she'd already done so. The man standing on the front step wore a flannel shirt with the top couple buttons undone, revealing a white undershirt and a hint of the chest hair beneath. His jeans were faded at the knees and his work boots looked well worn. Emmy recognized him quickly enough.

"Truck Guy."

He chuckled lightly. "I usually go by Paul, but you can call me Truck Guy if you want."

"No, sorry. I just... didn't catch your name last time," Emmy said lamely. She hadn't expected to see him again, and the fact that she could now see that he was tall and muscular made her wish she'd hunkered down on the couch and waited for him to leave.

"I didn't catch yours either," Paul said, raising his eyebrows expectantly.

"Uh..." Should she lie about her name? She didn't see how he could use it against her. "Emmy."

"Well, Emmy, I'm happy to see you made it wherever you were walking to the other day." He leaned on the doorframe, and Emmy tried not to feel like he was looming over her. Tried not to believe that was his intention. "Do you live here with Will?"

"Yes. He and I are involved," she said pointedly.

His smile didn't fade. It was accented by a hint of dimples beneath the scruff of his beard. "That's a shame. I suppose that means you and I aren't destined to run off together."

"Afraid not."

"Ah, well." Much to Emmy's relief, he stepped back from the door. "Is Will home?" He lifted a large paper bag off the ground and showed it to her. "I usually stop by this time of year to drop off some fresh vegetables. Farmers' market starts soon, but these'll go bad before I get a chance to sell them."

Emmy couldn't respond right away as she was busy having a mental argument with herself. Tell the big, strong man that *her* big, strong man was at work? Or lie and say he was home? Would he press her on it? Did he expect money for the vegetables? He wouldn't hurt her, would he? This was a romance novel. A sexy man wouldn't be... *couldn't* be dangerous in a romance novel, right?

"Uh..."

Paul raised an eyebrow.

"I can take them," she said quickly, trying to avoid answering the question altogether. "Does Will usually pay you?"

"Nah, nothing like that. I only charge if I'm at my stall." He handed over the bag and Emmy took it, relieved that he hadn't pushed for more information on Will's whereabouts. "You tell him there's probably more where this came from, okay?"

"Sure. Thanks." She opened the bag, saw a vibrant variety of peppers, carrots, squashes, and more. "They look delicious."

"Only the best from my farm." Paul winked, and Emmy had to make a concerted effort to stop herself from cringing. When she didn't say anything else, he rapped his knuckles twice on the doorframe. "I guess I'll head out now." His eyes stayed on her face. His smile was easygoing. All charm. "Should you and Will have any... trouble in paradise... you just walk in the opposite direction as last time. My farm isn't that far away at all."

"I'll keep that in mind."

"I hope you do."

Emmy didn't slam the door when he stepped back, but she badly wanted to. As soon as it felt socially acceptable, she shut the door quietly but firmly. Then she locked it. Then she gave the door a tug to double-check it was locked. Though Truck Guy... *Paul*... hadn't acted in any way threatening, she felt a little shaky. Her eyes fell on the bag of vegetables. They did look delicious, and she doubted they were drugged or anything. How could he drug a squash? And what would be the point? She took the bag into the kitchen and made an effort to put everything in the proper place. Carrots here. Tomatoes there. Will had a designated spot for everything. Just thinking about keeping her own apartment organized like that was exhausting.

And no good habits were formed that day, Emmy thought to herself, shutting the fridge.

She dropped the folded-up bag into the recycling bin and then flopped back on the couch. Mr. Woodworking was in the middle of assembling a fancy-looking chair. She told herself to change the channel, that she wasn't interested, but somehow got caught up in the process.

When the doorbell rang sometime later, she jumped a foot in the air. Pressing her hand to her chest to ease her galloping heart, she looked toward the entryway. He wouldn't have come back, would he?

Instead of rushing to the door, she walked quietly and made use of the peephole—something she absolutely should have done the first time around. Paul was not back. It was Bright waiting on the front step this time.

Emmy pulled open the door. Unlike with Paul, if Bright decided to attack her, Emmy was pretty sure she could win that fight.

"Hi!" Bright chirped. "Can I just say I love what you've done with the yard? It looks gorgeous."

"Oh, thank you. Do you want to come in? Will's at work, but he'll be back in a couple hours."

"I know. I texted him to ask if it was okay to come over since Jared didn't have your number. He said you'd be home."

"Oh. Okay. Yeah, come on in. I was just watching…" Emmy's voice trailed off. What was she watching? She couldn't call it *The Mr. Woodwork Show*. She gestured at the screen. "I don't know what it's called. A guy with a mustache is making chairs and stuff."

"Oh my God, I love public access TV! Have you watched any of the quilting shows? I can't get enough of them. They're so cheesy, but I can't help myself. I eat them up like… well… cheese. Really good melty cheese on a crispy cracker. I'm going to shut up about cheese now."

Emmy found herself laughing as she closed and locked the door behind Bright. "It's okay. I get it. My sister used to watch crochet tutorials on YouTube. She doesn't even crochet. She just liked watching other people do it."

Did May still watch those tutorials? Emmy wanted so badly to ask her. She would have given anything to be able to talk to her sister about anything at all.

"Your sister has good taste," Bright commented without an ounce of sarcasm.

Since she didn't want to think about May for a while—it hurt too much—Emmy decided to see if Bright would unwittingly provide a distraction.

"Did you want to watch with me? Or… did you need to talk to me about something?"

"I would love to watch with you. I came out here because I was curious. Will told Jared, who told me, that you were doing some work on the place. I wanted to see it for myself. You've got the touch, that's for sure."

Emmy blushed at the compliment. "Thank you for saying that. It's just a hobby."

"Not everyone excels at their hobbies. You do."

Since that was the nicest thing anyone had ever said to her, Emmy felt herself warming toward Bright. She even felt a slight sting of guilt over her manic pixie dream girl comment the other day.

"I was thinking about grabbing something to eat," she said, hiding behind the shield of small talk. "Just snack food of some kind. Do you have… allergies?"

"I'm happy with anything," Bright said. "No allergies. Bring on the snacks."

Emmy went to grab the bag of tortilla chips Will had bought at some point. She found a jar of salsa—unopened—in the cabinet with the canned and jarred goods. She didn't know if Will's need to organize bordered on obsessive, but it did come in handy. She remembered when he'd gone to find her a spare toothbrush, he'd had a sectioned organizer under his bathroom sink with toothbrushes neatly grouped together in one compartment. Meanwhile, back in her world, Emmy wouldn't have been surprised to find tortilla chips in her fridge and spare toothbrushes at the bottom of her purse. At work, she managed to keep things organized, but her home was another story.

"Chips and salsa," Emmy announced as she walked back into the den. "I hope you can handle spicy food because this salsa is medium, not mild."

Bright had already made herself comfortable on the sofa. "Wow, medium? That's pretty intense, but fortunately I'm a big fan of spicy food."

Emmy settled on the couch and opened the bag of chips. Then she spent a companionable forty-something minutes sitting and snacking with Bright.

"You just moved here, right? What brought you to Cobalt?" Emmy asked.

"A stolen car."

Emmy immediately hit the mute button on the remote, then turned to Bright with wide eyes.

"Okay, not exactly stolen," Bright amended with a laugh. "I was in my second year of law school when I realized I hated everything about my life, including my boyfriend. I broke up with him, dropped out of school, and started tending bar at a colorful little pub in Concord. It was the first time in my life that I'd worked for money. My parents had paid my tuition, bought me a car, and given me a stipend— that's what my dad called it—for expenses. Needless to say, they were not happy when they learned I'd dropped out... a full nine months after the fact."

"Oh shit. Not so close with the parents, huh?"

"Not so much." Bright crunched down on a chip. "They didn't find out until the tuition check they sent for the first semester of my third year got sent back. They'd still been putting their allowance—because that is what it was, no matter what my dad called it—in the account they'd opened for me, but I didn't touch it after I dropped out."

"What did they say when they found out?"

"Oh, we'll gloss over that part. Let's just say certain words were put out there such as 'ungrateful' and 'lazy' and 'unmotivated.'"

"Ouch."

Bright shrugged. "I've mostly gotten over it. Anyway, I told them I was sorry I'd disappointed them, but I couldn't be the daughter they'd planned to have. They responded to that by cutting me off financially and threatening to sue me for repayment in full of the tuition money they'd wasted on me."

In that moment, Emmy hated Bright's parents. She'd completely forgotten that neither Bright nor her parents were real people. She was too caught up in the story.

"I'm so sorry," Emmy told Bright, reaching out to touch the other woman's hand.

"Thank you, but I got through it. I figure they threatened to sue as a kind of ironic punishment. After all, if I'd finished law school, I would have been able to… represent myself or something. Anyway, I'd retained enough knowledge from my classes to hit them with some complex jargon about countersuing. I lied and said I had connections with lawyers who would represent me pro bono. They backed off, and I soothed their egos by telling them to take back all the untouched money from my 'stipend' account. Which they did pretty much immediately. That night, I packed up all my stuff—not that I had much—and hit the road. I spent some time finding myself and getting over what I felt was a pretty hefty parental betrayal. Then, I must have been just a few miles outside of Cobalt, a cop pulled me over. Apparently, they'd reported the car stolen. I hadn't even thought about how they still technically owned the car. They didn't put my name on it even though they'd bought it for me, their adult daughter."

"God, how could they do something like that? They're your *parents* for Christ's sake."

Bright shook her head, her smile wistful. "Parenting meant something different to them than it does to other people. To them, a child needed to be strictly disciplined. Controlled. If I stepped out of line, the punishment had to be harsh so that I'd learn my lesson."

"Psychopaths," Emmy muttered.

Bright laughed at that. "Possibly sociopaths, I'll give you that. But anyway, they were gracious enough not to press charges so long as I surrendered the car to them. I made the arrangements to do that, and then I just... walked the rest of the way to Cobalt. Figured I could at least find a motel or someplace to stay for the night, but then I saw the vacancy in the space that is now my shop. I took that as a sign... literally. There was a big For Lease sign in the window, right?" She giggled at the way Emmy snorted with laughter and rolled her eyes. "I know. I can be a bit much. But that's it. Now, I own my own car, and I'm in control of my own life."

"Have you heard from your parents at all?"

"They sent me an email confirming receipt of the car."

"Fuck that's cold," Emmy breathed.

"The coldest. But it's done now." Bright briefly squeezed Emmy's hand. "Thanks for letting me spew on you. It was all fresh on my mind since I just gave Jared the full story. His reactions were along the same line as yours, though his were a bit more... impassioned."

"Yeah, I'll bet. I guess that means things are going well between you two?"

"Yes they are." Bright's smile was that of a cat who'd gotten the cream. "I wasn't looking for a relationship, but that's just what I've got with Jared. And it's real." She didn't catch Emmy's wince at the word "real." "I feel more for Jared than I ever felt for my ex."

"I'm glad for you. You're like the poster child for 'All's well that ends well.'"

"Ha! I love that. Thank you."

"You're welcome. Do you want to stay for the next episode?" Emmy offered. "Learn how to build a credenza or something?"

"Tempting as that is, I'd better go. I don't want to leave Bianca alone too long. But thank you. This was super fun."

When Emmy stood, Bright pulled her into a hug. She was surprisingly okay with the gesture. Thinking of her own parents, their warmth and kindness, their guidance throughout her life, she squeezed Bright a little tighter.

"Seriously good job on the landscaping," Bright said again, looking out the window at the yard. "Are you in business? Should I spread the word? Or do you not have time to do it professionally and write at the same time?"

Write? Oh, yes. She was a romance novelist, according to Will. "I'm not in business. No need to advertise for me. Yet."

"I like the 'yet.' If you ever need tips on how to start your own business, hit me up. We can grab coffee."

"Thank you. I'll do that."

"Bye for now!"

Emmy watched Bright walk down the driveway to the slightly beaten-up Jetta she was clearly proud to own. The author hadn't pulled any punches when it came to Bright's backstory.

Reluctant to close herself back inside on such a beautiful day, she went out the front door to try to see what Bright saw when she drove up to the house. She looked at her own work, trying to be objective, and decided she was no amateur. The wind chime Bright had made was singing its song while the breeze carried the scent of fresh herbs from the window box by the kitchen. With a sigh, Emmy stretched out on the grass and closed her eyes. The sun warmed her skin and the breeze cooled it again. This was what she needed. Just a couple minutes of peace to shut her brain off.

Sixteen

Will found her like that when he came home from work. She was sleeping in the sunlight with the bright green grass and cheerfully colored flowers all around her. One leg tucked under the other. The breeze caused her hair to ripple gently over her face. A strand caught on her full lower lip, and he saw her mouth was parted ever so slightly. It was like some modern take on a fairy tale wherein Sleeping Beauty wore sweatpants and Prince Charming stank of hospital and sweat. Another big difference, Will thought as he set his shopping bag down on the front step, was that he wasn't going to kiss Emmy awake. It was tempting. *She* was tempting. But he didn't have the fairy tale prince's loose grip on morals that would allow him to kiss a sleeping woman. Instead, he sat down in the grass beside her and gently shook her shoulder. Her eyes fluttered open, and she frowned up at him in confusion.

"Hey," she said blearily.

"Hey, yourself. You often take naps on the front lawn?"

"Is that where I am?" She sat up and pressed a hand to her forehead. "Right. Yeah. I was admiring my work after Bright left. I just meant to soak up the sun for a second. Must have dozed off."

"You been sleeping okay?" Will asked, trying to subtly check her pulse and temperature. "Any headaches or dizziness?"

Emmy was not amused. "Put the stethoscope away, Nurse Watson. I'm fine." She pushed herself to her feet as he did, but as quickly as she'd stood up, she fell back down again, her leg evidently asleep from the way she'd been lying. Will tried to catch her a second too late and ended up overbalancing on the uneven ground. With an "oomph," a grunt, and several curses, Will landed on his back with Emmy draped over him. They lay there for a moment, both of them panting and trying to process what had just happened. He could feel her heartbeat with how close their chests were pressed together, could feel her warm breath ghosting over his face.

"Do you wish to amend your previous statement at all?" Will asked quietly, brushing some of her disheveled hair out of her face. He grazed his fingers lazily up and down her back, let his gaze flick down to her lips. It would be so *easy* to just lift his head slightly to kiss them...

All at once, the fondness on Emmy's face disappeared. "Oh God damn it, no. I am not doing this," she snapped, pushing herself off him.

She stood up just fine now, Will noted. In fact, she looked like she was bracing herself for battle. He rolled into a sitting position and looked up at her.

"Of all the dirty tricks," she continued, starting to pace as the tirade overtook her. Will didn't think she remembered he was there, she was so worked up. "That never happens in real life. I should've been ready for it. I should've expected it."

"Want to clue me in?" Will asked. "I didn't plan that at all. It wasn't a trick."

Emmy stopped pacing and planted her hands on her hips. "Not *you*. The book did this. I just know it. Motherfucker tried to pull a fast one, but I've got its number."

"What exactly did the book do?"

"I fell down on top of you!"

His smile was slow and a little cocky. "Yeah, I noticed."

"See? That's exactly the point. This always happens in romances. Books, movies, whatever. Somehow gravity affects people differently, and two adults who should be perfectly competent at balancing on their own two feet fall all over each other. And then there's the breathless gasps and the swooning as they realize they are basically in the missionary position but with clothes on. Then they start thinking 'Hey, we could do this with our clothes *off*,' but they don't because it's only the second act and they can't have sex until the third act even though they are both consenting adults."

He wished she could see herself, hair flying around her face in the wind, fists clenched as if she could punch the romance away. He had never met anyone like her. Probably because he'd never met anyone from the real world. Still, she'd hit his thought process pretty much spot on. How could he not think about getting her clothes off when she was nestled against him? He was only human. Rising slowly,

Will approached her. He saw the wariness in her gaze as he moved into her space. Her breath shuddered out when he reached up to run his fingers over the side of her face.

"And did you?" he asked quietly, his eyes searching hers.

"Did I what?"

"Start thinking about doing that with our clothes off?"

She turned her head until his hand no longer touched her face. "That's not the point," she huffed.

Will bent enough to intrude on her eye line again. "I'm curious. Come on, Em, I won't hold you to it." When she remained silent, he decided to wait her out. Finally, she sighed and looked back up at him. It was easy enough to read the turmoil and the desire in her eyes. He nodded, cutting her off before she could formulate words. "I won't hold you to it," he repeated quietly. "But I want to make sure we're, no pun intended, on even ground here. I want you to know I think about you that way."

"We can't." She said it like a plea, though she could no longer remember why they couldn't. Why they shouldn't. Any argument she thought of sounded weak, even in her own head.

"We can. We're both consenting adults, after all," he said, using her earlier words. His expression was somber, sincere. "I know what I feel for you, Emmy. I think you feel something, too." Emmy almost gave in at his words, but he stepped back. "I won't pressure you." He smiled a little, ran a finger slowly down the side of her face. "But think about it. Think about me."

How could she not? Just that one touch had left her skin tingling.

That was another problem. Who was to say she felt anything real for Will at all? Maybe it was the very air inside the romance novel that made her see him in that light.

And that argument was as weak as all the others she'd tried to come up with. She either believed in his realness or she didn't. She couldn't simultaneously believe in his validity as a person *and* that her feelings for him were manufactured. It was tempting to take that escape route, but she couldn't stomach it. Her feelings for him were as real as the man himself. But she was adult enough to deny herself what she wanted in order to find what she needed.

Will stopped after unlocking the door to pick up a nondescript plastic grocery bag that was weighed down with clinking bottles. Emmy felt a sense of trepidation overtake her, effectively wiping out her thoughts of intimacy, as they went into the house. He'd hit the liquor store before coming home? She knew the last few days had been rough for him. There were shadows under his eyes, and sometimes when he walked in the door, he had this expression on his face that made her gut clench. Grim. Defeated.

He went to the kitchen, set the bag down on the counter, and opened the fridge. He frowned as he noted the vegetables.

"Where'd these come from?"

Once again, her train of thought shifted. "Oh, some farmer named Paul came by to drop them off. He said this is a regular occurrence. It is, right?"

"Yeah, it is. I should've warned you about that." Will looked over at her, still frowning a little. "He didn't come on to you, did he?"

Emmy decided not to tell him how vulnerable and uneasy she'd felt. He didn't need her adding to his mental load. "A little bit. But he left without proposing to me, so I think we're good."

"Okay." He turned back to the fridge, stared at the produce.

Emmy held back a laugh. "Just rearrange them. You know you want to."

He shook his head. "No, it's fine. They're fine."

"Will." Emmy smiled indulgently. "I tried my best, but it's your fridge, not mine. I won't be offended if you move things around."

"Just the tomatoes," he muttered, reaching in to grab them. After arranging everything to his liking, he grabbed a couple bell peppers and shut the fridge. "It's not like I'm a freak of nature," he insisted, turning to Emmy and brandishing the peppers at her. "Lots of people like to keep their things organized."

"I didn't say anything!"

"Yeah, but I bet you thought plenty," he replied, setting the peppers on the counter.

"Maybe a little. Mostly I think it's cute. I swear."

The look he gave her told her exactly what he thought of being called "cute." She only smiled back at him. Until he reached for the bag on the counter and began to unload it, lining the liquor bottles up on top of the fridge. Emmy felt the smile slip off her face, and her stomach clenched.

"Rough day?"

He looked at her over his shoulder, noted her expression. Then he sighed and dragged his free hand down his face. "Yeah. You could say that."

"Was the liquor store having a sale?" she asked carefully.

"The liquor store had liquor."

"Okay."

"Look." He set the last bottle on top of the refrigerator with an impatient clank. "I don't need your judgment right now. Or ever. Yes, I had a rough day at work. I didn't mind coming home so much. We had a nice moment. I liked bantering with you about vegetables. Let's not ruin it."

"I don't want to ruin anything. I just... you bought a lot for one person. A lot for two, even."

"Relax, Emmy. I had a hard day, that's all. I'm going to have a drink to wash the bad taste out of my mouth. You don't have to worry. My liver isn't real, so it doesn't matter if I drink myself stupid."

With that, he grabbed a bottle of whiskey and strode out of the room. Emmy heard the TV going a moment later. She leaned back against the wall and stared at the ceiling, mortified to discover that she was blinking back tears. If he wasn't real, then why did this whole shitty situation hurt so damn much?

He was an asshole. Will was man enough to admit it. A part of him hoped Emmy would join him on the couch so he could share the cheap liquor with her and offer an apology. Another part of him hoped she'd give him space to wallow in peace.

The whiskey tasted like gasoline mixed with rubbing alcohol, but it burned magnificently on the way down his throat. He knew he could have sprung for the good stuff—his bank account was no more real than his liver—but he'd needed the cheap and caustic; the kind of drink that could double as paint thinner. In no time at all, his brain had a nice fuzzy blanket wrapped around it. The comforting warmth was almost enough to drown out the thoughts that had been plaguing him ever since the end of his shift.

Sure, his day had started out great. There had been the usual routines. Nothing engrossing about distributing pills or changing IV bags, but he found comfort in the familiarity. He'd also found time to entertain a pair of twins in the pediatric wing while one of them recovered from having her tonsils removed. Then he'd had a quick lunch with Jared who casually tossed out the idea of Will and Emmy joining him and Bright for dinner sometime soon. That one sure had thrown Will for a loop, but it was a happy sort of loop. His friend was starting a new relationship, and he didn't have any problem with the fact that the relationship was with Bright. All in all, it had been a fulfilling and productive shift.

Until Tabitha McGrady had started coding.

He knew this was the risk you took when you worked in a hospital. It was especially hard when you worked in peds. Sure, you got to hand out lollipops and make the kids giggle with silly faces. But you also had to deal with the other end of the spectrum. Things go wrong in hospitals. He told himself this. He told himself he was prepared to deal with the good, the bad, and the ugly.

But Tabitha, who preferred to go by Tabby, was in the hospital because she'd been in a car accident on the way to her best friend's birthday party. He had been there when she coded, and he knew the drill. Even as his mind balked at what was happening, his body went through the motions through sheer muscle memory. Crash cart. Compressions. Paddles.

God, she was so small.

He watched in a daze as a team of doctors and nurses tried to save her. That was when his brain hit him with the none-of-this-is-real sledgehammer again. Why was he trying to save this girl's life? Why did he care that he was *failing* to save this girl's life? Why did his heart feel like it was shriveling up into a wrinkled husk when he heard the doctor declare time of death?

It doesn't matter.
It's not real.
She's not real.
She's not dead because she was never alive.
Fuck!

He hadn't made a conscious decision to hit up Cobalt Wine & Spirits. His hands had just turned the steering wheel. Muscle memory. Like packing up a crash cart after time of death is official.

He hadn't made a conscious decision to bite Emmy's head off either—hell, he'd been in a pretty good mood only seconds earlier—but he'd done that just fine, too.

Will dropped his head into his hands. He could still hear the chaos of that little girl's hospital room echoing in his head, and he cursed the fact that it made his pulse race. The sound of his blood rushing in his ears grated on him. He was no more alive than Tabitha "Tabby" McGrady. Why couldn't he just accept that?

Reaching for the bottle again, he drowned everything out in the burn of cheap alcohol. Until even that faded away into numbness.

Then he slept.

Seventeen

The next morning, Will found Emmy in the kitchen fixing breakfast. The sun shone through the windows, illuminating her beautiful face, causing her hair to shine. He heard birds chirping. Puffy white clouds floated in a sky of crystalline blue. Flowers waved cheerily in the breeze. God fucking damn it, he hated that he was walking into a scene from a Disney movie when his head was pounding and grief was still a gaping wound inside his chest.

"Hey," Emmy said quietly, her expression wary.

"Hey," Will grunted. Then he cleared his throat and tried again. "Hi. Good morning. Sorry. I'm so sorry."

"It's okay. Here, have some coffee and painkillers."

"You're an angel," he murmured, taking the mug and the two pills from her. He burned the roof of his mouth as he swallowed the pills, but he didn't care. "Seriously, Em, you're a rock. I shouldn't have gone at you like that yesterday."

"I assumed you had your reasons. All is forgiven as long as you don't make a habit of it." She sat down at the table with her own coffee and a couple slices of buttered toast. "Did something happen yesterday? Are you alright?"

"I'm fine. Just a crap day at work. I let it get to me."

"Sorry to hear that."

She was still studying him, like she knew there was plenty more that he wasn't telling her, but she didn't press. For that, he was extremely grateful. He sat and sipped his coffee, willing the pain to recede just a bit so he could think of what he needed to do next.

"At least you don't have too many bad days left, right?" Emmy offered into the silence.

His head snapped up. "Why?"

"Because... your two weeks' notice is basically up, isn't it?"

Of course that's what she meant. Jesus, he needed to pull it together. She wasn't threatening him with a shortened existence. For a second, he thought she was going to say she'd found a way out of the book and was leaving him behind. But that was a stupid thought. She would have been way more excited if she'd found her escape route.

"Right, yeah. Friday's my last day. As long as nothing too catastrophic happens in the next couple days, I should be fine."

His phone rang, shrill and insistent. Will winced and picked it up, mainly to stop the sound from driving an ice pick through his skull.

"Hello?"

"Hello, stranger!"

"Oh. Hey, Mom."

Emmy watched his face change as he listened to whatever it was his mother had to say. Then he got up from the table and wandered away, talking quietly. She wanted to jump up, grab the alcohol off the top of the fridge, and dump it all down the drain while he was distracted. But that wasn't the right way to go about helping her new friend. She'd never had to confront addiction before—in herself or in others—but her gut knew he would only resent her for interfering like that. It might push him to drink more just to prove she couldn't control him. She sat and ate her toast as she contemplated what might have happened to push Will over the edge. Maybe Jared would know. Would it be treacherous to go behind Will's back and ask his best friend what was up? Probably.

"Uh, yeah... okay. Yeah, that works," Will said, returning to the table. "No, I swear, I'm fine. I just woke up, that's all. Yeah, love you, too. Bye."

He hung up and then just stared at his phone as if he didn't remember what he was supposed to do with it now. After a few seconds, he looked up at Emmy and smiled wryly.

"That was my mom."

"Yeah, I heard. Everything okay?"

"She and my dad want to have dinner on Saturday. Here. She would like the dinner to be here."

Emmy slowly put down her coffee mug as she took in this new development. "Oh."

"Yeah."

"Did you uh... did you tell her... we were...?"

"I told her about you, that you were staying here for a while. But I kept it vague. I didn't know how you wanted to play it. Would you rather tell them we're in a relationship or stick with being roommates? Not much danger of meet-cutes in my house."

"True. We could probably just go the roommate route. Except…" Her eyes went wide.

"Except what?" Will prompted.

"Well, like… what if it's a compulsion? What if your dad starts hitting on me?"

"What? No. He wouldn't. He couldn't. Not with my mom there."

"But that's what I'm saying!" Emmy insisted. "What if it's a curse and he can't even stop himself? Remember when I fell on top of you because the book willed it? I don't want your dad to hit on me, Will! This is going to be awkward enough!"

"Okay. Point taken. Don't panic. We'll tell them we're in a relationship. It's fine. Better safe than sorry, right?"

"Right." Emmy let out a relieved breath. "That's settled. Are you cooking for them? Is there something I should do or… wear?"

"Um… act normal and wear clothes."

Emmy rolled her eyes even as she laughed lightly. "Okay, I think I can manage that. Good thing I finished your landscaping. It'll give us something to talk about so things don't get awkward." She shrugged uncomfortably. "Bright seemed to think it looked good."

"That's right, you mentioned she was here. What did she want?"

"To hang out, apparently. I guess after she made the wind chime for me, she wanted to see it in action. She was really effusive in her praise, but that could just be because she's Bright."

"Why do you do that?" Will asked.

"Do what?"

"Make up reasons why your work isn't as good as people say it is. You landscaped my yard, Emmy. By yourself. What's wrong with being proud of that?"

"It's no big deal," she said quietly, her cheeks heating.

Will pinned her with a serious look. "It *is* a big deal."

Emmy stared into her half-empty coffee mug. Her light breakfast suddenly curdled in her stomach. She'd never told her family that she'd wanted to turn gardening into a career, rather than just a hobby. To this day, she didn't know what had stopped her. Sure, it had taken her some time to weave her way around to that conclusion, but that didn't make it less. Just because her parents had both stuck with the same career their whole lives. Just because May started watching makeup tutorials before she was even allowed to own makeup. Just because she couldn't come up with any good excuses or reasons for her waffling didn't mean she wasn't entitled to take a little time to decide what was right for herself.

Even as she'd drifted through college, she'd clearly had it on her mind. She'd run a few ideas by Andrew here and there during their relationship, and that had been a mistake. She felt shame—though she couldn't tell if it was deserved or not—for being more open with him than she was with her family. In this regard, at least. His responses hadn't exactly been encouraging. He never outright said, "This is a pipe dream. Don't pursue it." But whenever she tentatively brought the subject up, he asked leading questions, dropped innocent little comments.

Maybe you should look into taking a couple more classes. You've never pursued this seriously before, right?

It's kind of bad timing to start up your own business, isn't it? In this economy?

It's more than picking out pretty flowers, Emmy. Starting your own business is a huge responsibility.

Maybe give it a year and see if you're still interested. There's no rush.

This last said with a patronizing smile and a pat—an actual *pat*—on the head.

Emmy felt a rush of emotions overcome her. Andrew had had more to say on the matter of her "gardening habit" than she'd thought. Each instance on its own had been annoying, but had seemed ultimately harmless. Thinking of it all together like she was doing now, however... it was almost sinister. Andrew wasn't solely responsible for her self-doubt. She wished she could put it all on him because that would be easier, but she knew she had to own her part in it. Still, he certainly dug right into her insecurities and fed them regularly. How had she not seen that before?

The sound of the front door opening pulled her out of the sticky mire of her past. Was Will walking out on her? Was he that upset? But no, he came back in a minute later, holding out his phone to her. While she watched, he swiped through picture after picture of his yard. The early morning light perfectly accented every angle, every color. She found herself gripping her mug with white-knuckled hands.

"It looks like something from a brochure," Will said.

Emmy stared at his face. A single tear slipped through her defenses. Will smiled gently and reached to wipe it away. His caress lingered for a second before she lost the warmth of his hand again. Emmy dropped her gaze, suddenly realizing just how intimate this moment was. But Will gently tipped her chin up so she was looking at him again. He studied her face intently for a moment.

"Are you okay? I didn't mean to make you cry."

Emmy shook her head. "You didn't make me cry. At least not in a bad way. *Daijōbu*."

"That one I know. It means 'I'm alright' or something, doesn't it?"

"Yeah. Basically. 'I'm alright' or 'It's alright.' How'd you know?"

He gave her a sheepish look. "I may have watched some anime in the original Japanese when I was a kid. It always bothered me that their mouths didn't move with the words when I watched the dubbed versions."

She allowed herself a smile and the tears faded into the background in the face of a solid friendship that she was coming to treasure more and more every day. "The hidden depths of Will Barrett."

"Let me clear these dishes. I've got a little time before work. Wanna watch something?"

"Oh, absolutely. I'm learning to love public television craft shows. Just let me finish my coffee."

"Yeah, I could use another cup myself."

He refilled his mug and joined her at the table. It was clear he wanted to say something, but when he opened his mouth, no words came out. Emmy waited patiently for him to sort out his thoughts.

"So um... did you learn how to say some stuff in Japanese because... I mean... you're Japanese, right? I realized I assumed, and I shouldn't have. But I can't necessarily tell, and..." He let out a humorless laugh and ran his hand through his hair. "Man, I am fucking this up. For the record, I am trying *really* hard not to sound racist."

She laughed and touched his hand to stop him from babbling any more. "It's fine. I get it. Yes, I'm Japanese. I'm second-generation Japanese American, actually. The funny thing is, my parents were both born in America, but they met in Japan. They were both studying abroad at the same time, but they attended different universities. It was like... serendipity that they found each other. They spoke Japanese at home with me and my sister. English, too. We all kind of mix the two when we're talking to each other. I still understand Japanese really well, but I started to speak English more and more as I got older, so I lost a lot of my spoken vocabulary. But... but just because I don't speak it all the time doesn't mean I'm ashamed of my heritage or something. I've been to Japan. I want to go back on my own someday. My dad said he'd help me brush up on the language after May's wedding. I'm proud of who I am." She felt her voice hitch, tried to control it. "There's nothing wrong with that." Tears that had retreated during her initial battle now returned with a vengeance. She could feel them pushing for freedom.

Pressing her hand to her mouth, she tried to hold back the sob, but it broke free anyway.

"Aw jeez." Will pulled his chair around the table so he could put an arm around her shoulders. He squeezed, and then lifted his hand to press her head down onto his shoulder. Obviously panicked by the onslaught of tears, he began rambling at her. "Don't cry. Please don't cry. I'm so sorry. I never thought there was anything wrong with you being Japanese. And..." He took a deep breath, then exhaled slowly. "You'll get out of this. I promise. You'll see your family again. You'll practice Japanese with your dad.

And if you miss your sister's wedding, you can… make her do a reenactment or something."

"It's not that." Emmy wiped desperately at the tears, then murmured a quick thank you when Will grabbed her a box of tissues off the counter. She dabbed at her eyes and blew her nose. "Or not entirely. Fuck. I thought I was over this. It's been months."

Will frowned. "Over what?"

Emmy crumpled the tissues in her hands. She needed a second, so she got up to throw them out. Then she ran cool water in the sink and splashed a little over her face. Will rose and came to stand behind her, but she didn't turn around. Maybe it'd be easier to tell him if she wasn't looking at him.

"I was seeing a guy for a while. My best friend's older sister worked with him. He was the general manager at an upscale restaurant in Minneapolis. Hot guy. Single. Sarah's sister figured we had enough in common to make it through a first date since I'm a concierge. Some overlap in our jobs. Hospitality and service industries."

"Sure."

"Anyway, the first date was a winner. He was funny. We bonded over work stories. There are always weird or demanding customers to laugh at. We dated more. Then we started staying over at each other's places. It was going well, and we were talking about moving in together when his lease was up. But I thought it was weird that we were discussing such a big step when I hadn't even met his parents. He'd met mine already."

Emmy paused, thinking back on those tumultuous last weeks of her relationship with Andrew. It occurred to her that Lucy had been right. Again. *They'd* never discussed moving in together. *Emmy* had discussed it. Emmy had pushed for commitment. Andrew had evaded. He'd never had any intention of taking that step. How had she not seen that?

Will waited patiently while she sorted through her thoughts.

"I talked to him about it one night," she said finally. "We were at my place, and I brought up meeting his parents. I'd mentioned it before, but this time I was a little more direct about it. I gave him a kind of ultimatum, told him I wanted to move in together, but only if he finally brought me to meet his family. He smiled in this kind of… pitying way, I guess. He said we should hold off for a while longer. I asked why, and he said it was because they were traditional people. He said it like I was supposed to understand what that meant, but I thought he was talking about like… how his parents believed a man and woman shouldn't live together unless they were married."

"I'm guessing that's not what he meant," Will said quietly.

Emmy shook her head, leaned over the sink. She felt his hands on her shoulders. A gentle touch, but it was enough to bolster her. She had to finish this. Maybe telling him about it would free her of those last lingering demons.

"When I asked for clarification, he said they had certain expectations for him. He said… *Fuck*. He said they needed time to adjust to our relationship. That they needed to be prepared before he brought a Chinese girl home to meet them."

"Motherfucker," Will growled.

"Yeah. Motherfucker," she whispered. "I have absolutely no idea why I corrected him. I think I was in shock, or it was knee-jerk or something. But I told him I was Japanese. To this day, I can't remember if we'd ever talked about my background when we first got together.

But that's a problem right there, isn't it? We were talking about... No, *I* was talking about us living together, and he never once expressed an interest in *me*. Who I was. What my childhood was like. He never asked. You've known me for less than a month and *you* asked. I'm even meeting your parents this weekend. *God*." She pressed the heels of her hands to her forehead. "Why should it matter? It's not like I would have been *less* insulted if he'd gotten it right, if he'd said his parents wouldn't want him bringing a Japanese girl home, so what the fuck difference does it make?"

"Because it's... I was gonna say adding insult to injury, but that's not... big enough. It's more like... what am I trying to say? Bulking up? Bulking up the insult?"

"Heaping it on?" Emmy suggested.

"Yes! Thank you. It's heaping insult onto injury."

Emmy allowed herself a small smile and finally turned to look at him. "Truth. Got it in one. Bad enough to find out your boyfriend is a racist shithead, or that he barely knows you after months of being together. To find out both at once? Huge sucker punch."

"I'm so sorry, Emmy."

She thunked her head against his chest. He rubbed his hands up and down her arms. The movement soothed her enough to wrap up the story.

"Suffice it to say, he didn't see it as a big deal that he'd gotten two completely different nationalities mixed up with each other. He actually got this indulgent smile on his face, like he thought it was *so cute* that I would insist on making the distinction. And then he corrects himself with this tone like he's humoring his pampered girlfriend. He was all, 'Of course. I'm sorry. They would be uncomfortable to see me with a *Japanese* girl. I'd rather ease them into it.'"

"Please tell me you punched him in the dick."

"If I hadn't been in shock, I would have. I probably would have wasted my breath on a lot more talk, too, so I guess I'm glad for the shock in retrospect. It's not like I would have been able to convince him *not* to be a racist shithead. As it was, I just told him to get out. He looked genuinely surprised, and he pulled a lot of stuff along the lines of 'Don't be like that' and 'Let's talk about this.' I opened the door for him and waited until he got the picture. I almost told him to go die."

"Why didn't you?"

"I guess I'm a little superstitious. What if he got hit by a bus right after I said that? I didn't want that on my conscience, so I told him—in Japanese—that… uh…" She frowned as she tried to translate. "I basically told him he better never come near me again."

"Okay, saying it in Japanese was a good touch. Did he try to say anything back to you?"

Emmy turned so the side of her head pressed against his chest. "I slammed the door in his stupid face right after, so no."

"He got off easy."

"Yeah. I probably should've told him to go die and lived with the guilt if something bad happened to him." She sighed. "Not that he deserves to die, but… less than a week after I'd gotten around to throwing out the last of the things he'd left behind in my apartment, I heard he'd found himself a nice white girl to shack up with."

"I repeat: Motherfucker."

She nodded. "A couple days before I woke up in your bed, I stalked him on social media. They were still going strong. I bet *she* met his parents. Anyway, it messed me up enough that I went to see the stupid sex psychic who sold me the book that we are now in."

"I think I'm going to need to hear a little more about that."

"Yeah. Do you have any chocolate?"

"I think there are some Oreos left."

"Good enough."

She grabbed the Oreos from the snacks and sweets cabinet and poured herself a glass of milk. It didn't matter that she'd just eaten breakfast. Emotional upheaval called for chocolate, no matter the time of day. They sat at the kitchen table, and she told him all about May's romantic journey and how that had led to her drunkenly insisting that Emmy go see the same psychic. When she finished the story, she shoved the empty cookie package to the side and drained the rest of the milk.

"I guess her plan worked. I definitely got my mind off of Andrew." She grimaced. "Well… for a while anyway. Apparently there was still some stuff in there that needed to be exorcized."

"For the first time since this whole thing started, I'm glad I'm stuck in a book," Will told her.

"What? Why?"

"Because if I were in your world, I'd definitely track this guy down and punch his Hitlerjugend face in."

Emmy snorted out a laugh. "I'm not sure I would have stopped you."

"I wouldn't have given you the chance to stop me, but I would have expected you to post bail for me after."

She wrinkled her nose as she thought. "Still might be worth it." She sighed, then smiled wanly at him. "Thank you. For listening to all that, and for asking me about who I am. And for being on board with introducing me to your parents as your girlfriend. Even though it's a fake relationship, it matters to me."

He smiled back at her, reached out to take her hand. "No problem."

His eyes crinkled a little when he smiled. Emmy couldn't get enough of those eyes. That smile. He was such a solid, reassuring presence. Talk about being a rock. He was going through an emotional tornado unlike anything any human being should have to endure, and yet he still found the time to sit with her while she ate Oreos and told him about all her problems.

The warmth she felt in her chest was quickly followed by a wave of dread.

No. No warm feelings. She could not feel anything even close to warm about this guy. This guy, who might never exist in her world no matter how much he wanted to.

"You ready to watch some intense crafting television?" she asked, purposefully breaking the mood.

"Hell yeah. Let's do it."

Woodworking guy's show wasn't on, but Bright would have been delighted to know they passed the time watching a quilting program. After Will left for work, Emmy stayed on the couch, watched as the quilting came to an end and home cooking took its place. Because it was better than thinking about Will's crinkle-eyed smile or any feelings she may or may not have about it.

Eighteen

Will's last day of work was a double shift. He arrived home exhausted, his mind whirling with a strange combination of regret and relief. Yes, he was leaving his dream career behind, but at least that meant he was free to help Emmy explore escape options.

Speaking of Emmy, she was asleep when he got home. On the couch. Had she tried to wait up for him? He stood for a moment just looking at her, curled up on the couch, snoring softly. Was it bad that he found her snoring cute? There were very few things he disliked about this woman. She'd taken a hard hit with the last relationship, but he—

Will stopped himself before he could finish that thought.

Had he really been about to think of himself as a potential *real* boyfriend for Emmy? How could that possibly work?

It couldn't, of course. That was the answer, plain and simple. And it caused a wave of bitterness to wash over him, mixing with the regret that already lingered from the sendoff his coworkers had given him at the end of his shift. Jared had brought a cake that Bright had baked and decorated to look like an IV bag. Everyone had signed a card.

Disgusted with himself, Will carefully lifted Emmy off the couch and brought her to her room. He slipped her into bed, and she didn't stir once. Just kept on with her cute snores. Will wanted to linger, so he made himself leave. Except he detoured to the kitchen on his way to the bathroom. A glass of whiskey kept him company in the shower, and then he hit the mattress and conked out.

Emmy woke up in bed and blinked until her eyes adjusted to the morning light. Had she fallen asleep here? No, she'd been on the couch. It was coming back to her now. She knew Will was working a double shift, and she'd been hoping... God, she had to be honest with herself. She had been hoping to head him off before he "celebrated" being done with his job by polishing off one or more of the bottles that were on top of the fridge. The plan had been to encourage him to shower and then—if he didn't want to sleep—she'd been ready to watch late night television and discuss the impending parental visit.

Instead, she'd fallen asleep before he'd gotten home.

Whoops.

He must have carried her to bed. Her heart wanted to clench and her brain wanted to squee. She would *not* allow that. No heart clenches. No squeeing. So what if Andrew would have definitely left her sleeping on the couch? And, yeah, she wouldn't have minded if she'd woken up while Will was carrying her so she could enjoy the sensation of his strong arms surrounding her. But she needed to put a kibosh on all these wayward thoughts and... tingles.

When she got to the kitchen for breakfast, Will wasn't there. She guessed he was still sleeping off his double shift. That meant she had time to scrutinize the bottles on the fridge. They didn't look emptier, but it was hard to tell. Wait... the whiskey. Yesterday the liquid had been above the label. Now it was a little below. Worries crowded Emmy's mind. Not to mention the guilt she felt over the fact that Will was spiraling as a direct result of her appearance in his life. Maybe it was time to Google some intervention strategies. His parents were coming tonight, though, so she'd have to wait on talking to him. It wasn't like she could bring his parents in on the intervention.

Hi! Nice to meet you! I'm your son's fake girlfriend. Anyway, would you mind joining me this evening in discussing my growing concerns about your son's reliance on alcohol as a coping mechanism?

Yeah, not a great idea.

"What's the strategy?"

Emmy jumped at the sound of Will's voice. She'd been lost in thought, standing in the middle of his kitchen. If he asked what she was doing, she'd be hard pressed to come up with a believable explanation.

"Strategy?" she repeated dumbly. For a fleeting moment, she thought he was asking about his own intervention.

"For the parental dinner," he clarified. "I figured I would cook something. My mom usually brings dessert from this bakery she likes, so that's covered." His eyes found the bottles on the fridge. Emmy actually worried for a second that he was considering a drink before he said, "My dad likes gin and tonics, but my mom's a wine drinker. We can pick her up a bottle." He scanned the room, then nodded. "Yeah, dinner and wine. That should cover it, don't you think?"

Emmy didn't know. She wasn't exactly an expert on meeting the parents. Plus, these were romance novel parents. Maybe they had different standards?

"I can give the house a once over," she offered, trying to remember if she'd left any of her underwear in the bathroom. "Make everything nice and pretty for company. Do you have any candles?"

Will furrowed his brow. "I have Gordon if you need a light. Where are you going? The attic?"

Emmy let out a surprised laugh and shook her head in disbelief. "*Decor*, Will. Candles make nice *decor*. It's literally the root of 'decorate.'"

"Oh. Right."

"I'm going to take a wild guess and say you don't have any pretty candles with subtle, tasteful scents lying around."

"Good guess."

"Right. I'll make do without."

"We've got time, and I still have to grab food for dinner. Make a list and I'll take you to the candle store before we go grocery shopping."

"The candle store?"

Will stepped up to her and put his hands on her shoulders. She very deliberately clamped down on any and all warm tingles that might have resulted from the contact. "Emmy, it's time for me to confess everything. Not only do I not own candles, I don't even know where candles could be purchased. I have never once in my life bought a candle. I hope our relationship won't suffer too horribly now that you know the truth."

"Will." Emmy put a hand on his bicep, squeezed. Couldn't help thinking, *Wow, that is a firm bicep*. "I forgive you all your flaws. And I bet Bright sells candles."

"Oh yeah. They might be weird, though. She doesn't seem like the type to sell traditional smelling candles... like... peaches and cream or whatever."

Emmy shrugged. "We'll make it work. If your parents comment, we'll say we're supporting a local business."

"Sounds like a plan." He dropped his hands and made his way to the fridge to hunt for breakfast. "That reminds me, my parents weren't the only ones to try to set up dinner plans with us this week. Jared and Bright also extended an invitation."

"Jared *and* Bright? As in... Jared and Bright together? They're already at the dinner-invitation-from-both-of-us stage of the relationship?"

"Apparently."

"That is so weird. Maybe we should go and both of us can just talk endlessly about jellyfish. See if either of them notices."

His laugh was strained. "Let's just get through this thing with my parents first. Try to keep sea creatures out of the discussion for now."

"I'll do my best."

A short drive later, they were back in Bright Ideas looking at a display of handmade candles. The glass containers were artfully arranged on a counter along with paperweights that looked for all the world like... yep, they were glass boobs.

They looked handmade. Will resisted the urge to run his finger over a surprisingly realistic nipple.

"Maybe this one?" Emmy said. He turned to see her holding a green candle with three wicks sticking out of it. She gave it a sniff, shrugged, and offered it up to him. "What do you think?"

He obliged her even though he couldn't have cared less what scent of candle she purchased. "It's fine. What is that? It smells like…"

"Mojito," Emmy confirmed. "I like it. But maybe it's the wrong vibe for a meet-the-parents meal?" She put the lid back on the candle and selected another one that was a rich reddish brown color. After a sniff, she smiled with satisfaction. "This is the one. Masala chai. Very subtle and homey."

She grabbed two large candles and they headed up the counter. Bright greeted them with a genuine smile.

"Hey! I didn't know you were here. Did Jared remember to invite you guys out? We're free tonight if you don't have anything going on."

"He mentioned it," Will told her. "But we have to rain check. My parents are coming to our place for dinner tonight."

"Exciting!" She took the candles from Emmy and began wrapping them in gold-accented tissue paper. "Well, it's an open invitation. Seriously, I need very little notice. Just let us know when would be good for you."

"For sure," Emmy said. "Thanks for the invite. I'm glad things are going so well between you and Jared."

"Oh, me, too. I can't believe how well we clicked. It was just…" She did a happy shoulder wiggle. "… like a key in a lock. Instant connection. I'm definitely feeling saucy, sassy, and fancy these days."

She totaled up the two candles and Will had to swallow several remarks that popped into his head when he saw that they cost thirty-five dollars apiece. It wasn't like it was real money. For once, the knowledge that his world was fictional came as a comfort to him.

They said goodbye to the woman who was once supposed to be his soulmate and headed to the grocery store. After some brief deliberation, Will decided to make sweet potato fritters with goat cheese and a green salad with bacon crumbles.

"Damn. You're pulling out all the stops," Emmy commented. "You're actually buying lettuce. I don't know if I have ever bought actual lettuce."

"What have you been buying? Fake lettuce?"

"No, I mean, I buy bagged salads. Premade stuff."

"Oh, yeah. I usually do that, too, but this is a special occasion."

"Can I help you cook?" Emmy asked. "I wouldn't mind learning how to treat real lettuce right."

"Sure. It's a pretty simple meal."

"Says you."

Will bumped her gently with his elbow. "Trust me. Before the night ends, you will be an expert on real lettuce."

"I'm going to hold you to that."

Nineteen

When they got home, Emmy went around plumping pillows and checking for cobwebs—despite Will's insistence that the house looked fine—and otherwise making the place look presentable. She placed the candles strategically, one in the bathroom and one in the den, so the scent wouldn't get too strong or interfere with the cooking smells that would soon be coming from the kitchen. She could tell just from the ingredients Will had bought that the meal was going to have its own enticing and homey scent. Sure enough, by the time Will flipped the first fritter, she was salivating.

"I'm going to tell Bright to make a sweet potato fritter candle. I bet she could."

"I've never been complimented in the form of home decor before." Will smiled at her over his shoulder in that devastating way of his. "I like it. Thank you."

"Thank *you* for teaching me how to make this salad." Emmy popped a stray walnut into her mouth. "This is probably the first time in my life I've looked forward to a salad."

"You are very good for my ego."

His devastating, sexy smile melted seamlessly into one with such warmth and affection that she had no time to defend herself against it. Before she knew what was happening, her heart began to stutter. Fortunately, the sound of a car driving up meant that she didn't have to address what was happening.

"Show time," Will said, turning down the heat under the fritters. "Let's go say hello."

He opened the front door to reveal a smiling middle-aged man with gray-tinged brown hair and a carefully trimmed beard.

"Hey, Dad." Will embraced his father, then looked around for his mother.

Reading the question in his son's eyes, his dad said, "She's still out front admiring the view."

Will smiled smugly down at Emmy as her cheeks heated with a mixture of self-consciousness and pleasure.

"Dad, this is Emmy. Emmy, this is my father, Bill." After they'd shaken hands, he added, "Emmy is the one who redesigned the front yard."

"Did she now? You should go tell Will's mother. She'll be delighted."

"Oh... I don't know if I should—"

"Don't be shy. She's a gentle soul," Bill reassured her.

Will gave her an encouraging nudge, and she accepted her fate. Emmy stepped outside and walked to the woman who stood on the edge of the property, gazing at the house. Her expression was calm and relaxed, and Emmy saw a lot of Will in the shape of her face and the curve of her lips. When Will's mother spotted her, she smiled so warmly that Emmy forgot to be nervous.

"You must be Bright." She held out her hand expectantly.

"Ah... Emmy, actually." She shook the offered hand.

A look of bafflement briefly crossed the woman's face. "Oh, of course. Emmy. I don't know where my head is at." She dropped her hand, and the smile returned. "It's lovely to meet you. I'm Joanna." Her gaze shifted to the house once more, and she let out a wistful sigh. "I'm sorry. It was rude to stay out here instead of coming in to meet you right away, but my father loved this house, and he would have been delighted to see that Will got someone out here to give it a facelift." She paused, patted her chest. There might have been tears in her eyes, gathered just so as if she were putting on an act. Maybe she was, in a way, Emmy thought, though she was unaware of it. "Is that his old watering can being used as a planter? Oh, that's *lovely*."

Emmy figured she wasn't going to get a better opening than that. Steeling herself, she said, "Yeah, I hope you don't mind that I repurposed it like that. It just felt like it belonged out there."

Joanna gave her a look of surprise. "That was you?"

"Yeah, the whole thing was, actually. I got bored, and when I get bored, I garden."

"Well, color me impressed. Later, you and I are going to have a conversation about our place. For now, we should get inside."

Emmy allowed herself a quick moment to take a calming breath. That had gone well. So what if the woman spoke a little too much like... well... like a mom in a romance novel? The worst was officially over. Probably. She followed Will's mother into the house and waited while Will indulged Joanna with a long, tight hug.

"Missed you," he said.

Joanna stepped back, but kept her hands on her son's arms. "I love what you did with the place. Gramps would have loved it, too."

Will's smile was just a little pained. "I'm glad you think so."

"Honey, Bright, here, was the one who did the redesign," Joanna told her husband.

"Yes, I heard," Bill said. "Impressive, isn't it?"

Emmy cast a look at Will behind his mother's back that clearly said: Did you tell your parents you were dating Bright? He shook his head and shrugged in response. Clearly he didn't know what was going on either.

"Her name is Emmy, Mom," Will tried.

"Yes, I know. Why? Did I say it wrong?"

Joanna looked so horrified by the possibility that Emmy stepped in and reassured her. "No, you said it right. It's fine. Would either of you like a drink?"

Will followed Emmy's lead, grateful that she had taken over the hosting duties for the moment. He was still reeling from the reminder that his parents were just as much a part of this made-up world as everything else. The oblivious look on his mother's face when he'd corrected her about Emmy's name had hit him like a punch to the gut. All at once, he felt fatigued. He wanted nothing more than to cancel dinner and crawl into bed. But he was stuck, and he wasn't about to leave Emmy alone to carry the evening to its conclusion. She was holding up like a champ. It was a relief to him that she was there. He thought, not for the first time, how strange it was that he felt so comforted by her presence. She was the reason for his current predicament, but she was also his greatest supporter. He couldn't ignore that, nor could he overlook the fact that he felt drawn to her regardless of whatever part she'd inadvertently played in throwing his world into a tailspin.

They ate at the table, sharing the meal that Will had carefully assembled. Emmy dodged as many personal questions as she could, redirecting the conversation whenever it got dicey. She really was something else. Will barely paid attention to what was being said, and it surprised him when he looked down to see half his meal gone. He didn't remember bringing the fork to his mouth or tasting the food on his tongue.

"So how long have you been together?" Bill asked, snapping Will out of his own thoughts. "I have to admit I was a little surprised to learn Will was living with someone we'd never even met before."

"It is fairly new," Emmy said with a touch of apology in her tone. "I just moved into town, and I didn't have a place to stay. A friend of mine introduced me to Will, and we agreed to be roommates, but, well..." She paused to smile at him, and he got caught up in the look in her eyes—a twinkle of humor mixed with sincere gratitude. "Things evolved from there."

"Aww." Joanna pressed a hand over her heart. "Will, how can you not kiss the girl after she looks at you like that?"

He looked at his mother. "What?"

"You've barely touched since we've been here. You don't have to be so careful around us. Go ahead and give her a kiss."

Emmy covered a laugh with a cough. He could practically hear her thinking "I told you so" over and over again.

"Mom... no. It's weird that you'd even say that."

Joanna scoffed. "It's not weird."

"It is, though."

"Will, stop calling your mother weird," Bill put in. "She asked you to kiss your girlfriend, not recite a Shakespearean sonnet. Just give her a kiss."

"Dad..."

"Why are you fighting this so hard?" Joanna demanded with sudden distress. "Did we do something wrong? Do you not trust us?"

"What has gotten into you?" Bill asked. "You're upsetting your mother. Kiss Bright. Just once."

"It's Emmy, Dad."

"Kiss Emmy, then!" Bill slapped his hand on the table so hard that silverware rattled and Emmy jumped in her seat. "You owe us this much, don't you think? Are you really so ungrateful for all that we've done for you that you won't kiss your girlfriend when your mother asks?"

Will had no idea what was going on, but he was quickly losing control of the situation. He opened his mouth, thinking he might try a different tactic to defuse things, but Emmy squeezed his hand under the table. When he looked at her, she was transmitting a very clear message with her eyes. Immeasurably grateful to her, he leaned in and touched her lips with his. It was quick, barely a second of contact, but he felt the spark, the flare of heat that rose whenever they touched. He found it difficult to sit back again, but he did so, glancing warily at his parents.

"So, Willy, anything exciting happen at work lately?" Bill asked, as if nothing had happened.

"Willy?" Emmy repeated under her breath.

It occurred to Will that he hadn't told his parents that he'd quit his job. Given how they'd reacted to his refusal to kiss Emmy, he decided not to push them any more tonight.

"The usual stuff. I saved a couple lives, got to know a kid who beat pneumonia just in time for his tenth birthday."

"That's wonderful!" his mother chimed, sipping her wine. "Emmy, you simply must come look at our house. You see…" She glanced at her husband, got a nod from him. "Bill and I are thinking about moving, and it would be helpful if you could freshen up the curb appeal before we list it."

"You're moving?" Will asked. Bizarrely, he found himself wondering if this was a plot point that was going to happen regardless, or if he'd somehow triggered it by "dating" Emmy instead of Bright. Was it the kiss that had finally rewired his mother's brain enough to have her remember Emmy's name? He didn't like thinking that. He didn't like thinking of his mother as a robot.

"It's time," Bill said gruffly. "We love that old farm, but we're getting on in years, and it's a lot of land for two old folks like us."

"We're looking at some smaller houses… in Florida," Joanna said quietly.

"You're moving to Florida," Will said slowly.

"Preferably before winter," Bill confirmed.

Will didn't know what to say. It was hard to pin down what he felt about this revelation. A part of him felt terrified and guilty because he wasn't particularly sad or hurt. Shouldn't he feel sad and hurt? His parents were moving several states away.

"I'd love to take a look at your yard," Emmy said when he remained silent for a beat too long. "Do you have a budget in mind?"

"I hadn't thought of it," Joanna admitted. "Maybe you and I can discuss it. How does tomorrow morning sound? Is that too soon?"

"No, that's fine." Emmy's eyes tracked Will's movements as he topped off his wine and took a healthy swallow from his glass. "Will can drop me off. I don't have a car yet. Do you have any pictures of the house so I can start to form some ideas?"

Will took another drink of wine and let her carry the conversation until dinner was officially over. They ate the dessert his mother had brought—triple berry cobbler—with decaf coffee in the living room. His mother commented on the lovely scent of the candle Emmy had bought. Neither Emmy nor Will mentioned that Bright had sold it to them. They'd clearly both reached the conclusion that it would be best not to bring her up in case it confused Will's parents all over again.

"Well, it's getting late. We should be getting on," Bill said, pushing himself to his feet. "It was good seeing you, son. Thanks for having us."

Will accepted a hug from his mother. She kissed him on the cheek and smiled up at him. "We'll visit whenever we can," she promised. Then she looked at Emmy. "Tomorrow morning?"

"Yes, I'll come by early if that's okay. I'm looking forward to it. For now, I'm just going to get the dishes started."

Will almost told her not to leave him alone with his parents, but that was ridiculous. No matter the circumstances, they were the people who had raised him. He didn't resent them for who they were; it was the situation that was making him bitter.

Bill reached out to shake his hand. "Great dinner, son."

"Yeah, thanks for coming." Will dropped his father's hand and looked at his parents. He found he had to swallow against an unexpected ball of emotion that had lodged in his throat. "You guys know I love you, right?"

His dad looked at him with a kind of baffled amusement. His mother looked near tears. Shaking her head, Joanna stepped forward and hugged Will again.

"Of course we know that," she said. "We love you, too."

Will allowed himself to hang on for a moment longer than he usually would have. He very well might see his parents again, but something in his gut made him believe that this was one of life's big goodbyes. He didn't want to take it lightly.

They left, and he watched their car pull out the driveway before closing the door. When Emmy came back in a minute later, he was still standing there, looking a little lost.

"You okay?"

He shook off the mood as best as he could. "Yeah. We survived. That got intense there for a minute."

Emmy blew out a long breath. "Seriously. I wasn't expecting that. I think they just…" she trailed off.

"Malfunctioned?" Will offered.

"I didn't want to say it," she whispered guiltily. "Do you want to talk about it?"

He shook his head. "It is what it is. I'll process later." His thoughts were on the second bottle of wine they'd opened during dinner but hadn't finished. Digging deep, he worked up a smile for Emmy. "My mom's going to hire you. You're going to fix up the farm."

"Don't say 'I told you so.' I didn't say anything about your parents demanding we kiss."

"Yeah, but you were thinking it."

"True. I guess you're permitted to think it, then."

But he wasn't thinking smug thoughts at all. He was thinking about that kiss, and the other before it, about how he wanted to do it again. Maybe there was something of his thoughts on his face, because color rose in Emmy's cheeks.

"I'm going to finish cleaning up," she said quickly.

Smooth move, idiot, Emmy thought as she retreated back into the kitchen. She'd seen the look on his face. She had been so determined not to kiss him again. It was vital that she maintain a certain distance, both physically and emotionally. The quick peck during dinner shouldn't have messed her up like this. It had been perfunctory. It had been brief. It had been... wonderful, she admitted to herself, as she scrubbed a saucepan. The question was: Was kissing Will wonderful because of what they were together, or because he had some sort of romantic superpowers due to his origins? She hated that she was questioning that. She was basically calling him a robot just like she'd insinuated about his parents, and she knew very well he wasn't.

"I think we should take a trip," Will said, cutting into her thoughts.

"A trip?" Emmy repeated, turning to look at him over her shoulder. She couldn't hold back the wince when she saw he was sipping from a fresh glass of wine.

Will scowled, having caught the look, and deliberately took a big gulp of his drink before continuing. "I was thinking we should go somewhere. I'm curious if the world even exists outside Cobalt, you know? Like... if this place is the setting for a book, will the people and places that aren't relevant to the story even be there outside of town? If we fly to Paris, is the plane even going to land or is the pilot going to announce we have to turn around due to engine failure?" He drank again, instinctively. "I am officially jobless. Got all the time in the world. Let's go somewhere."

"We can't fly anywhere, remember?" Emmy told him. "Buying plane tickets requires ID, and I don't have any."

Will frowned into his wine. "Shit, I forgot about that. Okay, so we'll drive somewhere. Jared suggested I buy a motorcycle. We could just pick a direction and go."

Emmy had never been on a motorcycle in her life, and she didn't like the way her stomach clutched at the thought of spending hours pressed against Will's back, her arms wrapped around him. Women in romance novels never seemed to be able to maintain their self-control after a motorcycle ride.

"Motorcycles are dangerous." *In more ways than one*, she added silently.

Will shrugged. "I probably can't even die. It's not part of the book or whatever."

Emmy hung the dishtowel up and turned to face him fully. "And you're willing to test that? What if my being here changes that?" Worse, what if her being there meant that Cobalt would cease to exist if she left? It wasn't a real city. If the rest of the United States was the same as *her* United States, would they be able to navigate back? Even if the roads around Cobalt existed, there was nothing to say the turnoffs that led to the fake town would remain after her and Will's departure. Her presence was changing things left and right. There was no way to know what effect she had on the geography around her.

"Alright, relax." Will held up a hand for peace. "We'll take my car. Do you want to try to drive to Minneapolis? I know it would take a few days, but we've got time. You wanted to try to find the sex psychic right? To see if she can help us find a way out?"

Emmy shook her head. "I think I'm going to trust Google on this one. No such person or sex shop exists in Minneapolis or anywhere else in the U.S. It isn't worth driving for days just to confirm that she isn't hiding out in Minneapolis in secret or something."

"Alright, where should we go, then?"

Emmy looked into his eyes, noted his open and eager expression, then glanced down at his mostly empty wine glass. How many more blows could he take? He may have guessed that Cobalt wasn't a real place, but that was a big leap for him to find out definitively. It wasn't clear how he'd react. He might shrug it off, or it might make everything worse. Her eyes drifted back to the glass in his hand. Things had already tipped from bad into worse, if she was being honest with herself, and she dreaded what would happen if Will took another emotional hit.

"What?" Will asked when the silence had gone on too long. "What's wrong?"

"Nothing. You just put me on the spot." She took a moment. Took a breath. He was looking at her with a light in his eyes that she hadn't seen too often since she'd met him and thrown his world off its axis. They were in a romance novel. All bets were off. "Let's just drive. No destination, no goals. Just pick a direction and go. North. North sounds good, right?"

The light intensified, making Emmy want to reach out and hold him. Just hold on tight. "North sounds great. We'll hit the road and see what happens."

"Sounds like a plan. Tomorrow? I'm meeting your mother in the morning, but we can leave from the farm when I'm done."

"Sure, that works. Sunday is a good day for a drive with no destination. I'm looking forward to it."

"Me, too." She prayed Cobalt would still be there when they returned. There was just one other thing she had to clear up. It felt urgent and immediate; she couldn't let it go, no matter how hard the conversation might be. "Will." Emmy reached out and took hold of his arm. He looked down at her and she felt her heart give a little stutter as she realized how close they were. She could feel the ridges of muscle in his forearm and the warmth of his body. He was as real to her as her own sister, and his earlier words had made her desperately afraid that he didn't share her belief in his existence. "Promise me you won't... test the limits of your mortality, okay? Can we just agree that it's possible for you to die and that you shouldn't push your luck? Please?"

"Emmy, I'm not about to go driving off a cliff."

"Just promise me."

He smiled a little and reached out to run a finger lightly down her cheek. "Okay. I promise. No unnecessary risks. I'll look both ways before crossing the street and everything."

She breathed a sigh of relief. "Thanks."

It didn't occur to her that she was still squeezing his arm until his gaze dropped to her mouth. The warmth in his eyes made her pulse ratchet up. Time stood still as they both waited to see what would happen next. When he leaned closer, she found herself holding her breath.

"Okay... maybe one quick risk," he murmured, and lowered his mouth to hers.

His mouth was warm and gentle, but more insistent than it had been when they'd first kissed beneath the wind chime. Emmy sighed, a little sound of pleasure and acceptance, as he coaxed her mouth open, gently so gently. His arm came around her waist and he pulled her flush against him. Lips parted, they tasted each other.

And Emmy froze.

He tasted like wine.

Was he drunk? Was that the only reason he'd thrown caution to the wind? She didn't want to believe that of him, but she couldn't stop the frantic thoughts from forcing their way in and ruining the moment.

Sensing her retreat, Will stepped back. It was probably for the best that she'd held onto her self-control, because the first touch of his lips to hers had utterly undone him. She'd been warm and soft in his arms. Her mouth had fit his perfectly. She'd opened for him willingly, trustingly. Her taste lingered on his tongue. Never in his memory had a kiss affected him so much. He tried to gauge her reaction, to see if she was equally affected, but all he saw on her face was a guarded wariness.

"Sorry," he said even though he wasn't sorry at all.

She shook her head, made a visible effort to relax. "Don't be. That was... great. Wonderful. But we need to slow down. If we keep going down this path, it could lead to… complications."

"Right. Wouldn't want any complications."

She smiled apologetically, reached out as if to touch his arm again, then thought better of it and dropped her hand. "Tomorrow then?"

"Yeah. We'll leave from my parents'. Text me when you're ready to be picked up."

"I'll do that. Can't wait." Some of the tension was back as she said this. Now he saw no wariness. Instead, a kind of trepidation hovered on the edges of her expression. He decided not to push it—for now—and he would respect her wishes to back off on the kissing.

That didn't mean he wasn't going to try his damnedest to change her mind.

Twenty

The farm was a landscape designer's dream come true. Emmy spent her first few minutes on the property taking in the sights, the expansiveness of it all. The house had traditional charm: architecture that combined rustic sensibility and stately elegance. There were a few scraggly shrubs that looked well beyond saving, empty flower beds that begged to be filled, and some gorgeous ivy climbing up the northern walls. Overall, not terrible, but a lot of room for improvement. Emmy's fingers itched to start digging right then and there. Instead, she walked to the front door and rang the bell. Joanna answered with a welcoming smile.

"Emmy! So glad you came. Did you have a chance to look around yet?"

"Yes, a little. I'm going to do more, and take some pictures, but I wanted to stop by to let you know I'm here. Maybe you could give me an idea of what you're looking to have done?"

"Absolutely. Thank you again for taking the time."

They walked the extensive grounds and talked. Emmy saw potential everywhere she looked. Using her phone, she took pictures and googled different options for plants and rock, gave Joanna some rough price estimates. They focused on the front of the main house, knowing that would be the biggest draw for potential buyers.

"I can put some half-barrel planters in front of the barn to create a cohesive image," Emmy suggested as they wrapped up. "We'll use some of the same flowers as the front of the house, and it will barely bump the price point up because we'll be buying in bulk."

"That sounds just perfect. I'm so glad Will found you." Joanna surprised Emmy by pulling her into a quick one-armed hug. "You're good for him. I can tell."

"Ah…"

"Just an observation," Joanna added, laughing at the look of baffled distress on Emmy's face. "When do you think you can get started here?"

"As soon as you're ready. If you're okay with my estimate, I'll take twenty percent up front as a down payment, and I'll start gathering supplies."

Wow, I sound like a businessperson! Emmy thought excitedly. She fought to keep a friendly yet professional expression on her face, but inside she was squealing and dancing.

"Perfect. I'll text you after I discuss with Bill. You're a lifesaver, Emmy. Truly, you are."

"Tell me that after you see what I do. Besides Will's house, I haven't done anything like this before."

"You'll do spectacularly."

"I'll certainly try," Emmy said. "I can't wait to get started. This is going to be fun!"

Trepidations aside, she loved the idea of playing around in this expansive space. And though she'd never tell Will, she could admit to herself that he was right; there was a certain level of freedom in taking on this job knowing it didn't have any effect on the real world. When Joanna went back inside, she sent Will a text to let him know he could come pick her up. While she waited, she made notes on her phone, documenting ideas, saving images, comparing prices. She wondered how accurate the pricing information was as compared to the real world. Considering everything else she'd bought had been exactly as she'd expected, she assumed they were pretty much the same.

Then Will pulled up, and all thoughts of perennials and potting soil flew out the window as she took in his eager smile. He wore a pair of dark shades that added a bad boy edge to his appearance and made Emmy want very much to hop into the car and climb all over him. Instead, she buckled up and put her phone away, not wanting to give in to the temptation of googling a route or a destination.

"You ready?" Will asked.

"Sure." *Please don't disappear, Cobalt. Please!*

It took them less than two hours to cross the entire state of Massachusetts.

Will had wanted to drive east before heading north. The ocean was so close, and he thought it would be nice to see the beach as they drove wherever they were going. Emmy hadn't seen any reason to disagree. She had to admit to herself as they sat at Peggy's Diner, a little privately owned joint they'd discovered on the outskirts of Marblehead, that his instinct had been a good one. They were enjoying a late breakfast of pancakes, bacon, hash browns, and coffee while watching seagulls wing by out the window, their white bodies contrasting nicely with the vibrant blue of the cloudless sky. Emmy dabbed a bite of pancake into her syrup cup and wondered when it was that she'd been able to let go of the tension that seemed to have been with her since the moment she'd opened her eyes that morning.

Because Will's parents lived on the outskirts of town, it had taken no time at all before they'd approached, then passed, the sign indicating they were leaving the nonexistent town of Cobalt, Massachusetts, population 2,944. Emmy had had to concentrate on keeping her eyes on the road ahead. If she'd whipped around to look behind them and see if the town disappeared, Will would definitely have noticed and asked what was up. She'd sat rigidly in the passenger seat, glad at least that she could be sure of his sobriety on this trip, and allowed him to pick the music.

At some point between leaving Will's parents' house and stopping at the quaint diner for breakfast, the tension had seeped out of her. Perhaps it was the idyllic vista outside the car window or the distraction of the radio. Or she could be honest with herself and admit that it was all Will. Every now and then in the past couple hours, he'd turned to her and just smiled, or touched her arm to point out a particularly beautiful glimpse of scenery. He'd made small talk as well, but for the most part, they'd sat back and enjoyed a fast ride down an open highway. There was a freedom in it, once Emmy got past the worries and fears enough to enjoy it.

"Thinking big thoughts," Will said, cutting into her quiet reflection.

"Hm?"

He gestured with his fork. "You've been staring at that piece of bacon like you expect it to get up and dance."

Emmy snatched up the bacon in question and bit in. "I was just thinking about how I've never been to this part of Massachusetts before, so I couldn't say if this is an exact replica of the real world or not."

Will shrugged. "We'll find our way to some kind of landmark eventually. The point is that this place is here. There is a world outside the town of Cobalt. I was starting to feel... claustrophobic, I guess."

"I can understand that. I'm sorry for any part I played in your claustrophobia."

He fixed her with his gaze, and she was immediately lost in the mixture of pain and compassion she saw there. His face was so damn expressive. It was why he pulled at her even when she did everything in her power to fight any and all attraction she felt for him.

"You didn't play any part in it, Em. I hope I didn't make you feel like I resented you."

"You have every reason to. I upended your life."

Will reached out and took her hand in his. "It needed upending."

He didn't lean toward her, didn't increase their physical contact beyond his hand on hers, but she was reminded of their most recent kiss all the same. Neither of them had brought it up, and she was grateful to him for that.

Will looked on the cusp of doing or saying something, but his phone lit up with a text, and he let go of her hand. The moment was lost. She told herself she was relieved.

"Jared wants to know if we want to grab dinner with him and Bright tonight."

"Will we get back in time?" *Will we get back at all?*

"Depends how far we go. We can just drive for another couple hours, then head back. If we time it right, we can meet them at The Drowned Catfish around six or seven."

"The Drowned Catfish? How do you drown a fish?" Emmy asked.

"Ask Harlan. He owns the place. One of my favorite restaurants. You're okay with Cajun food?"

"I am very okay with Cajun food," Emmy assured him.

"Cool. It's in town, so we won't have a long drive home after. I know we'll probably be done with long car rides by then."

Provided they had a town anymore. "Okay. Sounds good. I like spicy food."

"Then you'll do Harlan proud." He texted Jared back. "Ready to go?"

Emmy drained the rest of her coffee, then they headed to the counter to pay.

They drove up the coast, stopped to dip their toes into the Atlantic, ate lunch at a seaside shanty that boasted handcrafted beers and an ocean view. Emmy still couldn't say if anything she saw would be exactly as it was in the real world, but she forgot to care. Everything was so beautiful and serene. It was an unexpected vacation that she hadn't known she needed. They kept going north up I-95—that was a real highway, Emmy knew—and ended up in Maine. Though lunch was only a couple hours behind them, they couldn't help but share a lobster roll. Will had Emmy in fits of giggles as he tried and failed to imitate the distinctive Maine accent, working his mouth around the word "lobster" like he was an alien trying and failing to assimilate smoothly into Earth culture.

It cost them an extra forty-five minutes, but they cut through Boston on their way back. Emmy had been there once when she was checking out some East Coast colleges. It had been years, but the city remained familiar enough. She'd spent a weekend there, exploring the sights and touring MIT. Her grades had been good enough to make it a viable enough reach school, but in the end, she hadn't been able to convince herself to stray so far from home. Added to that, she wasn't sure if STEM was the direction she wanted to go. She'd kept waiting for something to tug at her, some sense of rightness or belonging—like the proverbial lightbulb going on over her head. For years, she hadn't felt a single tug, until the day she'd turned an old watering can into a planter in Will's front yard. That bore some thinking on. Later.

Having confirmed that Boston was as it should be, they headed west toward home. With each passing mile, Emmy's nerves increased. The fears she'd been able to forget—or at least set aside—returned. Will sensed it, she knew. He glanced at her every few minutes, but he didn't attempt to engage her in conversation. Emmy twisted her fingers around in her lap and waited. She didn't know how close they were, but she did know that Will had predicted they'd get back to town a little before seven, in time to meet Jared and Bright. Her eyes kept flickering to the clock on the dash as the sun sank slowly behind the horizon ahead of them. It was almost full dark when the sign flashed past them. *Welcome to Cobalt!* She'd been so caught up in the anticipation, the tightness in her chest, that she'd nearly missed it. But it was there, and she felt her whole body go lax as she slumped back against the seat.

"I told you I wasn't going to go driving off any cliffs," Will said quietly, clearly noticing her relief. "I wouldn't do anything to put you at risk. You have to know that."

"Of course I know that. I wasn't worried about that at all."

"You were worried about something, though."

"Yes."

A beat of silence while he waited. When she didn't say anything further, Will made a frustrated sound in the back of his throat. "Just tell me."

"After dinner." It would be a brief reprieve, but she refused to ruin his night right before a fun meal with friends. "I'll tell you when we're back home. Promise."

"Fine."

"It's nothing, Will. I swear. Just set it aside for now. Jared's going to want a demonstration of your Maine accent."

He didn't smile as she'd hoped he would, but he did let out a long breath that took a lot of the rigidity out of his body. A couple minutes later, he pulled into the restaurant parking lot and found a spot. Though he turned off the car, he made no move to get out. Emmy waited, giving him the time he needed. Finally, he reached out and pulled her across the divider and into his arms. She held herself still as he buried his face in her hair and inhaled deeply. Though the position was awkward, she made no move to extricate herself. He still smelled like salty sea air. His body rippled with strength and emanated comforting warmth. She couldn't fight the way she felt about him when he was holding her like she was everything that mattered to him.

Finally, he spoke quietly, his lips against her hair. "You are not responsible for me, Emmy. Not when it comes to my mental health or my emotional wellbeing. You can't try to shoulder every burden for me. Let me take my share. I can handle it. Whatever else I am, I know I am a grown man who was raised with a solid support system. Don't treat me like I'm fragile."

"Okay."

He pulled back just enough to look into her eyes. "Okay?"

They were still so close. She could feel the whisper of his breath on her lips. Would he kiss her again? Would she let him? "Okay," she repeated quietly. She didn't know whether she was agreeing with his previous plea or if she was giving him permission to kiss her. Or both. All she knew was, when he pressed his lips against hers, softly and sweetly, it was more than welcome. It felt right. He pulled away instead of deepening the kiss. Probably for the best since she didn't want her hormones to ruin dinner.

They got out of the car and the sounds of the lively restaurant, the bright lights, the upbeat murmur of a hundred conversations, poured into her consciousness. Everything increased when they went through the door. Jazz music mingled seamlessly with the clink of glasses, the shouts and groans of people watching sports on the TVs over the bar, the laughter of the patrons, and the chatter of the servers as they swept past each other or stopped to check in at their tables. In place of traditional lighting, brightly painted mason jars had been placed over lightbulbs and suspended from the ceiling. The walls were covered in brass instruments, Mardi Gras beads, and splashy paintings.

Emmy was, quite simply, dazzled.

When she finally finished gazing around the space, it was to find Will watching her with a soft smile.

"What?"

"You're beautiful."

Emmy felt heat rush up her neck to settle in her cheeks. "Th-thank you. So are you."

Will laughed. "At least call me handsome."

"Sure, if you'll only accept gender-normative compliments."

"I don't know much about romance novels, but something tells me gender-normative is the name of the game."

"Yeah, fair enough. But only in the mainstream ones."

They saw Jared waving and wound their way around booths and tables to join him and Bright. His fingers were threaded through hers on the table in a casual and adorable gesture of affection.

"You guys get lost?" Jared asked.

"We were in Maine," Will replied as he slid into the booth.

"Uh… okay. I'll bite. Why were you in Maine?"

"Tah have the lobstah rolls, of cahrs."

Emmy burst into laughter and heard Bright giggling along with her. Jared just shook his head, but he was smiling. "I bet they took you for a native up there."

"Oh yeah. They all thought I was born and raised in Portland."

"A long way to drive for lunch," Bright commented, her eyes full of humor.

"I wanted an adventure," Will said.

"Uh huh." Jared gave him a knowing look. "Did you drive up there on your new motorcycle?"

"I talked him out of the motorcycle," Emmy interjected.

Their server came by to get their drink orders, and they put their conversation on hold while they ordered. Emmy must have read the menu a hundred times. She couldn't decide what to get; everything sounded so delicious that her mouth was watering. The two-and-a-half meals she'd already eaten that day were suddenly distant memories.

"You and I can share two entrees," Will told her. "Just tell me what you're thinking."

Filled with gratitude, she decided to get the catfish po'boy for herself. Will got the shrimp jambalaya with a side of homemade cornbread. Drinks were served and orders were placed. Then Bright asked them for details about their impromptu coastal adventure. Emmy couldn't help but like the woman. She was an active listener, her attention never wavering as they summarized their trip for her. Emmy pulled out her phone and showed off some pictures. When that topic was exhausted, Bright told them about some new artists she'd been working with to do a collection of upcycled jewelry and handbags for her shop.

The food arrived and Emmy dug right in. It was everything she was hoping for and more. When Will offered her a forkful of his jambalaya, she leaned forward and allowed him to feed it to her without a second thought. It only occurred to her afterwards that the exchange was quite intimate. When they'd spoken earlier about sharing, she'd assumed they'd put a bit of their meals onto each other's plates.

"Aw, you guys are positively glowing," Bright commented. "You are so good together."

Emmy opened her mouth to correct her before she remembered that she and Will were supposed to be pretending to be in a relationship. Fortunately, Will picked up the slack. Taking her hand, he placed a gentle kiss on her fingers and said, "I think so, too." Emmy swallowed. He was laying it on thick, but she couldn't stop the flutter in her chest.

The meal went well right up until they were sharing coffee and a platter of beignets so fresh that they let out little puffs of steam when pulled apart.

"Emmy, I haven't asked if you're working on anything new," Bright said.

Emmy's mind went blank. "Working on...?"

"A writing project," Bright clarified. Emmy's expression must have worried her, so she added, "Unless... is it not cool to ask? Do you want to keep it a secret?"

"No! No, sorry. I just... got a little turned around. Mentally." She barely resisted kicking Will under the table when he covered a snort of laughter by clearing his throat and sipping his coffee. He'd gotten her into this mess. And she knew just how to take her revenge. "I do have a new idea I'm working on, now that you mention it."

"Oo! Can I get the details?"

"Well, it's a work in progress, in the early stages, you know. But I'm thinking of setting it in a small town like Cobalt. Will actually inspired me, so I think the love interest is going to be a nurse."

"Aww, that is so sweet." Bright laid a hand over her heart. "You need to dedicate the book to him."

"Oh, I absolutely will."

"So does that mean the protagonist is based on you?"

That caught her off guard, but she rolled with it. "A little. I don't want it to be autobiographical, but if you don't pull in some of your experiences and emotions, it doesn't feel real."

"That is so true." Bright was eating it up. She leaned forward, resting her chin on her folded hands. Jared stole the second half of her beignet right off her plate and she didn't notice. "So how do the two love birds meet?"

Emmy barely resisted cutting a look at Will. "They wake up in the same bed and neither of them remember how they got there."

Jared barked out a laugh. "Love at first hangover?"

"Something like that."

"I like that. It's not something you see every day," Bright commented. "Which one of your characters has the tragic backstory?"

Beside her, Will stiffened. Emmy bought herself some time by taking a long drink of coffee.

"What do you mean?" Will asked, his voice quiet. Intense.

Oblivious to his tone and mood, Bright circled her hand in the air as she thought. "You know how these things go, even if you never read the books. It happens in movies, too. The guy—usually it's the guy—is all broodily sexy and sexily broody because of his dark past. Then his lady friend helps him come to terms with his past. Usually with her vagina. Then he loses the broody, but not all of it because that's what makes his character appealing in the first place.

And *bam*." She clapped her hands together for effect. "You have character development."

Emmy had a fleeting image of grabbing a trombone off the wall and whacking Bright across the head with it. That probably wasn't going to work; she imagined the instruments were bolted down. Besides, the damage was already done. She didn't have to look at Will to know that Bright's words had struck a chord with him. Their server chose that moment to drop off the check, and Jared whisked it off the table.

"My treat," he said, slipping his card into the folder.

"Thank you," Emmy managed. "It was great. My first time eating here."

"Happy to oblige. Thanks for squeezing us into your adventure today."

"Speaking of that," Emmy said, grasping at the opening Jared had unwittingly gifted her. "I think Will and I should get going. I'm exhausted. I feel like I haven't slept in a week."

They said their goodbyes, though Will's was wooden and perfunctory. Fortunately, neither Jared nor Bright seemed to notice his change in mood. After a quick hug from Bright, they went to their separate cars. Emmy got in and buckled up. Then she waited.

Will couldn't bring himself to start the engine just yet. He stared straight ahead, his hands resting loosely on the steering wheel. He could feel Emmy's anxiety rolling off her in waves. It wasn't like she was to blame for Bright's comment, but it still fell to her to fill in some gaps for him. She would hate that. No matter what he'd said to her before they'd gone into the restaurant, he knew she still felt responsible for every hard turn his life had taken since she'd appeared in it.

"It's after dinner now," he said, still not looking at her. "What was it you didn't want to tell me? The thing that was making you nervous about our road trip."

She looked down at her hands where they rested in her lap, and he heard her release her breath slowly. "Cobalt, Massachusetts, isn't a real town," she replied quietly. "I was afraid that if we left... I thought maybe the town would disappear. If the rest of the country was exactly the same as in the real world, I thought maybe leaving Cobalt would cause the inconsistency to... correct itself."

He absorbed this new revelation, let it roll through him, and he understood why she had wanted to keep it from him. But when compared to Bright's earlier words, the new knowledge about his hometown was negligible. It didn't matter that the town wasn't real. Nothing he knew or loved was.

Twenty-One

When Emmy woke up the next morning, Will was gone. There was no note stuck to the fridge, no dishes in the sink to indicate he'd eaten breakfast, and no car in the driveway or garage.

She refused to let her brain go to the worst-case scenario, though she couldn't help but remember her plea the other night. She'd asked him not to take unnecessary risks, and he had agreed. But that was then. It was impossible not to worry that certain new information had shaken him enough to break that promise.

To keep her mind busy, she made a list of practical steps she would take before jumping to the most extreme conclusions. She might not have a designated tomato drawer in her own home, but she was killer at making lists.

First, she sent him a quick text asking if he was okay. While she waited for a response, she went about making and eating breakfast. Through sheer force of will, she refused to look at her phone until after she'd put her dishes in the sink a good thirty minutes later.

No response.

Step two was to call him. It went straight to voicemail.

Step three was to contact Jared and see if he'd heard from Will, or if he knew where Will would go when he was caught in the throes of emotional turmoil. Then she remembered that she did not have Jared's number. The only contacts in her phone besides Will were his mother and Bright. She and Bright had exchanged numbers during their impromptu TV and snack session the other day, but Bright didn't seem like a good choice for this particular problem. She barely knew Will. Emmy saw that Joanna had texted her sometime last night, okaying the estimate for the landscaping. Her visit to the farm now felt like it had occurred a lifetime ago. But it was fortunate that Joanna had approached her at all, or Emmy would never have gotten her number. Who would know Will better than his mother?

Joanna picked up on the second ring. "Emmy! I'm so glad you called! Did you get my text? Bill and I are so excited to see what you come up with."

"Hi, Mrs. Ba—Joanna, I know you wanted to talk about the landscaping in your yard, but I have a quick question about Will."

"Oh, sure. Is everything alright?"

"I think so, but he seemed upset about something last night, and I was wondering…" She didn't know how to phrase the question. Bright's words had clearly been the trigger, but she couldn't exactly ask the woman if her son had a tragic backstory. "Did anything… bad happen to Will when he was younger? Something that might still be hurting him?"

There was silence for a moment. "If he hasn't told you, honey, I don't know that I should."

"Normally, I would absolutely agree with that. I don't want to invade Will's privacy. Please believe that. But yesterday I noticed something was bothering him, and today I can't find him. I'm worried about him, and I don't think he should be alone right now. If there's anything you can tell me…" She let the thought hang unfinished.

"The cemetery," Joanna said quietly. "Try looking in the cemetery."

Emmy spent five minutes trying to come up with a way of getting to the cemetery. She had no doubt there was only one in a town this small, except maybe the occasional little private one outside a church. The problem was she had no car, and Cobalt, she'd learned, did not have much to offer in the ways of ridesharing services. She did, however, have better walking shoes than last time she'd been stuck in the house without transportation. The only other issue she could think of was that she was about to be outside alone without Will to run meet-cute-interference for her. It was a risk she would have to take. Wearing her sturdy pair of sneakers, her hair tied back in a ponytail, she set out at a brisk walk.

It couldn't have taken a full fifteen minutes before she heard a truck driving up behind her.

"Third time's the charm. I'm going to have to say this is fate."

Emmy barely spared a glance for Paul as he leaned out the window, his smile a little smug, with just a touch of "I can't wait to be your white knight" thrown in.

"This is the only road into town. I think we can give fate a pass on this one."

"I could give you a lift this time."

"No, thank you."

She didn't make eye contact, didn't slow her pace. The fuck-off signals were in full effect. But she still wished she had a backup plan in case he didn't leave her alone. It worried her that he'd already brought fate into the mix. Why hadn't she asked Will to buy her pepper spray? She increased her pace, swung her arms in time with her strides to make it look like she was in the middle of a workout instead of wandering aimlessly. Breathing slow and deep, she tried to calm her thoughts. Just because the man wanted to flirt didn't mean she should jump straight to self-defense protocol. Not that she had any methods of self-defense. All she had was the ability to be bitchy and dismissive. It would have to do.

"You sure?" Paul asked patiently. "You gotta know by now I'm not a murderer."

"That's too bad. I only accept rides from murderers."

He laughed at that. She still didn't look at him, but she could feel him watching her. Her skin prickled, her chest began to burn more from nerves than exertion.

"You sure aren't like other girls. I like that about you."

"My goal in life," Emmy muttered, trying not to snap at him for pulling the "not like other girls" line.

"What was that?"

"I said…" Emmy tried to come up with a decent brush-off on the fly. Then she gave up. Looking at him directly for the first time since he drove up, she stated, "I'm still with

Will. And I'm trying to exercise. Thank you for the offer of a ride, but I'm good."

"Alright then." His smile didn't dim as he settled back inside the truck. "But I still say you should give fate some thought." Emmy held the shudder in check, but just barely. She caught Paul's quick wave out of the corner of her eye. "Until the next time we run into each other, Emmy."

She tried and failed not to hear those words as a threat. Then the gravel crunched under his tires as he increased his speed and passed her by. She let out a long, relieved breath, but she didn't allow herself to consider it a done deal until she caught sight of the town ahead of her. Paul's truck was nowhere in sight. A trickle of relief loosened her muscles and lifted some of the tension she'd held trapped somewhere between her lungs and her heart. Emmy found herself yearning for the safety and comfort of Will's presence as she entered the town proper. The next meet-cute could be waiting around any corner, and she had never before realized how much energy it took to ward off even the kindest of advances. It was time to start considering throat punches as an option.

Now she just had to find the damn cemetery.

Jared was clearly visiting Bright at her place of business during a day off or a break. When Emmy walked into Bright Ideas, he had his tongue in Bright's mouth. They were involved enough in the kiss that they did not stir at the sound of the bell tinkling over the door. Emmy took a moment, then opened the door again as violently as she could. The little bells sent up an insistent chorus of chimes, and the entwined couple separated abruptly.

"Oh! Emmy, hi," Bright said, her cheeks flushed with either embarrassment or arousal. Maybe both. "Did you come to do some shopping?"

"Not today, no. I'm sorry to interrupt. I know this is weird, but I was wondering if one of you could give me a lift to the cemetery? I won't need a ride back. I'm... meeting Will there." She didn't entertain the possibility that he wouldn't be there. Her gut knew that she'd find him. The only hitch would be if he was okay enough to drive her home, but by now she felt comfortable taking the wheel anyway.

"You're meeting Will at the cemetery?" Bright asked, concern shadowing her features. "Is he... did someone..."

"No, nothing like that," Emmy said quickly. "He's just... visiting. I told him I'd meet him there, but I forgot that I didn't have a ride."

They were too polite to question her further, and she was grateful for that because she was struggling to come up with a believable lie.

"I'll give you a ride on my way to the hospital," Jared told her. Fictional being or not, the look in his eyes showed genuine concern for his friend. "Is he alright? I thought he seemed off last night, but you had a long day. Figured he was tired."

"He's alright," Emmy said, fervently hoping she wasn't lying. "Just doing some deep thinking."

"Okay, you let me know if you need me."

He gave Bright a quick kiss goodbye and led Emmy out to his car.

★

The cemetery was a splash of bright green dotted with gleaming marble. While it was a sizable plot of land, it was small relative to cemeteries she'd seen in bigger cities. That was good because it meant she wouldn't have to spend a long time looking for Will or risk getting lost in the process. After thanking Jared for the ride, she stepped out and looked around. A graveside service was taking place nearby, but she didn't see anyone else until she had walked down the central pathway for a while. Then he was there, a single figure sitting on the grass, hunched over bent knees. She couldn't tell if he was staring at the gravestone in front of him, or if his mind had wandered off to the point where he no longer noticed or cared what he was looking at. The image broke her heart because he appeared... small. Wordlessly, she went up and sat beside him. The name on the marble stone in front of him read Trudy Elaine Novak. Some quick mental math had a jolt of pain spearing into Emmy's chest. She'd been sixteen when she died. Aching inside, she mirrored Will's position, resting her arms on her bent knees, and waited.

"Leukemia," Will said quietly, a minute or two later. "It came out of nowhere. I had to watch my aunt suffer as her daughter went through chemo, as she wasted away, as she died. I had to watch my mom suffer with her sister, try to comfort her—and me—try to hold it together when she probably wanted to break down. Sometimes I went to the hospital with them. I remember getting restless, wandering the halls. It was too hard to stay in the room with them. My cousin..." He broke off, swallowed hard.

"How old were you?"

"Twelve when she was diagnosed. Thirteen by the time she let go."

"I'm so sorry." There was nothing else she could say.

"She was the reason I became a nurse. Or part of it. Even at that age, I knew I wanted to do something with healthcare. Maybe be an X-ray tech. I thought bones were cool, but... nurse felt right." He turned to her then, his eyes red-rimmed and lost... so lost. "I meant what I said last night, how you're not responsible for my emotional wellbeing. But the things Bright said... I couldn't stop thinking about them. I think that's how I convinced myself to leave you this morning without telling you where I was going. Didn't want you to think I was a hypocrite, telling you it's not your job to care for me, then falling apart on you."

"It's okay to lean on me when you're hurting, Will. That's what friends are for. I won't think you're a hypocrite."

He stared at her for a moment, his throat working with the effort of keeping tears at bay. "I keep thinking of questions that split off into more questions. Was my cousin real? Was my aunt's grief real? Am I really a nurse? Did my cousin—" He broke off, choking on words and emotion. "Did my cousin die so I could be a well-rounded character? Is that what it all comes down to? A tragic backstory?" He gave in then, rested his forehead on her shoulder as he broke into sobs.

Tears streamed down Emmy's face as she cradled him against her. She could never take back what she had done to him. No matter what he said, this was her fault. She hadn't appeared in his world on purpose, but it was her appearance that had caused his pain nonetheless. A part of her felt like a fraud, offering him comfort when she was the source of his discomfort in the first place. Worse, she feared that he would never truly recover from this. Even if she somehow found a way to bring him back with her to the real world, his mind might not be able to handle it. For now, all she could do was hold him, grieve with him, and make sure he knew he wasn't alone. Even when he stopped crying, she held him, waited until he was ready to sit back. It took a while, and she didn't mind. There was a gentle breeze blowing and birds chirping. Comforting feelings, sights, sounds. Exactly what a cemetery was supposed to provide for the grieving.

He sat back eventually, rubbed his hands down his face.

"Tell me about her," Emmy requested softly.

"What's to tell?" he asked. "She wasn't real."

"She was real to *you*."

He didn't respond right away, and stayed silent long enough that she didn't think he'd speak again. But then he sighed, plucked a piece of grass to toy with absently, and spoke.

"She was older than me by a couple years, but she was one of my best friends. She laughed with her whole body, you know… threw her head back, held her stomach. It should have looked fake, but it was real with her. She always ate her French fries plain—no ketchup or dip of any kind. One time, when my aunt wouldn't let her get her nose pierced, she 'ran away' to our house. I think she was thirteen or fourteen then. My mom called my aunt—without telling us, so we could feel like we were doing something sneaky—and let Trudy stay the night.

"We used to challenge each other to competitions all the time. Just random shit that popped into our heads. Who can eat the most Lucky Charms without milk; who can climb this tree faster; who can watch this YouTube video of a kitten falling into a bowl of water without laughing."

Emmy smiled a little despite herself. "I think I would have liked her."

"Absolutely. She would have liked your sense of humor. If she were still alive, I think she would be the only person I would have risked telling about all this. Maybe it's best that she isn't, because I wouldn't have been able to leave her behind if I found a way out of the book."

He fell silent again, and Emmy's heart clenched. His pain was a sharp, aching wound in her chest. She cursed herself for ever picking up the book, for going to see a sex psychic just to make her sister feel better, for doing her best to convince him that he was a fictional character instead of leaving him alone.

"Can I ask you a favor?"

"Anything," Emmy told him.

"I need a little more time. Can you drive my car back to the house? I'll have Jared or somebody give me a ride back when I'm ready. I can't leave just yet."

"That's fine. Do you want me to call anyone for you? Or do anything else?"

He shook his head. "Just get yourself home safe."

She accepted his keys. It was difficult to get up and leave him alone in front of a young girl's grave, but she respected his wishes. She left. Tears dripped silently down her cheeks as she drove to the little house she was using as a temporary home.

Twenty-Two

Will found her asleep on his couch again. She was curled up under a blanket with her cheek resting on her hand. It was surprising how right she looked there. But she didn't belong in his world, no matter his feelings on the matter. Sighing, he scooped her into his arms and started carrying her to her room. She blinked blearily up at him as he set her carefully on her bed.

"Will?"

"Just putting you somewhere more comfortable. You can go back to sleep."

He started to rise, to pull away.

She grabbed his shirt. "Don't go away."

He put his hand over hers where it gripped his shirt. "I'm not going anywhere. I'm not going to disappear again."

Accepting his words, she allowed her eyes to close, and her hand slipped back down to rest by her side. Will indulged himself by brushing his fingertips over her hair, then pressing his lips to her forehead for just a moment. He had been selfish, he realized, asking her to hang around with him. She had a life—a *real* life—to get back to. Family and friends who loved her. A new business to start. An ex-boyfriend to get over. How could he keep insisting she stay with him instead of putting all of her focus into getting herself out?

Resolve settling in his gut, he went to the kitchen to work out some angles while she slept.

Emmy woke up to a quiet house a little while later. She struggled to sit up, pushed through the drowsiness left behind by her nap. It took her a moment to remember what had happened before she'd fallen asleep, but when she did, she jumped out of bed and rushed to find Will. Relief washed over her when she saw him sitting at the kitchen table, drinking a cup of black coffee and making quick notes on a legal pad. When she walked in, he looked up and smiled a little.

"There's plenty of coffee left."

"Thanks." She took a moment to pour herself a mug, splashed in some milk. "How are you?" she asked, sitting down across from him.

"Drained," he replied.

Emmy nodded, understanding that. She absently turned the mug around and around in her hands.

"How are *you*?" he asked.

"I guess you could say the same."

"I want to thank you for coming to find me. It meant a lot."

She shook her head, dismissing his misplaced gratitude and a fresh bout of tears. "I know what you said in the car,

Will, but everything you're thinking and feeling right now is my fault. I want you to know... I'm so sorry. Just so sorry that I put you through all this."

"Emmy, look at me." She did so, reluctantly. "You are not responsible for this. You had no idea reading a random book would fuck with everything you've ever believed to be true. You didn't ask for this. I'd like to think that if you knew what would happen, you would have chosen not to read that particular book."

She let out a tired half laugh. "Yeah, I probably would've browsed a different section."

His smile was fleeting, quickly replaced by a somber expression. "I don't want you to forget that you're a victim in this, too. You lost your home, your family, your reality. Honestly, I don't know how you've managed to keep it together all this time."

She sipped her coffee. "I don't know. I think you helped. Wanting to support you, help you find answers. And I clung to the belief that we'd get out. If I let myself think, even for a second, that I was never going to find my way back..." She didn't let herself finish the thought, knew she could not go down that route or the emotional pain would drown her.

"That connects with something I want to talk to you about."

Emmy raised her eyebrows at the sudden determined expression on his face. "What?"

"I asked you once to bring me with you when you found a way out. This morning, it occurred to me how selfish it was to ask you that."

"Will, no! Don't—"

He held up a hand. "I need you to let me finish."

Emmy felt words gathering to push their way out, but she pressed her lips together. She could give him a minute to talk before she let loose on him.

"What I said earlier is exactly what I believe," he continued. "You were hurt by events outside your control. You lost your life and your world. I can't ask you to set that aside for me. I need you to promise me that if you find a way out of this book without me, you'll take it. It was never right of me to ask anything different, and I need you to trust that this is what I really want. I want you to get back to your life without worrying about leaving me behind."

She was speechless. So many protestations and counterarguments flooded her mind at once that they all kind of crashed into each other and left her with nothing to say. Also, a small part of her—a part she felt immeasurably guilty about—felt relieved by his statement. She *did* miss her life and her family. More than she allowed herself to think about most days, knowing she'd lose control the moment she allowed herself to linger on her losses.

Taking her silence for a form of assent, Will tapped the pencil on his notebook. "I've been writing down everything I know about romance novels, which is not much. I've also been making a list of everything I know about Bright. You once suggested that the way for you to get out might be for me to carry the story to its conclusion. I think you might be right."

"But..." Why couldn't she *say* something? *Damn it, Emmy, stop this!* she urged herself. "Bright is with Jared now."

Good job, genius, she thought sardonically.

"She is, but she's not supposed to be," Will said. "I think the book probably wants her to be with me. Think about what happened with my parents. They kept calling you Bright, and it took them a really long time to comprehend I wasn't with her. If you and I put our heads together, I bet we can get this thing back on track. If I get Bright to leave Jared for me, it might ruin our friendship, or… I think it might hit the reset button. Everything will become as it should be, as it was… written."

Emmy's heart lurched at all the implications of this new plan of his. She stared at him like she'd never seen him before. "You'd do that for me, really?"

"Yes," he stated without hesitation. "You deserve your life, Emmy. I'm not going to keep you trapped just because I…" He shook his head. "I'm not going to be that selfish. I *can't* be that selfish."

How could he not see what that said about him? None of this had been written. The author hadn't meant for this display of selflessness to happen. It was all *him*. Everything about this thought process, this misplaced guilt, this heavy decision, was him.

She just had to make him see it.

"You told me you didn't read that much of the book," Will continued, studying his notes with a slight frown. "Did you read the back cover? Is there anything you can add to this?"

She stood up and walked around the table to him. He raised an eyebrow at her when she stopped to loom over him without even glancing at his notes.

"I'm not leaving you here," she stated.

"Emmy," he said on a sigh.

"No! I let you have your say, now it's my turn. So just sit there and listen." Anger probably wasn't the right way to go. Heaving out a breath, she stalked away from him and began pacing the short distance in a quick, agitated rhythm. When she felt like she had her thoughts under control, she stopped and looked at him again. "You are *real*, Will Barrett."

"No, Emmy."

"*Yes*, Will!" Tears were trying to make their way out again, but she'd cried enough. She blinked them back, wanting to be sure he heard her out and understood what she was trying to say. "I still have no idea how I got here, or where here is. I don't know how much of this place, aside from you and me, is real. It might all be an illusion. I'm sorry that it hurts you, the uncertainty I mean. I'm sorry that Bright put all that shit in your head about your cousin. Trudy may or may not have been created just so you'd have an interesting backstory, but your emotions about her are as real and as true as anything else in my world or yours. *You* are real, Will. I know you are. We aren't going through a script, you and me. I wasn't even supposed to be here. None of the thoughts or feelings you're having right now were created by an unseen author. The decision to be some kind of martyr for me can only have come from you, not a book character. Your feelings about your position in this world, about your past, about me… they're yours. And they make me sure you're real." She reached out, put her hands on his shoulders and squeezed. "I'm *sure* of it."

"I think therefore I am?" he asked, unable to hold back a smile.

"Yeah. You're joking around, but yeah, Will. You're thinking right now. You're making plans and working things out that were never supposed to exist for Will Barrett the character. Will Barrett the *person* is the one trying to do the right thing here. And I appreciate that." She smiled sadly at him. "I'm not going to let you make your noble sacrifice, but I appreciate it. It's the thought that counts, right?"

"Alright then. I *think* you need to consider my position a little more before vetoing it."

Emmy shook her head, shifted so she could lean down and gently press a kiss to his lips. "I'm not leaving without you, Will," she whispered, her face still close to his. "If I'm given that choice, if I'm not just ripped out of your world as abruptly as I was ripped out of mine, I'll choose to stay rather than abandon you. You're not going to be able to convince me to do anything else."

"Emmy," he said softly. Emotion stole his voice for a moment. He swallowed, then spoke again. "I don't want you to leave everything you love behind for me."

"Do you think I could live with myself not knowing if I'd ended your existence? No, listen," she insisted when he started to speak. "I meant it when I said you're real. I believe it with everything I am. I won't risk ending you. I can't."

"Your sister. Your parents. Your best friend."

He was right, and she knew it. She thought of her sister, her parents, Sarah. Her life. Her job. Her reality. She couldn't stay in the book forever, but she didn't need forever. All they had to do was find a way out.

Taking a breath, Emmy rubbed her hands over his shoulders, down his arms, in a brief caress. "I'm not saying I'll stop looking for a way out. I know I need to get back to my life and my family. Just... don't give up yet. I believe there's a way for us to get out together. We'll think of something. I'm willing to dedicate every waking moment to brainstorming a solution, because God knows I want to go home, but I want you with me. I *need* you with me."

He still looked doubtful. There were shadows in his eyes. She wished she knew the right words to convince him that everything was going to be alright, but she didn't have those words.

Sighing, she smiled sadly. "Will?"

"Yeah?"

"*Toile wa doko desuka.*"

He furrowed his brow. "Is that more Japanese? What does it mean?"

"It means 'Where's the bathroom?' I forgot how to say, 'I won't give up until I find a way for both of us to get out of this cursed book,' so you'll have to take what you can get."

Will expelled his breath on a surprised laugh and shook his head. "You are something else." He reached up to cup her cheek in his hand, ran his thumb over her skin. "You meant it, huh? You believe I'm real?"

"Absolutely," she whispered. "No doubt in my mind."

"Okay. Then this is real, too."

He gave her a gentle tug, pulling her toward him, and took her mouth in a kiss that went straight to her heart. She couldn't pull back from this, not now. He needed her in this moment, needed her to be unguarded and open to him, so she ran her fingers through his hair and held on. His lips lingered, not demanding more than she was ready to give, just giving her a taste of what she could have if she gave herself over to her feelings for him. Then, with one light nip at her lower lip, he pulled back.

Will took a second to catch his breath. He wanted more from her, but this was the wrong time. Maybe the kiss had been a test at first, just seeing what she would do, if she would put her money where her mouth was. But he'd lost that initial motivation in a wave of need for her. The problem was, his conscience wouldn't let him go further.

"I'm emotionally stirred up right now," he said, hoping Emmy would understand he wasn't rejecting her. He let out a half laugh and said, "Physically, too, obviously. But I think we should wait to… if you want to…"

"Will." She waited until he met her gaze. "I want to have sex with you. But I appreciate that you want to level out before we do that."

"Thank you."

"You're welcome." A teasing look came into her eye that he couldn't explain until she added, "You are going to be really good at sex."

"Wow… uh… thank you?"

She laughed. "You're the male lead in a romance novel, Will. You have sexual superpowers."

"I thought you said I was real and human."

"You're that, too. But you can't forget your roots," she said with a smirk. "I might be trying to take the man out of the romance novel, but you can't take the romance novel out of the man."

"Stop."

"I'm just saying, my quivering flower can't wait for your thick, pulsing, turgid… kielbasa."

"That's it!"

She squealed as he leaped at her, scooping her over his shoulder and giving her a quick, disorienting spin. The next thing she knew, he'd brought her into the living room and dumped her on the couch. Before she could catch her breath, he began to tickle her mercilessly.

"I'll kielbasa *you*," he growled over her giggles.

"Okay, okay! I yield!"

When he leaned over her, smiling and shaking his head, she reached up and pulled him down to her. This kiss was deeper. He took his time with her, coaxing her to respond, teasing her mouth with the tip of his tongue until she opened for him. Nothing had ever felt more right, more perfect, than her lips against his.

With a groan, Will pulled back. "You're making it hard for me to remember my reasons for not stripping you naked here and now."

"Emotional turmoil," she reminded him. "Very sad and broody."

"Right. Sad and broody." But he didn't feel that way with her. Not anymore. She had whisked away his bad mood with strategic genitalia jokes. "If we're not going to introduce my kielbasa to your flower, how do you want to pass the afternoon?"

"Scrabble picnic?"

"What is a scrabble picnic?"

She pushed herself up until she was sitting. "It's what it sounds like. We used to do it all the time when I was younger. We played Scrabble in the park while we ate a picnic lunch."

"I don't own Scrabble."

"What? How?"

"Because I live alone and, until recently, I regularly worked more hours than was healthy."

"We need to fix this," Emmy said resolutely. "Is there a Target around here? Do you guys have Target? Or maybe we can borrow something from Bright. You think she has like... vagina Scrabble?"

"What is it with you and genitals?"

Emmy did her best to look affronted. "*Me?* She's the one selling boob paperweights and beer bottle penises."

"Yeah, fair enough." He reached out and helped her to her feet. "Anyway, the nearest Target is in Springfield. We can just go to Grabby's."

"Grabby's?"

"Yeah, it's one of those secondhand stores where there's just a bunch of shit lying around and you can buy it. Books and games, outdated candy... no, that's not the word. What is it? Obsolete? Extinct?"

Emmy giggled as they headed for the door. "I think you mean discontinued."

"Yes! That's it. Anyway, if Grabby's doesn't have Scrabble, no one in town will."

"Sounds like a plan. Added bonus—we can get some dinosaur candy for our picnic."

Will rolled his eyes as he took his keys off the hook. "Misspeak one time and she busts your balls for life," he grumbled.

Twenty-Three

Theodore Grabby was an archetype. Emmy was sure of it. She wasn't sure what this particular type of character would be called, but she thought of him as a Jolly Wise Grandpa. Almost a Santa Claus. She couldn't help but love him, and that was probably the point.

"Scrabble, huh?" Grabby smiled through the fluffy salt-and-pepper beard/mustache combo that covered the entire lower half of his face. "I got three different editions. Are you looking for the '76, the '81, or the '89?"

"Whichever one you'd recommend, of course," Emmy told him, and got a chuckle in response.

"The '89. Can't go wrong."

He led the way, winding around shelves of books in various conditions, children's toys, gag gifts, novelty mugs, and license plate frames. The back wall caught Emmy's attention, and she stopped in her tracks.

When Will had spoken of discontinued candy, she'd imagined a little display by the register with a couple of spiral lollipops and a box of Bazooka bubblegum. Instead, she saw shelves upon shelves of confections, many of which she'd never heard of. Yes, there were giant rainbow lollipops in various twirling shapes. Yes, there was Bazooka—by the jar and by the tub. But there was also so much more. Chiclets, Fun Dip, Abba-Zaba, Payday, Pixy Stix, Walnettos, M&Ms bags that looked like they predated the Civil War, twenty-three different flavors of licorice, Warheads, Airheads, ring pops, push pops, baby bottle pops... not to mention the myriad shelves of bulk-buy candy in their individually labeled jars with attached plastic scoops.

"Jesus Christ. You're Willy fucking Wonka," Emmy breathed. Then slapped a hand over her mouth as she realized she probably shouldn't curse so blatantly in front of the jolly grandpa.

"If you're going to stock candy, you gotta do it right," Grabby said with a proud smile, clearly unfazed by her blue language. "My old man said it was like selling nostalgia."

"I'll say." Emmy was already selecting a colorful bag from the bulk buy shelf. Their picnic dessert was going to be handfuls of random candy.

"I'll just grab the board game and meet you up front," Will said, his tone a mix of exasperation and amusement.

"Sounds good," Emmy told him. "Prepare for a wait. Candy mixing is a science that can't be rushed."

"I'll stay strong for you."

She ended up filling two bags—one with chocolate and chocolate-adjacent flavors, one with fruit flavors. The sour candy was at the bottom of the second bag with a buffer layer of wrapped candies in the middle, so the sour flavor would have the least chance to adulterate the unwrapped non-sour candies on top. She carried her packages to the register where Will waited with a Scrabble board and Battleship. Grabby weighed the candy and bagged everything for them.

"You kids have fun," he said as he handed Will the receipt.

Emmy couldn't help feeling she was going to miss Grabby if—*when*—she and Will made it to the real world. Sure, there were novelty shops in her reality, but it would take her a while before she found one owned and operated by an adorable old man with an appropriately cute name.

They stopped at the grocery store to buy tubs of potato salad and coleslaw, the makings for sandwiches, and drinks.

"Should we get a bottle of wine?" Will asked. "Isn't that traditional for a romantic picnic?"

Emmy couldn't help the little tremor that went through her at the question. How could she tell him she didn't want alcohol anywhere near them?

"This isn't a romantic picnic," she said, hoping he didn't notice her hesitation. "For Scrabble picnics, we need pop."

His brow furrowed. "Pop?"

"Yes?" It took a second to figure out the source of his confusion. "Oh, for crying out... *Soda*. We need *soda* for our picnic."

"Ohh!"

"Wipe the smirk off your face, Massachusetts. In the Midwest, we buy pop."

"No problem." He continued smirking. "The *pop* aisle is right over here."

Emmy stuck her tongue out at his back and followed him. She thought the little linguistic hiccup had saved her from any uncomfortable beverage-related questions, but

Will stopped her in the middle of the aisle with a hand over hers on the handle of the cart.

"You didn't want me to buy wine."

She let out a long breath. "No, I didn't want you to buy wine."

He kept his eyes focused on hers. "You're that worried about me."

"Yes."

"God, what a wakeup call." He thought back over the past couple weeks, remembered all the times he'd restocked the liquor on the fridge, how often she'd seen him with a glass of something hard and strong in his hand. "I told myself I could destroy my liver because I wasn't real, so my liver wasn't real," he said quietly. "I told myself a fictional character can't develop a substance abuse problem."

"Yeah, but you're not a fictional character."

Will laughed weakly. "I guess you're right. I never thought that an unexpected dependency on alcohol would be the thing that convinced me, but here we are." He reached over and snagged a twelve-pack of soda at random, plunked it into the cart. Then, thinking about the sudden change in his future beverage choices, he grabbed two more. "If I'm going sober from here on out, we're going to need a lot more pop."

"Really?"

"Sorry, I was just teasing you. I'll say soda."

"No, I mean... you're really going to drink less?"

"Yeah, Emmy. Really." He saw the stark relief on her face and felt like the lowest kind of asshole. "Jesus, look at you.

I don't know if I can apologize enough for what I put you through."

Emmy turned the cart toward the checkout area, her hands trembling a little. "I put you through worse, so we're even."

It was perfect weather for a picnic. Emmy assumed that it was some kind of rule of nature that when two people in a romance novel went on a picnic, the weather would cooperate. Unless, she supposed, those two people needed a reason to kiss passionately—then it would rain so they would have to rush to the car and make out, soaking wet, while the rain drumming on the roof provided appropriate mood and ambience. But she and Will had already gotten the passionate kiss part out of the way, so the sun was shining. A few puffy white clouds drifted over them, borne by the gentle breeze. They found a quiet little patch of grass, spread out the blanket Will had snagged from a pile of clean laundry, and made sandwiches. They drank lukewarm soda/pop and ate two dozen varieties of candy while they played board games.

"Oh my God, I lost my E!"

"What?"

Emmy began searching the blanket, her lap, under her feet. "I had an E! I was going to put 'pearl' on that double word score. Where'd it go?"

"Hold on, I got you." Will pulled out his keys, found Gordon. He turned the little flashlight on and shined it around where Emmy was sitting.

"There you are!" She scooped the tile up from where it had been hiding, obscured by the shadow of her tile tray. "I must have bumped my letters at some point. I didn't even see it run away."

Will put his keys back in his pocket. "I don't know why I helped you when you're kicking my ass. I should've made you take a lost letter penalty."

"Too late now. Take that!" She put her E, A, R, and L down, using the P from his previous play: CLAP. "Fourteen points for me."

"No one likes a sore winner."

"Don't sulk. You beat me at Battleship."

"Only because you clustered three of your boats in one corner," Will pointed out.

"It worked for a while."

Will tallied her points, then fiddled with his letters. "I'd kill for a T or an S right now."

"Want to trade? I'd give you an A and an S for a D or a G."

"That's not allowed, is it?"

Emmy shrugged. "That's how we always did it."

She hadn't meant to bring up her family's house rules, but it had come out before she'd thought better of it. Now she couldn't help but remember all the times she had spent days exactly like this one with them. How she and May had joked that Japanese Scrabble would be way too easy since a ton of words were only one or two characters long.

"When did the Scrabble picnic tradition start?" Will asked.

"I don't even remember. We liked to play board games as a family. I think we were all feeling cooped up after a particularly long winter, and my mom just kind of suggested the idea out of the blue. It was the first warm day we'd seen in a long time. May and I helped my dad make bento boxes, and we packed up the car and drove to the park."

"Sounds fun. I'd like to meet them."

"You will," she said with conviction. "You absolutely will."

"I believe you."

She wasn't sure if he did, but she appreciated him saying it. He wanted her to feel better, and she did when he agreed to trade his G for her A and S. Even when he used the tiles she'd given him to earn a good chunk of points by playing FLAYS and using the S to simultaneously turn PEARL into PEARLS.

"What would you name a landscaping company if you had one?" he asked suddenly.

"I've never really thought about it before." No, it was time to come clean with him… and herself. She sighed. "I never *let* myself think about it before. Too… intimidating."

"You can think about it now," Will told her. "What happens in the romance novel stays in the romance novel. What would be a good name? Would you just call it Emmy's? Or Miura's?"

"Nah. I understand why Grabby's dad named the store Grabby's, but I don't think people should name their businesses after themselves unless their name means something to other people. Nothing against… what was it? Peggy's Diner. I'm thinking about SEO mostly. You want your stuff to come up on Google, so it has to be memorable and fairly unique."

"For someone who hasn't thought about this, you sure know your stuff."

She hesitated before answering. "I took some business courses in college, and I had to do projects and stuff. Sometimes I would use a landscape design business as the basis for a project. That was about as close as I could get to the idea without freaking out. I didn't even name the fake business because then it felt too real."

"I didn't mean to put you on the spot," Will said apologetically. "If it's meant to be, I'm sure a name will come to you."

"Yeah, I don't know. I think I spent most of my life waiting for some big lightbulb moment that would give me instant insight into my calling and how to go about achieving it. It gets tiring after a while, waiting around with a broken bulb floating over your head."

Will's keys jingled as he retrieved them once more. Leaning over, he turned on Gordon and shined him down on top of her head. "Don't be sad, Emmy. Gordon believes in you."

Emmy pressed a hand over her mouth and shook her head as she looked at Will. "How do you make being a dork look so sexy?"

"It's a gift."

He turned off the flashlight and dropped his keys onto the blanket beside him. Emmy looked at the little flashlight and immediately recognized the sensation that rolled over her, despite never having felt it before.

"Lightbulb," she whispered.

"Hm?"

"Lightbulb," she said, looking up at him in astonishment. "So *that's* what it feels like!"

"You had a lightbulb?" he asked. "Just now?"

"Yes! It's Gordon! He did it!"

"Way to go, Gordon!" He scooped up his keys and gave the mini flashlight an exaggerated kiss. "What's the lightbulb?"

"*Hikari*. It's Japanese for 'light.' If I named a landscaping business, I'd call it Hikari Landscape Design."

"That sounds… really good. I mean it, Em. It sounds professional and unique." He pointed at her. "Plus, when you get really big, you can always change it to Hikari Landscape Design by Emmy Miura."

"Oh man, that sounds good." Emmy sat back on her hands and looked up at the bright blue sky. For the first time, it felt real without feeling scary. She could actually *do* this. "I could incorporate kanji into the logo. I did some graphic design back in the day. Hell, I did some of *everything* back in the day. Will?"

"What?"

She pushed off the ground and tackled him. He caught her and fell backwards. This time, when she landed sprawled on top of him, it was her choice. She kissed him hard and smiled down at him. "I'm going to start a landscape design company. I'm going to make people's yards beautiful."

"Sounds great."

"Okay, picnic over. I win Scrabble by default. Let's go home so I can start drawing up a business plan."

"Hold on," he insisted as she pushed off him and began gathering tiles. "You win by *default*? I could have caught up. There's still a ton of space left on the board."

"Don't kill my buzz, Will. I win because I had a lightbulb moment."

"Okay fine, but I want a rematch someday where I can have my own lightbulb moment."

"Deal."

He helped her clean up their trash and pack up the leftovers. Together they made their way back to the car. She smiled over at Gordon dangling from Will's keychain as he started the engine. It occurred to her as Will pulled away from the curb and headed for home that those sexy Tarot cards had been right. This shitty situation had turned out to be the best thing to ever happen to her.

Because she'd finally had her lightbulb moment.

Because they *were* going to find a way out of the book.

Because she was falling in love with Will.

Twenty-Four

Will left her alone to start planning out Hikari and nailing down all the details, the to-do lists, and the technicalities. She sat cross-legged on the living room couch, a notebook in her lap, pencil working furiously to keep up with her thoughts. Every time she thought she'd wrapped up one aspect, she thought of a whole other facet that had to be explored. There were a hundred designs to think of. Logo, banner, website, business cards, brochures. Instagram and Pinterest would probably be her best friends when it came to displaying her work. She'd need to look into insurance, taxes, getting an EIN. Maybe she could work up to starting a YouTube channel with quick gardening tips and life hacks. A real YouTube channel with real advice, not the joke advice young Emmy and Sarah had once discussed. The memory of it made her smile.

Before she knew it, hours had passed. The sun had finished its descent beyond the horizon, and she had several sheets of paper covered with notes that she promised herself she'd type into a nice, organized document sooner or later.

She also had a few reject logo designs crumpled up beside her. Gathering the trash, she wandered into the kitchen to pitch them into the recycling bin. Will was at the stove. Whatever he was making smelled of garlic and onion, so she knew she'd love it. As she tossed the crumpled papers into the blue recycle bin, she noticed that it was nearly full of empty bottles. She stared down at them, then turned to look at the top of the refrigerator. Nothing up there.

"I dumped them out," Will said.

She jumped and looked at him guiltily. "I'm sorry. I didn't mean to notice... or... I mean..."

"It's okay that you noticed. I kind of wanted you to. I'm making a promise to you, Emmy. No more alcohol in this house. When we get to the real world, maybe we'll have a discussion about changing that rule. For now, though, I'm sober. A hundred percent."

"How does that make you feel?" she asked carefully.

"Good," he said. "I can tell it's the right decision for me, and I feel bad that it took so long for me to come around to it. How does it make *you* feel?"

She walked up to him and wrapped her arms around his waist, squeezed tight. "Happy and relieved."

His arms came around her and he returned the embrace. She felt warm and safe. The relief was still flowing through her, especially now that she could be certain his actions toward and with her had not been merely less-than-sober impulses.

After they parted, Will plated the chicken piccata he'd whipped up and took it to the table. Emmy took her time with the first few bites, savoring this man's otherworldly cooking skills, made that much better with the inclusion of the fresh herbs she'd planted—and labeled—for him. Will asked her to tell him about May's romance with Victor and the upcoming (or possibly recently completed) wedding ceremony. It was easy for Emmy to talk about, even though it caused her a few pangs in her heart. She believed firmly that she would find her way back to May soon. It was a sense of confidence that originated in her gut. Her sister would just have to have a second wedding when Emmy and Will got out of the book.

"Your sister is an optimist, huh?" Will said after he'd heard all about May's job, her friends, and the wedding she'd planned.

"Yes. Eternal optimist. Birds sing when she smiles and flowers bloom brighter when she walks by."

"That sounds like it could be... tiring, but I can tell from the way you talk about her that it's not."

"No, it's not. Sarah said something very similar to me after the bachelorette party." Emmy paused, remembering the party that seemed to be a lifetime ago already. She tamped down the worry, the sheer need she felt for her friends and family. "I can't say how she gets away with it. Maybe because it's so genuine. She doesn't put on airs or act cutesy for attention. It's just who she is. I used to think differently, but that was on me."

"What do you mean?"

Emmy thought about the wedding gift she'd set aside for May. It was something she'd been so nervous about giving to her sister, and now she wasn't sure she'd ever get the chance. *No*, she thought, and dug deep for that well of confidence inside her. *I'll give it to her whenever I get back. Better late than never.*

"May was always surrounded by friends," she told Will. "She was the type of person who was happier when she was around other people, but sometimes I felt like they were taking advantage of her, you know? So-and-so would call and bawl her eyes out because her boyfriend broke up with her... *again*. Then someone else would text her fifteen times in a row about... family drama or whatever. No matter what, she always listened, always made the time. If she hadn't made it as a makeup artist, she would have been a great therapist. But who could say if any of these friends would do the same for her, right?" Emmy looked at Will with a kind of desperate need for understanding. "People take advantage. Especially teenagers. They're all sociopaths."

"Sure. You have to be careful you don't give too much without getting anything in return."

Relief washed over her. "Exactly! Then, for her sixteenth birthday, my grandparents got her a gift basket with sixteen things in it. Some silly, some sweet. Makeup, of course. You know how sometimes people mention to one friend, one time, that they like elephants, and then for the rest of their lives, they get nothing but elephant gifts from everyone they know?"

Will laughed. "I know exactly what you mean. My mom has an entire collection of frog stuff that she feels too guilty to throw out."

"Right, you get it. So anyway... May's not like that. She loves makeup. She could have a thousand eyeliner pencils, and she'd still be delighted if you gifted her another one."

Will nodded in understanding. "Makes her easy to shop for."

"This is true. Since there was makeup in the basket, I thought she'd be all over it." Emmy took a moment to gather her thoughts. It still hurt to think about this. "She loved the makeup, don't get me wrong, but the first thing she went for was a Daruma. Do you know those?" She held her hands up as if cupping them around a baseball-sized object. "It's a little red guy you make wishes on. Well, they're not always little. But this one was."

Will shook his head. "I don't know if I've heard of that, but I am definitely interested in hearing more about the 'little red guy you make wishes on.'"

Emmy pulled out her phone and looked up a picture. She showed it to him. It was a hollow statuette of a head, mostly red, but with gold adornments painted on it as well. It stared out of the screen through two circular white eyes.

"Oh, I know those!" Will said, pointing at the picture. "I've seen those in a couple video games. I didn't know they were for wishes."

"Yeah, I don't know the origins behind it. Wikipedia could tell you. I just know the eyes are blank, and when you make your wish, you fill in the left eye with black ink. Then, when your wish comes true, you fill in the right eye."

Emmy turned her phone around, stared at the screen. She remembered wandering into May's room, seeing the doll on her shelf. Its left eye was filled in solid black.

"You actually made a wish?" Emmy had asked incredulously. "What did you wish for? To marry Josh Duhamel?"

She had expected May to blush and giggle like she always did. They'd had fun in the past concocting various scenarios in which they could "accidentally" meet the Midwest-born actor. Depending on their mood when they were inventing the story, they would either play it cool and get a quick autograph, or May would propose marriage on the spot.

But instead of the usual joking around, May shrugged. "You're kind of close. I wished for true love."

"Seriously?"

"Yeah, seriously. I mean... I wished to find it in the future. I'm not looking to get married quite yet. Not even to Josh."

Emmy didn't laugh. She just looked skeptically at the little doll head. Her sister had taken it seriously. She'd held that thing in her hand and made a wish. Did she really expect it to come true? She was practically an adult. What was she doing making wishes?

Emmy recounted what happened, absently pushing a piece of chicken back and forth across her plate with her fork. She wasn't quite sure if she'd properly conveyed the turmoil she'd experienced back then. The struggle to reconcile the older sister she'd admired with the fanciful young girl who dreamed of love and believed in wishes.

"It sat on her shelf for years," Emmy continued. She realized she was fidgeting and made an effort to eat her food, rather than playing with it. "Boyfriends came, and boyfriends went. She redecorated her room a couple times, too. But she never threw it out, even though she tossed plenty of other stuff. And one day... I got frustrated with her."

Will reached out and took her free hand. Didn't say anything, just listened. That simple connection gave her the strength to continue. She squeezed his hand once in thanks, then held on as she continued.

"She had a boyfriend in college. They were together over a year, which I think was her longest relationship at the time. Then he dumped her out of nowhere. I think he was probably juggling a couple girlfriends, but that's just speculation. I'd only met him a couple times. Didn't strike me as particularly interesting, but May was googly eyed over him."

The breakup had hit hard. May had been devastated, Emmy remembered. She'd come home from college that weekend to sit in her room and cry. Emmy was in college, too, at the time, but she had stayed local. Since she was still living at home, she had been there to sit on May's bed with her, holding her. She'd comforted her sister through breakups before, but this one was more intense. She could feel it. Emmy expected May to spend the whole weekend curled up in bed. She wouldn't have blamed her sister for blowing off a day or two of classes just to wallow.

But May was up early the next morning. Emmy found her eating cereal and reading something on her phone.

"Hey. How are you feeling?"

May smiled. Her eyes were still a little red from crying, and she hadn't yet worked her magic to cover up the evidence. "I'm okay. Thank you for being with me last night. I know it wasn't pretty."

"Breakups are hard." Emmy had been through only one herself at that point, and it hadn't been devastating so much as annoying, but she didn't mention that. "You'll get through it in time."

"I'm through the worst of it already," May told her. "He wasn't the one. I'm glad I know that now." She shrugged, went back to her phone.

Emmy felt something boiling up inside her. This was how it always went. May went through a bad breakup, cried for a day, then shook it off like it wasn't a big deal. Whenever Emmy asked her about it, she always responded with some variation of that line.

He wasn't my "It."

I tried to love him, but I clearly didn't.

He wasn't the one.

"You're deluding yourself." The words were out before she could call them back.

"What?" May looked up from her phone again.

"It's been *one day*, May. Why aren't you letting yourself feel?"

Keeping her eyes on Emmy's, May set her phone facedown on the table, her spoon in her half-empty bowl. Her expression was a little befuddled, but revealed nothing else about what she was thinking. "What do you mean?"

"You can't just pretend that you're not hurt by what Kayden did. You can't bottle it up like that. It's okay to be sad for two fucking days when a year-long relationship ends. Hell, you could go nuts and be sad for three days!"

"I'm not bottling anything up. Kayden did me a favor. Why would I want to stay with someone who doesn't want me? Yes, it hurt. But it also set me free."

Emmy ran her hands through her hair. "I'm not saying you should have stayed with him. I'm saying you're either repressing a whole lot of negative feelings, or you're moving on really quickly because you're on this endless quest for true love and believe Prince Charming is going to prance into your life any second. Either way, it's not healthy. It's not... reality."

May folded her hands on the table, met Emmy's gaze levelly. She didn't yell back, and that somehow made it worse. "I wouldn't say I'm waiting for Prince Charming. I'm just waiting for the right person. Someone who loves me wholly and completely. People fall in love every day. Why does it bother you that I want that for myself?"

"Because you're not letting yourself feel grief! Because you're going to throw yourself into the next relationship just as wholeheartedly as you did the last three. You're going to keep giving and giving and giving, May, until there's nothing left of you. All because... what? You believe a wish you made on your sixteenth birthday is going to come true? What kind of fairy tale do you think you live in?"

May got up from the table and went to rinse her cereal bowl. Emmy could still see the look on her face as she'd turned away. It wasn't sadness or anger she'd seen there. It had been pity. Maybe that was the part that had rankled the most, but Emmy had convinced herself that she was only feeling frustrated because she hadn't gotten through to her sister at all.

"She left Sunday night to get back to Duluth," Emmy told Will. Appetite gone, she set her fork down and sipped at her diet pop. "As soon as she was gone, I went into her room and took the Daruma. I don't know when I convinced myself that this little toy was the source of all May's misery, but it felt like it at the time. Maybe because it was always in plain view whenever May was crying over the end of one of her relationships. I don't know." Emmy shrugged, drew lines in the condensation on her glass. "When she next came home, she noticed it was missing immediately. I honestly thought she wouldn't notice at all, or it would take her a while. But it was instant. She asked me where it was." Emmy took a deep breath, let it out again. Her voice was thick with tears when she admitted, "I told her I threw it out."

"Did you?" Will asked.

Emmy shook her head. "I couldn't. Even though I told myself it was for the best, that I was doing the right thing for my sister, I couldn't bring myself to throw it away. I hid it in my room. But I told her it was long gone. In the garbage. The way she looked at me... I want to call it ironic. It feels ironic." She looked up at Will, her eyes full of remembered pain. "In that moment, I realized she had been telling the truth all along. She hadn't been bottling anything up. She hadn't needed more than a day or two to get over her exes. Not one of them had ever broken her heart. The only time I saw her look really, truly heartbroken... was when I told her I'd thrown out her wish." When her voice broke, Emmy fisted her hands, willed back tears. None of that now.

"Why didn't you give it back?" Will asked. There was no reprimand in his tone, only curiosity.

"I wanted to give it back to her a million times, but I didn't know if she would get angry at me all over again. And I hated the idea of admitting that I'd lied." Her lips turned up in a humorless smile. "I probably hated the idea of being wrong even more than that. I can be a little prideful at times." Her expression fell again. "The more time passed, the harder it became to think about giving it back. I did apologize, though. I drove out to her dorm to apologize to her in person. She forgave me, of course." Emmy shook her head, smiled again. With affection this time. "That's May for you."

"You're going to give it back to her now," Will said. "Wedding present?"

Emmy's eyebrows ticked up in surprise. "Maybe you're psychic, too. You got it. I was thinking of giving it to her sometime before the wedding. Maybe after the rehearsal dinner, when I could get her alone for a private chat. That was my plan, anyway." His hand was still on hers, warm and comforting. "Her wish came true. The least I can do is give her the chance to fill in the other eye. Hopefully she doesn't throw it at me instead."

"She won't."

"No, she won't. You've got a good sense of her already, huh?"

"You paint a pretty clear picture," Will said.

"Having her in my life... her and Sarah... it was all I ever needed. They were my two-person support system. I knew I could count on them without fail, and I recognized from a young age how valuable that was." Emmy felt Will squeeze her hand. She placed her free hand on top of his. "You'll like them. I can't wait for you to meet them."

She didn't miss his quick wince. He still didn't think he was getting out of the book. That was fine. Emmy was going to pull a May and be optimistic and positive until he had no choice but to get on board.

With dinner over, Emmy figured she'd take care of cleaning up as a way of thanking him. Not only had he cooked a fabulous meal, but he hadn't batted an eye when she'd failed to finish it due to emotional upheaval. It had hurt her heart to remember how she'd gone at May all those years ago, but she hoped the pain would remind her not to jump to so many conclusions in the future. At nineteen, she had felt like a proper adult who had already accumulated all the wisdom the world had to offer. Nearly a decade later, she could admit that she'd been a kid, and she had lashed out from worry. If the road to Hell was indeed paved with good intentions, plenty of hers were plastered on there with everyone else's. Though she hoped hers at least looked pretty. Paving stones were her specialty, after all.

Will was sitting on the couch unabashedly looking over her notes when she left the kitchen.

"Hey! Those are top secret." Emmy sat down next to him and snatched the notebook out of his hand.

"Top secret or not, it looks good," he told her. "I like the logo."

"It's a work in progress, but I know what I'm going for." Emmy let out a breath, savoring the words. "Finally," she added quietly. "I finally know what I'm going for."

"I'm glad."

Emmy sat back with the notebook resting on her lap. "You helped me get to this point. I won't forget it."

Will looked at her with an unreadable expression, then shifted a little, angling his body toward her. "Answer a question for me. Hypothetically."

She matched his position and placed her hands flat on top of the notebook. "Okay."

"Say I was the hero in a romantic book…"

"You *are* the hero in a romantic book."

Will groaned. "Yeah, I guess. But I don't want to be." He waved a hand in the air before she could speak again.

"Okay. Reset. Say I wanted to *act* like the hero in a romantic book. Hypothetically, what would I do to woo the heroine into having sex with me?" He reached out to toy with her fingers, and his eyes met hers. "Hypothetically."

"Wait… just checking… did you want this to be a hypothetical question?"

He chuckled. "Yes. It's hypothetical."

Emmy's heart raced. He was only touching her fingers, but her whole body reacted. Determined to play it cool, she raised an eyebrow. "Just asking out of curiosity?"

"Yeah." He maintained a straight face, keeping his expression politely interested. She gave him points for that. "I'm trying to share your interests. Get to know you better. That's all."

"Well," she said, watching his index finger journey over her thumb, to her wrist, and back again. Her nerve endings felt like they were sparkling at the contact. "First of all, you wouldn't call it 'sex.' You'd call it 'making love.'"

It was clear to her that the disgusted sound he made in that moment was completely involuntary. He tried to school his expression back to what it was, but his lip stayed stubbornly curled.

"Any um… alternatives to that?"

Emmy tried to look contrite as she shook her head. "Sorry. I don't make the rules."

He let out a put-upon sigh. "Okay, how would I go about convincing the heroine of a romance novel to…" He paused, grimaced. "… make love with me."

Her libido was all for putting the poor guy out of his misery and telling him she was already raring to go. But teasing him was proving to be fun, too. Decisions, decisions.

"Grand romantic gesture," she said.

His expression turned speculative. "Like... I hire a band to stand outside and play Elton John songs while I shower you with rose petals?"

Emmy stared at him. Finally, she managed to say, "I have so many questions. Why Elton John? Why outside? Can the band not go indoors?"

Will shrugged. "I don't know. It's always outside in the movies, isn't it? Kissing in the rain while the music swells or whatever."

"What am I supposed to be doing while you're dumping loose flower petals all over me?"

He contemplated the question. "Get naked, I guess. We can have sex... sorry, *make love* on the lawn while the band watches. If they miss a single note, they don't get paid."

She laughed at the image he was putting inside her head, and playfully slapped his shoulder. It was a good shoulder. A sexy shoulder. All strong and supportive.

"That sounds fun and... inventive, but I meant something like the Scrabble picnic. You were supposed to bring up the Scrabble picnic, and then I was supposed to pretend I'd forgotten all about it, and then we were going to agree you'd already been romantic so we could have sex." She pointed at him. "Don't say it."

"You were the one who told me I had to say it."

"Well, don't say it anymore. It's weird hearing it out loud. I guess it sounds sexier when you're reading it in a book."

"Yeah, it must." He ran his hand over her hair, stopped to tug gently at the ends. "Didn't you say you only ever went on Scrabble picnics with your family?"

"Yeah. So?"

"So... I don't think it counts as a romantic gesture. Not if you've been doing it with your family. Plus, it was your idea, not mine. I need to come up with my own thing."

Was he serious?

"No, you don't," she said quickly. "You don't need your own thing. The picnic was good. It was great. It can be our thing now. I'll tell my family to suck eggs."

"Nah, I can do better."

How had this gone off the rails so quickly? Had she really ruined her own opportunity for hot sex by choosing banter over sincerity? Blasphemy!

"Just to be clear," she said, "I am not asking you to do better."

"It's part of the rules. You said so yourself."

"I was joking. Or flirting. I was flirt joking." Emmy put her hand on his arm. His sexy, sexy arm. "You do not have to do anything to woo me, I promise. I'm wooed. I'm already there."

He narrowed his eyes at her. "You don't think I can do it."

"What?"

"You don't think I can be romantic."

"That is not true. You are so romantic," she said, a little desperately.

"That sounded doubtful. I think you doubt me."

"Will, are we really about to have our first fight?"

"No. Because I'm pretty sure we fought plenty before this."

Emmy groaned and collapsed back into the soft, welcoming cushions of the couch. "You're not going to let this go, huh?"

"No. I'm not. One, because I'm going to come up with something so romantic it'll knock your socks off. And hopefully everything else." He wiggled his eyebrows and Emmy snorted. "Two, because I just ate dinner, I'm tired, and I'm emotionally drained. And three, corny as it sounds, I want the first time between us to be meaningful."

Her heart turned to mush. How could she push back against that? She couldn't, of course. And he knew it.

"Alright, you win." She sat up once more. "What do we do in the meantime? More board games?"

"Maybe. First, I want you to tell me what you're planning for your business."

"Really?"

"Yeah, show me what you have so far. Take me through it."

She assumed he was using the readily available distraction to move the conversation away from sex, but it quickly became apparent that he was genuinely interested. Before long, she was fully immersed in her own plans, showing him more of her logo designs, the beginnings of her five-year plan, target audience, budget. In the back of her mind, she chastised herself for expecting him to brush her off. Those were the lingering effects of Andrew's influence, and she didn't want her ex anywhere near this place or this man.

Later, with the lights all turned off and her notes carefully tucked away in her room, Emmy lay awake and listened to the songs of insects outside her window. She couldn't tell how serious Will was with all his romance talk, though she hoped it meant he really did have romantic feelings about her. Maybe even love-type feelings. She knew she wanted to be with him soon, regardless of whether he could track down a voyeuristic Elton John cover band. To borrow a phrase from May, she had found her "It." In her own thoughts, she was able to admit that she wanted to make love with him.

She drifted off to sleep imagining his hands on her.

Twenty-Five

Emmy woke feeling energized and optimistic for the first time in weeks. Maybe years. She was riding high on that gut feeling that everything was going to work out, that she and Will would be together, that she would see her family again soon. There were three texts waiting for her, two from Will, one from his mother. She checked them while she brushed her teeth.

First, from Will:

Ive left you for my mistress Alessandrica we are moving to Tahiti to weave baskets and MAKE LOVE you can have the house

And then...

(jk bbs)

Emmy laughed to herself, spat toothpaste foam into the sink. The text from Will's mother contained more exclamation points and emojis than were strictly necessary. She and Bill were ready to go ahead with the landscaping, and they had the deposit check ready for her.

In that moment, Emmy didn't care that Will's parents weren't real or that she was in a book. Her heart skipped a beat. Pure pleasure swept through her.

This was what it could feel like. This could be her reality.

She found she was finally ready to *make* it reality.

Joanna's text concluded by saying she'd asked Will to swing by and pick up the check.

Aha.

So that explained his trip to "Tahiti."

After sending a quick response to Joanna telling her she'd get started right away, Emmy went to Will's office to begin researching native plants. Just because she intended to escape the book didn't mean she couldn't continue to practice being a business owner, right? A slight twinge of guilt dampened her mood. Was it really fair to ask Will to leave his parents? Wouldn't he miss them? What about Jared? His job?

Wouldn't taking him with her simply reverse their positions?

Emmy shook her head. There were no alternatives. If she left him behind, she might end his existence. And she couldn't stay with him indefinitely. Not only wouldn't she live without her family, but she would go crazy knowing she could never be alone in public for fear of being flooded by meet-cutes.

They'd work it out. She was sure of it.

Happy. Energized. Optimistic.

Don't kill the mood.

She began making notes on pricing for flowers and shrubs. Most of these species were familiar to her; Massachusetts and Minnesota had fairly similar climates. Still, she found herself going down a rabbit hole as she researched. There was no way she was going to come across a plant called Joe Pye weed and *not* look up its origins. Who was Joe Pye? Why did he get his own weed?

Then there was New Jersey tea. Why did it have New Jersey in the name if it grew all over the place? Did they actually use it for tea?

Before she knew it, early morning had retired and midmorning had taken its place.

Was Will coming back soon?

She saved her work and wandered toward the front of the house. Maybe he'd gotten back already, and she hadn't heard him.

Speak of the Devil, she thought when she heard footsteps coming up the front walk.

Already prepared with a humorous tirade about his betraying her for Alessandrica and Tahiti, Emmy swung the front door open.

Paul, fist raised to knock, startled at the sudden movement. Emmy felt all the words dry up in her mouth.

"Wow, you sure know how to keep a man on his toes," he said.

"What are you doing here?"

"I wanted to talk to you. Can I come in?"

Emmy's "no" was wasted on him as he had already wandered past her. She left the door open, not comfortable shutting herself in with him. He'd be leaving soon, she told herself.

Taking a deep breath, she turned away from the door and straight into a face full of flowers. Sputtering, she jumped back a step. Paul held out a bouquet to her, one that looked bedraggled and... familiar. Emmy stared from the wilting blooms that hung over his clutched fist to the tangle of roots that dangled limply from the stems.

"Those are mine," she blurted.

"Yes, they are," Paul replied with a grin, and pushed the flowers at her again.

Emmy snatched them out of his hand and brandished them like a weapon. "No, you idiot! I mean they're *mine*! You pulled these out of *my* landscaping. What is wrong with you?"

She didn't care if she was irrationally angry over this. Those flowers had meant something to her. They were the result of her hard work. And he'd ripped them out of the ground.

Paul looked confused. "They're Barrett's," he said slowly. "I thought they were pretty. He won't miss them."

The sound that ground its way out of Emmy's throat was more animal than human. "They're *mine*," she repeated. "I planted them. You just tore up my work!"

"Oh." Now he had the sense to look abashed. Slightly. "They'll grow back, won't they?"

Emmy nearly threw the flowers in his face, but held herself back. Yes, they were a lost cause, but she wouldn't debase them further by flinging them at him. She walked over to the trashcan and laid them to rest properly.

"I want you to leave now," she said, her back still to Paul.

"Emmy, wait, please. I know I messed up. Just hear me out."

She turned to him. "What could you possibly have to say to me?"

Paul ran his hand through his hair. "Ah, shit. You're mad now. I didn't want you to get mad. I'm just… I'm no good with this stuff. With pretty words and romance."

Emmy felt a pit form deep in her gut. "I don't need that from you," she said quietly. "I have Will."

"Damn it, Emmy, I said hear me out." Paul grabbed her hand before she could evade him. She felt callouses and sweat. "I'm no good with words," he repeated, "but I can tell you that meeting you changed my life. I couldn't get you out of my head. The last time I saw you, I told you I'd wait for fate to bring us together again. But then I thought, why not take fate into my own hands? I came here to tell you that I love you. I love everything about you."

"You do, huh?" Emmy asked.

If he noted her sarcastic tone, he didn't comment. "Yes. You're smart and you're funny. I love your sass and your confidence."

"What's my last name?"

That gave him pause, but he recovered quickly. "Details like that don't matter. My heart's in it, Emmy. You're what's been missing from my life. I need you. I need your laugh. Your voice. Your beauty."

Emmy snorted despite herself. Her heart was pounding because he still hadn't relinquished her hand, but she tried to keep a level head. The man didn't realize he was bespelled. Technically, none of this was his fault. She wondered if she should start rambling at him in Japanese. Would that stop his tirade long enough for her to gain control of the situation?

"You're beautiful, Emmy," Paul insisted, clearly taking her earlier snort as one of disbelief at the compliment. "You've got all this gorgeous hair, and your lips… and I… it's just… you're perfect. Lovely. Exotic."

"Oh, for the love of…" Emmy took a deep breath, tugged experimentally to see if she could free her hand, but he held on tight. "Do not call me exotic, Paul, for fuck's sake."

"What? Why not?"

Don't bother explaining, Emmy, she told herself. *It doesn't matter. He's a book character. Just get this asshole out of your house.*

"Because I'm not a freaking iguana! I'm a human being! Just like you. Being Japanese doesn't make me some kind of mystical, inscrutable creature, and I refuse to be flattered just because you chose to call me 'exotic' rather than 'foreign'!"

Good going, champ, she thought sarcastically. *Way to rein yourself in.*

Paul blinked at her, a bemused expression on his face. She found she could finally retrieve her hand from his grip. She wiped it not-so-subtly on her pants, and then sighed.

"Paul, you need to go. I don't know how else to—oh, for fuck's sake!"

Paul had pulled a small, velvet box out of his pocket. Though he faltered a little at her vulgar outburst, it didn't stop him from dropping down to one knee. When he opened the box, she saw a silver ring with a diamond big enough to put someone's eye out. At the moment, she was sorely tempted to try it… on the man who was apparently proposing to her right now.

"Emmy, I want you to be my wife."

"No, you don't," Emmy said. She was surprised to find that she felt more weary than anything else.

Paul frowned. "I do." His smile returned. "See? I already know my line."

"Jesus," Emmy muttered. "Paul..."

"All you have to do is say 'yes,'" he told her, his voice filled with what she had to admit was genuine emotion. "Say 'yes' and I'll spend every day of our lives together making you happy."

He really believed it, she realized. She didn't know anything about him as a character, what role he'd had in the story before she'd popped into it. All she knew was that right here, right now, he believed he was in love with her. He believed they were destined to be together.

"Paul," Emmy said again, relief filling her as she heard the telltale rumble of the garage door. The cavalry had arrived. She just needed to stall for another second. With Will here, they'd be able to get the guy back into his truck and on his way back to his farm in no time.

"Emmy," Paul said, his voice soft. "Marry me."

In the background, she heard the door open and close. Still stalling, Emmy said, "*Watashi wa kurage desu.*"

"That was beautiful. What does it mean? Is that how you say 'yes' in Japanese?"

Emmy heard Will's footsteps. A second later, the sound stopped abruptly in the kitchen doorway.

"It's 'no,' Paul," Emmy told him, trying to keep her voice gentle. "I'm sorry, but I'm not for you. We're not for each other," she amended. "I promise you, I would never make you happy."

He started to cry, and that was worse. Emmy finally looked at Will, would have laughed at his expression—part bewilderment, part disgust—if the situation were different. Her eyes pled with him. Will sent her a look that clearly said, "What the fuck?"

But he went to help a sobbing Paul to his feet.

"Alright, buddy. Let's get you out of here. I need to have a talk with my girlfriend about letting strange men propose to her when I'm not here."

"You'll never love her like I do," Paul whimpered.

"I think I agree with you there."

Emmy watched Will lead the distraught farmer out the still-open front door. Their voices carried back to her, indistinct, for a minute. Then Will returned—alone.

"Is he gone?" Emmy asked.

"Yeah. I watched him drive away."

She sighed with relief. "Good."

"Yep. Yeah." He paused, then said, "Uh… hey. What the fuck?"

"I can't help it if I'm popular with single white men," Emmy said wryly.

"I think I heard you telling him something in Japanese. What'd you say?"

Emmy gave him a small smile. "I said, 'I'm a jellyfish.'"

Will let out a surprised laugh. "I should have guessed." He shook his head. "I can't tell if I should find all this funny or go follow him to his farm and beat the shit out of him. I've never beaten anyone up before."

"Don't hurt him. His broken heart must be painful enough," Emmy said, her lips twitching. Sheer relief had her feeling just a little loopy. She walked herself into his arms, and the last nervous jitters died when he wrapped her in his embrace. "Thanks for rescuing me. I guess things didn't work out with your mistress."

"What? Oh, right. I forgot about that, what with the strange man in my kitchen proposing to you. Why'd you let him in? Not that I'm victim blaming," Will added quickly.

"I didn't let him in. Come on, I'm starving. I'll fill you in while we eat."

She hadn't had breakfast. She'd been too caught up in plant research. It wasn't quite lunchtime, but she decided to put together some sandwiches anyway, telling Will about her morning as she did so. Will sat patiently at the table and listened to the story. By the time she finished, the humor had died out, leaving him frowning with worry. He was likely thinking the same thing as her: How much worse was this going to get?

"I wanted to take you to dinner tonight," he said slowly.

Emmy set his lunch in front of him and sat down with her own. "Why? Not that I'm complaining."

"I thought it'd be romantic. Maybe not grand-gesture level, but romantic. And kind of celebratory. I got the check from my mom. Thought that was worth a night out. But now… I don't know."

Emmy thought about it while she ate. A part of her was still in mourning over the dead flowers, but she knew she had to let that go. He'd only killed a few of them. It could have been worse.

"Maybe we should spend the rest of the day brainstorming our escape plan," she offered between bites. "If we still haven't figured anything out before we leave for dinner, we can brainstorm and celebrate at the same time."

"I actually have some ideas," Will said. "Sure you want to risk going out?"

Emmy batted her lashes at him. "With you at my side, Will? I'll never be afraid."

He laughed and rubbed the back of his neck. "Sure. Okay. Just remember the part earlier where I said I'd never beaten anyone up before."

"Nonviolence is sexy."

"It's gonna have to be. Have you ever punched someone in the face? When I was doing my ER rotation, I stitched up plenty of people who'd gotten into fistfights. It's not pretty."

"I have not had the pleasure of fistfighting anyone, and I hope never to change that," Emmy told him. "I'll just take your word for it that it's not fun."

They finished eating and fell into the easy routine of cleaning up together, just like a normal couple. Emmy smiled to herself. "Normal" wasn't a word she'd had a lot of occasion to use in the past few weeks.

Once everything was in its place, they went back to the table. Will took out his phone and tapped on an app.

"Okay, hear me out."

"The last man who said that to me ended up crying his brains out in a pickup truck."

Will shook his head. "I'll try to keep my emotions in check. Look, I downloaded a romance novel." He showed her his screen, where the book cover was on display. "Let's call it research."

"Research for what?" Emmy asked. She nodded toward his phone. "I've read that one, and I can promise you, you're not going to learn any new sex positions from it."

"What? No. I don't want…" He took a breath, started again. "You've read it?"

"Yeah, it's pretty good."

"Okay, that might help." He put his phone down. "See… I was thinking… what if you were right? What if you need a book to get you back out to the real world?"

"I tried that, remember?"

"Yeah, you tried books that were already written, but what if… we wrote our own?"

Emmy's lips parted, but no words came out. Finally, she managed to say, "Huh?"

"It's not the craziest idea," Will insisted. "If we can write a story… maybe *our* story… with the ending we want, maybe that will create a… a portal. Or whatever."

"A portal."

Will scowled at her. "You have no idea how you got here. It could have been a portal."

Emmy carefully swallowed the laugh that bubbled up. "Fair enough. Uh… have you ever written a book before?"

"No, but I've read books. You've read romance novels." He tapped his phone. "I'll skim this one, so I can get the idea. We can work together. Maybe that's part of it. We create the story together, write an ending where we both get out of *this* book." He pointed at the floor for emphasis. "Maybe it'll work. Maybe when we write the ending, we'll *live* the ending."

Emmy thought it over. He was right; it wasn't the craziest idea. Certainly no crazier than a sex psychic sending her into the world of a novel, possibly by way of a portal.

"Okay. Sure. Let's try it."

"Really?"

"Yeah. It could be fun."

Twenty-Six

It was fun, Emmy decided later. Just not successful. Not even close.

They'd laughed at each other's poor creative writing skills, nitpicked over details they disagreed on, and continuously rewarded themselves for their hard work with rounds of Scrabble and Battleship. Hours passed, and they returned to their document only to find they'd written about four pages. Not a single word of it was useable.

"I think it's safe to say that this has no chance of becoming a best-seller," Will said.

"I have to agree with you. This is pure cringe."

Will sat back in the office chair. "Now what? Do we keep trying?"

"Maybe we should write an outline?" Emmy suggested uncertainly. They'd spent a considerable amount of time on this project already. Evening was approaching. But she hated the idea of giving up. It had felt good to take action. "We can discuss over dinner," she decided. "You promised to take me out."

"That I did," Will said.

He took her hand and pulled her to her feet with him. Then he just stood there, his eyes on hers. Emmy felt heat ripple over her skin. She knew that look.

Slowly, watching her all the while, Will lifted her hand to his lips. He laid a kiss on her knuckles, turned her hand over, pressed his lips to her wrist. Emmy's pulse kicked up. She was sure he could feel it.

"After dinner..." Will said huskily, his lips brushing her skin as he spoke.

"Yeah," Emmy agreed, though she wondered if maybe there was a case for *before* dinner.

Then her stomach growled audibly, ending the moment. Will smiled and pressed one last kiss against her palm.

"Let's eat."

They went to The Bell & Whistle. He'd taken Emmy there once before on a weekend. There had been live music and a huge crowd.

This time around, a weekday evening, was much calmer. They found a table easily. That is, they found a table after Will stopped to chat with a half dozen familiar faces. It was a small-town thing, Emmy knew.

Their server, who appeared to still be shy of his twentieth birthday, came up to them a minute later. His eyes landed on Emmy, and he froze. She watched his Adam's apple bob as he swallowed.

"Hi," he said.

"Hi," Emmy replied, trying for a polite smile.

"Uh... drinks? I mean... do you want to drink?"

"Water for me," Will said, capturing the kid's attention.

He blinked at Will as if seeing him for the first time.

"Same here," Emmy added.

"Yeah, okay. Yeah. Water. Two waters." He scribbled on his pad, though Emmy hoped he wouldn't need the reminder.

After he scurried off, Emmy looked at Will. "First day on the job?"

Will shrugged. "I've seen him around. I think he's on break from college or something. You made him nervous."

Emmy wasn't sure if that was the case or not. She thought of Paul's proposal earlier that morning, not to mention all the meet-cutes she'd staved off when she first arrived. Will's presence was supposed to have fixed that problem. Was his effect wearing off?

She tried to shake off the feeling of foreboding that had crept over her, but she kept noticing little things throughout the meal. Any time a man came in the door or left for the night, they seemed to take a moment to look at her. Even if they were with a partner or friends. She saw more than one significant other give a reprimanding smack on a boyfriend's or husband's arm. Feeling itchy, Emmy shifted her shoulders. The hairs on the back of her neck stood on end.

When their server came to drop off the check, he remained standing at their table, staring silently. Emmy pushed the little paper toward Will, but kept her eyes on the nervous teenager.

"Do you want to go to a movie?" the waiter blurted.

"Not right now, thanks," Emmy told him.

"Oh."

Will, fortunately, had cash with him. He slapped some bills on the table and stood up, purposefully doing so in a way that forced the young server to shift out of the way.

"Keep the change," Will said.

Emmy scooted out of the booth after him. She didn't let herself look anywhere but at the door as they left, but she felt eyes on her back the whole way there.

Back in the car, Will took a moment before starting the ignition.

"That was... awkward," he said into the silence.

"Yeah."

"Not exactly the romantic, celebratory dinner I'd been hoping for."

Emmy watched another couple stroll out of the restaurant. The man—old enough to be her father—craned his neck to stare at her as he passed.

She shuddered.

"Will... we have to get out of here."

Though he took that moment to put the car in reverse and pull out of the space, the weight of his silence told Emmy he understood she'd been referring to the book, not the parking lot.

"We'll figure it out," he said a minute later.

He took one hand off the steering wheel, laid it over hers.

Yeah, they'd figure it out.

It was full dark out by the time Will pulled up the driveway. He hit the brakes hard before they made it to the garage. Confused, Emmy followed his horrified gaze. Her jaw dropped.

The front yard looked like a war zone.

Shrubs had been torn apart. Clumps of dirt, broken branches, and stray leaves littered the lawn and the front walk. The siding of the house was stained with splatters of wet soil. Flowers, ripped violently out of the earth, lay like corpses all around the yard. Emmy felt her heart break when she saw the birdbath on its side next to the irreparably dented watering can. It looked like someone had stomped on it.

And the wind chime. Oh God, the wind chime was in pieces. She saw them scattered all over the place as if each individual part had been removed and deliberately thrown in a different direction.

There was no doubt who was behind the destruction. He was currently standing, half in shadow, at the side of the house, grinding the heel of his work boot into a cluster of daffodils.

"Emmy..."

She knew Will was going to tell her to stay in the car.

There was no way in hell.

She was out the door like a bullet. Will called after her, but she ignored him. Rage and grief were a maelstrom inside her, propelling her forward.

Paul saw her coming. The glow of the car's headlights washed over his face when he turned toward her, revealing the unfocused expression of someone highly intoxicated.

"Emmy. I knew you'd come back to me."

She didn't think. She simply drove her right fist as hard as she could into his unguarded stomach. When he doubled over, wheezing, she brought her left fist up and struck again. Pain exploded in her hand, but it faded into the background of her consciousness almost immediately. Paul stumbled back, pressing a hand to his bleeding nose. His eyes were wide with shock and betrayal.

"Leave!" Emmy shouted. She knew Will was standing behind her at this point, but kept her focus on Paul.

"Why are you doing this?" Paul asked. "I love you."

"I don't care," Emmy seethed. "I don't care what you feel or what you think you feel. What you've done here is unforgiveable."

"Emmy..."

"*Kiero*!" she roared. "Get out of my sight! Go back to your farm. Grow vegetables. Get therapy."

"I'd do what she says, man," Will added. "I don't want to get the police involved."

Whether it was his throbbing nose, his aching heart, or his need to stay out of jail, Emmy didn't know, but Paul shuffled off. She and Will watched him leave. Since she didn't see his truck anywhere, Emmy figured he'd either walked all this way or parked somewhere out of sight. She didn't care. As long as he got gone and stayed gone.

Will laid a hand on her shoulder. "Go inside, Em. I have to pull the car into the garage."

She looked up at him as sorrow rushed in to douse the flames of her anger. "The flowers..." She felt tears on her cheeks. "He killed all the flowers."

"We'll clean them up tomorrow," he said. "We'll buy whatever you need to replace what he killed. I'll help you fix everything. Just do me a favor and wait 'til morning."

Emmy thought of all the damage that had been done. It hurt. It hurt so much to know what had happened, to imagine what this mess would look like in the morning. But... maybe she could see this as an opportunity to build something *with* Will instead of *for* him. Maybe it could be symbolic or something. Maybe... maybe she just needed to leave it, like he said.

Will brushed the drying tears off her cheeks, held her face in his hands. "We'll fix it," he told her. "I'll help you. You won't have to do it alone. I'll be the best landscape apprentice you could ever ask for."

She found she could smile a little, and it was a relief. "Okay."

She went into the house and sat on the couch, cradling her left hand in her right. It was a shock to see the bruises and swollen knuckles.

"Told you so," Will said when he walked in after parking the car in the garage.

"Huh?"

"Fistfights. They're nasty. Let me see."

He crouched in front of her, gently probed at the reddened skin. Emmy winced when he hit a particularly tender spot, then felt her heart melt into a gooey puddle when he kissed the hurt.

"I'm sorry," he said. "I wanted to make sure you didn't break anything. It looks like all you'll need is some antiseptic and an ice pack. Can you move okay? Wiggle your fingers? Bend your wrist?"

Emmy slowly took her hand from his and rotated it, bent it forward and back. She watched him watching her, wondered why it was so sexy the way he focused on the movements. Apparently satisfied, he nodded, then took her right hand and helped her to her feet.

When Emmy looked up at him, Will simply forgot to breathe. Her brown eyes glistened with lingering tears, her expression soft and open. She was the most beautiful woman he'd ever seen. Then she wrapped her arms around his waist in a sweet, simple hug.

"Thank you for taking care of my hand," she said quietly.

"You're welcome."

He tried not to analyze the fact that one hug from her had left him almost astonishingly aroused. *Bad timing*, he told himself firmly. *Do not think about fucking her.*

Crap, now he was thinking about fucking her.

He redoubled his efforts to think about something—*anything*—other than sex. Then she pressed a kiss to his chest, right over his heart. Oh, man, he was already hard and there was no way she didn't feel it.

"Is that a penis in your pocket or are you just happy to see me?" she murmured.

Might as well own up to it since she didn't sound particularly appalled. "I guess my body thought that tending to your bruised knuckles counted as a grand romantic gesture."

"You know what?" she said after a brief pause. "It absolutely did." Her hand slid, feather-light, down his spine, then up again. "What do you think? Will it aggravate my injury further if we…" She dipped her fingers under the waistband of his pants and ran her nails over his skin. Slowly. Slowly. Back and forth. "… make love?"

Will didn't have it in him to laugh or continue the banter. Her skin was so soft. Her hands so busy. He was pretty sure she was trying to kill him. She pulled back a little to look at him as her fingers slid to the button of his jeans. "I'm going to take your silence as consent." In two quick motions, she undid the button and slid the zipper down. Her eyes stayed on his. "I need you, Will. Plain and simple. I'm glad you're on the same page."

Will let her push his shirt up, helped her lift it off him. She trailed kisses over his bare chest while her hands explored him. He could barely breathe, her touch was so sweet. Her fingers trailed fire over his skin. Then they snuck down again, slipped beneath the waistband of his boxers. With an oath, he scooped his hands through all that thick hair, grabbed hold, and took her mouth in a hard, hot kiss. He forgot to be gentle. Forgot to slowly caress and seduce. He was starving for her. Her hands left him—a brief disappointment—until he saw that she was moving to take off her own shirt. He parted from her long enough to help her with it, his movements frenzied and a little clumsy. She was in his blood, in his lungs, in his head, in his heart.

Her head fell back as Will trailed his mouth trailed from her lips to her neck. Her shirt hit the floor, followed quickly by her bra, and then his thumbs found her nipples. They circled and teased while he nibbled on the sensitive skin at the base of her neck. Heat gathered inside of him at the sound of her soft moans. When her eyes, glazed with passion, found his again, he lifted her into his arms to take her down the hall into his room. He dropped down with her onto the soft mattress and, gripping her hands in his, took her mouth again. The kiss stoked the flames inside him higher. He'd wanted to try to linger, to make this time with her last, but when she began to wriggle and writhe beneath him, he couldn't wait any longer. Groaning, he released her hands so they could both work on removing the rest of their clothing. Within seconds, they were both fully naked. In the glow of the hall light spilling into the room, they looked at each other. Her eyes slowly made their way down his body. Then she gulped. Audibly.

"Oh. Okay. I guess I should have expected that," she said, her voice trembling with a touch of nerves.

Will leaned over her, nipped her ear, and whispered, "Don't worry. My kielbasa won't hurt you."

He watched the nerves disappear as she laughed. Then she was running her hands over his shoulders, his chest, his hips. His hands were equally busy as they raced to explore each other. Somehow, she ended up sprawled on top of him. She slid her hands over his chest, then down. His eyes shut involuntarily when she took him in her hand, squeezed a little.

"I'm going to need to test your size real quick," she told him. "You know, just to reassure myself that we'll fit."

Whatever Will had wanted to say in response died as she took him into her mouth. His hips jerked, his hands found her hair. There was probably a hotter sight out there than Emmy with her lips wrapped around his dick, but he couldn't think of what it might be at the moment. She was a woman on a mission, that was for sure. Did his eyes just cross? They may have crossed for a second. Okay, he needed to stop her now. Hooking his hands under her arms, he dragged her back up his body, letting himself revel in the feel of her breasts rubbing against him, her smooth skin caressing his. Then he rolled them both once more so she was under him, smiling up at him with such trust and affection that he lost his breath for a second.

Staring down at her, he felt his heart lurch with a quick but intense jolt of emotion, and he knew in that moment that, if he could have one wish, he would wish to be real for her. To spend his life with her.

Emmy thought she might laugh when he brushed the hair out of her eyes—such a clichéd romantic gesture—but she couldn't find humor in the situation anymore. Coming from Will, it was the sexiest move any man had ever pulled. Then his fingers left her hair and found her center, and all thought fled.

When he leaned down and sucked her nipple into his mouth, her eyes closed on the wave of sensation. Then his tongue got to work, moving in perfect timing with the fingers between her legs, and her sighs became moans. She could feel herself growing wetter, her body practically begging for his. He removed his hand, hooked an arm under her thigh to open her wide for him. She felt him position himself, but he paused, holding them both on the brink. Confused, and a touch frustrated, she opened her eyes to look at him. He was looking down at her, his eyes focused and intense.

"You'll tell me if I hurt you," he said.

Frustration fled. Her heart melted. "You won't hurt me, Will."

"You'll tell me," he repeated.

"Yes."

He went slowly, taking care with her. Her body resisted for just the first instant, then opened for him as he slid inside. The sound of pleasure that she made echoed his. His first thrusts were measured, gentle. She expected him to pick up the pace, but he held back, gliding in and out of her, torturing her.

"Will!"

"I'm here, Emmy. I'm here."

He released her leg so he could drop down over her. She opened her arms to him, embraced him, held him against her as he began to pump his hips in earnest. Faster and faster until her moans sounded like music and her entire body drew tight with impending release. Her nails bit into his back, her hips arched to him in welcome, and then she felt the wonderful snap as the tension broke, flooding her with the pleasure of release. Her eyes closed again as the feelings overwhelmed her, but she could still feel it when Will followed her over, his body going rigid, his muscles hard as rocks beneath her fingers.

Emmy kept her eyes closed even when Will collapsed on top of her, pressing her into the mattress. She didn't feel smothered, though. Corny as it was, she felt safe with him over her. Protected. It was her lizard brain that felt this, she knew. The big, strong man surrounding her, covering her. Whatever the reasoning, she loved the feeling, and made no move to extricate herself.

"How's your quivering flower?" Will asked sleepily.

Just like that, she was laughing again. Her arms were still around him, his body still connected intimately with hers. She laughed, and she loved, and she knew she would never leave him behind. And, knowing this, she drifted into sleep.

Twenty-Seven

Emmy still felt sexually sated when she woke, but not sated enough to avoid grumpiness at having the sun intrude on her slumber. Blinking her eyes open, she frowned at the window like it was responsible for all the world's ills.

Then she frowned harder. Wasn't that the wrong window?

She bolted upright in bed, her sheets—*her* sheets—pooling around her hips.

The window was hers. The bedroom was hers. This was her apartment. They'd made it back! She swung around to see if Will was still sleeping, but her heart dropped into her stomach at the sight of the empty space on the bed. Feeling desperate, she touched the sheets, ran her hands over them, trying to feel some lingering body heat. But they were cool to the touch.

"No. No no no."

Scrambling out of bed, she searched her tiny apartment for any sign of him. Maybe he'd woken before her and gotten out of bed to look around or search for coffee. The kitchen and her makeshift office were both empty. The bathroom? Silly of her not to check there first, but she'd been sure he would go for coffee first thing. She went down the short hallway and saw that the bathroom door was cracked open. She didn't hear any sound from within, but knocked just the same.

Nothing.

"Will?" She pushed the door open slowly, revealing another empty room.

She stood in the doorway of her bathroom, wearing her rubber duck pajamas, staring at the unoccupied shower as if Will would appear if she waited long enough. Somewhere on the street, somebody honked their horn. She heard the gentle swish of tires on asphalt and, a few seconds later, the distant wail of an emergency vehicle's siren.

Inside the apartment, she heard nothing but the frantic beat of her own heart.

She went back to her bedroom and found herself standing uselessly in one spot again. He wasn't there. The thought kept repeating itself in her head, but she found she couldn't process it. At no time in the last couple days had she really, truly considered the possibility that she would leave the book and he wouldn't. She'd had her doubts once, but they had been quashed when she realized Will was her true love. He was her It, for God's sake! They were supposed to get married and have babies and live happily ever after!

So where was he?

Maybe he had gone out for a walk. It was his first time in the real world. He'd definitely want to get a look at it. But... he wouldn't leave without telling her. At the very least, she knew he'd leave a note. Did he even have clothes? He was naked the last time she'd seen him.

That thought quickly led to another. She had also been naked when she'd fallen asleep.

Why was she wearing her pajamas?

A new and terrible thought entered her brain. So now the endless refrain of *He's not here* expanded to: *He's not here. And I was never there.*

What day was it?

She went to her nightstand and grabbed her phone. Her breathing picked up as the screen came to life, revealing that it was... Wednesday. The morning after she'd gone to sleep. She had lost no time. She hadn't missed May's wedding. She hadn't even missed the rehearsal dinner. Or a single shift of work.

She should be thrilled.

She felt like she was going to shatter.

Her eyes tracked down to the book. That fucking book. It was on the floor next to her side of the bed. No, she thought a little manically, not her side of the bed. Both sides were her side because *Will wasn't there.*

No problem, Emmy thought, snatching the book off the floor. *No fucking problem.*

She blinked back tears, imagined weaving a thick sheet of gauze around her heart to keep it from breaking. *Not a problem*, she thought again, sitting on the side of the bed. She cracked the book open and flipped through. She'd start over at chapter one. If she'd gone in there once, she could go in again. This time she'd find a way to get them *both* out. And if she couldn't find a way, well...

Emmy paused, her thumb holding the book open, and felt her breath hitch.

Well what? she thought bitterly. *If I can't find a way to get him out, I'll just stay? Live my life with him? Grow old together?*

Even if that were a viable possibility, she hadn't made it a full month in the book before one of the characters had gone absolutely insane. How long could she last before she was stuck in the house, afraid to leave or even open a window for fear of staving off yet another misguided declaration of true love?

She couldn't go back.

Her breath hitched again. The gauze loosened and slipped off her heart. Her lungs burned like she was trying to breathe broken glass.

She couldn't abandon her family, live her life in a literal fantasy world. Not even for true love.

He wasn't coming to her.

She couldn't go back to him.

The first sob broke free as she fumbled for her phone, and the book tumbled to the floor once more. She tapped May's name in her contacts.

May picked up on the second ring. "Hey, you. What's up?"

The sound of her voice made Emmy nearly dizzy with grief and love and relief. She pressed the phone to her ear, willed herself to respond. Her voice croaked on the single word she managed to get out. "*Onēchan.*"

Big sister.

It was an endearment she hadn't used since she'd been a child. She didn't need to say anything else.

"I'll be there in ten," May said, and hung up.

Emmy let her arms fall limply into her lap. She put all of her energy into breathing in and out. Slowly. In and out. No thinking. No feeling.

Not yet.

Twenty-Eight

Time passed in a haze. May didn't knock. She used her spare key to let herself in and found Emmy still sitting on the bed. When May sat beside her, pulled her into a tight embrace, Emmy felt herself begin to crumble.

"May... I can't..."

"Shhh..." May stroked Emmy's hair. "It's okay."

Emmy let the sobs break free. She keened like a wounded animal while her sister continued to stroke, to rock her, to make reassuring noises.

It took a long time for the tears to run their course. When they had, May gently led a hiccupping Emmy to the couch in her little sitting area. Emmy lay down on her side, feeling numb. She welcomed it after so much pain. May went into the kitchen. Emmy heard her clinking around, muttering to herself in a mixture of English and Japanese.

"Why is your tea never in the same place?" May grumbled, more to herself than to Emmy, but Emmy smiled a little anyway. Will would be equally frustrated if he saw her lack of kitchen organization. And that thought brought on a fresh tremor of pain.

"Emmy, *ocha wa doko*?" May called.

Trying to remember which random cabinet she'd shoved her tea into was a good use for her brain. It kept her thoughts off other things for the moment.

"Uh... try the cabinet to the right of the fridge."

"That's where I'm looking."

"Oh." She paused, tried to remember. It had been weeks, technically. She couldn't remember when she'd last had tea in this apartment. Which cabinet would be her next go-to? "Corner cabinet by the stove."

She heard May rifling around, then a kind of baffled, "What the..."

At that moment, Emmy remembered what else she'd stuck in the corner cabinet by the stove. She sat up on the couch in time to see May walking toward her with the Daruma cupped in her hand.

"Emmy... *kore wa nandesuka*?"

Obviously, May knew what it was. Emmy was sure she'd asked, "What is this?" because it was more polite than asking her emotionally wounded sister, "Is this the Daruma you stole from me back when we were kids?"

She wished she'd thought of a better hiding place. In no way was she prepared to have this conversation. She couldn't read May's feelings from her expression. She looked a little confused that she'd found a little red wishing guy in the cabinet with the tea. But what else was going on inside her head? Was she angry? Emmy didn't think she could stand to have her sister get angry at her now.

"It's your Daruma," she answered, her voice raw and hoarse from crying.

"*My* daruma? The one from my sixteenth birthday?"

"Yeah."

"Didn't you say you threw it out?"

"I lied. I kept it." When May said nothing, Emmy began to fidget with the hem of her ducky pajama top. "I wanted to tell you about it so many times, but I couldn't handle the shame." That wasn't it, she knew. She had to come clean. Be completely truthful. "I probably had more trouble swallowing my pride than anything else. Admitting I'd kept it meant admitting that I…"

Now May smiled a little. As if she'd read Emmy's mind, she finished the thought. "That you believed throwing it out would somehow ruin my chances at love?"

Emmy shrugged, feeling like her teenage self all over again.

When the kettle beeped, May set the Daruma on the coffee table and went to prepare the tea. Emmy stared at the little red guy. He stared back at her out of one good eye. He always looked so angry. Why should he be angry? He could grant wishes.

May returned a few minutes later with two cups of green tea and a couple slices of buttered toast. She set the tray next to the Daruma and sat again, taking Emmy's hand in hers.

"I need to tell you something," May said.

"Okay." It usually wasn't difficult to meet her sister's gaze, but she found it a little awkward at the moment.

"I know I believe in things more easily than you. I know you think that makes me naïve. Don't deny it!" she added quickly when Emmy opened her mouth to argue. "I won't lie. I was angry and hurt when you told me you threw the Daruma away. It took me a couple days, but I eventually figured out that it *would have* been cruel if you'd thrown it out just to hurt me, to try to…" May paused, searching around for the right words. "To try to deliberately crush my dreams, my wishes. It would have been cruel, and you're not cruel. Once that thought hit me, I was like 'Oh, duh. She wasn't being mean. She was trying to protect me.'"

Emmy tried to speak. Her lips parted. But words failed her.

May smiled, then, without warning, shoved some toast into Emmy's open mouth. Emmy coughed once, grumbled, and took a quick bite. At least it gave her something to do instead of fidgeting under her sister's knowing gaze.

"You've always tried to protect me," May continued, brushing stray crumbs from her hands. "You felt like you had to look out for me, didn't you, Emmy? Because you're not cruel, but you convinced yourself the world was. Cruel world; naïve sister. You thought I'd get hurt when I realized that Prince Charming wasn't coming for me, that I wouldn't be able to handle it. *Daro?*"

Emmy bought time to compose herself by taking another bite of toast, then washing it down with hot tea. "Yeah, you more or less nailed it."

"I can't tell you how loved I felt after I got my thoughts sorted out. I remember you came out to apologize to me. You apologized for throwing away the Daruma because it was easier than admitting you hadn't thrown it away. If you told me the truth, you'd also have to tell me why you hadn't thrown it out. You would have had to admit to having some fanciful, unrealistic thoughts." May's kind expression kept the sting out of the words, but Emmy felt sufficiently chastised anyway. May cocked her head to the side. "Were you planning on giving it back to me now? Because I'm getting married?"

"*Un.* Your wish came true. You should get to fill in the other eye. I was going to give it to you after the rehearsal dinner, but... you're here now."

Emmy pushed to her feet. She was a little shaky, but she didn't have to go far. She made it to her desk, noted that the cup she kept on top of it for pens was completely empty. She never did remember to put the pens back once she'd taken them out. It took a bit of searching, but she eventually found a permanent marker in the drawer. When she handed it to May, she saw her sister was already holding the Daruma in her free hand. Emmy sat next to her again and watched as May uncapped the marker and filled in the right eye. Something inside Emmy lifted at the sight. The Daruma still looked angry, but at least he could see properly now. May capped the marker and handed it back. Without looking, Emmy tossed it in the direction of her desk, causing her sister to roll her eyes and shake her head.

"I want to thank you," May said. "Seriously big *arigatō*. This is the sweetest thing." She looked at the little wishing toy, then got up to set it by her purse, which she'd dropped just inside the door when she'd first come in. She returned to the couch, sat down, nudged the teacup back into Emmy's hands. "I need to tell you something else."

"*Masaka!* You're pregnant already?"

"What? No! Why did your mind go there? No, don't answer that. I need to tell you that I enjoyed making a birthday wish when I was sixteen, and seeing Lucy for a psychic reading before I met Victor, but I didn't think that the course of my life hinged on those things. I didn't think, not even for a second, that you throwing out the Daruma put my chances at happiness in jeopardy. I don't even think I have Lucy to thank for the fact that I'm getting married this weekend."

"You don't?"

"No, Emmy. Lucy didn't make love happen for me. She basically just confirmed that it would, that I'd find my guy. But even if I hadn't seen her, I still would've found him. Because I lived my life the way I wanted to, and in doing that, I put myself on the path to meet him."

Emmy sat with that for a few seconds. She felt foolish now. Not to mention terribly ashamed for doubting her sister, for thinking May lived with her head in the clouds, waiting for life to hand her what she wanted.

"Why did you do it then?"

May shrugged. "It was fun. Like I said, I enjoyed it. Beyond that, I was… impatient, I guess. The older I got, the more ready I felt to put down my own roots. You'd understand about putting down roots." A small smile broke through her serious expression, and Emmy wondered at the fact that she'd never before noticed it was a duplicate of their father's post-joke smile. "I had established my career. Living the dream, in that part of my life. Ando is a great boss, and I get to do what I love every day. My other life goals needed to catch up, and sometimes I got frustrated or discouraged waiting for them. It helped to do something silly or impulsive every once in a while."

How could she have known her sister her whole life, but not known her at all?

"I'm sorry, May." Emmy borrowed her sister's earlier words. "Seriously big *gomen nasai*."

"*Dōshite?*"

"I underestimated you. A lot. I didn't trust you could take care of yourself."

May waved that away. "Nobody's perfect, Emmy. You're harder on yourself than you ever were on me. I'm glad we got that all cleared up, though, because I want to know what's wrong. Are you up to talking about it?"

It all came back to her at once, and her hands shook around the rapidly cooling tea in her grip. She didn't want to cry again. Physically, it felt like she couldn't produce more tears. She swallowed back the rising panic and heartache.

"I'm not sure you'll believe me."

May gave her a look. "Emmy... who are you talking to?"

"Oh... right."

She started with the visit to Lucy. It was surprisingly easy once she got going, especially if she pretended she was simply telling a story, a tall tale to amuse her big sister. She summed up the Tarot reading, moved on to browsing for a new romance novel, and remembered at the last second to skip over seeing the vanity set in all its glory. No need to spoil anything there.

May listened without interruption. Even when Emmy got to the part where she woke up in Will's bed, inside the world of the novel. May laughed a little, then sat forward and gestured for Emmy to continue, like she was excited to hear what happened next.

Then Emmy got to the part where she'd looked at Gordon the flashlight, and May stopped her for the first time.

"I guess I can accept he'd name a flashlight since it was from his grandfather or whatever, but why Gordon?"

"It's a reference to *Flash Gordon*."

May gave her a blank look.

"It's an old TV show from the eighties."

"Never heard of it. How do you know about it?"

"Sarah's uncle had it on DVD. We got a kick out of watching it. It's ridiculously cheesy. I never told you about it?"

"I, too, am shocked that there's something about you I was not aware of, but more interesting to me is the fact that this particular obscure show was referenced in a magic book you happened to pick up. Almost like it was made for you. Or Will was." When Emmy frowned at that, May added, "If it had been me, I probably would have thought he was a basketball fan or something."

Now Emmy wrinkled her nose in pure confusion. "Why basketball?"

"Because of the famous basketball guy. Come on, everyone knows him. His last name is Gordon."

Emmy let out a bark of laughter as she connected the dots. "*Baka!* You mean Michael Jordan?"

"Yeah, him! Wait... Michael *Jordan*? Oh."

Emmy had thought it would be a long time before she could laugh again, but as her sister's face turned red, and she began to giggle at her own mistake, the joy bubbled up. They laughed together, drank cold tea, ignored the remaining slice of toast. Emmy sat back against the couch and tried to pick up the threads of the story. She opened her mouth, and, without any warning, burst into tears all over again.

Then she was lying with her head in May's lap, sobbing until she thought she'd die.

"You fell in love with him," May said quietly, her hand rubbing soothing circles on Emmy's back.

Unable to speak yet, Emmy nodded.

"Do you want some water?"

Now she shook her head, got her breathing under control. "I need to finish it. There's so much more."

She didn't bother to sit up as she resumed the story. Once again, May listened without question, without offering censure, or judgment, or incredulity. Her lap was comfortable, and Emmy could smell some kind of delicate body spray. Honeysuckle maybe. May always had one or two scents in her purse. As well as deodorant, lipstick, mascara, a compact, cold cream, hand lotion, nail clippers, eye drops, tissues, and peppermints.

Emmy breathed her sister in and took comfort in it. Until she got to the part of the story where Will had encouraged her to try landscaping professionally, and she'd balked. She admitted now what she'd only thought to herself at the time—that Andrew had played a big part in her hesitance.

And May simply exploded.

Emmy jumped back as her sister sprang off the couch like someone had jabbed her butt with a pin. Hands fisted, May let loose with a string of Japanese that had Emmy's eyes going wide. She had no trouble translating, but she didn't think May even knew those words, let alone felt comfortable using them.

"That *cocksucker*!" she screamed, switching to English. She began to pace furiously. "That absolute fart cloud! I could kill him! I *will* kill him! I fucking *knew* it!"

"Uh…"

Emmy was so bewildered that her heartbreak actually receded, temporarily forgotten as May fumed and swore. Then she swung back to Emmy, perfectly styled hair whipping around her face, eyes blazing with fury.

"I *knew* it!" she repeated, jabbing a finger at Emmy. "We were all waiting for you to tell us you wanted to go into gardening… landscaping… something like that. Dad thought you were going to be a florist. He even suggested I talk to Ando to see if you could shadow Yvette," she added, referring to the florist who worked exclusively for Elegancia.

"Really?"

"Yes! It was obvious you had a knack for growing things, and you lit up whenever you talked about it. You didn't freak out when you saw earthworms or when you got dirt under your fingernails." May stopped, took a long, deep breath. "But you never went for it. Not a word from you. I always wondered if that asshole had something to do with it. I could tell something was off, but you never mentioned anything. I just had a feeling. I almost tracked down Beth to pump her for information, but she couldn't have helped. If she'd known he was a slimeball, she wouldn't have set you up with him in the first place. She's not malicious like that. A little… dim, but not mean. She's sweet."

"May… you just insulted someone."

"I said she was sweet." She ran her hands through her hair. "Don't tell Sarah, but I could tell Beth never clicked with you guys. I like to think we clicked. Not just you and me, but Sarah as well."

"Yeah, we absolutely clicked. Definite clicking," Emmy said quickly. It was true, fortunately, but she would have lied without compunction in that moment if it meant May remained calm. She'd never seen anything like this from her sister. It was fascinating and scary.

"I just knew..." May shook her head. "There was never anything I could point to, but I *knew* he was wrong for you. I felt so guilty when you broke up because you were hurting, but I was secretly glad to see him go."

"I never knew any of that. You never said anything to me."

May deflated a little. "Like I said, there was nothing to say. It was just a gut reaction. Anyway, it's done now. And I can finally tell you I'm glad it's done." She sat next to Emmy once more. "Tell me the rest. I want to hear all of it."

Emmy finished the story with no more surprise outbursts from her sister. The heartbreak crept back in, making some parts harder to tell than others. But she simply squeezed May's hand and pushed through until she'd made it all the way back to waking up in her bed that morning.

Her throat was dry. Her eyes were swollen. She felt like a dishrag that had been wrung out and left on the counter in a damp heap. Then May hugged her, and she felt the soothing sensation of being believed.

"Can I see the book?" May asked quietly.

"Sure. Just don't read it."

"No chance of that. You said it was on the floor in your bedroom?"

"I can get it."

May shook her head. "Go drink some water. Splash some on your face if you need to. I'll be right back."

Because she desperately needed to hydrate, Emmy didn't argue. She got herself a glass of water and downed the whole thing in one breath. Then she fumbled in the tea cabinet until she found a bottle of ibuprofen. All that crying had left her with an insistent, throbbing ache in her temples.

"Is this it?" May asked.

Emmy looked over, saw the unfamiliar cover, and shook her head. "No, that's... wait." She frowned at the book cover as May held it out to her. Then she snatched it out of her sister's hands. "What the *fuck*?"

The model who had portrayed Will was no longer entwined with Bright beneath the swirling script of the title. While Bright remained the same, she now gazed lovingly up at a Black man with a chiseled face and appealingly defined arm muscles. He looked back at her with equivalent love in his expression.

It was Jared.

Emmy flipped the book over, read the synopsis. Bright's section was, like the image on the cover, exactly as it had been. But the paragraph that had been dedicated to Will was now entirely about a divorced anesthesiologist named Jared.

"What the fuck?" Emmy repeated.

"What's wrong?" May asked.

"It's different. The book changed." Taking a risk, she flipped open to the first chapter and skimmed a few paragraphs. Different here, too. The narrator followed Jared as he navigated a hectic shift at the hospital. "It's not about Will anymore. It's about Jared, his best friend."

"The one who fell for Bright?"

Emmy closed the book and looked at the cover again. "Yeah. The one who fell for Bright." She looked up at May again. "What does this mean?"

"I don't know, hon. At the very least, we can say you definitely did experience something. It wasn't a dream.

The book is some kind of magic. I guess Lucy would know more. Do you want to go ask her?"

"I... yeah. Maybe. But..." Emmy squeezed her eyes shut. "I'm trying not to get my hopes up. If I get my hopes up, and I still can't get to him... May, I don't think I can go through that heartbreak all over again."

She felt her sister touch her shoulder, opened her eyes again.

"One step at a time," May said soothingly. "Do you have work today?"

"I..." Emmy let out a half laugh. "I don't remember. It's been weeks for me. I'm a little screwed up."

Clutching the book to her chest, she grabbed her phone to check her schedule. She did have work that afternoon, and would get off well after Lucy closed up shop for the day. She told May as much.

"Do you want to call in today? You're definitely entitled."

Emmy shook her head. "Better to have the distraction than sit around here noticing how empty my apartment is." She studied her schedule. "I have an evening shift tomorrow, so I'll go in the morning. I don't know what Lucy will say, but you're right that I should talk to her."

"Do you want me to go with you?"

Emmy pulled May into a quick hug. "I want you to get ready for your wedding. Be excited. Sext with Victor. Whatever it is you do."

May laughed. "Okay. Will you call me after you talk to her? I want to know what she says."

"That I can do."

May had to get to work herself, so she reluctantly left Emmy a few minutes later. Emmy stared at the book, was almost tempted to read it. Was Will in it at all? If he was, what would that mean? But she couldn't risk getting sucked into the book again. What if it tried to make her fall for Jared this time around? Best to leave it be. For now.

She focused entirely on her work. It was good to have something familiar as a distraction. In her downtime—and she had plenty on a Wednesday afternoon—she doodled ideas for Hikari. It was a relief to know that she still felt wholly committed to the idea of starting her own business. It was still a kind of wonder to her that her family had known all along. The one thing she took away from May's rant was that her family never doubted her, not for a second. They had talked about when she was going to make her career official and how they might be able to help her with it.

Two thoughts floated through her brain in quick succession.

God, she was lucky.

Fuck, her notes were in the romance novel.

She remembered most of them, fortunately. What did it say about her that she was a little excited about rewriting them with more organization this time around? She decided not to analyze it too much.

It was clear from the projections she'd jotted down on a pad of hotel stationery that she couldn't think about putting in her two weeks right away. In fact, she might do better keeping the day job—so to speak—for as long as possible. It would give her an income to work with while she was getting Hikari up and running.

It would have the added benefit of keeping her mind as occupied as possible during all her waking hours.

No room to think about romance.

The apartment was dark and quiet when she returned to it that night. She hadn't realized how accustomed she had become to having someone living with her, having a companion. Not wanting to think about that, she checked on her various plants, watered a couple. It felt like years had passed since she'd woken up alone in bed that morning. She was physically and emotionally exhausted enough to crawl into bed and fall immediately to sleep.

Twenty-Nine

Emmy let out a frustrated breath as she searched for a spare binder. She had to have one. She *loved* binders. Just as she loved the colorful tabs and dividers she could use to separate them into different sections. Yet a thorough search of her desk, her nightstand, and even some of her kitchen drawers turned up no binders, no tabs. It had been such a perfect plan. She'd spend the morning getting started on rewriting her notes, finalizing her business plan, organizing and color-coding everything. Then she'd go see Lucy. Then she'd go to work. Somewhere in there, she imagined she would take some time to burst into tears. But the main game plan was simple: Distract, distract, distract.

And now she couldn't find a damn binder.

The kicker was, she knew if she went to buy more, she would immediately find a million of them in the freezer or something.

Oh, well. She'd use everything eventually.

Emmy was like a kid in a candy store when she was surrounded by office supplies. It took a lot of self-discipline to ignore all the highlighters, the rainbow-colored binder clips, and the dry erase boards. She pretended she had blinders on as she took her small bundle of supplies to the front of the store.

There were a couple people in line ahead of her, and she couldn't help scanning the impulse-buy shelves. Just to have something to do.

That was when she saw it.

A small display of flashlight keychains.

Was this a sign? Or was she so desperate for a sign that she was ready to believe fate had sent her a flashlight?

Either way, it felt wrong to walk away without taking one. She chose the blue one.

By the time she reached the register, she'd named it Barry.

There were several people browsing the various displays and shelves in Lucy's shop when Emmy walked in. She was a little impressed that the store was doing such good business on a weekday morning. Lucy stood at the cash register, ringing up two college-age girls. Emmy hung back, waited for the transaction to finish. Once the girls had left, Emmy stepped forward. She watched in utter astonishment as Lucy's eyes filled with tears.

"Oh, God. Can you give me a second?" Lucy asked, holding up a hand. "I just need to... block some of this out."

Emmy waited while Lucy took a few deep breaths, blinked back the tears, and visibly pulled herself together. When she got the go-ahead gesture, she approached the counter.

"What happened?" Lucy asked, her voice quiet, and so full of pity that Emmy nearly teared up herself.

"I was hoping you could help me figure that out." She slipped the book out of her purse, placed it on the counter, and slid it across to Lucy.

"Is this the one I sold you?"

"Sort of."

"You didn't like it?"

Emmy studied Lucy's face, but saw no signs of deceit. She seemed interested, a little confused, but neither concerned nor smug. "I spent weeks inside that book."

Lucy raised an eyebrow. "Is that your way of saying you liked it? Or didn't like it?"

"No, I mean… I went inside the book. Or it pulled me inside. And I lived in there."

Lucy gave her a weary look. "Are you trying to mess with me or something? Are you that angry that I gave your sister a reading?"

Emmy stared for a moment. "You really didn't have anything to do with it. You didn't know it was magic when you sold it to me."

Lucy made a frustrated sound. "I don't have time for this. Do you mind?"

When she reached to take Emmy's hand, Emmy simply shrugged. Lucy laid a hand on top of hers, frowned, and then picked up Emmy's hand to hold it sandwiched between both of her own. Her eyes flickered back and forth, almost like she was in a waking kind of REM sleep. Emmy waited. Finally, Lucy released her and looked at her with shock.

"You're not—" She stopped herself, her gaze sweeping her shop, no doubt noticing there were plenty of people around to overhear their conversation. "You're not bullshitting me," she said in a hushed voice. "You went through something."

"What did you see?"

"I didn't see... not the way you mean it. I could tell you weren't lying to me, and I got flashes of some emotions, some images. I'm better at looking forward, not back. You really thought I sold you some kind of magic romance novel?"

"You *did* sell it to me."

Lucy waved her hand in a quick, impatient motion. "I sold you a book. I didn't know it was possessed or whatever."

"Is it? Possessed, I mean," Emmy clarified.

"How should I know?"

"You're psychic!"

A couple heads turned.

Lucy massaged her forehead with the tips of her fingers. "Do you have to be somewhere?"

"Not until this afternoon."

"Can you come upstairs to my apartment so we can talk in private?"

"Sure."

Lucy looked over at a young woman with long, black hair and a pentagram tattoo on the side of her neck. "Selene, I'm going to grab a cup of tea with my friend. Can you mind the store for a bit?"

"Gotcha covered," Selene replied, smirking a little.

Emmy picked up the book and followed Lucy to a door at the back of the store. Lucy unlocked it, allowed Emmy to walk through, then locked it behind them. They went up a narrow flight of stairs to another door, which Lucy also unlocked and then locked again behind them.

"Your employee definitely thinks we're about to have sex," Emmy informed Lucy as she looked around the cozy space.

"Yes, probably," Lucy replied. She slipped out of her shoes and left them by the door, so Emmy did the same.

The apartment was cute, clean, and homey. She had expected a lot of velvet cushions, crystals dangling from windows, beaded curtains, and maybe a cauldron on the stove. Instead, the decor ran to simple and homey. The colors were bright and inviting, the kitchen a little cluttered. There wasn't a beaded curtain in sight, and the windows were covered by standard-issue slatted blinds.

"I save all the commercial trappings of professional psychics to the shop," Lucy said in answer to Emmy's thoughts. It was unclear if she'd read her mind or simply guessed what she'd been thinking based on her expression. "Would you like some coffee? Tea? Pop?" She opened the fridge, scanned the contents. "Never mind. I don't have pop."

Emmy thought of Will teasing her over that word. Everything was going to remind her of him, wasn't it? For how long? How long would hearing people talk about soft drinks make her heart hurt?

"Maybe some water," she said quietly.

Lucy poured two glasses, brought them to a small, round table. "You're hurting again. I'm sorry." She placed the water on the table. "Let's see what we can see."

Emmy joined her and set the book down. She sipped water and tried to breathe through the worst of the pain in her chest. Lucy ran her fingers over the book, opened it, flipped through it, closed it again, laid her hand on it. Emmy focused all of her attention on that, on the surprisingly smooth and soothing motions, like a dance of hands, fingers, and pages.

"I do feel something," Lucy told her. "I felt something when I sold it to you, too. It was almost like it was alive. I started talking to it, didn't I?"

"Yes. I made fun of you for it."

"You sure did." Lucy paused to take a drink of water. "It feels different now. Still alive, but… sleeping? Dormant?"

"What does that mean?"

Lucy smiled wryly. "You're still waiting for my eyes to roll back in my head and for a thousand voices to sing from my open mouth, delivering answers to all your questions in terrifying harmony, aren't you?"

Emmy shrugged petulantly. "It would be nice."

"Sorry. It doesn't work that way. I'm psychic, yes, but I'm not some kind of all-knowing, all-powerful time and space wizard."

"So you can't help me at all?"

"I didn't say that," Lucy replied patiently. This time, when she put her hand over Emmy's, it was a gesture of comfort and nothing more. "I had to put up a lot of mental blocks before I could stand to be near you. You're not just hurting. What you feel is anguish. My heart breaks for you. I want to help."

Damn it. She was so sincere, so full of empathy and understanding, that Emmy wanted to weep. Again.

"Will you tell me about it?" Lucy asked. "I only got vague images when I read you earlier." She paused, smiled as if listening to a voice only she could hear. "You already told May. That's good. Would you mind going over it again?"

"It's a long story," Emmy warned her.

"I've got time."

She went through it much as she had done with May, but Lucy interrupted more often to ask clarifying questions. At least she didn't have any emotional fits over Emmy's epiphany regarding Andrew. At some point, Lucy took out her phone and typed into it. When Emmy faltered, Lucy gestured for her to keep going.

"Just taking some notes."

"Oh. Okay."

While she picked up the thread of the story, in the back of her mind, Emmy felt like she was at a doctor's office getting an evaluation. It was all very professional and clinical. That helped a great deal, as she was trying to keep her emotions out of it. Best to stay detached. She still had to get through a shift at work after this.

"It's clear that you didn't lose any time while you were in the book." Lucy looked back at it, tapped the cover as she thought. "You didn't read this version?"

"No. I almost did. I didn't notice it had changed at first. I wanted to go back in, go back to Will, but I... I couldn't. It wouldn't have been right. I just... closed the book. I left him." Emmy blinked furiously as the guilt ate at her. "I told him I wouldn't leave him."

"I think you can forgive yourself for that one. You didn't choose to leave him. He would have known that."

The words were true enough, but Emmy felt like the worst kind of traitor.

Lucy picked up the book and flipped steadily through the pages. "If Will is mentioned in here, even as a side character, he doesn't seem to come up a lot," she said after a minute.

"I see a lot of Jared, a lot of Bright. Maybe Will is here, but it would be very interesting if he weren't." She went back to the beginning, paused on one of the first couple pages. "Interesting dedication."

"'For you.' Yeah. I read it."

"It said 'For you'?" Lucy asked, her eyes laser focused on Emmy's face now.

"Yeah. I remember because I thought it was a little hokey. Why?"

"Read it again," Lucy said, and slid the book across the table.

Emmy placed her fingers on the page to hold it open. She read the dedication. Blinked once, hard. Read it again.

For someone else

"What the fuck does that mean?" she demanded.

"I told you the book appeared to be used," Lucy said slowly, like she was working out some answers on the spot. "I'd say you're not the first one who took a trip through it."

Now the tears that sprouted from Emmy's eyes were angry. "So it just... what? Sucks random, helpless women into a romance universe, dangles their one true love in front of them, and then yanks them back? Why? What's the point of that?" Emmy swiped at her eyes, then turned her glare on Lucy. "What is the goddamn point?"

Lucy didn't flinch at Emmy's ire. She simply drummed her fingers on the table, her head tick-tocking back and forth a little as she thought of how she wanted to respond.

"You'll get frustrated if you keep asking questions and I keep telling you I don't know," she said after a while.

"Especially since you've equated 'psychic' with 'omniscient,' which I am not. So let me hit you with all the I-don't-knows at once." She began to count on her fingers. "I don't know who wrote this book. I don't know if the book was ordinary once, and someone other than the author enchanted it. I don't know if the book itself has taken on a kind of sentience of its own. I don't know if the magic within the book is benevolent or malicious. Is that it?" She looked up at the ceiling, tilted her head. "I think so."

"You're saying someone did magic to the book. Like a spell. Abracadabra, wave the magic wand."

Lucy looked back at Emmy with a perplexed expression. "Not 'abracadabra' necessarily, but words can have power. Not waving a magic wand, but certain gestures or actions can take on great meaning. There are forces and energies in this world that can be tapped. It takes a certain amount of belief. Or faith, you could say. With that, some people can manifest things. Can make their wishes a reality." She raised a sardonic eyebrow, leaned her head on her fist. "You can't tell me you're still skeptical. Not after all you've been through. What did you think pulled you into the world of a novel? Too much salty food before bed?"

"Okay, yeah. Fair enough. It's just... a lot to take in."

"Let me ask you something. Did you really think there was only one psychic in the world, and that you happened to meet her? You didn't wonder, not for one second, what else is out there that you've never thought to believe in before?"

She hadn't, Emmy admitted to herself. It hadn't even crossed her mind that the existence of one psychic definitely meant that there must be others out there. She wouldn't admit it, though. Her pride had taken plenty of hits lately, and it wasn't ready to handle another one.

"There's something else," Lucy said quietly. "It's not quite an I-don't-know."

"Okay."

"I'm not sure why or how this book found you, or why it feels it is no longer for you, as the dedication indicates. But I find it interesting that Will doesn't appear to be in it anymore." She paused again, this time to let her words sink in. "If he's not in the book, I'd be interested to know where he is."

Hope felt more dangerous than heartbreak in that moment, but Emmy felt it swell inside her despite her attempts to remain neutral. "But he wasn't there. When I woke up, he wasn't there."

"That's true. You didn't manage to get him out of the book. I guess I'm wondering if he was ever in the book to begin with. Or maybe it's better to say the book character you fell in love with only existed because the book... took inspiration, we'll say, from reality."

"You're saying... Will might be here... somewhere. The real Will."

"'Might be' is all I can offer you," Lucy told her. "It's something you should think about."

"Why?" Emmy asked. "Why would it trap me like that? If Will is here somewhere, and I'm destined to fall in love with him or whatever, why not just let me?"

"You ask good questions." Lucy drank some water, the ice cubes clinking gently in the silence. "Let's go with a hypothetical. Hypothetically, you never met me, never bought the book, never fell in love with Will in a fictional world. You've been going about your life as normal, and today, tomorrow, next week, you meet Will. He's attractive and open to starting a relationship. How would you respond? Would you feel ready to take that step with him? To be vulnerable again?"

Emmy sat with that for a while, turning it over, trying to remember the person she'd been only a few days ago (in real time). If Will had reached out, tried to get close to her, would she have let him in? Or would she have run in the opposite direction?

"I guess it's my turn to say, 'I don't know.'"

"Something to think over, then," Lucy said with a decisive nod. "Do you want to keep the book? Or should I?"

Emmy looked down at the image of Jared and Bright on the cover. It wasn't her book anymore, apparently. It had told her as much. And she didn't see herself reading it. Not now, not ever.

"Can you keep it?" she asked Lucy. "But not in your store. Can you keep it up here?"

"Sure." Lucy scooped it back off the table.

Emmy stood when Lucy did, then felt her eyes go wide as a thought struck her. "Don't read it!"

Lucy laughed lightly. "Why not? What if I want to find true love?"

"I... I can't explain it. It feels wrong to have someone else read it right now because I don't know the ending yet. The real-world ending."

"I'll keep it safe and unread. Promise."

"Thank you. For everything. I'm sorry for the way I treated you."

"You're forgiven," Lucy said, and Emmy could tell she meant it. Just that easy. "Let me walk you out."

They went back down the stairs and out into the store where Selene was restocking a shelf of multi-pronged sex toys. Emmy swore she saw four prongs on one of them. That was too many prongs, wasn't it?

Lucy stepped outside with her and put a hand on her arm. "I hope you find your answers. I hope your love is waiting for you somewhere. But if you get frustrated, I want you to know you can come back here. I can try another reading. Pro bono, since the last one led to a little more chaos than I'm comfortable with."

Emmy laughed at that. "Thanks for the offer. May's wedding is right around the corner, and I'd like to concentrate on being happy for her. Afterwards, maybe I'll take you up on the reading."

"Deal. Enjoy the wedding. Tell May to come by sometime and tell me about it. I'd love to see pictures."

"That won't be a hardship for her. I'll tell her."

Work was gloriously boring. Emmy used her downtime to process her conversation with Lucy. She wanted to see Will again. She wanted to believe she would. But she hated thinking that her happiness depended entirely on whether a magical work of fiction was on the side of good or evil. Unfortunately, she leaned heavily toward the evil possibility. Hadn't the damn thing put her face-to-face with true love and then spat her out without him? And *then*, as if it hadn't already put her through enough, it had dumped her!

For someone else.

Not just evil, but rude. Childish. Petty. Conniving.

Emmy was still trying to think of more insulting words when the front doors slid open, meaning she had to put her customer service face back on. She returned to the front desk with a falsely cheerful smile that froze on her face. Her jaw dropped just a little and then she stayed like that, a deer in headlights. Apparently, the forces and energies in the world weren't quite done screwing with her yet.

"Okay... you definitely know who I am," said the blonde woman who approached the counter. "I don't know if that makes this easier or harder."

"I... um..."

Yes, she recognized her. Andrew's girlfriend wasn't wearing makeup, and she was in a comfy-looking black hoodie with her hair tied back in a messy bun. She looked quite different from the polished image Andrew had presented on social media, but Emmy recognized her just fine. The problem was, she had no idea what to say, couldn't fathom why she was there.

"I'm going to admit to the creepy part first. I stalked you on social media to figure out where you worked. Andrew wouldn't tell me."

"That's okay. I stalked him on social media, which is why I know who you are. I guess we're even."

"I'm not so sure about that, but I'll take it." She looked as awkward as Emmy felt. "Look... you don't owe me a damn thing, but I'm going to ask you to meet me sometime. Just to talk. I have a couple questions, and... it would ease my mind if you'd answer them. I'm sorry. I know this is weird. If you want me to go, I'll go."

Emmy found herself shaking her head. She'd expected a bitchy snob, and that had been on her. It hadn't been so much a women-hating-women thing as a presumption that anyone who dated Andrew had to be as bad a person as he was. She chastised herself for that. After all, *she* had dated Andrew, hadn't she? And she wasn't nearly that bad of a person. To prove it, she smiled genuinely at Riley—social media stalking had long ago provided her name.

"I'm off at eight. Do you want to grab coffee?" She thought about how most people didn't consume caffeine at all hours of the day. "Or... a decaf alternative?"

"Coffee would be great. Thank you. Sincerely."

"I haven't answered your questions yet."

"You're giving me the time. I'm already more grateful than I can say. Where should I meet you?"

"You know Coffee Fix?" Emmy asked. "They're open late."

"Yes, I do. Eight o'clock?"

"Make it a quarter after. It'll take me a few minutes to finish up my shift and get there."

"I'll be there."

She was there. Emmy decided to order a half-caf latte, figuring she'd feel less awkward with a drink, and also the ordering and waiting for it would give her time to settle. What could Andrew's girlfriend possibly have to ask her? That question had rolled around in her head all through the remainder of her shift. It was time to find out. Taking her drink, she joined Riley at the table.

"Thank you again for meeting me," Riley said.

"It's no problem."

"Okay, I'll jump right into it." Riley paused. Frowned. "Or I won't. I don't even know where to start. Or how. Um... okay, you know that I am seeing Andrew. He's your ex."

It wasn't a question, but Emmy said, "Yes."

"You broke up with him?"

"Uh huh."

Riley leaned forward, her expression serious and a little pleading. "Can you tell me why?"

That threw her for a loop. "You want to know why I broke up with him?"

"Yes. If you feel comfortable telling me."

"Why didn't you ask Andrew?"

"I did. Several times. To the point where he accused me of nagging. And I'm like... I'm like listening to my gut, okay? It's like... the topic of our exes came up, and I told him all about my most recent ex. I fully unloaded on him. Just—" She opened her hands and turned them over to mime dumping a heavy load. "I figured he'd reciprocate a little, you know? The funny thing is, I wouldn't have found it so important if he hadn't acted all evasive and stuff. He told me he'd been seeing you for a while, how you met, all that. But then when it came to the breakup, suddenly it was all vagueness. He said you 'wanted different things.'" She did air quotes to add emphasis. "I pushed a little, and he said you weren't ready to commit."

Emmy couldn't help the snort. Riley jumped on it.

"See!" She pointed. "See! Right there. Okay, so..." She took a deep breath, laughed at herself a little. "Sorry. I've been working myself up into a tizzy over this. The thing is,

Andrew is pushing for Serious with a capital S. And I am like… eighty-seven percent there with him. But my gut told me I shouldn't take another step forward with him until I knew more about you."

Emmy sipped her coffee as she considered. It was an awkward and strange position to be in, but she didn't blame Riley for wanting to know what went down. Andrew had screwed himself with his own evasiveness. She knew that he must have been caught unprepared by the question. If he'd known it was coming, he would have come up with a comfortable lie, and Riley wouldn't be sitting across from her right now.

"Okay. Here's what I'm going to do," Emmy said. "I'm going to tell you my side of things as objectively as I possibly can. And I want you to promise me something."

"Sure. Whatever. As long as it's not illegal. I'm aiming for a promotion at work."

The laugh was a surprise, but welcome. Emmy shook her head. "Nothing illegal. I want you to promise me that if, after you hear what I have to say, you decide it's no big deal for you, then that's fine. You promise that we can both walk away from this with no hard feelings, no judgments, and if you want to move forward with Andrew, you go for it. Don't hold back on my account."

"That's fair. That's absolutely, totally fair." Riley looked earnest and eager. Emmy wasn't sure she was the best judge of character, but she appeared to be committed to this. The question was, how would she react when she knew the truth? Despite what she'd said, Emmy realized she'd be a little crushed if Riley reacted with an, "Oh, that's it? Psht. That's nothing." Then again, she never had to see this woman again after they parted ways, so it was no skin off her back.

She told Riley everything, trying to include as much detail as possible without injecting too much emotion into it. She found it surprisingly easy to rehash. No lingering pain or resentments. It was what it was. No matter how Riley reacted, Emmy realized she was grateful for this moment. Without this conversation, she wouldn't have known for a long time—if ever—that she'd truly gotten over this part of her past.

She also couldn't help thinking about what Lucy said. The book had given her time to get to this point, hadn't it? She was fairly certain this conversation, this whole encounter, would have gone differently without her brief sojourn into the pages of a novel.

When she finished talking, she sat silently and waited. Riley stared at her, eyes wide, upper lip curled slightly. Finally, she took a deep breath, let it shudder through her, as if shaking off a trance.

"Ew," she said. "I was trying to prepare myself for some worst-case scenarios, and racism didn't even factor into it. Ew. *Ew!*"

"I know it's weird for me to say this, but I'm sorry," Emmy told her.

"No. No apologies from you." Riley dismissed Emmy's words with a flick of her hand. "You did me a favor. Seriously. Hold on one sec." She pulled out her phone. "I'm breaking up with this fucker by text."

Emmy let out an incredulous laugh. "Um... you don't want to think about it?"

"Not even a little," she replied, still typing. "Nothing to think about."

"What are you telling him? Would you mind leaving my name out of it?"

"No worries there, girlfriend. I'm telling him I've decided he and I want different things, so he should text me when he's out of the apartment so I can go get my stuff. There. Sent." She placed her phone screen-down on the table and reached for her coffee. She shook her head as she drank, stared blankly out the window. "I want the whole deal. The marriage and family thing. Whatever. But I'm young. There's no rush. Except sometimes I get so sick and tired of the dating thing, you know?" She looked back at Emmy. "I won't bore you with the details, but the ex I told Andrew about? The most recent one? He fucked me up. Now this. It makes me want to give up. Adopt a Jack Russell terrier, focus on my career, take up a new hobby." She shook her head again. "Sorry. I shouldn't dump all this on you."

Emmy didn't know who was more surprised when she reached out and took Riley's hand. "You can dump on me. Trust me, I've been there."

Riley looked down at their joined hands, then back up at Emmy's face. She cocked her head. "I guess it would be weird if I asked you to get coffee with me again sometime. Or dinner maybe?"

"Oh. Um... no, it wouldn't be weird. We'd certainly have plenty to talk about. Something tells me neither of us would have any qualms about venting about our most recent exes." Riley laughed at that and toasted Emmy with her coffee. "The thing is," Emmy continued, "I... I'm in love with someone." That seemed to be the safest way to put it, and it was the absolute truth.

"Oh." Riley squeezed Emmy's hand once, quickly, and let go. "Well, it was worth a shot. You're lucky. I'm so petty because all I feel right now is envious of you and sorry for myself."

Emmy studied her for a moment. "How open-minded would you consider yourself?"

"Well, that sure is a question. Not open-minded enough to consider any kind of throuple situation. You're hot, and I'm sure your partner is, too, but…"

Emmy laughed hard enough to draw the attention of nearby patrons. "No, not that kind of open-minded. I was wondering how you would react if I told you I'm in love right now because I paid a visit to a local s—*romance* psychic."

Riley snatched up her phone. She snorted in amusement. "Fucker is not pleased. Good." She swiped away a number of texts and missed call notifications from Andrew and opened her Notes app. "Where do I find the psychic?"

Feeling lighter after her chat with Riley, Emmy returned to her apartment with some new clarity and some semblance of hope for her future. Good timing, because the wedding was right around the corner. It was time for May to shine, and Emmy wasn't going to let any of her own bullshit intrude until the happy bride and groom drove off into the sunset.

After a quiet dinner for one, she pulled the things she'd bought earlier out of the plastic shopping bag. Barry went into her purse. She'd attach him to her keys later, if she remembered. With her new binder, her trusty highlighters, and an assortment of pens, she began the process of planning

Hikari anew. She enjoyed every moment of it, the planning, the number crunching, the color-coding. By the time she went to bed that night, she'd recreated most of what she'd come up with when she was in the novel, and even added a bit more. Plus, it all had tabs and section headings now. Much more official.

She fell asleep feeling more content than she would have thought possible only a day ago. If she dreamed, she didn't remember.

Thirty

The "rehearsal" part of the rehearsal dinner went smoothly. Emmy allowed herself to be guided, instructed, reminded. She smiled for her parents when they held up their phones to document it, pretended to hold May's bouquet while her sister pretended to get married. There was more pretend, more reminders.

They ate well. The meal was full of laughter and nervous jitters, inside jokes and updates about work, family, friends. They'd booked a private room in an upscale restaurant. Waiters passed in and out unobtrusively to deliver food and refill drinks.

Then, before dessert was served, two of Victor's groomsmen wheeled a furniture cart into the room. The vanity was covered by a lacy, white sheet. May's mouth dropped open. Victor, like Emmy, smiled in anticipation.

"What is this?" May asked.

"A present for the bride from the bride's parents," their mother said. "Come and see."

May rose to her feet, along with her mother and father. Emmy got up, too, because her parents had entrusted her with picture duty. She had her phone ready to go, and felt she did an admirable job capturing the look of utter joy on May's face when she pulled the sheet away. Then there were the hugs and kisses for her parents, layered with effusive praise and gratitude for the gift.

Then it was time for dessert and departure.

At one point, while saying her goodbyes, Emmy felt a lightning-quick jolt in her chest. Out of the corner of her eye, she thought she'd seen Will. But when she turned to look more fully, she saw that it was a stranger, a tall man with brown hair who was older than Will by several years. Not him. Just another patron of the restaurant heading out to his car. Emmy shut her eyes for a moment, pulled back on the pain. She chastised herself silently. It wouldn't do her any good to start seeing him everywhere she looked. That probably wasn't healthy.

When she opened her eyes again, she had a smile ready for her parents, who had approached her to finalize plans for the following morning.

The night flowed into day, flowed into afternoon. Emmy didn't remember eating breakfast—or lunch for that matter—but the nearly empty basket of pastries in the bridal suite indicated she'd probably gotten some calories in her at some point. Though she knew everybody who was in the wedding party, as well as everyone who was helping them to prepare for it since they were all May's coworkers, she still felt better when Sarah arrived. Emmy, hair and makeup already perfect, took advantage of the moment to sit on the plush, velvet divan with her friend and observe from a safe distance.

"She's happy. It's nice," Sarah commented before biting into one of the few surviving pastries. She washed it down with a sip from the giant Coffee Fix to-go cup she'd brought with her.

"She's in her element," Emmy replied. "Makeup, socializing, fashion. All her greatest loves in one room."

"Victor isn't here."

Emmy shrugged. "Fourth place ain't bad. He gets a participation trophy."

Sarah laughed and finished her pastry while the wedding whirlwind continued around them. Eventually, it was time for Emmy to slip into her dress. She approved of May's choice for her maid of honor gown. A simple, strapless design in pale green silk. The ruching around the bodice added both elegance and structure. Emmy waited while her mother zipped her up, then turned to the nearest mirror. Her hair fell in loose curls down her back. A simple, antique clip held it in place so that her face was unframed. There was no doubt the makeup was perfect; May had done it. She shimmered just a little. It gave her an almost ethereal look. When she turned back, she saw her mother dabbing at her eyes with a folded tissue.

"I thought you got all the tears out during the rehearsal dinner," Emmy said quietly, pulling her into a careful, one-armed hug. She felt like one false move would smudge her makeup or stain her dress.

"Those were rehearsal tears."

Emmy laughed and leaned her head lightly against her mother's. The photographer moved in to capture the moment, and she was grateful for it.

Finally, it was May's turn to get dressed. Emmy and her mother helped to clip, pin, and zip while the photographer spun around them like a satellite. When they were finally able to step back, Emmy felt tears of her own forming.

May was stunning. Her dress was also structured more around the bodice and hips, with the addition of delicate lace and floral appliques that wrapped around the upper part of the dress and fanned out at the back to run down the middle of the brief train. The whole dress glimmered with tiny sequins that mirrored the hairpiece she wore instead of a veil.

Emmy grabbed a tissue from her mother and dabbed at her eyes. If she smudged her makeup, May would fix it.

Then it was time for pictures, and Emmy was whisked along to stand and smile. Shift this way, shift that way. Hold the flowers like so. Tilt her head just a bit more.

Before she knew it, she was walking down the aisle, smiling for all she was worth, keeping her strides long and elegant, just as she'd been instructed. When everyone rose to watch May walk down the aisle, Emmy thought she caught a glimpse of Will's face again. Just for a second before he was lost in the crowd. She refused to be distracted. Swallowing down the jump of anticipation she'd felt—*it wasn't him, damn it*—she focused all her attention on watching her sister marry her true love.

The ceremony tumbled into a glorious reception in the hotel's ballroom. The chairs were decorated with green and silver bows. Ferns adorned with fairy lights acted as centerpieces. There was a screen behind the DJ station that played a looped slideshow of pictures of May and Victor. Emmy watched from her table as her father and her sister swayed their way through the father/daughter dance. Sarah sat next to her, picking the tomatoes out of her salad.

"Don't look now, but I think there's a hot guy two tables over who would like to *dance* with you," her friend said without looking up from her task.

Emmy was prepared for the jump of hope now, so she gave herself a second to calm down before she turned to look.

It wasn't him.

The man was attractive, and did seem inclined to let his attention wander her way more often than anywhere else. How Sarah had noticed him while staring at her salad, Emmy couldn't say. All Emmy knew was, if the guy was looking for a wedding hookup, he was going to be disappointed. She told Sarah as much.

"Why?" Sarah asked. "You're unattached, and sex is nice."

Emmy hadn't told her anything about Lucy, Will, or the book. Unlike May, Sarah was completely and wholly disinclined to believe in the supernatural. Until recently, Emmy had considered herself to be in the exact same camp.

"Sex can be nice," Emmy agreed, starting in on her own appetizer. "But I'm not looking to hook up at May's wedding."

"You're not still thinking of The Asshole, are you?"

"No. Not even a bit." Emmy was delighted to realize she meant that. Sarah had also unwittingly given her the perfect opening for a distraction. "I didn't tell you, but his girlfriend paid me a visit at the hotel the other day."

Sarah slammed her fork down, eyes wide. "The fucking chutzpah! Did you murder her?"

"No, but by the time we were done talking, *she* was ready to murder *him*."

"I am very intrigued by this. Hold on. Gregolas is here."

"What?" Emmy turned, saw the photographer, and laughed. She obligingly leaned into Sarah and smiled for a couple pictures.

"Okay," Sarah said when he'd gone on his way. "Tell me everything."

By the time she'd wrapped up the story, they'd finished their wine and most of the main course.

"Well, well," Sarah said, looking like the cat who'd gotten the cream. "I'd still prefer a more physical form of revenge for him. Just a couple broken fingers. Maybe some itching powder in his hair gel." She leaned out of the way so a passing server could refill her water glass. "Still, this is pretty satisfying. I'm glad you gave her the time."

"So am I."

Sarah dropped her napkin on the table. "With that, I must inform you that I have to pee."

"Okay. You want me to go with you?"

"Do you have to pee?" Sarah asked.

"Not particularly."

"In that case, can I ask you to do me a favor while I am relieving myself?"

"Yeah, sure," Emmy said.

"May told me she has that pomegranate body spray I like in her purse. She left it in the bridal suite. Would you grab it for me? I would maybe like to attract a sex partner for the evening, and while I understand that men will overlook body odor if it means they get sex, I'd prefer to give off a more pleasing kind of aroma."

"Oh, yeah. No problem. Meet you back here?"

"Sounds like a plan." Sarah tapped the tip of her finger to Emmy's. "See you soon, lover."

Emmy stood just inside the door of the bridal suite, her mouth agape. How could so few women create such an enormous mess? She found her little evening bag right where she'd left it and slung the thin strap over her shoulder. It only contained her keys, her wallet, and Barry, but she figured she might as well take it with her. The ceremony was over, so there was no risk of having the bag ruin the lines of her dress, or damage her silhouette, or whatever it was fashionable people said.

She scanned the room around her. There were wraps, shawls, purses, cosmetic cases, garment bags, various articles of clothing, a box of tampons, a to-go bag from whatever bakery had provided the pastries. This was going to take a while.

Emmy took a quick picture of the room and texted it to Sarah.

> I will find ur body spray but it might take me a couple years. Pray for me.

Sarah's reply came a moment later.

> People still eating main course. u got time. God be with ye

With Sarah's blessing, Emmy stuck her phone in her tiny clutch. Yet another benefit to keeping the purse with her for the rest of the night—she wouldn't have to carry her phone around wherever she went. The zipper only closed about halfway with the new addition, but that was okay. She set the bag down against the wall by the door, then turned to begin her search. With no better idea of how to go about it, she started to wander the perimeter of the room. Maybe she had a better chance of finding the Ark of the Covenant than her sister's purse, but Sarah was counting on her. She poked around, found her mother's purse, but nothing of May's. It didn't help that she was pretty sure her sister had had at least three different bags with her when she'd bustled into the suite that morning. She found those, finally, piled against the wall beneath one of the vanity mirrors. One of them looked more purse-like, though it wasn't her sister's usual, and she felt what she believed was a well-earned surge of triumph when she located the pomegranate spray within its cavernous depths.

Now, with her quarry in hand, she noted how quiet it was. Part of her wanted to flop down on the nearest comfortable surface and bask in it, but a more dominant part of her knew it would be a bad idea to have too much alone time with her thoughts. Also, many people considered it uncouth to dip out of a sibling's wedding and hide in the changing room. Holding the body spray in one hand, she carefully scooped up her bulging clutch in the other. She managed to use her elbow to press the door handle down enough to release the latch, and then she bumped it open with her hip.

Should've opened the door and then *grabbed the purse,* she told herself, feeling a little foolish.

She stepped out of the bridal suite, kicked the door shut behind her, and promptly dropped everything. The plastic bottle of body spray bounced a couple times, losing its cap in the process, and rolled off somewhere. Her clutch hit the floor and vomited out its contents.

Will—not an illusion, not a hallucination, but *Will*—winced at her reaction and the ensuing mess. "Sorry. Didn't mean to scare you. I wanted to talk to you, so I... followed you up here. That sounds bad. I swear, I'm not going to hurt you. Shit, that sounds bad, too."

She knew she should say something, needed to say something, but she couldn't find her voice. He looked at her expectantly, his eyes pleading with her to let him off the hook. She opened her mouth, but no sound came out.

Letting out a breath, Will ran a hand through his hair. "Look, I know it sounds like a line, but I swear this is the truth. I saw you earlier, and you looked familiar. I wanted to ask if we've met somewhere before."

He was really there, was all Emmy could think. He was there, physically standing in front of her, wearing a dark gray suit and a striped green tie. For a second, right when she'd first seen him, it had been a dream come true. Now it hit her that he didn't know who she was. He remembered nothing. This wasn't the Will from the book. To this Will, she was a stranger.

She wanted to weep, but she'd done too much of that lately.

She wanted to throw herself into his arms, but he would think she was a lunatic.

He'd said he recognized her, or felt he should. She clung to that.

"Did I bully you in high school or something?" Will asked. "If I did, it was an accident. I mean... I don't think I ever bullied anyone. Not on purpose anyway. Victor and I go back. He can vouch for me."

"You didn't bully me," Emmy managed.

"Oh. Good." He knelt down to gather her things. "I'm just gonna clean this stuff up. Least I can—" He stopped midsentence. Her purse was still in his hand. He'd already put her keys and wallet back in it. His eyes were fixed on the tiny flashlight. Slowly, he picked it up, lifted it for a better look. "You have a flashlight keychain."

"Yes."

A new thought occurred to her. Did *he* have a flashlight keychain? It was suddenly vitally important to her that he have one. If he did... and if it was named Gordon...

He was still kneeling on the floor. Emmy wondered vaguely if he was aware that it looked like he was proposing to her, down on one knee, holding a flashlight up to her like an offering. It would be funny later, she promised herself. One day, she would look back on this moment and laugh.

"I also have a flashlight keychain," Will said slowly, finally pushing himself up to stand.

Emmy's heart skipped a beat. She stopped herself before she could ask its name. He didn't know her. She reminded herself that, to him, they were meeting for the first time.

Trying for surprise, she said, "Really? That's a freaky coincidence. But I bet you didn't name yours."

"You... named your flashlight?"

"Yep. Barry. Don't judge me."

"You named your flashlight," Will repeated. His hand took another quick journey through his hair. If he kept doing that, he was going to look like he'd taken a break from dinner to go skydiving. "Why Barry? I guess it doesn't matter, but..." His face lit up when realization hit. "Barry Allen. The Flash."

"You got it."

Somehow this conversation was far more surreal than any she had had with him when they were both literally living inside a novel. She felt detached from herself, like she was having the conversation but also observing the conversation from afar. A defense mechanism, she supposed. If she let herself be a hundred percent present, she would probably start crying. Or begging.

Not happening.

Will took a deep breath, then reached into his pocket and pulled out his keys. "My flashlight is Gordon."

Emmy's heart leaped with joy at the sight of the familiar little gadget. It really was him. This was real-world Will.

"No way! Like *Flash Gordon*?"

"Yeah." He paused. "What's going on here?"

That was a tough question to answer. She couldn't very well tell him the truth.

Emmy shrugged helplessly. "I don't know. You said I looked familiar. Maybe it's just... fate?"

He studied her for a moment. "If you'd suggested something like that before I saw Barry, then I would have told you I don't believe in fate."

"And now?"

"Now? I think we gotta at least grab a cup of coffee or something."

She wanted to ask him so many things. He didn't remember her, so he wasn't the Will from the book. But he had a flashlight named Gordon, so he *was* Will. Did he still have a friend named Jared? Was he a nurse? What about his cousin?

No, a wedding was not a good time to ask if he had lost a cousin to cancer.

He'd suggested coffee. That was good. That was a start. She would have time to ask her questions. She needed to stay calm, take everything one step at a time.

How long had she been gone from the reception? She couldn't linger here any longer, no matter how much she wanted to stay with him, talk to him, figure out this version of him. She'd promised May, and herself, that she would be there for May's wedding. She wasn't opposed to getting to know this Will, to seeing if that spark was there, but her sister came first. This was May's night.

For now, it was enough to know that Lucy had been right. Will was here. There was hope.

"I have to get back," she told Will. "I don't want to miss more of my sister's wedding than I already have." She looked up at him, at his familiar face, his hair—a little shorter than she remembered—his chiseled jaw, his green-tinged hazel eyes. She looked at him, and she realized she loved him still. Even as a stranger, she loved him.

Lucy had also told her that there were forces at work in the world that most people didn't know of or understand. She didn't know if they were… listening, or paying attention? Did they think? Did they make decisions?

Was true love's kiss a thing?

"Can I kiss you?" she asked quietly. "Just once? I can't explain why."

"Uh… sure. I guess." He shifted uncomfortably and looked at her like she'd sprouted a second head.

She pointed a finger at him, couldn't help it. "You got to be weird for like five full minutes, so I get to be weird, too. That's fair."

He let out a quick, startled laugh. "You're right. Fair's fair."

"Okay. Lean down. I'm short."

He leaned down. She put a hand on his shoulder to balance herself, stretched up, concentrated on the love inside her, and touched her lips to his. When she pulled away, she searched his face, looking for some sign of recognition.

"Thanks, I guess," Will said.

Emmy deflated a little. So much for true love's kiss. She was going to have to start from the beginning.

"There's something there," she told him, and smiled genuinely. "Just doing a quick chemistry check."

Take two, she thought.

Emmy slipped her arm through Will's and walked with him back toward the reception. "You mentioned coffee? I know a place. It comes with free cake and a great view of drunk people attempting the Electric Slide."

Will chuckled. "Sounds great. I'm in."

So am I, Emmy thought, smiling to herself as she walked arm in arm with her One. *I'm all in.*

Epilogue

The house was nestled in a quiet neighborhood, just a few blocks south of a little playground, and close enough to the highway to make commuting easy. It featured a sturdy front porch, a fenced backyard, and a finished basement with heated flooring. The freshly landscaped front yard had taken full advantage of spring to become one expansive bouquet of fluffy pastel flowers that perfumed the air with each sweep of the gentle morning breeze.

Emmy surveyed her work with pride. The house was perfect for May—Victor deserved credit for catching it the moment it came on the market—and May had been correct to choose Hikari Landscape Design to fix up the bedraggled exterior. Emmy was relieved to note that she felt no lingering doubts, no fears or anxieties. It had taken her a long time before she could look at her own work without being self-critical or worrying that she was two bad days away from failing. Last year, when she'd started getting enough interest to quit her day job, she had thought her confidence would naturally rise to the occasion. But she'd still felt echoes of her old insecurities.

Not anymore.

She'd done some soul-searching, and she'd accepted that, for all that Andrew was an asshole, he wouldn't have been able to get so far under her skin if she hadn't been mired in her own fear to begin with. Now, Emmy let herself float on the bliss of success, and genuinely believed she deserved it.

Her sister's yard featured a few extra design elements, just for today. Crepe paper ribboned its way around the porch rail. A cluster of balloons was tied around the mailbox. A fresh floral wreath—created by a local florist Emmy had collaborated with before—hung from the door. The word "Congratulations" was carved into a thin plank of repurposed driftwood that slashed its way diagonally across the wreath. It was going to be a good party.

But first...

Emmy swung her messenger bag and her purse onto her shoulder, then grabbed the small plastic bag from the pharmacy. She walked up to the door, knocked twice, and opened it without waiting for an answer. She dropped her purse and bag inside the entryway closet and took a quick look around.

Party prep was clearly going strong. The banister was already draped with streamers. A table had been set up by the door with a delicate cloth and a small sign that indicated shoes, purses, and bags could be placed there for guests' convenience. The smell wafting from the kitchen was enough to draw Emmy down the hall. Emmy found May arranging plasticware, glittery paper plates, and napkins—embossed with "Congratulations" in the same script as the wreath outside—on the island. The Daruma was sitting on a decorative shelf beneath the window alongside a few other keepsakes and knickknacks. Emmy smiled to herself when she noticed that May had added some sparkly eyeliner around the black eyes. Fully ensconced in her role as party planner, May didn't notice Emmy, even when she swung around to put a pile of extra supplies in the cabinet. Saying nothing, Emmy put the shopping bag on the counter and pulled out the little cardboard box. When May turned back around, she squealed in both surprise and excitement.

"I didn't hear you come in!"

"You were too deep in party mode," Emmy said. She took the folded instructions from inside the box and casually flipped them open. "It says here that one line means 'Not Pregnant,' two lines means 'Pregnant,' and three lines means 'Extra Pregnant.' Wow. You don't even want to know what four lines means."

"Stop it," May said, laughing. "You're a tease."

Emmy slid the test out into her hand and held it up. "What are we hoping for? One line or two?"

"Two! Obviously two!"

"Okay." She handed her sister the test. "The bathroom awaits."

"Yay! I've never been so excited to pee!"

The white stick clutched in her grip, May dashed off to the powder room to pee excitedly. Emmy threw the box and instructions in the trash, leaned against the counter, and waited. Her heart had been fluttering with nerves and excitement ever since she'd gotten the text from May requesting that she stop off to buy a test on her way to the house. The instructions had said it might take as long as three minutes for results to appear. She was pretty sure not even half that time had passed before she heard excited noises echoing down the hallway. She smiled to herself, allowing a couple tears to slip down her cheeks. She'd cried a lot of happy tears lately.

The bathroom door opened, and Emmy heard her sister's hurried footsteps as she clambered up the stairs to find Victor. They had agreed ahead of time that he had to be the first to know. Since Victor had been hanging in the office with Will (something about a video game tournament), Emmy wasn't surprised to hear her fiancé enter the room behind her a minute later.

He wrapped his arms around her waist and rested his chin on the top of her head.

"From the sound of it, she's pregnant," Will said.

Emmy placed her hands over his, enjoying the way she could feel her engagement ring pressing ever so slightly into her finger. A rose gold band with an arrangement of colorful stones that looked just like a little sun, it was the perfect fit for her in both size and style. Better than that, Will had proposed with not only the ring, but a necklace with a V-shaped pendant that doubled as a nifty ring holder. Just like that, he made it so she always had a safe place to keep the ring, even when she was wrist-deep in mulch and soil.

"She's pregnant," Emmy confirmed. "I can't believe it. She's going to be such a great mom."

"You're going to be a great aunt, too."

"Heck yeah. I can't wait."

Will pressed a kiss to the top of her head. "How do you say, 'Congratulations on being pregnant' in Japanese?"

"*Ninshin omedetō gozaimasu.*"

There was a pause.

"Is there a shorter way to say congratulations?" Will asked.

"You can just say *omedetō*."

"Okay. That'll be my backup plan. Let me try the long one. Say it again."

Emmy repeated it for him. He fumbled it. She repeated it again.

"Okay, I got this," Will said after repeating the phrase several times. He turned her around and rested his hands on her waist. "Are you wearing sweats to our engagement party?"

"I thought about it, but no. I brought a change of clothes."

"You can wear your comfy pants. It's your party."

"It's *our* party," Emmy corrected.

"It's our party, and I will still love you if you wear sweatpants."

Emmy lifted herself up on her toes, wrapped her arms around his neck, and kissed him. His lips had become familiar all over again. It had taken very little time for them to start seeing each other regularly, and she'd enjoyed falling for him—the real him—and watching him fall for her. Even better, this Will was a little happier, a little more carefree, than the one she had met in the book. Probably because he wasn't currently going through a soul-wrenching existential crisis.

It had been extremely difficult, at first, not to tell him that they'd met before the wedding, that she knew him and didn't know him at the same time. But even that struggle had faded over time as she had come to see him as a person who lived in her world, solidly grounded in reality. Plus, May knew everything. Being able to confide in her sister had made a huge difference.

The book was a distant memory now, and she had to admit she was grateful to it.

"Break it up, you two!" May ordered sternly as she marched back into the room.

Emmy abandoned Will without a second thought as she turned and flung her arms around her sister. "Say the words. I know you want to."

"I'm pregnant!"

Emmy pulled away from the hug, beaming. "I'm going to spoil your kid rotten."

"Get in line."

"Uh… *Ninjin omedetō gozaimasu*," Will said carefully.

Emmy managed to hold back the laugh.

May didn't even blink at his slight—but significant—mispronunciation. "Aww! Thank you, soon-to-be-brother-in-law!"

She broke away from Emmy to hug Will. Emmy looked on, her heart absolutely bursting with love, wondering if she should tell her fiancé that he'd just congratulated her sister on her carrots.

Nah. May understood. No need to ruin the moment.

When Victor came in a moment later, grinning from ear to ear, Emmy hugged him and congratulated him.

"May said I'm not allowed to announce it at your engagement party," he told her. "I promise not to steal your thunder."

"I appreciate you and May for thinking of us," Emmy said, "but…" She glanced over at Will, correctly interpreted his expression. "Steal away. It's a party. There's more than enough thunder to go around."

"You sure?" May asked.

"Yeah, I mean, maybe wait until after everyone has had a chance to fawn over me and Will for a bit."

"Okay!" May squealed again. "I'm pregnant! You're getting married!"

"We need to toast!" Emmy announced. "Before the party. Just us four."

They uncorked a bottle of white wine from the party supplies. May filled her glass with seltzer and added a twist of lime. All four held their glasses up and then paused.

"I think you're supposed to say something since this was your idea," Will said, his eyes alight with humor.

"Oh! Right uh…" Emmy cast a desperate glance in May's direction.

May smiled knowingly. "How about this?" She lifted her glass of fizzy water. "To happy ever afters!"

Emmy couldn't think of a more accurate statement as they all echoed May's words and sipped their drinks. Victor pulled May into his side and kissed her temple. Whatever he whispered into her ear made May's face light up. Emmy looked at Will. He was looking right back at her, his expression full of warmth and love. He raised his glass once more, this time to her.

"To happily ever after," she said quietly, and tapped her glass to his.

Acknowledgements

Sometimes, on *American Idol*, a contestant would respond to negative feedback from the judges with, "But... but... my friends and family say I'm a great singer!" I took this with a grain of salt because the type of person who thinks their arguments will succeed where their *singing* failed is... not necessarily a reliable narrator. But this type of assertion stuck with me for years. I find myself thinking that this is a strange way for family and friends to show love. Surely it's more loving to give them the harsh truth—perhaps even an honest critique—than to let them embarrass themselves on a massive scale?

On that note (no pun intended), here is a list of people I am extremely grateful toward because they never took the easy, dismissive route of telling me I could definitely win *American Idol* (metaphorically speaking).

Mom – Never once in my life have I questioned your belief in me. Creativity and outside-the-box thinking are strengths that I am proud to say I inherited from you.

Dad – Any time I self-consciously told you that my books weren't for you, that you weren't the intended audience, you steadfastly insisted that you wanted to read them. In this way, you validated and supported me and my writing.

Tamara – You are the thoughtful, incisive critic I needed throughout the years. One of the best pieces of writing advice I ever received came from you. To paraphrase, you told me (many moons ago) that I was writing something that appeared to be cathartic for me, but wouldn't necessarily have the same effect for a wider audience. It taught me to differentiate between personal writing projects and writing for others.

Daniel – I'm assuming you understand that Tamara got to go first because she is the oldest, and not because I like her better than you. You are my sounding board. My writing conscience. My "What about this?" guy. I feel like I should put some sort of sophisticated inside joke here now, but most of our inside jokes are just *Spongebob* quotes, so I'm afraid I can't follow through on that.

Liz – I still remember multiple instances in high school when we were discussing one of my writing projects, and you were like, "Hey, what about this?" And I was like, "NO! No, that's impossible! That could never work!" And then you patiently waited forty-five or so minutes for me to go, "Well... actually... that could... huh. That's... perfect. That's what this book needed." I was, and am, lucky to have you. Here's to another 94 years of friendship.

Martyn and Zero – I'm sorry I had to lump you in with Martyn, Zero, but this list is getting long. You are the reason there is an offhand mention of adopting a Jack Russel terrier in this book. I'm sorry I tried to kiss the top of your wee little head once. It made you *so* angry. I still feel bad about it years later. Martyn, I never tried to kiss the top of your head, but I can if you want. When we brainstorm together, you are like the Navi to my Link, guiding my way and highlighting important details. But you do all that without making me want to trap you in a bottle and lob you out to sea like I've always wanted to do with Navi. She is very annoying. You, in contrast, are clearheaded and patient.

Alan – You are the one person who told me I could definitely win *American Idol*, but you weren't just saying that to spare my feelings or offer generic support; you genuinely believed it.

Kate – It must have been some form of fate or cosmic coincidence (which is just fate by a different, cooler-sounding name) when I saw the link to Greene & Heaton pop up on the site I was browsing. I felt the click right away when I read your profile on the website, and I am eternally grateful that you felt the click right back. Thank you for believing in me, and in Emmy and Will. I know it sounds cheesy, but it is simple fact that you helped make my lifelong dream come true.

Aubrie – I once told you (and Kate) that I queried this book despite knowing it still needed… *something*. When we began the editorial process, you had such a clear-cut vision for the book that it felt like kismet. It was simply… right. I had this feeling like, "Oh! There it is! That's what was missing." Many thanks to you (and Holly!) for believing in this story and unlocking its full potential.

Honorable Mention: To my sons, Warren and Ari, thank you for lighting up my life. Warren, your love of trains gave me the name for the pub in the book—The Bell & Whistle. (Ari, your Easter egg is in Book 2). To Adele, Adrian, Suni, and Gift, I didn't know writers could have cheerleaders! Thank you for making me feel cool!

About the Author

BEX GOOS started writing at the age of thirteen on an old laptop that weighed as much as a compact car. A Los Angeles native, she currently lives in North Dakota with her two sons and doofus dog. She has several hobbies, including glass art, podcasting, blogging, and acting weird around Midwesterners.

See more at bexgoos.me

Thanks for reading!

Want to receive exclusive author content, news on the latest Aria books and updates on offers and giveaways?

Follow us on X @AriaFiction and on Facebook and Instagram @HeadofZeus, and join our mailing list.